Deliver Us From Honor
by S. E. Valenti

© Copyright 2015 S. E. Valenti

ISBN 978-1-63393-106-0

This is a work of fiction. The characters are both actual and fictitious. With the exception of verified historical events and persons, all incidents, descriptions, dialogue and opinions expressed are the products of the author's imagination and are not to be construed as real.

Published by

◤ köehlerbooks™

210 60th Street
Virginia Beach, VA 23451
212-574-7939
www.koehlerbooks.com

DELIVER US FROM HONOR

S.E. VALENTI

VIRGINIA BEACH
CAPE CHARLES

To my beloved Chito, who taught me everything I have come to know and love about Sicily: her people, her traditions, her culture, and her enduring passions!

To my son Matteo, who filled his father's life with joy and pride and who continues still to fill mine with joy, love, and inspiration!

And to all the women in my life who have, in one way or another, influenced my writing of this novel! Each of you, whether through your personality, your loving heart, your understanding and forbearance, your passion, your stoicism, or your strength, have guided my hands across the keyboard to create a story about survival and triumph over the trials we have to face in our everyday lives.

Thank you all!

CONTENTS

CHAPTER I
REVENGE

5 MAY 1911

SEVARIO VAZANNO BROUGHT his arm back ready to strike. *Only a coward attacks a man in his sleep!* he thought, as his mind abruptly transitioned from sleep to sudden wakefulness.

"Sevario! Sevario!" urged the voice standing over him. "It's me, Santo! Stop fighting me! Wake up!"

Sevario relaxed his fist, blinked, and then blinked again as he suddenly recognized the voice of the man standing over him. "Santo! What are you doing, you jackass? I nearly knocked you out!" he shouted. "What do you want? It's the middle of the night, you fool!"

"Sevario, wake up!" his brother Santo Padua urged. "There's trouble. Come on . . . get up!"

Groggy with sleep, Sevario looked around the room. Realizing he was still holding onto Santo's arm, he let go of his grip and said nervously, "What's wrong? Who's here?"

"There's no one here . . . but there's smoke coming up from over the ridge. It looks like it's coming from Giuseppe's place."

Immediately, the expression on Sevario's face turned serious; throwing back the blanket, he swung his feet down onto the floor and stood up facing his brother. "Are you sure?"

"Yes! Can't you smell the smoke? It woke me a few minutes

ago; I ran outside thinking our barn was on fire. But then I looked up and all I could see was this black smoke coming up over the ridge."

Sevario ran past Santo and out the open doorway. Dawn was still several hours away. A full moon illuminated the night sky but an unmistakable black cloud hovered over the ridge that separated Sevario's farm from the farm of his older brother, Giuseppe Vazanno. Suddenly, Sevario was aware of an acrid smell drifting over the ridge along with the cloud of smoke.

"Get the horses. I'll get the shotguns!" Sevario told Santo as he ran back inside to get dressed.

Santo had already finished saddling the horses when Sevario entered the barn carrying three shotguns and two sets of pistols in their holsters. He tossed a holster to Santo, who was standing next to his horse ready to mount.

Sevario got on his own horse; his mind was racing. He thought about what they might find at his brother's farm; turning back to face Santo, he asked, "Do you think we should bring the wagon?"

Santo knew instinctively what his brother was suggesting. He got down off his horse, strode to the wagon, and began tying his horse to the back of it. "Go on, Sevario. You go ahead; I'll be right behind you. I can handle this."

Sevario kicked his horse hard. The horse bolted and then took off at a full gallop toward the ridge. As soon as Sevario reached the top of the ridge, the smell of charred wood mixed with kerosene filled his nostrils. He covered his nose and mouth with his kerchief. The usual morning winds were picking up off the Castellamare coast and were carrying the ash directly towards him, causing him to cough and gag; his eyes teared at the sting of it. His horse whinnied and shook his head back and forth, rebelling against the ash filling its own nose. Sevario's mind was whirling; he prayed his brother and his family were able to get out of the farmhouse and that they all were safe. The more his mind raced, the harder he rode his horse towards the fire.

***

By the time Sevario reached the top of the ridge the entire landscape before him was a black blur. The smoke had entirely filled the valley below him where his brother's farmhouse stood. Barely able to see ahead of him, he kept rubbing his eyes, trying to focus on the ground in front of him. He pulled back on his horse's reins, slowing the animal to a walk. He knew he was close to the road leading up to his brother's house, but with the smoke blurring his vision, recognizing even the familiar was nearly impossible.

Suddenly, the smoke started to clear; a stronger wind came up and started to blow the smoke higher into the air and away from the ground.

There, he said to himself as he finally spotted the road leading to his brother's farmhouse. He pulled his horse hard to the right and started down the road; suddenly the house came into his sight. The closer he got to the farmhouse, the more he realized the extent of the devastation.

"Whoa! Whoa!" he yelled, pulling his horse to a stop.

Sevario took in the sight before him and gasped. His throat tightened immediately; he felt as if his lungs could receive no air. He groaned and opened his mouth to scream but nothing would come out. There in front of him were the burned-out, charred remains of his brother's farmhouse. There was nothing left but the stone hearth, still engulfed in flames and ready to collapse.

The sight of the ruination sickened him; he jumped down off his horse and emptied what little he had in his stomach. He grabbed a kerchief from his back pocket and wiped his mouth; then he gagged and vomited again. *That smell . . . what is that smell?* he thought. *Wool? Hair? Something else?*He tied his kerchief around his nose and mouth to ward off the putrid smell.

As he looked into the charred rubble in front of him, without warning his legs gave out beneath him. He instinctively put his shotgun out in front of him to prevent himself from falling forward. After a few moments, Sevario regained his strength, took a step back, and stared at the sight before him. Dawn was just breaking over the horizon, and now in the clear light he could see his brother's farmhouse was gone; the only thing left standing and seemingly untouched was the barn.

"Giuseppe!" Sevario screamed out, falling to his knees in anguish. "Giuseppe, where are you, brother?"

Feeling a hand on his shoulder, Sevario jerked his head around quickly, ready to fight. Instead he saw Santo staring out at the rubble in front of them, his face wet with tears. "How could this have happened, Sevario? How?"

"I don't know, brother. I don't know." Sevario shook his head back and forth in disbelief.

Looking up again, he noticed once more the odd quiet of the barn. Nothing had been disturbed there. The only unusual thing was the quiet, the total absence of the bleating of goats and squawking of chickens.

"The animals," Santo whispered to Sevario. "All the animals are gone. No goats, no sheep, no horses . . . nothing; they're all gone."

Sevario nodded in agreement and said quietly, "I know, I know. Come on, we better take a look."

Turning away from his brother's farmhouse, now a smoldering heap of rubble, Sevario suddenly realized what had made him so sick. *That's it! It's the smell of burning wool. Those bastards burned the farm animals in the house fire!* His stomach turned again, but this time he refused to give in to it. As he and Santo got closer to the barn, he felt a sudden rush of adrenaline. *What if those responsible for the burning of Giuseppe's farmhouse are still here and hiding in the barn? That would explain why the barn is still standing!* Sevario thought as he cautiously walked towards the barn.

As the brothers approached the barn, they cocked their shotguns. They approached the barn, slowly and carefully scanning the perimeter for any signs of movement. Sevario pointed to the barn door, which was still wide open; he motioned to Santo to go around the back side of the barn while he, pointing to himself, would go in the front way.

Sevario approached the open doorway. As soon as he was near, he backed up against the wall next to the door and peered around the opening. He saw nothing unusual except that all of Giuseppe's horses were gone. Immediately, Sevario thought that Giuseppe might have escaped with his wife and daughters. *No,* he told himself, *if Giuseppe had escaped, he would have ridden to either my place or Gaspano's farm. Wherever my brother and his family are,* Sevario reasoned further, *they did not get*

*there on horseback. Even the wagons and lemon crates are in
the exact same place where Giuseppe and I left them yesterday
when we returned from the orchards.*

Leaving Sevario at the entrance to the barn, Santo walked
slowly around towards the back of the barn. Nothing looked out
of place to him at first; the fences were intact and even the grass
looked undisturbed. But, as he walked further around the back
and towards the other side of the barn, something white caught
his eye. Cautiously, Santo walked over to get a closer look. The
tall, dry broom grass appeared trampled in one particular area
and there, lying just off to the side, was a piece of clothing. He
picked it up. It was a white linen chemise—a woman's garment,
not a girl's. He held it in his shaking hands, noticing the ragged
edges as if it had been ripped off. Quickly he put the chemise into
his jacket as he continued to inspect the area. That's when he
saw it. A small area of grass, bent, and still wet with blood. Now
with physical evidence in his hand, he felt overcome. His mind
raced with fear and apprehension. He shook his head back and
forth. Something bad had happened here last night. Something
very bad. For the first time now, Santo was convinced harm had
come to Giuseppe and his family. Santo finished looking over the
entire area. He found nothing other than the chemise and blood.
He went around to the front of the barn to join Sevario inside.

Not seeing Sevario in the immediate area of the open
doorway, Santo entered the barn cautiously. But once in, he saw
his brother standing in the middle of the barn. "Have you found
anything?" he asked Sevario as he walked towards him.

Sevario turned and put a finger to his lips, pointing toward
the stacks of hay piled one upon another towards the back of
the barn. Santo nodded, understanding that Sevario suspected
someone might be hiding there. The two men walked closer to
the haystacks, stopping just in front of them. Sevario yelled out,
"Anyone in here?"

Only the deafening sound of silence came back to Sevario.
The two men looked at each other, feeling an immediate sense
of relief. But suddenly they both heard the sound of something
familiar—the jingling of a bell.

"Come out! Come out now! Come out now or I'll come in
shooting!" Severio yelled out, thinking someone was holding

Giuseppe's goats to keep them quiet.

As soon as Sevario raised his voice, the jingling got louder. Then, a small white tuft of hair poked out from behind one of the haystacks. Sevario and Santo breathed a sigh of relief and smiled: it was one of Giuseppe's pet goats, either Pepe or Fiore.

At least they were spared, thought Sevario. Then both Pepe and Fiore bolted out from behind the haystacks and ran directly towards the men. They began nudging the brothers' hands and rubbing their bodies up against their legs as if completely relieved to see them. "So, how is it you were spared, my friends?" Sevario asked quietly, disbelieving anything could have survived the apparent horror of the previous night.

* * *

Sevario and Santo looked through the remains of the barn but found nothing more. Sevario turned to Santo and asked, "Did you find anything out back?"

Santo averted his eyes from Sevario. It was painful for him to show the chemise to his brother. "I found this behind the barn," he said, pulling the white garment out from the inside of his jacket. "It looks as if something happened there. I found some blood on the grass, too."

"Show me where you found it," Sevario whispered almost inaudibly.

As Santo took Sevario to the place where he found the chemise, he could feel sweat starting to drip down his forehead, and his hands started to shake. He stopped when he found the patch of blood-soaked grass. When he looked up, he saw Sevario with a kerchief over his mouth as if holding back a scream: tears were running down his face. Sevario shook his head in a gesture of despair.

"Something terrible has happened here, Santo. Something terrible," Sevario said as he tried to choke back tears, but then began to weep bitterly.

Santo put his hand on his brother's shoulder and waited for him to stop crying. Once he regained control of his emotions, Sevario said, "Tie the goats to the back of the wagon. We better ride to Gaspano's farm. I pray to God he and his family are all right."

On their way back to the horses, they couldn't help but stop and inspect the still-smoldering farmhouse. They stood staring at it in disbelief. "Surely nothing has happened to Giuseppe," Santo said with conviction. "I know Giuseppe. He and Maria have escaped."

"I, too, know my brother. There is not a man alive who would have been able to do this to him—if he was alive. The only way all this," Sevario said, gesturing towards the ruins in front of him, "could have happened would have been for Giuseppe to have been taken by complete surprise or shot dead first."

"Brother, you are wrong! Giuseppe is not dead!" Santo shouted. "Surely he would never let anything happen to his family, to Adriana . . . to little Francesca." Santo stopped his rant, knowing it served no purpose. "Who could have done such a thing, Sevario? Who?"

Sevario had no answer. He stepped closer to the charred ruins and stared down at several large black lumps still smoldering in the rubble; it was impossible to tell what exactly they were. Sevario took a step closer towards the objects.

"Sevario!" Santo reached out and grabbed his brother's arm, stopping him from taking a step further. "What are you thinking?" But he knew exactly what his brother was thinking. "Those are animals! Smell it! It's the smell of burned wool. It's the animals, Sevario–that's all, it's the animals." He pulled on Sevario's arm. "Come on with me. We have to go to Gaspano's farm. Giuseppe and Maria are not here."

"I need to know for sure, Santo. I need to know for sure," Sevario said as he started to cry again, falling to his knees.

"Believe me, Sevario! Believe me! I know the difference between wool and flesh! If Giuseppe and Maria are dead, their bodies are not here. I promise you!"

Sevario looked at Santo and believed he was right. The murderers might have disposed of the bodies somewhere else, but they were not here.

"We have to go, Sevario. I have a feeling whoever did this is not going to stop here at Giuseppe's place. I think all of us are in danger. We have to get to Gaspano's farm. There is nothing more for us here."

Sevario turned to face his brother, nodding his head in

agreement. "Come on, I'll ride ahead of you to Gaspano's place. If you see or hear anything, don't even try to fight them off—fire a shot into the air twice. I'll double back to help you."

* * *

Gaspano, the middle Vazanno brother, was only four years younger than his older brother Giuseppe, who at forty-one was now the patriarch of the family since the death of their father. All the Vazanno brothers were very close, but Gaspano and Giuseppe were inseparable. In fact, Gaspano had married Giuseppe's sister-in-law. It seemed only reasonable to Giuseppe and his wife Maria that they should arrange a marriage between Gaspano and Maria's younger sister Adanella, whom everyone called Nella. Once Gaspano and Nella were married, they built their own farmhouse just two miles from Giuseppe's, solidifying the strong bond between the two brothers and the two sisters.

Sevario mounted his horse and headed towards his brother Gaspano's farm. He had only gone a short distance when suddenly he remembered: *the tunnel! Yes! The tunnel, that's where they are!* He turned his horse around and began to gallop full speed back towards Santo.

"Santo," Sevario yelled out as he rode close to the wagon, "the tunnel!"

Santo knew immediately what he meant. He waved up at Sevario and felt a surge of hope. He stopped the wagon immediately, turned it around, and headed back in the direction of Giuseppe's farm.

* * *

The outer hinges of the wooden door looked as if they had been recently opened. Sevario, in a rush to get into the tunnel, pulled at the door latch so hard, he nearly broke it off. One of the hinges did come off, causing the door to fall backwards onto the ground with a loud thud. With the sun behind him now, Sevario peered down into the partially lit tunnel but could see no sign of life there.

"I'm going in," Sevario said to Santo. "Keep a cautious eye out. If you see anyone suspicious, just shoot!"

Sevario jumped down into the tunnel and felt an immediate change in temperature. The tunnel was cool, clammy, and musty. The cold clay walls caused a shiver to run down his spine. He put his hand out, reaching for one of the walls still visible from the open doorway above. He touched the wall to steady himself and immediately felt cold water drip down his arm. He steadied himself and then called out, "Giuseppe? It's me, Sevario."

No answer.

He began walking slowly into the tunnel. As he moved along a slight curve, he lost the little bit of light he had from the doorway—and no longer had any light to help him maneuver through the cold darkness.

"Maria? Giuseppe? It's me, Sevario," he said as he walked further and further into the dark. "It's safe now. Come out if you're in here."

Still, there was no answer.

He tried to adjust his eyes to the darkness but it was nearly impossible to see anything in front of him. He walked cautiously, continuing to press his hands against the tunnel walls to steady himself. As he neared what he knew to be the midpoint of the tunnel, Sevario was suddenly overcome with a feeling of hopelessness. In desperation, he shouted out, "Is anyone here?"

Not a sound came back to him. He put his head down in despair. Discouraged, he turned to walk back towards the light. But just as he started to move away, he heard a faint voice: "Uncle?"

Sevario stopped; he stood as still as possible and held his breath. *Did I imagine someone speaking out to me?* he thought as stood in the darkness.

"Uncle, it's me, Adriana. I am over here."

Sevario turned and rushed back to where he had just been standing. "Adriana? Is it you? Is it really you?"

"Yes, Uncle. I am here . . . over here . . . with Francesca."

"Keep talking to me, girl, so that I can find you in the dark."

Adriana kept repeating, "Here, Uncle. I am over here."

In the pitch darkness he followed Adriana's voice and finally reached her. He knelt down, feeling for her body. Then he felt the familiar curly hair of little Francesca sitting on Adriana's lap, enveloped in her arms. "Oh, my God!" Sevario exclaimed. "What has happened here? What has happened, Adriana? Where are your mother and father?"

"Many men came last night; I saw what they did, Uncle . . . I saw everything! So did Francesca, Uncle . . . so did Francesca," Adriana said weakly as if the life had been drained out of her.

"Did they take your father and mother away?"

"I don't know what happened after I closed the door. Mamma was screaming . . . I couldn't bear it any longer; I could not let Francesca listen, Uncle. Mamma made me promise to take care of Francesca . . . I could not go out to her, Uncle! I could not go out and help her!" Adriana said, on the verge of hysteria.

Sevario could feel Adriana's entire body shaking as if she were reliving the previous night's terror, and then she began to cry uncontrollably. "Shh . . . shh. Hush now! Don't talk right now," Sevario urged. "Santo is here. Let me take Francesca from you first and then I will come back for you. Can you wait for me for a moment, Adriana? Will you be all right if I leave you for a moment?"

"NO! Don't leave me, Uncle! Please don't leave me!" Adriana screamed, grabbing desperately at his arms in the dark.

"Everything is all right, child. I promise you I won't leave you."

Then he called out loudly in the direction of the tunnel opening, "Santo! I've found them! Come and help me!"

Santo's heart began to pound in his chest as he jumped down immediately into the tunnel. The distance between the tunnel opening and where Sevario found Adriana was more than several yards, but it took Santo only seconds to reach them.

"Santo, here, take Francesca out. I will help Adriana."

Santo picked up the five-year-old from Adriana's arms. The little girl tried to hold on to Adriana but Adriana told her soothingly that it was Santo who was taking her. Francesca let go her grip on her sister's arms then and went to him. Santo felt an intense impulse to rush to Adriana, but he knew he could not–he should not. Instead, he said before taking Francesca out, "Adriana, are you all right? Did they hurt you?"

When Adriana did not answer him, he turned to take Francesca out of the tunnel.

Sevario asked Adriana "Can you stand?

"I will try, Uncle," Adriana said weakly.

As soon as Santo reached the opening to the tunnel, he easily lifted Francesca up so she could climb out onto solid ground. He felt Sevario's presence right behind him. Immediately, Santo jumped up and out of the tunnel himself, turning quickly to reach down and help Adriana out. Sevario jumped up right behind her.

"Hurry, Santo. Get the wagon," Sevario said as soon as he stood up. "We have to get out of here as soon as we can."

Santo immediately began to run towards the wagon. Adriana was holding Francesca in her arms, and Sevario had his arms around the both of them. As Adriana turned her head away from her uncle, for the first time in full daylight she saw the devastation that had occurred during the night. Immediately she put her hand to her mouth to stifle a scream. Unable to control her emotions, Adriana let the scream escape from her throat and then another as she broke away from her uncle's arms, running headlong towards the charred ruins screaming, "Mamma! Papa!"

Santo jumped down off the wagon and began running towards her. He caught up to her just as she was about to step into the burning embers. He put his arms around her shoulders to stop her. She struggled against his restraint but finally gave in to him as if completely defeated. He turned her body around to face him. He held her tightly as she buried her face into his chest, and she wept bitterly. He let her cry as he stroked her hair, trying to console her the only way he knew how. When she had stopped crying, he said softly, "We have to leave now. We have to go to Gaspano and Nella's farm."

Adriana moved her head away from Santo's chest and looked up to his face. She nodded in agreement and turned then to walk back to the wagon.

***

Sevario rode hard toward his brother Gaspano's farmhouse. He had wanted to ride ahead of Santo, knowing he could get there far faster on horseback than Santo could with the wagon, but then he slowed his pace, thinking better of it. Leaving Santo alone with his nieces—even though Santo had a shotgun and a pistol—was still foolish. If more than one or two men tried to ambush Santo and the wagon, he would be unable to fight them off. Instead, Sevario rode ahead but not so far ahead he could not see the wagon if he looked back–at all times.

As Sevario came near enough to see the front landscape of Gaspano's farm, his breathing became labored; instinctively he felt something was wrong. A sudden chill ran through his body. He slowed his horse to a canter as he approached the front of the farmhouse. The house looked undisturbed. Empty. Quiet . . . too quiet. *Where are the children? Where's Nella*? he thought. As he got closer he could see that the front door had been left wide open. Sevario's hands started to shake. Cautiously, he got down off his horse and walked to the doorway. As he stepped in, he yelled out, "Gaspano, it's me, Sevario!"

There was no reply.

Sevario cocked his shotgun and leaned it up against his shoulder with his finger on the trigger; then, he took his pistol out of its holster and held it in his other hand. He walked into the sitting room first—nothing looked disturbed. Sevario continued towards the kitchen—again, nothing looked out of place. But, as he walked through the kitchen and towards the hallway leading to the back of the house, he heard a cry. An infant's cry! *Angelo!* he thought. *The baby is here!*

Immediately Sevario began to run down the short hallway that connected the kitchen to the back bedrooms. As he ran past a small window in the hallway, he stopped suddenly and retraced his steps. Staring out the window, he could not believe his eyes. He saw his sister-in-law, Nella, kneeling on the ground, crying and beating her fists into the body of his brother, Gaspano. To his horror, he also saw his nine-year-old nephew, Alfredo, and his five-year-old niece, Cinzia, kneeling on the ground just a few yards from their mother. They too stood watching her in horror as she hysterically tried to beat the life back into her dead husband.

"Oh, my God!" screamed Sevario as he ran back towards the kitchen and to the door leading out to the back of Gaspano's farm. Just as he was about to go out the door he saw Santo standing in the doorway leading into the kitchen.

"What is it?" Santo asked, seeing Sevario's face drained of color.

"Get Adriana and Francesca. Bring them into the house, but keep Francesca in the front of the house. They've killed Gaspano! Nella's out back with his body! Hurry, Santo! Gather up some things for Nella and the children. We have to get everybody out of here fast!"

"Where are Alfredo and Cinzia? Are they safe?" Santo asked frantically.

"Yes, I will get them and bring them in; they are outside with their mother."

Sevario ran out the back door towards Nella but stopped and put his hands on Alfredo's shoulders first.

"Uncle, they shot Papa! They shot Papa!" Alfredo cried.

"Go inside now, son, and take Cinzia. Santo and Adriana are waiting for you. Gather some things together. I will bring your mother in."

Alfredo could not take his eyes off of his mother as he reached down to take his sister's hand. Slowly, he turned and led her back into his farmhouse.

Sevario went to Nella and knelt down beside her. To his horror, he could see his brother had been shot in the head and in the chest. His brother lay in a pool of blood so vast it covered the entire area around his body.

"Nella," Sevario said gently when he had regained his own composure, "I am here to take you and the children to a safe place."

Nella pushed him away and then threw herself down on Gaspano's body. Again, she began to beat his body while screaming out hysterically, "Gaspano! Gaspano! Get up, Gaspano! Get up!"

Sevario let her cry for a moment but he knew they had precious little time. He reached out and with all his might pulled Nella up. "Nella, listen to me!" Sevario said sternly. "Gaspano is dead. We have to leave here. We are all in danger—even your children."

Nella, as if stunned to hear Sevario's voice for the first time, turned to him and said, "They killed my Gaspano, Sevario; they killed my husband in cold blood."

"Shhh . . . shhh . . ." Sevario whispered as he held her close to him, trying to soothe her. "We have to leave here, Nella. It is very dangerous right now for all of us. We have to leave right away."

* * *

Adriana had helped Santo push clothing haphazardly into bundles. As she was walking out with one bundle to put in the wagon, her uncle came into the kitchen holding Nella in his arms. Adriana shrieked as she saw the blood-soaked skirt of her aunt. She knew immediately her uncle had been killed. Adriana went to her aunt and put her arms around her shoulders. "Oh, my Zia!" she said as she held her aunt tightly in her arms. "Come with me, Zia, I will take care of you."

"Let me take her for a moment, Adriana. Can you go and fetch some water to clean her up first?"

Sevario helped Nella to sit down in a chair in the kitchen. Adriana turned immediately and ran out the back door towards the well. But, as soon as she was within a few feet of the kitchen doorway she could see the dead body of her uncle. She gasped, feeling as if her limbs would not carry her a step further. Her first instinct was to scream out in horror, but she controlled herself in an effort to spare her aunt more anguish. Quickly she filled several leather flasks with well water and took them back into the farmhouse. Her aunt was still in hysterics.

"I'm not leaving here without my husband! I will never leave Gaspano here alone, Sevario. You cannot make me leave him!"

Sevario looked at Santo who had come back into the house with Alfredo. The little boy was shaking as he watched his mother's hysteria, her skirt covered in blood. Seeing the terrible state Alfredo was in, Sevario knew he had to get the child out of the house.

"Santo, take Alfredo to the wagon. I will bring the rest of the bundles myself while Adriana helps Nella to dress."

Adriana ran immediately into one of the back rooms and came back with a clean skirt and blouse for her aunt. She changed her stockings and shoes and then her chemise. Finally, Nella was ready to go, too. Adriana called for her uncle to help Nella out to the wagon.

By the time Adriana, Sevario, and Nella had reached the wagon, all the children were safely inside the wagon's bed. Bundles were piled up high against its walls and supplies of water, bread, and cheese were put beneath the wagon in a holding place. Everyone was in the wagon but Nella. She stood behind it, clutching the railing, seemingly reticent and determined not to be moved from the spot where she stood.

"Nella," said Sevario, "we will take Gaspano with us. I promise you we will. Please let Santo help you into the wagon now. Please Nella, we have to go as quickly as possible. These terrible men could be back at any time."

"You will bring Gaspano with us, Sevario?" Nella said hopefully as she looked at her brother-in-law.

"Yes. We will take Gaspano with us."

Santo reached out to take Nella by her arm. She let him help her into the wagon. As soon as Nella was safely settled with little Angelo in her arms, Santo left her to help Sevario with Gaspano's body.

"Should we take both of Gaspano's horses?" Santo asked Sevario.

"No, we'll just take one. We already have two pulling the wagon, your horse and mine; we also have the two goats. They have to be fed, too; it's going to be hard enough to feed all of us—much less all the animals. We can let Gaspano's horse go once we've buried his body."

"Where are we going, brother?" Santo asked.

Sevario shook his head. He wiped his brow with his kerchief. "I don't know. All I know for sure is that we can't go anywhere near Palermo. Whoever did this knows the Vazanno family—all of us. That means they are probably from here—they are at least from the west." He shrugged his shoulders and shook his head in bewilderment. "But, one thing is for sure, we have to get away from here and the sooner the better. Whoever they are, I'm sure they are looking for us right now."

Santo climbed up onto the driver's seat of the wagon. He turned to his brother and said, "I'll follow your lead."

"Let's follow the Fiume Freddo River from here; it's completely dry by now and it will lead us toward Calatafimi and the wheat fields; from there we can go towards Salemi and then down to Partanna."

"You want to go south, then?" Santo asked.

Sevario shrugged his shoulders. "I don't think it's safe to go east or north . . . too dangerous . . . too close to Palermo. Let's head southward for now; by the time we reach Partanna it will only be a short distance then to Campobello di Mazara."

"Mazara? You want to go to the sea? Are you thinking of crossing over to Tunisia or Malta?" Santo asked, knowing the inherent danger in trying to cross the Mediterranean Sea from the western coastline of Sicily. The boats were small and sudden storms were common in the springtime.

"We have to get to the coast; once there we can decide where to go. I know the danger, too—but we will have to see what happens over the next couple of days—maybe over the next couple of hours. I figure if we can make it to the coast, there is more of a chance of meeting people who do not know us or our family," Sevario said. He put his hand on Santo's arm and said again, "I don't know where to go, Santo. But one thing I do know for certain—we have to leave Balastrate and we have to get as far away from Palermo and the west as we can—right now."

Santo nodded in agreement. "Let's go, then. I trust your judgment, brother."

CHAPTER II

ESCAPE TO SALEMI

5 MAY 1911

THE SUN BEAT down relentlessly on the covered wagon. Not wanting to take a chance on being seen that first day, Sevario decided to hide the wagon and horses in the middle of an olive grove during the daylight hours. Once night fell, Santo and Sevario took turns driving the wagon all night across the back roads; one would drive the wagon while the other led the way on horseback. That night the sky was coal black as the moon was nearing the end of its cycle. Using the stars to guide them and grateful for the added cover of darkness, Sevario led his brother due south. The south central part of Sicily was familiar to Sevario; he had traveled this part of the country as a boy many times with his own father, who often took him and his brothers with him when he looked for work.

Sevario's memory served him well. Even though most of the trails he remembered were now covered by wild grass and tangled barberry bushes, he did find one that was passable and led directly to the town of Salemi. *Once we make it to Salemi,* Sevario reasoned, *we will be very close to Mazara—and from Mazara, little more than a half day's ride to the sea.*

By morning they had reached the valley just to the south of Salemi. Sevario recognized the towering castle of Normanno, two square towers with a circular tower between them. The sight of it was exactly as he remembered it from childhood. Down in the valley, Sevario found a large grove of pine trees. "Santo, look there," Sevario said, pointing out a grove of pines. "We can stop there to rest and water the animals."

Santo nodded in agreement. But first he waved Sevario over closer to the wagon. When Sevario was within a few feet of the wagon, Santo jumped down and went to him to avoid shouting: "We have to find a place to bury Gaspano. It's been over a day and a half now . . ."

Sevario nodded. "Take the wagon over there; find a place where you will be hidden and surrounded by trees. I'll ride out and find a temporary place to bury Gaspano."

Santo drove the wagon into a perfect niche between several towering pines. He removed the covering over the wagon, allowing a stream of fresh, clean air to the fill the wagon bed.

Grateful to finally breathe in fresh air, Adriana closed her eyes and took a deep breath. When she opened them she saw Santo standing in front of her. A moment of awkward silence fell between them; Adriana looked away from Santo when she felt a sudden feeling of attraction stir within her. After a few moments, Adriana forced herself to look up at Santo again and asked, "Where are we now?"

"In a valley just below the town of Salemi. We'll be safe here."

"Where is Uncle?" she asked, looking around behind Santo to see if he was nearby.

Santo did not want to speak in front of Nella and her children about Gaspano. Instead he changed the subject and said, "You and the children and Nella should get out of the wagon for now. I'm going to go over that ridge there and see if I can find water."

Adriana stood then. Her legs were shaky after being curled up in the cramped confines of the small wagon bed. Santo, seeing her instability, jumped up into the wagon to help her down. As soon as Adriana was on the ground, he turned and called out to Cinzia and Francesca to come to him so that he could lift them out, too. Alfredo defiantly refused Santo's help. Instead, he jumped out of the back of the wagon by himself and started to run off toward a grassy knoll nearby.

"Alfredo!" Adriana yelled out firmly. "Stay close by!"

Only Nella remained in the back of the wagon. She seemed

oblivious to the activity around her. Concerned over Nella's lethargy, Santo asked Adriana, "Is she any better?"

Adriana shook her head, indicating she did not think her aunt was doing well. Then she went closer to the back of the wagon and said calmly, "Zia, would you like to get down out of the wagon for a while?"

When Nella did not answer, Adriana climbed back into the wagon and took Angelo from her aunt's arms. She handed the infant to Santo and then went back to Nella and knelt down next to her. "Zia, I want to help you. You need to get some fresh air. You need to get out of the wagon for a little while."

Nella looked up at her niece. "Leave me be, Adriana. Please, just take care of Angelo for me."

"Please Zia, it will do you good to get out of here and move about for a while."

Nella said nothing; instead she turned her head away from Adriana, pulled the thin blanket covering her body up to her face, and then over her head.

Adriana, frightened by her aunt's reaction, looked back at Santo in helpless desperation.

"Come, Adriana," Santo said. "When Sevario returns perhaps he can coax her out."

Adriana hesitated; her instinct was to insist her aunt leave the wagon, but then she thought perhaps that would make things worse. Reluctantly, Adriana got out of the wagon and attended to baby Angelo and the two girls while Santo went looking for water.

"There's a creek just over the other side of that ridge," Santo told Adriana excitedly, obviously relieved to have found water so close. "The water is shallow and clean. It looks to be a safe place for you and the children to refresh yourselves."

Just then Sevario rode up. He said to Santo, "I've found a place not far from here."

Santo nodded. "I found water just over the ridge there," he said pointing in the direction of the ridge. "Adriana can take the children and get cleaned up."

"What about Nella?" Sevario asked.

"Zia refuses to leave the wagon," said Adriana. "I'll take care of her when I return with the children, Uncle. I'm sure she will recover from the shock of all of this soon."

Sevario shook his head in frustration. "I'm not so sure, Adriana. While you take the children down to the creek, Santo and I are going to bury Gaspano . . ." Sevario spoke quietly so that Nella would not hear him, but he could not control the tears that welled in his eyes. The thought of burying his brother in the Salemi valley—without a proper burial and Mass—caused his heart to ache. He also knew they could not mark the site with a headstone for fear whoever was after them would discover it— and then follow their trail and kill them all.

Adriana knew how painful it was for her uncle to bury his brother and did not want to prolong his agony. "Uncle, I'm going to take the children now." As she turned to walk towards the water, she caught a glimpse of Alfredo walking not far from her and called out to him, "Alfredo, come with me and the girls. We're going down to the water's edge to get cleaned up."

Santo picked up the large covering that he had removed from the wagon with the intention of carrying it down to the creek's edge for the children to sit on. As he passed Sevario, he whispered to him, "As soon as Adriana and the others are settled at the creek, I will be back to help you bury Gaspano."

Sevario nodded in agreement.

The stream was not far from the wagon but the path leading down to it was steep. About halfway down, the ground seemed to level off, leaving a steady path to the creek. Santo, seeing the steepness of the downward path, called out, "Wait for me, Adriana. I'll help you with the children until you get to level ground."

Adriana carried baby Angelo in her arms, and her little sister, Francesca, walked next to her holding onto her long skirt. Behind Adriana was Alfredo, who was holding his sister Cinzia's hand.

Just moments after Santo called out to Adriana, she suddenly lost her footing; without warning her left foot gave out under her and she slid down to the ground. Santo was next to her in an instant. He took the baby from her as he helped her back up to her feet.

"Hold onto my arm, Adriana," Santo insisted. "I'll carry Angelo and you can take Francesca's hand. Just keep a good hold on my arm on the way down."

Adriana put her arm through Santo's arm. The warmth of his

body felt good against her bare arms. She took Francesca's hand with her other hand and noticed for the first time Francesca wasn't speaking—to anyone.

"Francesca, are you all right?"

The little girl looked up at her sister and nodded.

"What's wrong, Francesca? Tell me how you feel," Adriana urged.

Francesca put her head down. She quickly pushed her face into the folds of Adriana's skirt, hiding her face.

Adriana released her grip on Santo's arm and knelt down in front of her sister. "What is it, Francesca? Are you afraid of something?"

Francesca started to cry. Adriana took her into her arms and held her tightly.

"Shh . . . shh. Don't cry, my darling. You don't have to talk to anyone if you do not want to. Everything is going to be better. I promise you." Adriana stroked Francesca's curly hair. "I promise you, child, everything is all right. No one in this world will ever frighten you again. I promise I will never let anyone scare you ever again."

Francesca pulled her head away from her sister, smiled, and then kissed Adriana on the cheek lovingly.

"Come on then. Let's go down to the water," Adriana said as she stood up, taking Santo's arm again and Francesca's hand.

Santo laid the large covering on the ground near the creek bed as soon as they arrived at the water's edge.

"You will be alright here, Adriana. I'll be back as soon as Sevario and I are done burying Gaspano's body," Santo said firmly.

Adriana noticed Santo had left two blankets atop the canvas for them. Before he started up the incline he hung another blanket between two nearby trees so that she and the two girls had privacy for changing their clothes.

Santo stopped just before he headed up the incline, walked back to where Adriana was standing, and said, "Here, if you need this—use it." Santo handed Adriana his pistol.

Adriana looked up at Santo. For the first time it seemed she noticed how much taller he was than her. Their eyes locked for a moment, but this time it was Santo who looked away first.

"Thank you, Santo." Adriana said sincerely. "I'm sure we will be safe here."

Santo turned from her then and started up the embankment.

Adriana felt a gripping compulsion to call out after him. "Santo!"

He stopped and turned immediately. "What is it? What's wrong?"

"Nothing . . . everything is fine." Adriana lowered her eyes, embarrassed to have given in to such a foolish impulse. But then she raised her head and said, "Thank you, Santo. Thank you for everything you are doing for us . . . thank you."

Santo smiled. His look lingered on her face for a while longer and then he turned and continued up the hill.

She walked over to baby Angelo, lying contentedly on the covering Santo had put out for her and the children. His thoughtfulness touched her in a way she had not experienced before. *He thinks of me . . . us . . . before he thinks of himself,* she mused as she looked back and watched his retreating figure climb the hill and disappear out of sight.

* * *

Santo and Adriana were not natural siblings, as he had been adopted by her father when he was just a five-year-old boy. Santo's own father had brought him and his mother and infant brother to western Sicily looking for work because he had heard rumors of poor men like himself becoming rich—working in the sulfur mines in the Sicanian mountains. His father sold what little they had accumulated during their six-year marriage, and with that money bought a wagon and one mule. Leaving family, neighbors, and friends, Santo's father packed up his family's belongings and left the little town of Nicosia in north central Sicily, finally settling in the small village of Balestrate.

Only three months after Santo's father began working in the mines, there was a massive explosion that could be heard all the way back to the village of Balestrate. Within hours of the explosion, the man in charge of Santo's father's work crew rode towards Balestrate with a list of the names of the known dead and of those men who were still missing—and presumed dead. The man rode directly to the church and handed the list of names to the village priest. The priest posted the names of those killed on the front door of the church and then began ringing the church bells. Since it was mid-afternoon, the townspeople knew some men from their village had been killed. The church bells are only rung for morning Mass—and when a disaster has occurred.

Dong! Dong! Dong! Dong! Dong!

The church of Santa Anna was situated right in the middle of the small town with a large piazza in front of it. It took only minutes before the townspeople started rushing towards the front steps of the church.

Santo's mother was hanging laundry out to dry, behind the village butcher shop where her husband had rented a small room for her and her children, when the church bells started to ring.

"What is that all about?" she asked the butcher's wife.

"A mine accident, signora. The church has posted the names of the men who have been killed."

Santo's mother grabbed her infant son and yelled out to Santo to follow her as she made her way through the crowded streets. As she reached the main street leading to the church, people were everywhere. Running in between a crush of villagers now, Santo's mother shouted back to Santo, "Hold on to my skirt! Don't let go!" The closer they got to the church, the thicker the crowd became. Suddenly, Santo's mother stopped along with all the women and children surrounding her at the very entrance to the piazza. Silence fell over the crowd. The villagers who had arrived first at the church doors were now reading the names of the men missing and presumed dead, and the names of those identified as dead.

Sorrowful moans and screams of agony started to rise from the front of the church. The people who were in front of Santo's mother started to gasp and cry, putting their hands to their mouths, even though they still did not know the men whose names were read. The reaction was one of sympathy for their neighbors and loved ones—who surely, they knew, had lost someone.

Within minutes of arriving at the piazza in front of the church Santo's mother could barely move forward because of the large crowd. She pushed and struggled against the crowd until she was within a few feet of the church's door, looking back constantly to make sure Santo was still holding on to her skirt.

The scene she saw there was horrific; women were fainting dead away and lying on the stone steps leading into the church, surrounded by relatives trying to revive them. Everyone else was crying and screaming out the names of their loved ones lost to the explosion. Finally, other villagers began to physically remove people from the doors of the church so that others could approach and read the fate of their own loved ones.

Santo's mother finally reached the top step leading to the church entrance upon which the names of the dead were listed. Women were kneeling and praying their rosaries everywhere as they sat crying and moaning inconsolably. Stepping in between the mourners, some lying prostrate on the ground, Santo's mother slowly approached the church doors. A sudden chill came over her; she wrapped her shawl tightly around her as she approached the death list.

Giovanni Padua—Morto

Giovanni Padua, dead! Santo's mother let out a scream, clenched her fist to her mouth, and then she, too, fainted dead away. Santo caught his baby brother just before his own mother would have surely crushed him in her arms. Not knowing what else to do, Santo sat down next to his mother and waited for her to wake up.

* * *

After the shock of her husband's death and the realization she had no money to support her two children, Santo's mother fell into a deep depression, refusing to leave her bed. The butcher's wife took pity on her, begging the butcher to let the woman stay for at least another couple of weeks until she could recover from her shock and find a way to return to her family in Nicosia. Begrudgingly, the butcher agreed, but only under the condition Santo's mother leave his household in two weeks' time.

Santo's mother was so distraught she refused to nurse her infant son; the butcher's wife, unbeknownst to her husband, paid for a wet nurse to feed the baby until the mother, hopefully, recovered from the shock of her loss. But Santo's mother did not recover; in fact, her state became so grave she refused to eat or drink anything. By the time the two weeks had passed it was apparent to the butcher himself that the widow could not possibly live much longer in her current condition. And he was right.

Santo awoke in the middle of the night, not more than three weeks after his own father died, to the sound of his mother moaning and rasping.

"Mamma! Mamma! Wake up!" Santo screamed as he pulled his body up close to hers from his sleeping place at the foot of her bed.

Then Santo watched as mother took one more deep breath and then gasped. Her head fell to one side, her eyes wide open, staring, emotionless.

Santo ran screaming to the butcher's wife. But, by the time he and the butcher's wife returned to Signora Padua's side, she was dead.

* * *

When the priest came to administer last rites, the butcher's wife took him aside to talk about the children. "Father Licolli," she explained, "their mother and father are both dead. I cannot care for them. My husband will kill me! We already have six little mouths to feed. You will have to take them to the orphanage in Palermo. Take them to the Sisters of Charity there; they can take of them—after all, they are orphans now."

"The sisters will not take an infant. They will take the boy, but not the baby. They do not have the means to nurse an infant, signora . . . you of all people should know that!"

"What am I to do? I cannot take in another child, Father."

Father Licolli thought for a moment. He remembered a young couple that had just come to visit him, begging for his blessing and prayers because the young woman had still not conceived after three years of marriage. The problem was that the couple would be traveling all the way across Sicily to the mainland because the young husband had found work in the south of Italy.

"I will take the boy to the orphanage—to the sisters. But please take care of the infant for just a couple of more days until I can try to find a solution," Father Licolli begged.

"All right, Father, but please, only two more days; my

husband will beat me if I keep these children any longer," the butcher's wife lamented.

The young couple was happy to take the infant, but not his five-year-old brother, Santo. They had just enough money to travel to the mainland and then a small amount more to tide them over until the young husband established himself in his new job. Tearfully, the young woman explained her situation to the priest as Santo stood staring up at her, holding his baby brother.

***

They all met in the priest's rectory. The butcher's wife brought the baby, along with some papers she had found among Santo's mother's belongings. One paper verified Santo was five years old, born in January of 1890; another said the boy had been baptized one week after his birth in *La Chiesa di Angelus* in Nicosia, Sicily. The priest shook his head in disbelief and sorrow for young Santo's predicament as the butcher's wife handed him the two pieces of paper she held in her hands. The young barren couple turned and walked out of the rectory to leave for the mainland of Italy, tenderly carrying Santo's only brother.

The next day, Father Licolli took Santo by the hand to start the long walk to Palermo to the orphanage of the Convent of the Sisters of Charity. The two had not gone far when Giuseppe Vazanno happened along the same road. He was taking a large shipment of crated lemons to the Palermo dock to send them off to the mainland. Seeing Father Licolli walking under the hot Sicilian midday sun, Giuseppe stopped immediately and offered to give the young priest and the boy a ride to wherever it was they were going.

"Please, Father! You cannot walk in this heat! Come with me; I will take you to wherever it is you must go."

Gratefully, the priest climbed up and sat beside Giuseppe. Santo climbed into the back of the wagon and sat atop the lemon crates.

"Who is this young fellow, Father?" Giuseppe asked curiously, having never seen him before in the village.

The priest, not wanting to cause Santo any more pain than necessary, leaned in close and started to tell Giuseppe of

Santo's troubles and that he was on his way to take the boy to the orphanage in Palermo.

Giuseppe was shocked and at the same time heartbroken to think such a small boy had suffered so much already in his young life—not only losing his father and mother, but also his only brother! Giuseppe looked back at Santo sitting with his legs crossed and holding on to the crates for dear life, so as not to fall off as the wagon rambled along the dirt road.

"Father, would you mind if I talked to my wife about this terrible situation?"

Father Licolli looked at Giuseppe, surprised. "What are you thinking, Giuseppe? Are you thinking of taking the boy in yourself?"

"To be honest, I'm not sure, Father. I will have to discuss it with my wife first. She has just given birth to our daughter . . . I don't know for sure what she will agree to. But, if you could just wait a day or two before taking the boy to Palermo, I will try my best to see if I can find him a good home."

Father Licolli agreed. Since they had not gone very far from the village, Giuseppe turned the wagon around and took the priest and the boy back to Balestrate. When Giuseppe told his wife Maria, Santo Padua's story, she broke down in tears at the thought of Santo's losses at such a tender age.

"Oh Giuseppe, my Peppino, we have to do something to help the child. We have to!" Maria urged sincerely. "We cannot let that innocent child go to an orphanage—not now, after everything he has already been through."

"Do you agree then we should take the boy in with us?" Giuseppe asked hopefully.

Maria sat back in her chair. She had a thoughtful look on her face for a long time. Finally, she said, "I love you, Peppino, and I know you very well; I agree entirely with you that we must do something for the boy, but my concern is that we now have an infant daughter ourselves. I don't know if it would be proper to raise a male child with her in the same house—since he is not our blood relation."

Giuseppe took on a thoughtful look of his own now. He started to speak but Maria interrupted him.

"Giuseppe, the boy is nearly the same age as your little

brother Sevario. Sevario is eight and this Santo Padua is five. I have no doubt your mother will be very happy to take the boy in as a brother and companion to Sevario."

Giuseppe smiled. He kissed his wife on her forehead and said, "Not only do you have all the beauty in this family, but you have all the brains too." Giuseppe kissed his wife again and told he would be back soon; he told her he was going over to his mother's house to talk to her.

***

"Of course I will take the boy into my house! Of course!" Giuseppe's mother answered excitedly. "Go on! Go and get him now and bring him back here to me! While I wait for you—I will ready a warm bed and some good food for him. Go on now. I will tell Sevario the good news!" she exclaimed happily.

Giuseppe rode directly to Father Licolli's house.

"Would you like to come and live with me at my farm, young man?" Giuseppe asked Santo Padua.

Santo put his eyes down; he shoved his fists into his pocket. He did not know Giuseppe and his heart was crushed at the loss of his entire family.

Giuseppe knelt down in front of the boy who was sitting at Father Licolli's parlor table. He put his hands on Santo's shoulders. "Listen, son," he said soothingly. "I know you have suffered a great deal and I cannot take that away from you. But, you trust Father Licolli here, don't you?"

Santo looked up at the priest, who returned the look with a broad, comforting smile.

Santo nodded his head up and down.

"Good. Father Licolli will tell you that I will take very good care of you. I have a brother nearly your age—just a few years older—and he lives with my mother. My mother was very happy when I told her I would bring you to her so that she could take care of you. And, I promise you this, if you are at all unhappy living with my mother, my brother, and becoming a part of my family, I will bring you back right here to Father Licolli—just as soon as you ask me to." Giuseppe smiled, placed his hand under Santo's chin, tilted the boy's head to look at him, and said, "I promise you that."

Santo smiled up at Giuseppe, who even though he was kneeling down in front of the boy still towered over Santo.

Without saying a word, Santo got up from his chair and went to the back of the door where his cap was hanging on a hook. He put the cap on his head and said, "I will come with you, signor."

***

By the creek, Adriana knelt down next to baby Angelo, changed his diaper, re-swaddled him, and then placed him carefully between the two rolled-up blankets so that he could not move one way or the other.

"Francesca . . . Cinzia . . . come with me. We're going to the water to get cleaned up." Just as she was walking down towards the water with the two girls, she happened to look over a few yards and saw Alfredo throwing rocks into the stream.

"Alfredo," she called again to him, "come here to stay with your brother while I help the girls to wash."

Reluctantly, he turned to walk towards her but stopped; instead, he kicked a stone with his foot out towards the creek. Watching it hit its mark, he smiled, and then continued over to where Adriana was waiting for him.

"It's just for a little while, Alfredo; I'm going to wash the girls quickly and then you can take your turn farther down the creek." Adriana told the boy as she started off for the creek. Suddenly, she stopped noticing a look of sadness—maybe loneliness—in Alfredo's expression. She walked back to him and said gently, "Thank you, Alfredo, for helping Santo and Uncle Sevario. I know this is very hard for you." Adriana put her hand under his chin. "But I for one am very grateful to have you here with the other men in the family."

Alfredo smiled broadly. Then he sat down next to his little brother and continued tossing stones out over the grassy area that surrounded him.

"Francesca! Cinzia!" Adriana called out to the girls who were now chasing each other playfully. "Come with me now."

***

"How far is the burial site from here?" Santo asked Sevario as they watered and fed the animals.

"Down in the valley, not far from here. I carved out notches in several trees standing over the spot . . . this way, when we return we will be able to find his grave."

As soon as the last horse was watered, Santo and Sevario mounted their horses, took the reins of the one carrying the body of their brother, and rode off in the direction where Sevario had found a burial place for Gaspano.

It took the two men over an hour to dig a deep enough grave to cover Gaspano's body with earth and keep it from being found by wild animals. When they reached a depth of about five feet, Sevario wiped his brow with a kerchief and said, "I think this will do."

Santo went to get Gaspano's horse and walk it to the crude grave site. As they took the body down and were ready to put Gaspano into the ground, Nella appeared from between the trees.

"You could not tell me you were burying my husband, Sevario?" Nella said calmly.

Sevario and Santo looked up immediately, stunned to see that Nella had followed them all the way into the woods.

"How did you . . . ?" Sevario started to ask, but then simply said, "I'm sorry, Nella. Please forgive me. I thought . . . I thought . . ."

"He is the father of my children, Sevario. Gaspano has been a good and faithful husband to me. It is only fitting I am here with him as you lay him to rest."

Sevario looked at Santo, giving him the sign to proceed.

The two brothers slowly slid Gaspano's body down into his grave. Its loud thump broke the silence around them in the dark green Salemi forest. Nella came forward and stood over her husband's grave; then she knelt down and put a bouquet of wildflowers on top of his body. She showed little emotion as she slowly bent down, pulled back the covering over her husband's face, and kissed the top of his head. She pulled out two small bottles: one of oil and the other water. She cleaned Gaspano's face as best she could and then she made the sign of the cross with water over his body. She stood up then as Santo and Sevario lowered their brother's body into the ground. Nella took the shovel out of Sevario's hand and put into the pile of earth next to her husband's grave. Slowly, she lifted one shovel full of earth and let it fall down on Gaspano's body Then, she handed the shovel back to Sevario, "You can bury our Gaspano now, brother."

***

Adriana had brought olive oil soap, clean towels, stockings, and undergarments for the two girls. She helped them wash up in the cold water and then quickly change into clean clothes. As soon as they were done they returned to Alfredo. "Here, Alfredo," she said, handing the boy a piece of soap and a clean towel, "take these and go down a ways to get cleaned up." She pointed in the direction of the stream just as it made a slight turn away from sight, but yet close enough so Adriana could still keep an eye on him.

Alfredo took off happily in the direction Adriana had pointed out.

Adriana instructed the girls to take a nap while she returned to the water to clean up. She put the baby in between them for safety. "I'm just a little way down. If you need me for anything, call to me," she said firmly before turning to return to the water.

The mountain stream was not more than a half mile across and seemed to Adriana to be quite shallow. But she discovered that the look of it was deceptive, once she entered it. Past the rocky shoreline, where she had the girls sit and clean up, she ventured out into deeper water. Here the water seemed colder and flowed more rapidly. She braced herself against a large rock sticking up out of the stream, letting the silky softness of the sandy bottom caress her bare feet. She had tied up her skirt and underskirt around her waist and wanted more than anything to completely immerse her entire body in the water. The water was up to her hips, and the ice-cold feel of it was invigorating. She bent over, carefully maintaining her footing, and washed her upper body.

Suddenly, without warning, she was gripped with chills and she started to shiver uncontrollably. She knew she had to get out of the water, and quickly. She made her way gingerly to the shoreline. She reached for her shawl to wrap it around her; she pulled her underskirt and skirt down around her. But still she continued to shake violently. She sat on the ground to put her stockings back on when suddenly she was gripped with nausea. Her head began to spin; it seemed the entire forest around her was whirling about her. She closed her eyes against the sensation but then the dizziness intensified. A flood of nausea came over her again and without warning she emptied her stomach. Having had little to nothing to eat over the past two days, there was little to come out of her, causing her to gag and retch. It was so intense she thought she would faint.

Afraid of becoming unconscious, Adriana lay her head on the cool earth, hoping she would recover enough to make it back up to the blanket where the girls were. After no more than a few minutes, her strength returned. The nausea left her and she felt entirely relieved. From behind her she could hear Angelo's cries.

Quickly, she finished dressing and ran up to the spot where she had left the girls and the baby. To her surprise, Santo was just approaching the blanketed spot himself.

Immediately, Santo noticed how pale Adriana appeared. "Is everything all right? I heard the baby crying . . . what's wrong? Are you sick?" he asked Adriana.

"No . . . that is, yes, I am fine." But then Adriana made a quick assessment of her surroundings. *Where is Alfredo?* she thought.

"Is Alfredo with Uncle?" The tone of Adriana's voice suddenly alerted Santo.

"No. I haven't seen him since he left with you and the girls early today."

"He's gone, Santo. Alfredo is gone."

***

"Alfredo! Alfredo!" Santo called out as he walked along the water's edge.

The forest next to the creek bed was thick with pines, filled in with low-lying shrubbery and gnarled thickets. *The chance of Alfredo going back into the pine forest or the thickets isn't very likely,* reasoned Santo, who then continued to follow the creek around its natural curve where Adriana had last seen Alfredo.

But as Santo went around the curve of the stream, suddenly the creek looked more like a river. It had widened, and the water flowed more rapidly as it rushed over rocks and boulders jutting out of it. Santo's anxiety grew as he realized Alfredo would be no match for the current if he had fallen in at this point.

Santo started yelling out the boy's name now in the hope he was somewhere close enough to hear him.

Santo walked some distance along the water's edge when suddenly it narrowed back into a shallower creek; he felt some relief now, thinking if Alfredo had crossed the creek to the other side, at least he would not be drowned in the rapids upstream.

Then, just as suddenly, the pine forest cleared. Santo found himself next to an open field of dried winter grass. He walked up a bit from the creek's edge and inspected the grass to see if it had been trampled recently by the likes of a young boy running through it. Standing in the sunlight now, his eye was caught by something in the distance; it was just a small glint but enough to make Santo take notice. He stood very still. *There! There it was again.*

Santo made his way up through the thick grass toward the top of a hill and to whatever was glinting in the distance. Intuitively, he knew that if the glint had caught his eye and interest, it most likely would have caught the eye of an adventurous nine-year-old boy, too. As soon as Santo got to the top of the hill, he could see what looked like an abandoned structure of some sort in the distance.

He saw the glint again. It was coming from something hanging on a wall of the structure. He picked up his pace to get to the building, but as soon as he got within several yards of it, he heard the sound of voices—men's voices, not a child's.

Santo crouched down. He listened intently. He couldn't make out what was being said. He needed to get closer. Slowly, he circled around to the back of the old building, which was made of wood and stone. He could see that only three walls were still standing and that the wooden roof was held up precariously by one lone wooden beam in the center of what looked like an abandoned barn or shed. The missing wall had been apparently made of stone, as a large pile of them lay where it had likely collapsed. The pile was high enough, though, for Santo to crawl on his belly, unseen by whoever was in the it. Slowly, he crawled closer towards the pile of rocks.

"I told you I'm not lying!"

That's Alfredo's voice! Santo told himself; he was sure of it!

Suddenly, a feeling of panic came over Santo; no one with good intentions would be holding a child!

Santo looked up to inspect the building more carefully. He realized he needed to get to the back of it so that he could peer through the wooden boards and see who and how many men were with Alfredo. He rolled over several times until he thought he would be out of sight of those standing inside the structure. Getting on his knees, Santo crawled around the rear of the dilapidated building. He reached down to take his pistol out, but then remembered he had given it to Adriana. The only thing he could use for a weapon was a four-inch pruning knife he usually used in the orchards.

Then he heard a man say, "You're lying to me, you little *bastardo*!"

"I told you, I'm with my father! He's looking for me right now! We were hunting rabbits and I got lost, that's all. He's looking for me, though; I promise you that!"

"Tie him up!" the voice said. "I'll get him to talk."

"Get your hands off me! Stop it!" Santo heard Alfredo yell out.

Santo felt sweat running down his forehead and between his shoulder blades. He made his way to the back wall, and luckily found a small gap between the boards. Santo lay down on the ground again and looked in.

One man sat on a small wine barrel. Another man stood next to him with a shotgun trained on Alfredo, and a third man had Alfredo by the arms and was in the process of tying him to the center pole of the structure. The man sitting on the wine barrel seemed to be in charge and had a pistol in one hand that he rested on his lap. Alfredo looked scared to Santo; he could see his lips quivering. But, that didn't stop Alfredo from standing up to the man in charge.

Alfredo is a Vazanno through and through, Santo thought. *But he needs to learn to keep his mouth shut!*

A loud crack rang out. The man sitting on the barrel had suddenly taken out a long whip that he had attached to himself at his belt and cracked it.

"Start talking, you *bastardo,* or I'll peel every inch of skin off of you! Where are you from and who are you with?"

"I told you . . ."

The whip cracked again, but this time the tip of it hit Alfredo's leg. He cried out in pain. Then he screamed at the man with the whip, "Stop it! Stop it, you're the *bastardo!* My father's going to kill you!"

Santo had to act. There was no time to waste now. He crept backwards away from the back of the barn.

"Nobody talks to me like that, especially a *ragazzino* like you! Now, tell me what you're doing in this valley. Nobody comes into these parts unless they're thieves or beggars. You look too well dressed to be a beggar. So, what is it then: you a thief of some kind?"

"No! I told you, my father and me were hunting; that's all. Just hunting!" Alfredo screamed.

"You got a different way of talking. You are not from Salemi, that's for sure. You sound like you come from the west . . . Palermo. That's it! You are from Palermo. Nobody goes hunting for rabbits in these woods—especially from Palermo!"

The man on the barrel handed his whip to the man standing next to him. "Go ahead, beat the *merda* out of him!"

The man cracked the whip once, and then he cracked it against Alfredo's legs again.

Alfredo screamed and slumped down against the ropes that held his chest to the post.

The man with the whip walked over to Alfredo and slapped his face hard. The boy jerked his face upright in defiance. The man stood back from Alfredo and was about to thrash him across his chest.

"I wouldn't do that if I were you, signor!" Santo said calmly.

Startled, the three men looked up at Santo, standing only feet away from them. The sun was directly overhead but its glare surrounded Santo's body, making him appear gigantic as he stood in front of them.

The leader of the men yelled, "Who are you?"

"It doesn't matter. Leave the boy alone. We'll get out of here and you won't have to worry about either him or me."

The man eyed Santo up and down. "I don't think so, signor."

Then he turned to the other man, who was standing nearest to him and said, "Shoot him."

The sound of shot blast echoed in the air.

But instead of Santo, it was the man sitting on the barrel who fell over onto the ground. For a moment there was total silence, and then the man on the ground started to scream out in agony, "My knee! My knee! That *bastardo* shot me in my knee!"

Santo turned to see Sevario standing behind him. He threw Santo a pistol. "Get Alfredo out of here."

Santo ran to the boy and sliced the ropes that were holding him to the post in the middle of the building. He put his arms around Alfredo's shoulders. "Can you walk?"

The boy nodded.

The man with the whip threw it down and started to pick up his shotgun.

"If you're smart, you'll throw that shotgun to me," Sevario ordered.

The man threw the gun towards Sevario. It landed just a few feet from him. Sevario motioned for Santo to pick the shotgun up.

"Get going," Sevario said to Santo. "I'll be right behind you."

Santo looked at Alfredo and said, "Can you run?"

Alfredo looked down; he was bleeding badly from the whip marks across his legs.

So Santo picked the boy up and ran with him tucked under one arm as he carried the shotgun in the other hand. Santo had gone no more than a hundred yards when he heard a gun blast and then a loud crash. He stopped running for just a moment and then continued on. By the time he and Alfredo reached the wagon, Adriana had everything packed and was ready to leave.

Sevario had known when Santo and Alfredo did not return quickly that something was wrong. He had told Adriana to get everything ready because as soon as he got back, with or without Santo and Alfredo, they would be leaving.

"Where is Uncle?" Adriana asked anxiously when she saw only Santo and Alfredo return.

"Is everything ready to go?" Santo asked Adriana.

Before she could answer him, Sevario came running up the incline at breakneck speed. "Come on, we have to get out of here now!" he ordered.

Santo jumped up on the wagon. He looked down at Alfredo who was limping back towards the wagon bed. "Hey, Alfredo!" Santo yelled out.

The boy stopped and looked at Santo.

"Ride up here with me!" Santo ordered.

"Follow me!" Sevario yelled to Santo as he jumped up onto his horse.

CHAPTER III
THE ROAD
TO CATANIA

6 MAY 1911

SANTO FOLLOWED SEVARIO'S lead for over an hour, but when the terrain became rough to the point of being nearly impassable, he shouted out for Sevario to stop.

Sevario pulled his horse to a halt right away and then doubled back to Santo.

"I'm afraid if we keep going on like this—along this trail—I'm going to crack a wheel or lose an axle; either way, we would be in a lot of trouble. Is there another way out of this forest?"

Sevario nodded in agreement, but he knew the only other way out was to get onto one of the main roads leading out of the province. His fear was that the Salemi bandits who tried to torture and most likely kill Alfredo were on their trail by now—if they had survived the collapse of the structure on top of their heads. "Stay here," he said to Santo. "I'll ride out and find a way around this area. If I'm not back by nightfall, take the wagon and head south toward the coast."

Santo nodded in agreement and then said, "Take care to come back, brother! I can't make this trip without you!"

Sevario rode out, looking for any sign of an old trail that was in better condition than the one they were on. After an hour or so, he came upon a dried-up river bed; he had no idea of its origin or its name but at least, he told himself, it was as straight as an arrow and so dry that the clay bottom was like stone.

It was just after nightfall when Sevario rode up to the wagon.

"I've found a good trail we can take. Let's rest here for the night and leave at dawn."

"You think it's safe right here?" Santo asked.

"No," Sevario sighed. Santo was right; they needed to get away from where they were. "There's a wheat field I passed not far from here. No one will find us there. Then at daybreak we can head out again. Follow me."

Santo drove the wagon into the field as Sevario directed. But the animals were leery of going into the six-foot-high wheat, so Santo had to lead them in. Once they reached the middle of the field, Santo sat down next to the wagon and put his head in his hands, exhausted. Sevario looked at him and knew Santo needed rest badly.

"I'll be back. I'm going for water," Sevario told Santo.

"Wait, I'll go with you," Santo answered.

"No, stay here, brother. I'll be back as soon as I can. You and the others will be safe here." Sevario said as he rode off, but then came back within minutes. "Alfredo!" Sevario yelled out.

"Yes, Uncle," the boy said excitedly.

"Come on with me. We have to go for water."

The boy quickly jumped up onto Sevario's horse behind him.

* * *

Sevario found a small stream not far from the wheat field; he and Alfredo filled several wine skins with fresh water and then filled two tin buckets as well for the horses. When they returned to the wagon, not more than a half hour later, they saw Adriana sitting up front in the wagon with a shotgun, and Santo fast asleep on the ground under the wagon. Adriana had laid out a blanket for him there and he had fallen asleep within seconds of putting his head down. When Adriana had seen him asleep, she took his shotgun and had sat up on the wagon with it, waiting for Sevario's return. Alfredo and Sevario watered and fed the animals together, letting Santo sleep. Adriana insisted that her uncle sleep for a few hours, too.

"I can keep a watchful eye as well as you or Santo, Uncle. Go and sleep for a while and I will wake you before dawn. I can rest all day while we're on the move," Adriana insisted.

Grateful for the chance to sleep, Sevario kissed Adriana on the forehead, leaving her to keep watch. He knew as well as Santo did that Adriana was as capable as either of them when it came to handling a shotgun.

At dawn, both Sevario and Santo were up and ready to get moving again. But Santo had a question for his brother: "What happened back there with those bandits, after Alfredo and I left? I heard the gunshot and then a loud crash," he asked.

Sevario smiled. "You know that single wooden pole? The one holding up the roof in the middle of the barn?"

"Yeah, the one where they tied up Alfredo."

"Well, I shot the damn thing down! One shotgun blast and the whole roof came down on top of those *fili di puttana*!" Sevario was laughing now.

Santo started to laugh, too. "Well at least, brother, your heart was in the right place! You didn't want to kill them outright . . . you just wanted to hurt them bad enough so they couldn't do any more damage! You can tell that to the priest next time you go to confession!"

* * *

The town of Salemi was only two days' ride on horseback from Palermo but the news of the Vazanno farmhouse fire, Giuseppe and Maria's disappearance, and the murder of Gaspano Vazanno spread like wildfire. Within one day of the incident, the news had spread throughout western Sicily all the way to Salemi.

* * *

Two of the Salemi bandits were not seriously injured when the roof collapsed down on their heads. But the leader of the three men, the man whom Sevario shot in the leg, was bleeding badly and needed a doctor right away.

"If we don't get him back to town," said one of the uninjured men, "he's goanna bleed to death."

Once out from under the roof, the two uninjured bandits rigged a litter from the wood of the destroyed building. They dragged the bandit with the bleeding leg out from the rubble and placed him on the litter. His leg was bleeding profusely. One man took off his belt and tied it tightly around the bleeding man's thigh. The bleeding seemed to stop. Finally, the wounded bandit passed out from the pain and the other two bandits tied the litter behind the man's horse and took off headed for Salemi.

Just outside the town of Salemi there was a brothel by the name of *Il Core Nero*, "The Black Heart." It wasn't a place frequented by the locals of Salemi, but rather it was a hideout for the bandits who lived in the forests around Salemi. And, of course, a place filled with the prostitutes who made a good living off of them. The owner of the brothel, a peculiar man by the name of Gerome Fellini, always wore a tall, black, top hat on his head for reasons known only to him. For the most part, Fellini was the laughingstock of the town and disrespected even more by the bandits and thieves who hung out in his establishment.

The two bandits carried the wounded man into the bar.

The owner, Fellini, yelled out, "What the hell are you doing? Why are you bringing that filthy piece of *merda* in here bleeding all over my floor?"

"Shut up and bring a bottle of whiskey over here!" yelled one of the men carrying the wounded bandit.

By this time, the wounded man was awake and writhing in pain. "Sit me down, you fools!" he shouted.

The two men followed his instructions and sat him up in a chair. One tried to prop the wounded leg with another chair.

"What the hell do you think you're doing to me?" he screamed as he kicked the man with his leg, which resulted in more blood gushing out onto the floor.

"Get a doctor, whore!" the bleeding bandit screamed at a woman sitting at the bar. "Don't you see I'm going to die?"

The woman immediately jumped down off of the barstool and started to run towards the door. Then the man took out his pistol and laid it on top of the table, looked over at Fellini, and yelled, "I thought I told you to bring a bottle of whiskey to this table!"

Four men who had been in the bar when the bandits came and were at a table playing cards opposite the bleeding bandit's table, suddenly put their caps on and got up to leave.

Fellini, already angry because of the lack of business in his place, immediately grabbed two bottles of whiskey. He brought one bottle to the foursome who were about to leave. "Here, friends; this one is on the house! Stay and enjoy yourselves!" Then he winked at one of the men and said, "I got plenty of girls upstairs for you! It's a slow night! You can stay as long as you like for the same price."

The card-players looked at one another and shrugged. "Let's finish our game. We're in no hurry," one said, laughing.

Fellini smiled. Then he hurried to the table where the bleeding bandit sat. He put the bottle down on the table and said, "That'll be *tre lire*."

"Collect it at the end of the month, you jackass!"

"You already owe me *venti lire*, signor! You need to pay up!"

The bandit stared at the bartender. After a few moments, the bandit grabbed his pistol on the table. "The next bullet that comes out of that gun," he said, glancing down at the weapon, "has your name on it, you fat pig! Now get away from me. I told you, I'd pay at the end of the month."

When the bartender saw the gun he turned to walk away, but there was so much blood pooled around the bandit's chair that the bartender slipped and fell backwards, hitting his head on the stone floor. His black hat went flying across the room, leaving his few strands of hair sticking out from his head. When he tried to get up, he slipped again. Now his greasy apron was covered in the bandit's blood.

The bandits laughed as the bartender's face turned bright red; the more they laughed, the more Fellini's face became swollen with rage. He struggled to his feet, all the while slipping and sliding on the filthy, blood-splattered floor. As soon as he managed to get on his feet, he hastily moved to the back of the bar and pulled out a shotgun from its hiding place.

He walked slowly and deliberately to the bleeding bandit's table. He stood in front of the man and cocked the shotgun. "You owe me twenty *lire*, signor. I want it now or I swear I'll blow your brains out all over this table."

The bandit, already weakened by the loss of blood from his leg, had little fight left in him. He knew his pistol was no match for a cocked shotgun aimed directly at his head.

"Pay the man," he said to the other two bandits sitting across from him.

"You want me to pay . . ."

"Shut up, you jackass! I said, pay the man!" he growled through clenched teeth.

The man pulled out the money and handed it to the bartender. "Here," Fellini then said as threw a white envelope down on the table in front of the bandit. "This came for you today."

"What the hell is it?" the bandit asked.

"Some man from Palermo came in looking for you; when he didn't find you he gave this to me to give to you."

The bandit opened the envelope and started reading the piece of paper inside of it. Just then, the woman who had run to get the doctor came rushing in. She pointed to the bandit, his bleeding leg propped on a chair, and said, "There, that's the man."

"Let me take a look at your leg," the doctor said as he approached and knelt down on the floor next to the man's chair. As soon as he pulled the man's dirty, blood-soaked pants leg away from the wound, the leg began to bleed profusely again. "This is bad, very bad," the doctor said to the bandit. "You need to have this wound cleaned out and stitched up properly. It might already be too late."

"What the hell are you talking about?" the bandit screamed at the doctor as he reached for the bottle of whiskey, took a long drink from it, and then pushed the doctor away from his leg.

"The wound has severed blood vessels, signor; lucky for you—you still have a kneecap!" the doctor said without looking up. Then he turned to the girl who was still standing behind him. "Go and get clean water and more bandages."

The girl left and returned quickly with a bucket of cold water and a bed sheet; she started to tear the sheet into long pieces. When the bartender saw what the girl was doing he screamed out, "Now you owe me for the linen, you stinking *bandito!*"

The doctor removed the belt above the bandit's knee; immediately, the wound gushed blood again. He quickly tied several pieces of linen around the man's leg, making sure they were bound tightly enough to finally stop the bleeding wound.

"I need to clean all the buckshot out of this wound," said the doctor as he examined it. Then he looked up at the bandit and said, "You better take a few more drinks of that whiskey."

The bandit took a long drink of whiskey and then set the bottle down on the table. As soon as he put the bottle down, the doctor grabbed it. He poured the alcohol directly into the wound.

The bandit screamed out in agony. The shock and pain of the burning liquid draining into his open wound was unbearable. Suddenly, the man's eyes rolled back in his head, his body went limp, and he fell over onto the table.

The two other bandits got up out of their chairs immediately and tried to revive the man, but it was too late. He had lost too much blood. "I think he's dead!" shouted one of the men to the doctor.

The doctor felt for a pulse. Nothing. He put his ear close to the man's mouth to see if he could detect any breathing. Nothing. "You are right, signor. This man is dead."

* * *

Through all of the confusion, Fellini kept a watchful eye on the white envelope on the table in front of the wounded bandit. When the doctor finally pronounced the man was dead, the bartender shouted, "Get that *bastardo* out of my place! Get him out of here before the *autorita`* send the *polizia* out here to investigate! Hurry up, you good-for-nothing *bastardos!*"

The two men picked up the bandit and carried him out of the bar. The doctor ran out after the men, yelling, "I want my money! You owe me for taking care of your friend!"

The bartender turned toward the young girl and screamed at her to start cleaning the blood off the floor. As soon as the girl left and the table was empty, Fellini went over and pretended to inspect the girl's work; he looked around to see if anyone was watching him, and when he knew they weren't, he slipped the envelope meant for the bleeding man into his pocket.

> *To my men in Salemi, Balastrate, Capo di Vito,*
> *and Corleone*
> *REWARD £10,000*
> *I'll give £10,000 to any of my men who capture or*
> *kill Sevario Vazanno or Santo Padua from the town of*

Balestrate. My men in the west are watching Trapani, Marsala, and Selinunte. These bastardos have black hair and are with two women and some children. They come from the province of Palermo and you will recognize their accents if you find them. Your reward money is for information about their whereabouts. They are probably headed for a coastal town so they can get out of Sicily. I want them dead or alive. But you have to bring proof of their killing to Paolo Aiuto in Palermo if you kill them.

> *Turiddu Vanucci*
> *05 May 1911*

Fellini was elated. *Ten thousand lire! I could be a rich man!* He ran to the bar and tore his apron off. He yelled out to the girl cleaning up the floor to take care of the bar until he returned. Then he ran upstairs. In his excitement, the envelope with the note in it fell from Fellini's pocket as he bolted up the stairway.

One of the men playing cards noticed the bartender's sneaking interest in the dead bandit's envelope. He also watched as the envelope fell out of the man's pocket. As soon as Fellini was out of sight, he got up and retrieved the envelope from the floor. He read it, walked back to his playing partners, and threw the note down in the middle of the table. The other three men looked up at him. He looked down at them and said, "Read it."

"Turiddu Vanucci?" one of the men who read the note said rhetorically. "That bastard must be behind the burning of Vazanno's farm!"

"The burning of Giuseppe Vazanno's farmhouse is one thing, but what about the murder of Gaspano Vazanno?" echoed another one of the men.

"I have no doubt he's behind all of it," said the man who had picked up the piece of paper off the floor. "We have to get back to Palermo. Turiddu's father has to be told about this as soon as possible."

"That stinking bastard is crazy! He's offering a reward to anyone who can give him information about the rest of the Vazanno family! We have to stop him before it's too late," said the third man sitting at the table.

"We can be back in Palermo midday tomorrow," said the man still standing next to the table. "Let's ride."

All four men got up at once and headed for the door. They worked directly for Turiddu Vanucci's father, Vito Vanucci, the Don of Palermo. They, like most of Vito Vanucci's men, hated the Don's only son, Turiddu, but tolerated him out of respect for the Don. As they walked across the floor, the cardplayer stuck the note into his pocket; he wanted proof of Turiddu's treachery.

* * *

"The sun will be up in less than an hour. We have to get out of this wheat field," said Sevario to Santo.

"How long do you think it will take us to get to the coast from here?" asked Santo.

"I've been thinking . . . actually I couldn't sleep very well because that's all I've been doing all night. I think we'll be making a big mistake going to the western coastline. Whoever is after us now knows we're not going into Palermo. They know, as well as we do, we're going to try and run as fast and as far away from Balestrate and Palermo as we can. They probably know by now—since they haven't found us—we are on the run, and, since Nella and the children are nowhere to be found in Balestrate, that we have them with us. They'd be fools to think we are still anywhere near Balestrate or Palermo. No, I think they think we are headed for the western coastline. And, up until now, they would be right. We have to outsmart them, Santo. They know our family. They know we're not educated and they know none of us has ever been any further east than Corleone. No, for sure, they are looking for us along all the western coastlines. I say we go east. I say we go all the way to Catania, the exact opposite direction from where they are looking for us right now."

"Do you even know where Catania is?" Santo asked nervously.

"Look at it this way: what separates the west side of this island from the east? Nothing, brother, except the ground beneath our feet! We just keep following the North Star and keep bearing east of it. I think that makes as much sense as heading directly to the coast and into the hands of whoever is after us."

"I don't know, Sevario. I've heard men talking about the mountain ranges in the middle of this island. They're not like the Sicanians. I heard some of them are so high, you can see snow on top of them—even in the summer months! How in the hell are we going to travel across mountains with a mule, two horses, two goats, and a wagon full of women and children?"

"You worry too much, brother! It's easy! We just go straight until we reach a mountain and then we go around it." Sevario shrugged his shoulders, indicating the simplicity of his plan.

Santo started to laugh. "So let's say we make it all the way to the east—how are you going to find this place called 'Catania'?"

"I'll ask somebody! How else do you find what you're looking for?" Sevario answered jokingly. "Come on. Let's get a move on. I'm going to ride up on the wagon with you for a while. I marked a trail not far from here; it's a dried-up riverbed; the bed of it is as hard as stone. It looks fairly flat and, lucky for us, it's heading due east!"

Santo and Sevario pulled the wagon out of the wheat field just before dawn. Adriana, Nella, and the children were sound asleep in the back of it. Sevario's estimation of the riverbed was correct; the river had been dried up for years and the soil in the bed was baked hard as stone, as it had been exposed day in and day out to the merciless Sicilian sun. The two brothers rode in silence for several hours, Sevario keeping a sharp eye out for trouble and Santo concentrating on keeping the wagon in the middle of the riverbed trail—avoiding the occasional boulders that kept appearing in front of them.

Finally, it was Santo who broke the silence. "Seriously, brother, why do you think we should go to Catania? I know you too well. It is not just because it is situated as far away as possible from Palermo, of that I'm sure."

"I started thinking about it when we left Salemi. For some reason, I remembered a man who once came to visit Giuseppe at the farmhouse. Do you remember as a boy there was an occasion when two men came to visit with Giuseppe? They came on a Sunday afternoon—it had to have been many years ago because I think I was only Alfredo's age at the time."

Santo thought for a moment and then shook his head back and forth. "No. Whenever Giuseppe had visitors, it was usually about business, like when Don Vito would come to the farmhouse. I always felt it was none of my business so I would busy myself with other things."

"I agree. I always did the same when Don Vito would come to visit. But this time was different. I happened to be in the front of the house when Giuseppe caught sight of me and waved me over to come and meet his friends. Don Vito I knew, of course, but the other two men? I had never met them before. I remember how Giuseppe introduced me to the men. The one man, whose name was Manricco, I think, with the first name of Alfonzo, was the maker of a black-colored liquor. The reason I remember is because Giuseppe insisted I have a drink with him and the other men! Can you imagine it? I was just a kid but he poured me a glass right along with the men. He made me drink it down, too—I remember they all laughed when I nearly choked to death on the thickness of it.

"Then there was the other man, the man from Catania. His name was Battaghlia, and–I cannot recall for certain his first name–I remember thinking he was just as important as Don Vito. I remember watching our brother Giuseppe kissing this man's hand when he left the farmhouse that day. As you know, it was a shock to see Giuseppe give another man as much respect as he does Vito Vanucci. I tell you, Santo, this man Battaghlia is an important man and he is a friend to our brother Giuseppe. Something tells me if we go to him and ask for his help he will not refuse us."

"So you think this man Battaghlia from Catania might help us because of his friendship with Giuseppe?"

"I don't know who we can trust. But at least this Battaghlia fellow isn't a part of the *Famiglia* in Palermo. He may be our only hope. We have no papers and no money to travel to the mainland or anywhere else. We are in desperate need of help from someone who has the power to help us."

"Why can't we go to Don Vito, Sevario? After all, he and Giuseppe are like brothers! I can't believe he would ever have anything to do with this."

"Whoever attacked Giuseppe knows him. This wasn't a random act. I do not know who we can trust here in the west, including Don Vito. I do not believe he would ever harm Giuseppe and Maria—or Gaspano for that matter–but until we know for sure who's behind all this, we cannot trust anyone. I don't think we have any choice but to go east and try to get help from Battaghlia. If anything, he knows Don Vito better than us. He can get more information than we are able to get right now."

"So where do we go to find the man called Battaghlia once we get to Catania—if we even make it there?" Santo asked.

"I remember the men talking about the east the day I met Battaghlia; they talked about Etna."

"Etna? What do you mean, Etna?'"

Sevario laughed, "Etna is the name of a mountain. It's one of the biggest mountains in Sicily—maybe even all of Europe. The only reason I know about it is because I remember Giuseppe and Don Vito laughing about how one day it will blow its top and swallow up all of the east, including Catania!"

"A mountain? How the hell am I supposed to know they give a mountain a name?" Santo was laughing so hard he could hardly finish his sentence. "Who on earth gives a mountain a name? Only jackasses with nothing better to do!"

"I guess we'll have to wait and see just how big this mountain is, brother; maybe there's a reason they named her. I figure if we ride hard we can make it across country in a week, maybe less." Sevario said.

"Well," said Santo, "it looks like we are heading east to Catania. We'll just keep going until we run into the mountain they call 'Etna.'"

At dusk, Sevario knew they had to be close to Corleone. The countryside was still fairly wide open, but here and there were olive groves and patches of pine trees. "Pull over there," Sevario said to Santo, pointing out a small grove of trees. "We can stay there until dawn; I can go into Corleone and get some supplies."

"I think I should go to town," answered Santo. "You've been in the town many times more than I have; we shouldn't take a chance on you being spotted."

Sevario nodded his agreement.

* * *

Adriana's sleep was fitful. The wagon bed was small and cramped and arranging two adult women, three children, and an infant in it, comfortably, was impossible. Adriana saw that Nella and the others were all sleeping soundly and, rather than move them about to find a more comfortable place for herself, she decided to get up and get out of the wagon for a while. She could hear her uncle and Santo talking outside the wagon, and not wanting to surprise them, she spoke as she approached them. "Uncle. Santo," she said.

The two men looked up to see Adriana walking towards them.

"Are you hungry? I brought some cheese and bread," she said.

"Ah, thank you, Adriana," Sevario said, taking the food from her. "But you should be thinking of yourself, child. Why aren't you sleeping with the rest?"

Adriana didn't bother to explain her discomfort—after all, everyone was uncomfortable in one way or another. Instead, she began cutting the cheese and breaking off pieces of bread for the two men. Santo ate a small piece of cheese and some bread and then told Sevario and Adriana he was going to ride in to Corleone to try and get some more supplies.

"Be careful, brother." Sevario warned. "First sign of trouble, forget about the food and get back here right away."

"I'll be fine. I'll be back before dawn for sure." Santo got up and mounted one of the horses tied near the wagon.

"Why is this happening to us, Uncle? What could my father or poor Uncle Gaspano have ever done to anyone to deserve all of the terrible things that have happened?" Adriana asked Sevario.

Sevario closed his eyes, rubbed his forehead, and then shook his head back and forth. "Nothing. I can't think of anything at all. Your father has helped more people than I can even count. Gaspano was much loved by everyone in the town." Sevario shook his head again. "I do not have an answer for you. I don't know, " he said finally, shrugging his shoulders. "Your father, me, Gaspano—we don't have enemies; we only have friends! At least, that is what I thought until the day before yesterday."

Adriana stared at the ground in silence; she knew every word her uncle spoke was the truth. Her family was well respected in their village of Balestrate; and for that matter, everywhere across the western provinces of Sicily.

"Adriana . . ." Sevario asked, concerned, "can you think of

anything or anyone—in the last few months—that perhaps came
to your father's house and was angry with him for some reason?
Perhaps a stranger, someone you did not recognize?"

Adriana's heart began to beat harder in her chest. Suddenly
and unexpectedly she felt anxious. "No, Uncle," she answered.
"I do not know of anyone who may have been angry with Papa."

"I am shocked . . . I don't think these things that have
happened were by accident. They are too vicious . . . too hateful.
It is as if someone had a vendetta against our family," Sevario
said, confused.

Adriana felt the palms of her hands start to sweat; her heart
continued to beat harder and faster. She stood up suddenly and
said, "I am sorry, Uncle, but suddenly I do feel very tired. Would
you please excuse me?" Adriana said, as she turned to walk away.

"Wait, Adriana. Please, just a few more minutes. I know this
is hard for you, but you are the only one who saw what happened
that night at your farmhouse. Can you remember anything about
the men who came there? Do you remember anything at all that
might help me to know who is behind the murder of Gaspano
and the burning . . . ?"

"No!" Adriana fired back. Immediately, she regretted
shouting at her uncle. "Please forgive me, Uncle. I did not mean
to be disrespectful," she said "If I remember anything at all, I
promise I will tell you right away." Then she turned away from
him and walked to the back of the wagon.

The truth was, she remembered everything. She saw her
father tied to a tree and yelling out, desperately and helplessly, to
the men there to stop their madness. She watched as they threw
the farm animals into the blazing fire—alive. She remembered
the sound the butt of the gun made when the men kept hitting
her father in the head with it. She did not see her mother; she
only heard her screams and pleas begging for the men to stop.
She heard her mother cry out to strangers, "Kill me! Kill me,
you cowards!"

Adriana climbed back into the wagon using every ounce of
strength she had left in her small body. Her head was pounding
and she could feel each beat of her pulse throbbing in her
temples. The pain was so intense she had to close her eyes
against it; she laid her head back against the hard sideboard

of the wagon, praying for relief. Her stomach started to churn; nausea overwhelmed her, and the burning taste of acid rose in her throat. She swallowed hard, trying to rid herself of the taste, but nothing seemed to help. She knew she couldn't vomit even if she wanted to; she had not eaten anything since the day they left Balestrate.

"I'm back, my friend," she heard Santo say to her uncle Sevario.

"Already? How far was Corleone from here?"

"Not too far, but I didn't have to go all the way to the town. There is a farm not far from here. Look," he said, showing Sevario a bag full of hen's eggs and a large piece of smoked pig. "It's not bread and cheese, but it will feed us well into tomorrow."

"You did good, brother!" said Sevario, happy to see the meat and eggs.

"Go to sleep, Sevario. I'm wide-awake now. I'll wake you in a couple of hours so that we can get out of here before dawn—and before the farmer finds his pig missing!"

Adriana heard her uncle get up off of the ground. She heard Santo settle down right under the wagon where she sat. It comforted her to know he was there so close to her. Gradually, that feeling of comfort brought her body and mind a sense of relaxation; she closed her eyes and pulled a blanket up over her for warmth. She listened intently for a moment; she suddenly recognized the sound of her uncle's snoring. Gradually, the tension holding her body hostage began to dissipate; her eyes closed and her body seemed to relax all at once. Between the warmth of the blanket, knowing Santo was so close to her, and a state of complete exhaustion, Adriana finally fell into a deep sleep and began to dream.

Her dreams at first were pleasant and full of happy memories: her brother Antonio, her uncle Sevario, and Santo, too. The boys were running ahead of her. She watched as they climbed the steep wall leading up to the top of the bridge that led into and out of the village of Balestrate. She could hear her mother's voice in the background warning Antonio not to climb the bridge—it was too dangerous.

"I want to come, too!" Adriana heard her own voice call out to Antonio.

Antonio looked at Santo and motioned for him to climb down so that Adriana could climb up between them.

"Santo," she heard Antonio yell out, "make sure Adriana doesn't get too close to the edge!"

"Stay in the middle, Adriana! Don't worry, I'm right behind you. I won't let you fall," she heard Santo telling her.

Abruptly, her dream changed. Now she was running through a field of vibrantly colored wildflowers along the edge of the creek; she knew it was spring time. She watched as she came to the lemon orchards her family owned. She saw her mother then bring the men their supper at midday; she could see herself pouring wine into her father's cup. Everyone was sitting on the ground under the cool shadow of the lemon trees. Suddenly it was midday and time to rest. The branches of the blossoming, fragrant lemon trees swung back and forth in the warm breeze that came across the orchards from the Gulf of Castellamare.

Adriana loved midday in the orchards! She saw herself lying under a large lemon tree; she could smell the aroma of the lemon blossoms surrounding her; she watched as thousands of white, soft, delicate petals poured down on her as she slept, safe and peaceful, next to her father.

Suddenly, she was no longer a child but her own age. She was walking through the north orchards looking for her father and her uncles. She was carrying their supper to them and it was just before the midday siesta time. *What a beautiful day for Antonio's celebration!* She said out loud as she walked through the orchard, *Thank you, God, for making his day a perfect day!*

Suddenly, even in her sleep Adriana felt cold. Her mood became somber and a feeling of doom came over her. She was frightened. It was coming back again! She tried to fight it, but she could not rid her dreams of the terrible nightmare that came to her every night since that fateful day in March.

CHAPTER IV
THE LEMON ORCHARD

4 MARCH 1911

MARIA VAZANNO WOKE earlier than usual on the morning of Antonio's big celebration; the sun was shining through her bedroom window and the warmth of it felt good against her bare skin. It was the first Saturday in March in the year of 1911—a day Maria had been planning for a very long time. Her only son, Antonio, would be leaving Sicily, perhaps forever, on the day after Easter—exactly six weeks and one day from now.

Antonio, home from his seminary studies in Milan, had arrived one week before Christmas and was not scheduled to return to the mainland until after Easter. Returning to the seminary this time would be different from all the other times he was granted short leaves to visit his parents—this time, once he left Sicily and returned to the seminary, he would be sent immediately to Rome to prepare for the final phase to accept the sacrament of priestly ordination in December.

Maria had planned this celebration very carefully for a very long time. She had invited all of the villagers from Balestrate and many of their family and friends from the surrounding villages and towns throughout the Province of Palermo. Antonio would be the first native son to be ordained a priest from their small village—and to the people of Balestrate, Antonio was no longer just the son of Giuseppe and Maria Vazanno. Now he belonged to everyone!

The day she chose was a Saturday, exactly six weeks and one day before the Feast of Easter—but more importantly, it was a day just five days *before* the start of the Lent. And to the villagers living in Balestrate, and all of Sicily for that matter, the Lenten season is taken very seriously. It is six weeks long and marked by long hours of prayer, self-reflection, fasting, and personal sacrifice. Church attendance usually doubles during Lent—mainly because the men of the village are shamed into attending Mass by their wives and mothers.

Because Antonio was leaving to go back to the seminary the day after Easter, Maria knew she had to have a celebration for him before the start of Lent. After all, what kind of celebration would it be without wine and alcohol, *dolci, biscotti, lemone tortes,* and every sort of pasta with meat sauce—all things prohibited for consumption during the Lenten season? Maria strategically planned the date for her son's celebration very carefully indeed!

***

Maria lay still, enjoying the feel of the warm sun on her face; she turned lazily toward Giuseppe. His back was to her; the familiar sight of his strong, muscular body still stirred her after twenty-two years of marriage. She craved the feel of him next to her and reached out to put her hand on his shoulder. *What a pity so many Sicilian women are forced to marry men they do not love,* she thought as she began to caress his arm. He turned to her immediately.

"You're not asleep?" Maria whispered.

"I love you more today than the day I first set eyes on you," he whispered. "You are my one and only."

Maria smiled. "We are married for twenty-two years now in September and still you say the same thing to me every morning . . . just as you did that first morning."

"Of course I say the same thing! It is another day and I love you more today than yesterday."

Maria laughed out loud then; immediately she put her hand over her mouth. Then whispered, "Shh . . . we will wake the children!"

He pulled her to him; his strength was overpowering and without any effort at all he pulled her on top of him and kissed her passionately. Immediately stirred to passion, Maria began to kiss him back but then stopped and pushed him away. "We can't, Peppino," she whispered. "Nella and the others will be here any time; Nella is coming early to help me with the preparations today."

Giuseppe was not deterred. He continued to kiss her neck.

"Not now, Peppino! The children! The children!"

Giuseppe stopped. He sighed deeply. "Maria, Maria, Maria!" he said tenderly. "This is your fault." He pushed his body against hers.

They both started to laugh. To stifle her voice, Maria buried her head in Giuseppe's chest. "I'm sorry, my love," she said. "There is nothing I want more than you, but today is going to be a very long day and there is so much to do."

Maria rolled off her husband's body, got out of bed, and quickly put on a white linen chemise. "Come on, Peppino! We have to get up." She smiled warmly at her husband.

"If I must, I must. But I warn you, when I see Father Licolli tonight, I'm going to tell him how you are neglecting your wifely duties."

"Knowing you as I do, you will probably say that exact thing to someone tonight! And, I am warning you now, Peppino, if you do it will be a good long time before I do perform my wifely duties if you dare embarrass me in such a way!"

Maria pinned up her long, curly blonde hair atop her head; it was so thick and wavy that invariably a few long wisps of unruly hair fell out of the pins and down around her face. Giuseppe stared at her, thinking how beautiful and innocent she looked and at the same time intoxicatingly erotic.

"You are the most beautiful woman in all of Sicily," he said sincerely.

Maria smiled back at him. "And that is because I am from Milano."

Giuseppe turned over onto his back. "How did such a beauty from Milano fall for a poor lemon farmer like me? It is against nature."

"You have to get up, Peppino. Your brothers will be here any minute."

"Can you believe our son is to be a priest, Maria?"

Maria averted her eyes from her husband. When she looked up and saw the look on his face, she knew he was about to ask her what was troubling her. Instead of letting him say anything, she spoke first. "Get up, Giuseppe. We have so much to do!" Then she turned and walked out of the room. Giuseppe could hear her calling out to Adriana and then to Antonio to get up, too. "The rooster is crowing! It must be getting late! Everyone has to get up now!"

* * *

It hurt Giuseppe to think of the pain it caused his wife to know that once her son was finally ordained a priest, he might never return home again. He wanted to assure her that would never happen, but he knew he could not promise. Once a priest, Antonio belonged to the church and would be subject to her first, before his family.

Still, Giuseppe told himself, *I made the right decision.* Better he become a priest in Italy than to become an Honorable Man in Sicily. Giuseppe knew Antonio was different. From the time he had completed his four years of lessons in the village, he could be found reading all the books his mother brought with her when she left Milan to marry Giuseppe in Sicily. Antonio had his mother's keen intelligence and gift for language; he spoke fluently his mother's northern dialect, along with Sicilian. He would much rather spend his time reading or debating politics than waste his time chasing girls or riding his horse in the gulf waters of Castellamare like the other twelve-year-old boys in the village.

Giuseppe's love and concern for his son's welfare went deeper than Maria knew. Giuseppe had grown up with men who, like himself, had fathers who fought hard to bring about the Society of Honorable Men in Sicily—but he also knew what was required of men who joined that movement. He did not want that for Antonio, and was determined his son would never have to kill a man for the sake of Sicilian honor.

For years, Giuseppe debated what to do before making the

final decision to send his son to the seminary in Milan when he was just a boy of thirteen. He thought perhaps Antonio could take over the lemon farm from him, but—he told himself—Antonio truly has no talent for the business. *And besides that,— what about my brothers? They make their livelihoods in the orchards, and when I die, the property and orchards should go to them—after all, they have been working in them as long as I. Plus,* Giuseppe reasoned, *Vito Vanucci gave me all this land—out of loyalty to me. What happens if I should die? Would he honor that loyalty and let my son and my brothers have the land? After all, Vito has a son of his own! Perhaps once I die, he will take the land back and give it to Turiddu, his own son.*

No! Giuseppe told himself! *My son will be a priest and live an honorable life for God. He will be well taken care of by the church. More importantly, he will not lose his immortal soul to a life of crime and allegiance to a society other than to God.*

* * *

Giuseppe walked into the kitchen after dressing. Maria, her back to him, was already kneading dough for bread. He immediately walked up behind her and wrapped his arms around her tightly. "I love you with my whole heart and my whole soul," he whispered as he kissed her neck tenderly.

She turned and smiled up at him. "I love you too, Peppino," she said softly.

The kitchen door opened with a bang. Maria jumped automatically at the sound of the door banging against its hinges. It was Giuseppe's brother, Gaspano, and his wife and Maria's sister Nella, and their three children.

"*Buongiorno,* brother!" boomed Gaspano in his deep baritone voice.

"Be quiet, you jackass!" Nella said with irritation. "What's the matter with you? You're so loud you could wake the dead."

Everyone laughed except Gaspano, who put his eyes down, embarrassed by his wife's admonition in front of his brother and Maria.

"Come, everyone, let's sit down. We have a big day ahead of us and an even bigger night!" Giuseppe said as he put his arm around his brother.

Maria kissed her sister on both cheeks. Then she whispered, "Leave Gaspano alone! He's not hurting anyone." It angered Maria to hear her sister belittle her husband so, especially in front of other people and their own children, Alfredo and Cinzia. Nella's constant criticism of his brother bothered Giuseppe, too, but still she was Maria's sister and he did not want to start trouble between them. He knew her tongue bothered his brother, but Gaspano's good nature overpowered Nella's criticism of him—as he always managed to make a joke out of her stinging remarks.

"Yes, come and sit here, my love," Gaspano said to Nella as he pulled a chair out for her, "right here next to me, your loving and adoring husband."

Everyone laughed; Nella cast her eyes down but then pushed Gaspano gently against his chest jokingly. The tension, once again, was completely dissipated by Gaspano's sense of loving humor.

Adriana then entered the kitchen; Maria turned and embraced her daughter affectionately. Adriana could smell the rose and lilac water her mother used to rinse her hair and wash her body—the scent, so comforting, always made Adriana feel as if she were a small child again. Maria gently put her hand on Adriana's head and stroked her hair tenderly. "What can I make for you to eat, my sweet girl?"

"I'm not hungry, Mamma. All I want is my espresso."

"Nonsense!" her mother replied. "Today is going to be a long day; you are going to be very busy helping me today, daughter! You have to eat something."

Adriana reached for a large platter of sugar-coated biscotti and picked out the smallest one she could find. She dipped one end into her espresso and took a small bite of the dripping delicacy. Her mother smiled at her.

"Good girl," Maria said.

"Come and sit down, everyone!" Giuseppe announced. "I want to read a letter I received from Antonio's rector at the seminary before Antonio gets up. It arrived yesterday in Palermo and I thought I would save it for tonight to read to everyone," he said, turning to his wife, "but instead, I have decided this letter is only for our family."

Giuseppe pulled the letter out of his pocket.

Caro Signor Vazanno,

I hope this letter finds you and your family in perfect health! I am writing this letter to you because your son will take his ordination in December. I know he is with you now and will be with you for some time to come before he leaves his home for the last time to give his life to God. Yours is a great sacrifice! Only parents of a priest know how much they truly give back to God when they give Him one of their children. So, I write this letter to you, the parents of Antonio Vazanno, hoping it will bring you some consolation for your loving sacrifice, but will also bring you a great deal of holy pride in its knowing!

Your son, Antonio Vazanno, is one of the most impressive candidates for the priesthood this school has ever had during our long history. It has been many years since a young man with his intelligence, insight, and piety has graced our seminary and held fast his faith to see his vocation come to fruition. He excels in every subject with a particular gift for mathematics and science, not to mention his mastery of Latin, Greek, and German. He, in fact, far surpasses some of our most gifted professors! Never in our long history have we had such a protégé to guide and nurture.

Therefore, it is my pleasure to tell you, Signor Vazanno, that your son, Antonio Vazanno, has been chosen from among all of his classmates to continue his studies, after his ordination, in Rome. He has been selected to work and study in the household of the Holy Father himself, Pope Pius X.

May God bless you and your family, and I look forward to meeting you in Rome for Antonio's ordination.

Yours in Christ,
Pietro Provinzano, Rector
SS Peter and Paul Major Seminary
Milano, Italia

As proud as she was of her brother, a feeling of profound sadness came over Adriana. Sitting at the large farmhouse table with her aunt and uncle, she observed her mother's eyes fill with tears; she watched as her father wiped tears away from his face as he read the letter. She knew how embarrassed her father became when he was overcome with emotion—always taking great care to hide his weaknesses from his family. Her mother was outwardly crying, pulling her apron up to her face to hide her wet cheeks. Adriana knew, in her own heart, Antonio's leaving was breaking her mother's heart, even though that same heart was swollen with pride at the thought of her son becoming a priest.

Giuseppe looked up to see his wife covering her face with her apron. "Don't cry, Maria! Today, our family has much to rejoice over." Then he got up out of his chair went to his wife and kissed her tenderly in front of everyone.

Maria pulled away. "Stop, Giuseppe. What are you thinking?" She pushed him away, gently smiling at him.

***

Adriana sat across the table from her aunt Nella and uncle Gaspano. The table ran the entire length of the kitchen, in front of the open hearth.

"Do you want bread and butter or *dolci*?" Nella asked Gaspano.

"Of course I want bread and butter, and after that—*dolci!*" he said as he laughed heartily. "Do you think I got up before dawn just to come to work?"

Giuseppe laughed and answered, "I hope so! That's what you do every day, brother!"

"No, of course not! I'm here for Maria's delicious *dolci!*"

Nella looked down immediately. Between the two sisters, Maria was always the better cook—even though no one would speak such a truth out loud in front of Nella. Her husband's compliment of her sister's sweets and cookies hurt her to the quick.

Nothing that happened or was said in Maria Vazanno's household went unnoticed by her. She knew her sister's feelings had been hurt. "There is not a *Sicilian* woman anywhere who can come close to the delicious delicacies my sister bakes! I tell you, her *crème torte*, the exact recipe of my own mother, is famous throughout all of Milano! I can't shine my sister's shoes when it comes to her *torte riempito con crema!* And I never will because she, like my own mother, keeps the secret of it to herself!"

Giuseppe smiled broadly—not at Nella, but at his own wife. No one in all of Sicily could compare to Maria's generosity of spirit, much less her natural northern Italian beauty. He knew Nella did not deserve the compliment but it cost his wife nothing to give it, and he knew she expected nothing for it. Nella also smiled broadly, enjoying the attention—neither returning a gratuitous thank-you to her only sister, nor giving a reciprocal compliment in return.

Adriana's eyes were drawn suddenly to the warm colors dancing across the stone floor, colors created by the yellow sunlight coming through the kitchen window joining the golden-orange colors of the blazing fire in the cooking hearth. The colors seemed to dance and intermingle, creating shadows and images of unknown shapes. The heat of the stone floor felt good against the bottom of her bare feet; her body completely warm and cozy made her throw her shawl off of her shoulders and lay it across the back of the chair.

Sevario and Santo Padua had not yet arrived. Leaving her hair fall about her shoulders in front of her uncles was perfectly acceptable, but Santo Padua—even though as close to her as her own brother—was not blood-related, and once Santo arrived, Adriana would have to immediately cover her hair.

"How long do you think we will work today, Giuseppe?" her uncle Gaspano asked.

"We should be done after supper, early afternoon. We can work just a few hours—maybe six at most. Today we have to finish the pruning that we started yesterday."

"One day isn't going to make that much of a difference, Peppino," Adriana's mother remarked as she stood in front of the hearth, her back to her husband.

Still, he heard her. "I know, my love, but there is so much to get done before April sets in. I promise you, we will only work a half a day."

* * *

"Nella," Adriana heard her mother say, "Adriana will take the girls to their lessons this morning in the village and then she will take the men their supper. After that she will come right back here to help me with the preparations for tonight."

"Then who will pick Francesca and Cinzia up from their lessons?" Nella asked.

"You, if you are able to do it for me. I need the meat to be picked up from the butcher market, too. It will be ready about the same time as the girls are done with school. You can pick it up and then bring it back here with the girls."

But Adriana sensed that her aunt was not happy about what her mother was asking her to do.

Her aunt's face took on a look of disappointment. "Well, if Adriana is taking the girls to school, why can't she pick up the meat while she's there and wait for the girls to finish their lessons?"

"Nella." Adriana heard her mother's voice change, adopting a tone of impatience. "If Adriana waits for the girls and goes to the butcher, then you will have to go into the orchards and bring the men their supper today."

Everyone knew Nella hated going into the orchards in the early part of spring; it was a time when much of the immature fruit would fall off the trees and then mix with the fruit petals, making the ground altogether dirty and slippery with lemon juice and dirt. Nella had little love for lemon growing and a true dislike for the unsavory, messy parts of it. So no one was surprised when she said suddenly, "I think I will be happy to go to the village for you, sister; I promised Pina, the baker's wife, that I would bring her some sweet oil for her daughter who has been suffering from earaches for three days now."

Adriana quickly glanced at her mother. She knew what Nella was up to, just as her mother did. Both knew if Nella met up with Pina in the piazza, she would sit and gossip all day, and it might be hours before she returned to help Maria with the preparations for the evening's celebration.

"Nella," Maria said impatiently, "please return here immediately after you pick the girls up from their lessons and the meat from the butcher. I have sweet oil here and I will give it to Pina tonight when she comes here with her family."

Adriana smiled at how clever her mother could be.

Antonio walked into the kitchen just as Sevario and Santo arrived. Giuseppe stood up. "Let's go, men!" he said as he took one last sip of espresso. "We have to get to the orchards. I want to be back here no later than four o'clock today."

The sound of chair legs being pushed back across the stone floor echoed throughout the room, drowning out the chance of any other conversation being heard. The women stopped what they were doing and watched as the men filed out the back door, one by one. And like the silence that befalls a concert hall after the last note of music is played, the room became amazingly quiet.

Maria put her hand to her head as if suddenly reminded of something important that must be done immediately; she ran straight away to the back door and yelled out after her son, "Antonio!"

Antonio, hastily crunching one of the *biscotti* he had grabbed on his way out the door, stopped and turned to see his mother standing in the doorway, "What is it, Mamma?"

"What orchard are you working in today? Will you be working in the north or the south orchard?"

Giuseppe, just coming out of the barn, heard his wife asking Antonio about the orchards. He yelled out to them in answer: "The north orchards; we have to get most of the pruning done today, if we can."

* * *

Giuseppe, Gaspano, Sevario, Santo, and Antonio rode off together toward the road leading to the orchards. They were just about to turn to enter the north orchard when they encountered a group of laborers standing at the entrance, apparently waiting for their arrival.

"What's wrong?" Giuseppe asked as he rode towards the men.

"All the irrigation pipes have been broken in the south orchards," the leader of the men told Giuseppe. "It looks to me like someone has deliberately broken the pipes."

"Are you sure?" Giuseppe asked with a look of surprise on his face at the man's assumption.

"They were sawed at the elbows—and every one of the pipes are broken, not just one or two."

Giuseppe looked at his brothers and shook his head. "Who would deliberately break the irrigation pipes?"

Gaspano and Sevario shrugged their shoulders. Santo and Antonio looked at one another, and then Santo said, "Now that you mention it, when Antonio and I were out riding through the orchards last week, we noticed something strange, Giuseppe: there were some wooden crates left in the north orchards. But when we went to pick them up–thinking perhaps they had fallen off one of our wagons—we noticed immediately they weren't our crates."

"Why didn't you tell me sooner?" Giuseppe asked curiously rather than accusingly, knowing Santo would never keep something important from him.

"To be honest, I just thought perhaps we forgot to mark some of the crates with our 'V' trademark."

Giuseppe nodded in agreement. Then he took off his cap and wiped his brow with a kerchief. He stood silently for a minute or two, then looked up and said to his men, "Well, it looks like our plans have changed. We'll be working in the south orchards today; the irrigation pipes have to be fixed before pruning. Come on, let's go; we don't have any time to waste."

* * *

Adriana took Francesca by the hand and then held out her other hand to Cinzia. The three started out of the kitchen when suddenly Adriana remembered she had to go and retrieve the meal her mother had prepared for her father from the cellar. She asked her mother, "Is Papa's supper ready, Mamma?"

"Everything is in the tunnel."

The tunnel, located beneath Adriana's bedroom, was a large room and the starting point of a longer tunnel that ran the full length of the Vazanno farmhouse. In centuries past, this tunnel was used as an escape route when conquering invaders came onto the island and seized land and property. Having secret tunnels under the larger manor houses was a common way for the owners of the household to escape with their lives.

Adriana climbed down the steps of the ladder into the

darkness. She reached instinctively in the dark for the oil lamp that sat on a shelf near the ladder. Finding it, she moved her hand further down the shelf to find the sulfur sticks kept next to the lamp. *Ah*, she thought, as she found the sticks and struck one to start a flame, then putting it to the wick of the lamp. The room lit up immediately.

Her eyes fell upon the two satchels of bread and cheese hanging on a knob across the room from where she stood. Once she retrieved the bags, she turned to go back up the ladder but stopped, remembering she needed to get some wineskins, too.

She found herself remembering another day when she was a little girl. She had gone deep into the tunnel to get a food satchel for her mother. She had been with Antonio and Santo, and the three of them wanted to venture further into the tunnel to see how far it led. Before they had gotten very far, she heard her brother Antonio whisper to Santo, "Did you hear that?"

"No," Santo had answered, "what did you hear?"

"There's someone coming down the steps!" Antonio whispered. "Come on, grab the satchel and Adriana's hand and meet me in the cellar room."

Antonio started to run ahead as Santo grabbed for the food bag, looked at Adriana adoringly, and then took her little hand.

"Ah, Santo," Adriana had heard her father's voice say, "I see you have been placed in charge of my little Angel. Come over here and join Antonio and me. I have something I want to share with all of you."

Antonio and Santo glanced at each other; neither of them had ever seen Giuseppe in the cellar before. Even stranger, why wasn't he scolding them for being in the tunnel part of the cellar, a place which was forbidden to them?

"What I have to tell all of you is very important. Even though it primarily concerns Antonio," Adriana watched her father draw in a deep breath, "my decision will affect all of us."

Antonio swallowed hard, as if he knew the news was not going to be good news.

"As you know Antonio, your thirteenth birthday is just a few days away." Adriana remembered the tone of her father's voice and how it had made her feel apprehensive. "And thirteen is a very important age for boys and girls in this village; it marks the

beginning of your manhood and it is a time of independence."
Her father had moved to her brother and put his hand on
Antonio's shoulder. "Sometimes, son, in order for a boy to come
into manhood, independence means a boy must leave his family
and home."

"What do you mean, Papa, 'leave his family and home'?"
Adriana had seen the color drain from her brother's face.

She watched her father smile warmly at Antonio. "For most
boys here in the village, it means they will no longer have to take
lessons and most of them will go to work for their own fathers. "

"Yes, and that is what I want to do, Papa. I want to work with
you and my uncles in the orchards." Antonio retorted.

"Well, that is what I want to talk to you about, son. I have
decided that working in the orchards is not for you. You are too
intelligent and you have too much promise, my son, to waste
your life in the orchards like a common laborer."

Suddenly Antonio had looked hopeful. Many years later he
told Adriana that when her father said he would not be expected
to work in the orchards—that he was too intelligent—he had
thought, happily, that his father was going to send him to school
in Palermo.

"Antonio," Adriana could hear her father's words as clearly
as if he were talking at that very moment, "I am sending you to
a school on the mainland. I have made arrangements for you
to enter the seminary, son. Everything is complete; I paid for
everything already and you will be leaving within a month."

"But, Papa, why?" Antonio protested.

"You will understand perfectly well when you are older,
my son. But for now you must trust that I have made the right
decision for you—for your future."

"No, Papa, please!" Antonio pleaded.

"If I do not do this," Adriana's father had said, "this country
will not only take your soul away from you—it will take your life."

* * *

Adriana climbed the cellar steps and reentered the kitchen.

"I have everything, Mamma. Where is Papa working today?"

"Antonio told me the north orchard. And, that is good
because it is on your way back from the village."

Adriana took Cinzia and Francesca's hands and walked out of the kitchen to take them to school.

"Adriana!"

She turned around and look at her mother. "What is it?"

"Stay on the village road today, Adriana. I do not want you walking alone through the orchards."

"Mamma . . ." she began to protest.

"I want you to listen to me today. Bring your father his supper and then come home."

"Yes, Mamma."

"Adriana!" Her mother was now walking towards her. She reached out and untied the shawl that was tied around Adriana's waist, put the shawl over her hair, and then turned her around to tie the shawl under her hair at the nape of her neck. "You are no longer a girl, Adriana. Keep your hair covered when you go out now and are not here in this house. Do you understand me?"

"Yes, Mamma."

* * *

As Adriana walked through Balestrate, she found herself smiling and talking to several of the villagers about the celebration dinner for Antonio that night. Everyone was excited! It seemed suddenly the entire village had claimed her only brother as their own! Their expression of happiness for him made her feel very proud of him.

After dropping the girls off at school, Adriana approached the bridge leading into and out of the village. She felt the warmth of the sun on her bare arms. As she walked, the sun rose higher in the sky and she knew it must be exactly noon because the sun was directly over her head. The bridge was built to traverse the creek bed once a year in the early spring when it filled to capacity with snowmelt from atop the low-lying Sicanian mountains.

She could hear her father's warning in her mind: *This time of year it is at its most dangerous because the water is more than four feet deep; there is nothing but rocks and boulders below! Be careful you don't fall in!*

Adriana looked up at the wild vine that completely covered the stones stacked one atop another to create the two massive walls on both sides of the road. She was shocked to see all the flowers in full bloom; bougainvillea and white lily of the valley were everywhere! It was a magnificent sight. She had often climbed this wall with Antonio in front and Santo Padua behind her. It was very easy to climb to the very top because the stones were so thick—at least two to three feet wide in some places—and the stones were built like steps, gradually becoming higher and wider as they neared the top. Climbing the wall was dangerous enough, but a fall from the very top would most likely kill the unfortunate climber. Both she and Antonio were strictly forbidden to climb the wall.

But they did climb it—many times! And when they reached the very top they would yell out as loudly as they could, just to hear their echoes come back to them from the valley below.

* * *

The heat soon became unbearable. Sweat rolled down Adriana's scalp under the heavy woolen shawl her mother had tied around her long hair. She wore wool stockings beneath a heavy linen skirt, and although her thin chemise was made of light cotton, under her outer skirt she wore another heavy underskirt! *Why did I wear such heavy clothing today?* Adriana wondered.

The girl put down her satchels of food and wine and untied the shawl from behind her neck. She took it off and tied it at her waist. She shook her hair out, letting the cool breeze blow over and through her hair. It was instant relief! Then she took her leather shoes off—but left her stockings on. Still, the relief of removing the heat of the leather felt just as good as the shawl taken off of her head.

You are no longer a girl, Adriana. Keep your hair covered when you are not here in the house. Do you understand me? Her mother's voice rang out.

She picked up her satchels and began walking into the orchard.

* * *

"Paulo," Turiddu Vanucci ordered, "take two men and ride the full length of the orchard. Keep an eye out for any sign of Vazanno or his men. If you see anybody, get out of the orchards as fast as you can and head for Alcamo. If I don't see you back here in one hour, I'll know you ran into trouble and I'll head out to Alcamo to meet you."

"Don't you want me to warn you, boss? Maybe Vazanno might find you here if I don't warn you," Paulo Aiuto, Turiddu's right-hand man, asked.

"Vazanno isn't smart enough to find me. I can take care of him, that's for sure. Besides, he is too busy today in the south orchards trying to repair all the pipes we destroyed last night. That will keep him busy for a while!"

* * *

Turiddu Vanucci, the only son of Vito and Apollonia Vanucci, was a man who was feared in Palermo. Even though just twenty-three years old, his reputation for ruthlessness and cruelty was already well known to everyone—including his father and mother. Don Vito Vanucci knew his son *should* be the obvious choice to take his place leading the Society of Honorable Men when he died—but he also knew his only son did not have the courage and character to do it. Unlike Turiddu, Vito and his own father before him were both beloved by the peasants in western Sicily. They were loved not because of their power and position but rather, because they had earned every man's respect by leading the way to freedom from foreign domination for the Sicilian peasants.

Turiddu, on the other hand, felt entitled. He knew what his own father and his grandfather before him had done for his country—but in his mind, the work was done! Now, it was time for the people to pay back to his family what they owed them for the sacrifices his father and grandfather made. Now it was time for him to enjoy the fruits of his grandfather and father's hard work! And to that end, he felt his father was *stupid* not to take advantage of his power and position. Even though Vito Vanucci collected protection money from the shop owners, bankers, and farmers throughout the provinces around Palermo, he only took a small percentage, preferring instead that his countrymen themselves enjoy the fruits of *their* hard work.

But, Turiddu Vanucci disagreed entirely with his father's philosophy on how to run Sicily. Turiddu, although not spoiled by his iron-willed father or his loving but firm mother, had grown into someone his father did not like. And the more he made it known to Turiddu he did not like his behavior, the more angry and hateful Turiddu became.

"My father doesn't know how to run this country anymore!" Turiddu would complain to Paulo Aiuto.

"Why do you say that?" Paulo would ask.

"Because he's weak. He only takes a pittance from the rich shop owners and farmers—and that lousy friend of his, Giuseppe Vazanno, owns the best land in the country—all because of my father's generosity and weakness!"

"But maybe your father wants to help the people, Turiddu, and not take from them," Paulo would answer.

"This country is rich in everything! My father could be sending everything to the mainland, even America. No, instead, he sends just enough for each man to make a living and no more. He lives in this fantasy that he and my grandfather saved Sicily for the Sicilians, that *la cosa nostra* is the only way to be happy. I tell you Paolo, my father is stupid now and he will die stupid. When I take over this land, things will be different. I will live the life of a king!"

Vito Vanucci knew every step his son took. He knew every word that came out of his mouth criticizing the way he ran the Society of Honorable Men. He knew everything his son did to try to undermine the security of Sicily and the Sicilian people. He also knew he would never allow his son, Turiddu, to become the next Don of Palermo. It broke his heart and brought him to tears more times than he wanted to think about—but—he was too intelligent to let a man like his son have control over all the power and wealth his people had finally earned. Everything was for the people—not his family alone. That's how much he truly loved his country.

As often happens with fate, Turiddu, already enraged over his father's generosity towards the *Sicilianos* and in particular Giuseppe Vanucci, happened upon a document that served to seal his destiny.

"Turiddu, while you're here, would you mind taking this document to your father? I have had it for some time now and when I saw your father yesterday, he asked if I would send him a copy of it," Signor Carlo Petronni, Palermo's Court Magistrate, asked.

"Yeah, sure. I'm on my way to my father's house now," Turiddu said as he took the envelope from the magistrate.

As soon as Turiddu was out of sight of the city, he stopped his horse and took out a cigarette. He eyed the package time and again, wondering what was so important that his father would ask the magistrate of Palermo to keep it for him. Finally, his curiosity got the better of him and he opened the envelope, being careful not to tear the paper or destroy the seal; this way he could easily melt the wax back into position and his father would never be the wiser.

It was a deed. It was a property deed made out to *Giuseppe Vazanno*.

Turiddu read it over and over again in disbelief. His own father had *given* him all of the land south of the town of Balestrate, west to Trapani, east to Alcamo, and south to Calatafimi!

"That's thousands of acres!" he said out loud to no one but himself. "That *bastardo* gave my land away! That *bastardo* gave my land to his *bastardo* friend, Vazanno!"

As Turiddu started to push the document back into the envelope, several receipts fell out onto the ground. Turiddu picked them up and started to shove them back into the envelope along with the deed. Then he stopped. He read one of the receipts. It was made out to SS Peter and Paul's Seminary in Milan, Italy. The receipts were made out every month starting in January of 1911. Then he found another bundle made out in 1910, and another 1909.

"Is he out of his mind?" Turiddu screamed out loud.

Turiddu could not believe his eyes! *Not only did he give my inheritance away, he's paying for Vazanno's son's education on the mainland.* Turiddu was enraged. He felt as if his head would explode. He jumped on his horse and started to gallop toward his father's house to confront him. But the closer he got to his father's house, the more he changed his mind about confronting him. He knew his father too well—and he was afraid of him.

If I confront him, he will know I read his private papers; he may be so angry with me he'll take back all that I have managed to get from him. No, better I think about a better way to get back at him—short of killing him, Turiddu thought.

And so it wasn't long before Turiddu found an opportunity to get back at his father and at Giuseppe Vazanno!

* * *

"So, you're looking for a partner in Sicily? Is that right, signor?" Turiddu said to Benjamin Meyer, a businessman from America visiting Naples.

"Are you from Sicily or Naples, signor?" Meyer had asked.

"Oh, no, I am from Sicily. Palermo, Sicily. I am in Naples on business. What type of business are you in, signor?"

"Fruit, produce, olive oil. I'm here in Naples looking for someone who will work exclusively with me to export their own fruit to me in America."

"What in particular are you looking for, signor? You know Sicily grows the best fruit in the world," answered Turiddu.

"Oranges, figs, grapes, the yellow tart fruit—*lemon.*"

Turiddu knew this was his opportunity to get rich on his own, without his father and without Vazanno—that is, *with* Vazanno but without him knowing anything about it! *It was perfect!* he told himself.

"I have hundreds of acres of lemons, signor. Would that interest you?"

"Really? Where are your orchards?"

"Just outside of Balestrate in western Sicily. We have been sending the fruit to mainland Italy for some time now, but we have never thought about America."

And so it was that Turiddu and Meyer formed a partnership. Turiddu would send him—and only him—lemons from western Sicily and Meyer would give Turiddu a 40 percent partnership in his business. If everything was successful, after a year, they would become full partners and he would rename the enterprise *Meyer & Turri Produce.*

When Meyer received the first shipment and saw that the lemons were stamped with a "V" and under that, *Product of Balestrate Sicily,* he immediately questioned Turiddu about the symbol.

"We have a crew of men who pick and crate for us; we pay them a small stipend for their work but they insist on putting their business label on the lemons, that's all," Turiddu explained, and Meyer accepted it.

After all, Benjamin Meyer, a gangster whose headquarters was New Orleans, America, was only using Turiddu anyway. Once he received the fruit, he marked up the price without letting Turiddu know and then paid him what they had originally agreed upon for each crate of fruit—so, unbeknownst to Turiddu, he was only handing over 25 percent of the American profits to his Sicilian partner.

The Vazanno orchards were so large it was easy for Turiddu to watch where the men were working. If they were in the north orchards, he would go at night and steal from the south orchards and then vice versa. It was easy enough to steal the "V" stamp from the steelsmith who designed it; and it was next to nothing to steal the crates from the docks in Palermo.

*　*　*

"Buongiorno, signorina!"

Adriana felt her heart leap inside her chest at the sound of a man's voice. She looked immediately in the direction where it came from, and saw a tall man standing next to his horse. Adriana answered nervously, *"Buongiorno, signor."*

She did not know this man standing in front of her and staring directly at her. Men from Balestrate do not do such things. They take off their caps, always averting their eyes from young girls and women they do not know.

The man started smiling at her.

Adriana's mouth went dry; her hands started to shake; she was afraid of him. "Are you looking for my father, signor?" she asked.

"And who might your father be, signorina?" Turiddu asked sarcastically.

"Giuseppe. Giuseppe Vazanno," answered Adriana. "Giuseppe Vazanno is my father and he is working here—here— in this orchard today."

"Really?" asked Turiddu mockingly. "I've been here all morning and I have not seen anyone—just me and my men. That's all—not another soul; except, of course for you now. And, what, may I ask, signorina, is your name?

Adriana couldn't speak; her mind was racing with confusion. He did not look like a good man and she wanted nothing more than to get away from him. She turned from him and started to walk away when suddenly he yelled out to her.

"No! Wait! Wait, signorina. Please. Don't be afraid! I do know your father. I know him very well."

Adriana stopped and turned to the man. She felt for one split second she did know this man; it was his voice. She knew his voice.

"Do I know you, signor? How do you know my father?"

"Oh, yes, we have met. It was a very long time ago. You were just a small girl. Tell me your name and I will tell you if we have met before, signorina."

"Adriana. My name is Adriana Vazanno."

"Ah yes! We have met. I do recall now," Turiddu said as if in thoughtful remembrance. "I rode to your farmhouse to see my father who was meeting with your father and some of his friends. You were picking flowers just off the main road to your house—I remember you were sitting in the middle of a patch of bright yellow flowers! You had two goats who were grazing next to you." Turiddu finished the recollection smiling broadly. Then, he continued, "You sat with your legs apart and your skirt pulled up about you. If you had not been such a tiny little thing, I would have thought you were quite naughty—the way you sat."

Suddenly Adriana remembered. She was picking wildflowers and sitting not far from where her own father sat with his friends. This man rode up on a huge, black stallion. He steered the animal to stand directly over her. She remembered the fear she felt; she thought him about to trample her with his horse. The sound of his voice, the cold blackness of eyes; they were still exactly the same.

If it had not been for her father, she would have surely been trampled. She remembered looking up and seeing her father ride between her and this black-eyed horseman. Her father was so forceful, he pushed the other horse backwards as he drove his own smaller horse—like a wedge of steel—between her and the stranger

"What do you want here, signor?" Now Adriana asked angrily.

"Well, I was hoping to see your father, but seeing you is all the better."

Adriana turned and this time walked away with conviction.

"Wait! Wait!" Turiddu called to Adriana. "Where are you going? Come and sit with me awhile. The sun is high above us and the coolness of the clearing is calling us to rest. I see you have bread and cheese with you. I'm very hungry. Come now, bring it over here to me."

Adriana kept on walking, ignoring him—which made him angry.

Suddenly, he rode his horse up next to her as she walked. Adriana stopped and shouted, "My father and my uncles will be here any time now, signor. This meal is for them. I think you had better leave before my father finds you here, trespassing on our property."

Turiddu got down off of his horse and caught Adriana by one arm, causing her to drop the satchels with the cheese and bread. Some of the bread spilled out onto the ground. Now her anger turned to terror.

"Please, signor," Adriana pleaded, "you are preventing me from taking my leave. My father will be very angry when I tell him of your behavior."

"Do you know who you are talking to?" Turiddu said as he grabbed her other arm and stood her in front of him. "My name is Turiddu . . . Turiddu Vanucci. Do you know who I am?"

"Yes, signor, I know who you are. You are the son of Vito Vanucci, my father's friend. Your father and mine are as close as brothers . . ."

"Don't bother me with that *merda*, it makes me sick to hear it; no, worse than that it makes me *pazzo* to hear it," Turiddu said through clenched teeth.

"I have to go, signor. Please let me go! My father is waiting for me. As you can see, I am bringing my father and uncles their supper." Adriana tried to free herself of Turiddu's grip but he only held onto her tighter. "Please, please signor! Please let me go!" she started to scream.

Suddenly, she felt the back of his hand across her mouth. "Shut up!" he seethed. "Shut up, you stupid Vazanno *puttana!*"

Shocked, Adriana put her hand to her face. She turned again

and tried to run but Turiddu jumped on top of her. "I thought you said your father is coming here . . . now. Isn't that what you said?" He looked around the orchard. "I don't see another person in this orchard except you and me."

Turiddu got up then. Adriana started to try and crawl away from him when suddenly she felt her head being pulled backwards by her hair. He had grabbed her hair and was trying to pull her across the ground. Adriana screamed out in pain and terror. Turiddu stopped and kicked her hard in her side. "Shut up, I told you!"

"Take your hands off me!" she screamed as loudly as she could.

Suddenly, he was on top of her again—the weight of body crushing her breathless. She screamed out again.

"Shut up!" he seethed.

But Adriana continued to scream for her life, hoping someone—anyone—might be happening through the orchard and hear her.

She felt his fist go into her mouth this time. Pain burst out and threw her head back as if something exploded inside of it. Then, everything went black.

Turiddu felt her body go limp beneath his. But within seconds, she started to blink; she tried to open her eyes to the glaring sunlight over her head. The sting of the light pierced her already throbbing head.

Wait! Wait! What's happening? she asked herself but then, she knew; her body was being dragged across the rugged ground by her feet. The devil was pulling her by the feet! When she tried to react, she realized immediately her hands were tied together; her feet too! Her feet were raised up off the ground—*My God,* she thought, *he's pulling me behind his horse!*

She glanced down at her body and could see her skirt and undergarments were all up around her waist. Feeling the humiliation unbearable, Adriana begged God to take her. *Please, let me die, dear God, please take me!* she begged.

"Stop it! Stop it!" she pleaded. "Please, I beg of you; please I beg you," she screamed and then began to cry and sob uncontrollably knowing it was futile to try and reason with a devil who was finding his pleasure in torturing her.

Suddenly she lay still on the ground. She saw him approach her from the side and she tried to move her body back across the rocky ground but it was useless. With one fell swoop, he picked her up and started to carry her back further into a clearing.

"Please, please," Adriana pleaded, "please don't hurt me. Please don't touch me. I beg of you. My father is a rich man! He will pay you whatever you want . . . but please just leave me alone. I promise you . . ."

"Shut up!" Turiddu screamed.

He had taken her to a grove of cypress trees that had some low-lying shrubbery in front of them. He laid her down between the shrubbery and trees near a stone bench. She felt him untie her feet and try to spread her legs apart. She began kicking him with all her might. One good kick landed on his face between his mouth and his eye. He fell backwards, the blow was so intense. He got up off the ground and crawled back to her; his mouth was bleeding and his eye in a squint from the blow. Adriana began kicking again and he knelt down on her tiny legs that were no match for his brute force. Adriana screamed out so loud then that Turiddu's horse whinnied and jumped back.

"I told you to shut up, didn't I? But, you're just like your father! You just won't listen to anyone, you bitch!" Turiddu slapped her again across the face; it was so hard she was stunned into silence momentarily. But then when he ripped her chemise open with his two hands, she started to kick all the harder again. He tried to put his hand over her mouth but she bit down into his flesh. He pulled his hand back to see it bleeding.

"Son of a bitch!" Turiddu screamed. "Son of a bitch!" He shook his hand and blood flew across Adriana's face. Without warning, he pulled his arm back forming his hand into a fist and in an instant, his fist landed on the side of Adriana's face.

Finally, through the mercy of God, everything went black. Adriana no longer felt any pain.

* * *

She tried to open her eyes but could not. She felt the warmth of the sun on her body; she smelled the earth beneath her; she felt a light breeze cross over her body and the aroma of lemon blossoms around her. She tried to move her hands but they were still tied over her head; she tried to move her legs but she could not; she could just turn her feet at her ankles. But, the pain from just that tiny movement shot a searing pain up her legs into her thighs.

I must still be alive, she thought. *I can feel pain again.*

She tried again to open her eyes; this time only one eye opened. But as soon as the sun's light filtered into it—she immediately closed her lid because of the shock of it—it burned straight through her head like a knife had pierced it. Even the slightest twitch of a muscle caused her pain. She lay perfectly still hoping the pain would go away.

She heard something.

Terrorized beyond anything she had ever known, her first thought was that the devil was coming back to torture her again. She lay as still as death. She willed her lungs to stop taking in air. She willed her heart to beat slowly and softly. *Please dear God,* she prayed silently, *please let him think me dead. Elsewise, take me Father, I beg of you this one last favor.*

The sound of boots hitting the rocky earth around her rang in her ears; the clanging of metal hitting something. *A belt buckle,* she thought, *yes, a belt buckle.* But, she dared not turn her head or open her eye for fear he would know she was still alive. *I must be on my side,* she thought suddenly, *because the noise is coming from behind me.*

She heard the sound of a horse moving as if a rider was trying to mount; then she felt the earth beneath her head pound in her ears. It was the sound of hooves; the horse was moving away from her. But just as suddenly, she felt the movement of the earth again—but this time the horse was coming closer to her.

"Oh God, no," she whispered fervently, "Please don't let him come back. Please help me, God!"

Turiddu stood over her. He stared down at what he thought was her lifeless body. The sight of her disgusted him. She belonged to Giuseppe Vazanno, whom he hated beyond anything or anyone—except for his own father.

"You bitch," he seethed as he kicked her in her side with the steel tip of his boot. "I hope your own father finds you! I want him to die at the sight of you!"

Then, just as he came, he was gone.

A breeze crossed over body. She felt chilled to the bone suddenly. She felt gooseflesh rise on her arms and legs; her thighs. Suddenly, aware of her humiliation, she prayed again to die.

* * *

"Hey boss, what's going on?" Paulo said to Turiddu as he looked over his shoulder in the direction of the cypress grove.

"None of your business," Turiddu said angrily. Then he added, "Do you understand me? Nothing in my life is your business. Ever!"

"Sure boss. I understand."

"Where are the men?" Turiddu asked.

"They're already on their way to Messina," Paulo said looking over Turiddu's shoulder.

"What are you looking at?" Turiddu asked menacingly.

"Nothing, boss. Nothing."

"Shut up, then. Come on, let's get out of here."

* * *

Adriana drifted into blackness. She felt her body being transported away; there was a warm light above her. The closer she got to it the warmer she felt. The scent of lemon blossoms filled the air. It was intoxicating and made her forget about her broken body. *How wonderful it is to die at last,* she thought. *Thank you, God, for answering my prayer.*

* * *

Adriana woke from her nightmare to the sound of screaming. Within moments of waking, both Santo Padua and her uncle were next to her, and she realized the screaming she was hearing was her own. "What is it, Adriana? What is it?" asked her uncle, frightened she was having a nightmare because of everything that had happened over the last two days.

"I'm sorry, Uncle. It's just a bad dream. I am recovered now. I promise you, I am recovered," Adriana said sincerely.

Santo brought her water and put a cold, water-soaked cloth on her forehead.

"How long have we been traveling, Uncle?"

"Since dawn. I'm hoping we can make it to central Sicily by nightfall. The roads are not very good though. I'll try to find another way just as soon as we get out of this rock-strewn territory we're in right now."

Nella's infant started to cry as soon as Adriana began to scream. Now Nella was feeding him and he seemed content. But the other children were up and hungry.

"Santo, let's stop for a little while. Everyone can take some refreshment before we start off again."

Adriana had no way of knowing for certain it was Turiddu Vanucci who was the one responsible for the burning of her farmhouse, the torture of her parents, and the murder of her uncle Gaspano. In fact, no one knew for certain except for her own mother Maria and her father Giuseppe.

CHAPTER V
DON VANUCCI'S FARMHOUSE

TURIDDU VANUCCI WAS enraged. It angered him the girl had put up such a fight. *That damn Vazanno whore just kept fighting me,* he thought as he rode through the countryside next to Paulo Aiuto. *It's her own fault I had to beat her to death!*

"Hey, where are we going boss?" Paulo asked. "I thought you said we were going to Trapani to meet the other men." Paulo noticed Turiddu was riding towards Palermo rather than Trapani where he had told the other men to meet him and Paulo.

"I forgot I got business to take care of in Palermo tonight. You can go on to Trapani and check everything out. Meet me back in Palermo tomorrow," Turiddu ordered.

"Who was the girl back there, boss? Where did you find her?" As soon as the words left Paulo's lips he felt immediate regret: he remembered how Turiddu hated it when any of his men asked about his personal life.

Turiddu's expression turned to stone. "None of your business! Who are you to ask me about my business?" Turiddu's face was flushed with anger. "Shut up and mind your own business, you stupid jackass!"

"Sorry boss. It's just that she looked as if she was . . . well, you know . . . dead." Then Paulo stopped. Once again, he knew he had said too much.

"What do you care if that *puttana* is dead or alive? All the Vazannos are nothing but whores and bastards . . ." Turiddu turned his head away from Paulo now; he too immediately felt regret; not for his crime but for revealing it to Paulo.

"Vazanno . . ." Paulo was stunned. He could not help but to ask Turiddu about the girl now. "You mean that girl back there was Giuseppe Vazanno's daughter?"

"How is my business any of your business?" Turiddu asked sarcastically. "Didn't I already warn you once today to stay out of my business?" he shouted.

"Whatever you say, boss. It's none of my business," Paulo answered as he turned his face away from Turiddu in disgust. "See you back in Palermo."

Paulo kicked his horse hard in the flank with his boot. The horse bolted forward. As he rode off he kept kicking the horse harder and harder—as if by kicking his horse he satisfied his urge to kick Turiddu. *How could he attack a maiden! No Sicilian in his right mind would ever dare commit such a heinous crime! Vazanno's daughter is just a young girl! I hate him! I swear I hate Turiddu Vanucci.*

From that moment on Paulo Aiuto began to plan how he would escape Turiddu Vanucci's control.

* * *

Turiddu turned down the dirt road leading to his father's farmhouse; he slowed his horse to a walk. He was nervous. He knew if his father was back from the docks in Palermo, he would have a lot to answer for—considering his clothing was filthy and bloodstained. He saw no sign of his father's horse; he knew the animal would be out grazing in the winter grass next to the barn if his father was home. Not seeing the animal, Turiddu felt immediate relief. All he would have to contend with was his mother—and he had no fear of her whatsoever. Suddenly, his stomach growled. He remembered he had not eaten anything since the evening before; nor had he slept since then. He kicked his horse to pick up his gait. All he wanted now was to get off the animal, get something to eat, and then go to sleep.

Turiddu rode into the barn and jumped off his horse. He took the saddle off of him but did not bother to cool him down;

a habit that enraged his father who had respect for everything including his faithful horse. Turiddu looked at the foam all over the horse's flank and sides and thought briefly of watering the animal and wiping him down—but quickly dismissed the idea as soon as his stomach started to growl again.

As Turiddu approached the back of the farmhouse, he slyly peeked in the window off the kitchen making sure no one was in the room before he went in. He opened the backdoor quietly, not wanting to arouse his mother's attention. He stepped into the kitchen and went directly to a large wooden cabinet where his mother kept her freshly baked bread and wheels of cheese.

He opened the door and, to his chagrin, the cupboard door creaked; the sound seemed much louder than he remembered and reflexively he put his head down and closed his eyes hoping his mother did not hear him.

"Turiddu!"

He recognized the familiar voice immediately. He turned around to face his mother. "Mamma! I'm so sorry. I was trying not to disturb you, thinking you were napping before Papa comes home." he lied.

Turiddu's mother walked closer to him. She turned him around by his arm to face her. She looked him up and down staring at his filthy, bloodstained shirt. "What's all this?" she said, pointing to marks on his shirt.

Turiddu's face turned red—not from embarrassment but rather from anger. *How dare she ask me about my business! I'm a grown man!* Ignoring her question, he pulled his arm away from his mother's grasp and started towards a washroom off the back of the kitchen.

"Where have you been, Turiddu?" his mother asked angrily as she followed him towards the washroom. "Look at you! Your shirt is covered in blood!"

Turiddu stopped. He looked down at his shirt and trousers; blood and dirt were smeared across the front and bottom of the shirt; even his shirtsleeves were smeared with Adriana's blood. Now he was furious. *That stupid whore has even managed to get me in trouble with my own mother,* he thought.

"What does it matter to you where I've been, Mamma?" Turiddu walked closer to his mother and stared her in the eye.

"Huh? Do you have to know everything I do? Do you have to know everywhere I go? My business is my business and no one else's!" he said through clenched teeth.

Turiddu felt the back of his mother's hand across his face. He immediately brought his hand up to where she slapped him and stared back at her now in shock.

"Enough! I'm your mother!" Turiddu's mother seethed. "If your father heard the way you talk to me he would beat you until you could no longer talk. I'm your mother, Turiddu, and don't ever forget that! Now, tell me where you have been and what filthy business you have been up to."

Turiddu felt an immediate urge to hit his mother back, but he dared not. That would definitely seal his fate and he knew it. His father would not hesitate to kill him if he ever laid a hand on his mother.

"Mamma, why do you worry?" Turiddu said calmly suddenly trying to soften his aggressive demeanor to calm his mother down; he knew if his father came home while she was angry at him—she would tell him everything. "Me and my friends went rabbit hunting. We left late yesterday evening and finished up this morning. That's all. I'm sorry for raising my voice to you, Mamma. But, when you accuse me of doing something wrong, it makes me angry."

Turiddu's mother stared at her son knowing full well he was trying to manipulate her with another lie. "Rabbit hunting, eh? Where did you go rabbit hunting then?" she asked.

"Where we always go . . . to the valley around Salemi. The catch was good! We caught nearly seven rabbits but one got away when the snare snapped." Turiddu laughed out loud trying to convince his mother he was telling the truth. "You should have seen that rabbit try to hobble away on three legs!"

Hearing such a cruel statement come from her own son hurt Apollonia Vanucci more than the lie he was telling. She put her eyes down so she would not have to look into his face any longer. She felt nothing but disgust for him at that moment, and wanted more than anything to be rid of the sight of him. "Get cleaned up, Turiddu," she said quietly as she turned her back on him.

Sensing his mother's disbelief in his story, he stammered, "Mamma, wait, don't go."

But without hesitation, his mother quickly continued to walk towards the doorway to leave the room. Turiddu's face turned red now with anger as he yelled out to her, "Where is Papa?"

"I don't know where your father is. But you had better get cleaned up before he comes home." She left the room without bothering to turn and look at him.

Turiddu, enraged by his mother's disapproving attitude towards him, turned away then to leave the kitchen. He slammed his hand so hard against the back door that it banged against the back of the house loudly. The sound caused his mother to stop and turn in fright. Turiddu looked back at neither his mother nor the door but rather continued to walk angrily towards the barn.

His mother went to close the door. She watched her son walk away. Her eyes followed his defiant body as he stomped across the dry ground; she watched as she remembered how many times she had seen the same behavior when, as a small child, he couldn't get his way.

Turiddu's anger reached a fever pitch by the time he got to the barn. He continued to brood over his mother's refusal to believe his story. *Even my own mother doesn't know how to respect me! One day I'll be the head of the family—things will be different then. Things will be different then . . .* His uncontrolled anger became so charged he did the only thing— at that moment—his head told him to do: he pulled his arm back and punched a wooden pole with his bare fist; immediate, excruciating pain coursed through his fist and up his arm. He pulled his fist back, shaking it in the air to try and dispel the pain. He felt tears sting his eyes but he controlled the urge to scream out in pain. Instead, he ran towards the well in back of the barn and shoved his throbbing hand into a pail of cold water.

He caught sight of his horse as he stood in front of the well; the animal was still thickly lathered in a foamy sweat. *If my father comes home now and sees I haven't properly taken care of the animal, he'll kill me,* he thought. He whistled for the horse to come to him. He began pouring jugs of water over the back of the animal, and then rubbed him vigorously to try and cool him down properly. Satisfied, the animal didn't look as if he had been ridden hard for hours—he then led his mount over to a trough to drink heartily before slapping his rump and causing him to bolt out of the barn again.

Turiddu looked down at his clothes. The front of his white shirt was filthy with blood and dirt. His hands started to shake as he stared down at them; the skin was crisscrossed with deep scratches; his fingernails were black with caked mud and blood. Suddenly a feeling of panic came over Turiddu. If his father did happen to come home now—come into the barn now—and see the way he looked, it would be impossible to convince his own father he had been rabbit hunting. His father was no fool and would see right through the lie. Frantically, Turiddu began pumping the handle on the well. Water began to gush out into an open stone trough. As soon as the large basin was full, he took off his clothes down to his undergarments and knelt in the dirt in front of the well. As soon as he splashed the cold water up onto his arms and chest, he felt immediate pain from the sting of the cold water on the numerous lacerations on his arms and hands. He looked down at his body in disbelief.

Look at what that whore has done to me! he seethed as he looked at all the bruises already forming on his arms and chest. He began to wash his face and noticed fresh blood dripping into the now murky water. He got up and went over to a small mirror nailed to the wall. As he stared at his reflection, he could see scratches all over his face and then opened his mouth to examine his tongue; it was bleeding profusely from the left side. *That's where the whore bit me when I tried to kiss her!* He looked back at his face. Discoloration encircled his right eye; it was turning an angry black and blue color and was swollen to nearly twice the size of his left eye. Suddenly, he remembered. He was holding her down when her foot came up and hit him squarely in the face. That's when he stopped and pulled off her stockings.

Suddenly Turiddu was smiling. He felt himself becoming aroused as he thought about how he attacked the girl. He recalled her helpless screams for mercy, her whimpering pleas to be released.

A horse whinnied in the front of the barn breaking Turiddu's thoughts; the smile left his lips as he quickly turned from the mirror to see who was in the barn.

* * *

Turiddu's mother had continued to watch Turiddu until he was out of sight. *Where I have I failed, dear God?* she thought.

She felt her heart was breaking. Tears welled in her eyes; she covered her face with her apron and walked from the kitchen. She wanted to prepare a meal for her son but could not. She felt empty; once more on the verge of despair, she slowly walked to the front parlor feeling defeated and weak. She dropped down onto a chair and began to weep bitterly.

"What's happened? Why are you crying?"

Startled, Apollonia looked up, shocked to see her husband standing in the doorway. She had been crying so hard, she did not hear him come into the house. Quickly, she wiped her face and stood up to go to him. "Nothing, Vito; nothing!" she said as she continued to wipe her face with her hand and then greet him with a kiss.

"Don't tell me there is nothing wrong when I can see clearly there is something wrong! Now tell me what has happened to cause you so much distress," Vito said with genuine concern and love for her.

"I'm fine, Vito. It's just sometimes I feel lonely in this big house; you know with you gone most of the day on business and Turiddu rarely home . . ."

Vito stopped his wife midsentence. "The only time I ever see you cry is when Turiddu is home. Is that what this is all about? Is Turiddu home now? What did he say to you?"

"No, no, Vito! I promise you, everything is fine!" Apollonia said urgently. She knew there would be a terrible confrontation between father and son—if Vito knew Turiddu had caused her to cry. She stood in front of him and put her arms out to him.

He ignored the gesture.

Apollonia became anxious; she knew her husband did not believe her. Quickly, she tried to distract her husband. "Would you like an anisette? Let me make you a *tazzini di caffè;* you must be very tired after the long ride back from Palermo."

"No, nothing. Come and sit here with me." Vito walked to a divan and sat, gesturing for his wife to join him.

Obediently, Apollonia sat down next to him. Vito put his arm around his wife's shoulders and then took her face in his hand turning it gently to face him. "Now tell me." he said. "What has Turiddu done to upset you?"

* * *

"Turiddu!" Vito screamed out as he walked into the barn. "Turiddu!"

Turiddu was startled to see his father coming towards him. He thought the horse whinny was from his own animal coming back into the barn.

Vito looked at his son standing shoeless and shirtless with a filthy pair of underwear hanging from his waist. "What the hell have you been up to?" Vito demanded. "Where have you been the last three days? And don't even try to tell me the lies you told your mother!"

"Papa! I swear it's the truth! My friends and me were rabbit hunting in the valley around Salemi. We left a few days ago and just came back today. That's all. Mamma was upset because I had blood on my clothes; but what am I supposed to do? You know rabbits have to be skinned right away!"

"So, where are your clothes then?" Vito demanded.

Turiddu nervously looked back over his shoulder at the pile of clothes lying near the water trough. "They were ruined, Papa. I was just about to burn them in the smithing hearth.

"What makes you think I do not recognize your lies? Do you think I have never come home and found it necessary to burn my clothes because of blood . . . of course I have! But I will tell you this . . . I never had to burn my clothes because they were covered with rabbit blood! What do you take me for, a fool?"

Turiddu stood speechless now. He knew when his father was enraged and had learned long ago to shut his mouth on those occasions. He knew very well if he tried to spin the same story again, his father's anger would only intensify. Instead he said calmly, "Then you of all people should know better than to ask why I have burned my clothes."

In the blink of an eye, Turiddu found himself flying backwards toward the ground. His father's fist had struck him hard in the face; he was a very powerful and strong man—absolutely no match for Turiddu.

Vito walked over and stood over his son. Now, Vito could see all the scratches, cuts and bruises on his son's chest and arms. "I see the rabbits fought back hard," Vito said mockingly as he pointed out the scratches on Turiddu's chest. "They must have put up some fight, eh Turiddu?"

Turiddu rubbed his jaw. He tried to sit up but his father pushed him back down with his foot. Then Vito moved away from his son and picked up an iron rod that was propped against a post. He scoffed at his son as he walked past him and over to the bloody clothes lying on the ground. He picked up Turiddu's shirt and eyed it suspiciously. "So then, Turiddu," he said holding up the bloody shirt in front of his son, "if you were not killing rabbits today, where did all this blood come from?"

Turiddu began to sweat; his mouth went dry. His first reaction was start to move away from his father—push his body backwards across the damp, dirt floor. But he did not move a muscle. He knew better. His mind began to race. He needed to think of something . . . anything to calm his father down. But his head was pounding from the punch he received to the side of his face; his brain, it seemed to him, was incapable of rational thought. The only thing he could think of to say was "I gotta go, Papa; I still got all of my collections to get done before tomorrow." Then he started to get up.

Vito walked closer to his son and stood over him; he took one of his heavy leather boots and pushed it against Turiddu's torso. He pushed him back down onto the ground and stood over him with one foot on his bare chest. "Tell me why you made your mother cry," Vito demanded.

"I don't know why," Turiddu stammered, "she was upset when she saw the blood . . ."

Vito reached down and picked his son up by one arm. Turiddu staggered to his feet. Then Vito dropped the iron rod and slapped him again hard across the face. Turiddu fell to the ground again.

"What's the matter with you? What kind of an animal makes his sainted mother cry all the time? Go ahead . . . tell me about the blood. Tell me the truth, Turiddu! Where did the blood come from?"

Turiddu got up and faced his father squarely, "I told you, it came from skinning rabbits!" Suddenly, Turiddu felt a rush of adrenaline; he wanted to hit his father back but controlled the urge. Instead he stood up taller and took in a deep breath. "If you want to beat the *merda* out of me—then go ahead. I was rabbit hunting for three days and the clothes on my back were the only clothes I had! Of course they are going to be bloody and full of filth."

"That is not what I asked you. I asked you why you made your mother cry," Vito demanded.

"I don't know why she was crying. She wasn't crying when I left the house. She always cries—it's nothing new. I came home after hunting rabbits this afternoon and had some blood on my shirt. She got upset and asked me—no, she accused me—of doing something even she could not think of. I explained why I had blood on me—but it didn't satisfy her, I suppose." Turiddu shrugged his shoulders in a false gesture of uncertainty.

That was the last straw. Turiddu's cavalier attitude and disrespectful remarks about his mother infuriated his father. With clenched teeth, Vito walked over to Turiddu and put his huge hands around his neck. He pushed him backwards up against a wall and started to choke the life out of him.

Turiddu began grabbing at his father's hands trying to get him to release the pressure around his neck.

"Where were you the past three days and whose blood is on your shirt? Answer me or I swear I will kill you with my bare hands and bury your body where no will ever find it." Vito let his grip loosen around his son's neck so that he could answer.

"I told you . . ."

"Don't lie to me!" Vito let go of Turiddu and let his body slump to the ground. Then he walked over and picked up the iron rod and turned back to Turiddu. He raised his arm and let the rod come down on Turiddu's knees.

Turiddu screamed out in agony.

Vito raised the iron again but Turiddu put up his hands and begged, "Please, Papa! Please! I will tell you everything but please don't hit me again."

"Start talking," Vito said between clenched teeth.

"I picked up your collections for the last three days. Papa, I swear it. Two days ago I went to Trapani and after that I headed back towards Palermo picking up the money owed us along the way. I swear it!" Turiddu pleaded. "But then, we stopped in Salemi . . . in a bar there. There was a bunch of drunken *Siciliano* peasants who started a fight with us. I'm sorry, Papa, I didn't mean to do it but I beat up one of the men. I don't know if he's alive or dead; I swear that's what happened. You can ask Paulo Aiuto if you don't believe me. He and few other men were with me. They will all tell you that's what happened."

"Why didn't you tell your mother that?"

"Because she gets upset when I fight, you know that! You know that, Papa."

"So you weren't rabbit hunting . . . you were brawling in a bar in Salemi. You may have killed a man . . . but you don't know for sure." Vito stood back from his son; he rubbed his chin and then said, "Men die all the time in fights . . . it happens. What I want then is the money and all the receipts from your collections for the past three days. I want them in my office in Palermo in the morning. Every last receipt and every single lire you collected."

"I put the money away already. You can check on the receipts yourself in the morning; they're in the safe in my office on the docks," Turiddu said, now pleading with his father to believe him. "I was just getting dressed so I can go back to the docks and finish my collections; now it's too late. I'll have to finish collecting tomorrow." Turiddu felt his father's wrath waning; suddenly, he felt a surge of confidence.

"I want the money and the receipts in *my* office in the morning—not yours. And who didn't you collect from yet?"

Turiddu slowly stood, still leaning against the wall. "The leather shop owner," he said, "and the registrar down at Immigration, and a couple of the whiskey dealers who sell to the bars over on via Giogonollo." With his sudden surge of confidence—having never learned to keep his impulsive mouth shut—he added, "I could be collecting from that rich-ass lemon grower Vazanno if you would only let me! You know better than I do that he has more money than everyone in Balestrate put together!"

Turiddu watched as his father's face turned red; he could see the veins in his neck start to pulsate. Suddenly he knew, once again, that he had gone too far.

Vito walked to Turiddu and stood just inches from his son's face. "You listen to me and listen well! I . . . only me . . . not you or any of those ignorant banditos who follow you around like stinking jackasses . . . decides who pays and how much they pay, *capeche*?"

"Yes, Papa . . ."

"Shut up!" Vito roared. "I'm the head of this family and every single Honorable Man in Sicily; you have absolutely no power whatsoever in this country—and if you keep it up, Turiddu, you will not live to see the day I *do not* choose you to carry on your rightful heritage. Unless you change your ways, you will never become the head of the family in Sicily, *capeche*?"

"I will change, Papa . . . I promise you I can change my ways . . ."

Turiddu's father moved back away from him; he stood several feet away with a look of thorough disgust on his face. He stood with his feet apart, still holding the iron rod in his hands. "Go on and get out of my sight. Find yourself some supper elsewhere tonight. You don't deserve your mother's food." He turned to walk away from Turiddu but suddenly stopped. He turned around slowly and said, "If you so much as raise your voice to your mother again—my beloved wife—I'll kill you with my bare hands."

Vito turned and walked out of the barn leaving Turiddu standing there alone.

Turiddu's jaw was clenched now as he watched his father leave; his hands were folded tight into fists as he stared at his father's back.

"You stupid old bastard! I hate you more than you could ever imagine . . . more than you will ever know. Someday . . . someday things will be different! The shoe will be on the other foot! That's a promise, old man!" Turiddu whispered through clenched teeth.

* * *

"Turiddu, where have you been? I been waiting for over two hours . . ." Paulo Aiuto asked, but then sheepishly fell silent seeing the look Turiddu gave him as he entered the room.

"Something came up," Turiddu said absently, as if Paulo was the least of his problems.

Turiddu walked past Paulo without so much as a nod; he walked over to the window and looked out. "Go home," he said to Paulo behind him. "We can finish the rest of the collections tomorrow."

"Your father's not going to be happy if we don't get the collections to him early tomorrow."

"Shut up!" Turiddu screamed. He turned around then to face Paulo. "Who are you to tell me what I need to do for my own father?" He started to walk to Paulo—his fists were clenched. Paulo backed away. "I said, get out of here. Go on! Be back early. I got a job for you to do in the morning," Turiddu said, stopping himself from going any further.

Paulo put his cap on his head and pulled it down hard over his forehead. He wanted to say more but his years of experience taught him better. He knew when to shut up when it came to Turiddu. Instead, he got up and walked out of the office, pulling the door shut behind him.

* * *

It was just after nine o'clock in the morning when Turiddu heard a knock at the office door.

"Come in," Turiddu yelled out.

Paulo came in with his cap in his hand. "Hey boss . . . you said you got a job for me this morning."

"Come on, let's go." Turiddu pushed past Paulo as he walked out of the office; Paulo followed him without saying a word.

By midmorning the sun was already beating down on the docks of Palermo. The glare of sun on the pale blue Tyrrhenian Sea caused sharp flashes of light to continuously pierce Turiddu's eyes. He swore under his breath as he pulled down the lid of his cap to cover his eyes. Then he shoved his hands in his trouser pockets and walked with determination towards the leather and smithing shops to finish his collections along the docks.

* * *

Not long ago, Sicily had been ruled by foreign landowners, none of whom had ever put one foot on Sicilian soil. Instead, they sent the dreaded *gobliotti* (ruthless overseers) who beat the Sicilian peasants into working their own land and made them settle for little pay—only scraps of food—for all their backbreaking work.

But all that changed when Vito Vanucci's father led a Sicilian peasants' rebellion to overthrow all the foreign landlords and take back the Sicilian land for the Sicilian people. Let the Sicilians keep the profits of their labor! Give Sicilians back their dignity! Let all things Sicilian be kept for Sicilians! That Sicilian rebellion became known as *La Famiglia,* or *La Mafia.* And *La Cosa Nostra* became their battle cry, and that of Vanucci's son, Vito, who inherited his father's legacy and became the first Don of Palermo.

Vito's followers, known as the Society of Honorable Men, were loyal to him and his vision of the new Sicily: free men owning their land, property, and positions. The only condition associated with this newfound freedom was that a percentage of their earnings must be paid to the Don as protection, to keep the Sicilians safe from ever being invaded by foreign landowners again. The Sicilian people agreed joyfully to the Don's request. But Vito Vanucci's only son, Turiddu, did not resemble his father in stature, looks, or generosity. Turiddu, the grandson of the man who fought to give Sicily her freedom, hated the ideals of the Society of Honorable Men. In his mind, his father was a fool to give so much back to the Sicilian people.

* * *

As they walked onto the docks, Paulo followed Turiddu in silence; he wanted to ask him what type of special job he had for him but decided not to risk getting Turiddu upset so early in the day; he knew that would make for a miserably long day. Instead Paulo just kept his silence.

Turiddu was an imposing figure; he always wore silk suits imported from Milan and leather shoes from Naples; he put a silk handkerchief in his breast pocket so that he could pull it out and cover his nose and mouth when he had to talk to the poor people he collected money from. In fact, he was the complete opposite of his father, who never brought attention to himself by dressing in a fashion other than what the common dockworkers or the poor peasants around him wore. He preferred instead to be thought of as an ordinary *Siciliano*—working hard, just like them, to make a living.

Turiddu hated that, too, about his father, thinking it disgraceful his father looked and acted like nothing more than a poor, ignorant peasant!

This morning was no exception. Turiddu wore a starched white shirt over which thick black leather suspenders held up his trousers. He wore a black silk vest, unbuttoned, over his shirt. He carried his suit jacket over one shoulder. His white shirt was unbuttoned, too; he left it open to his midchest so that the customers he collected from could see nestled in his thick chest hair the large gold cross he wore on a fine chain around his neck. Exposing oneself in such a way was considered disgraceful by both men and women of the day, but Turiddu had absolutely no respect for or loyalty to anyone—much less the ignorant *Sicilini*, as he called them.

My father is the most powerful man in all of Sicily, and yet he treats the Sicilian people like his equals! When I become Don of Palermo, things will be different! I will become the richest man in all of Sicily—Italy—no, all of Europe! People will fear me, not sit with me and eat as if I were a peasant like them. Turiddu thought as he walked next to Paulo.

The two men walked past several storefronts on their way to the places they still needed to collect from. As they passed one leather shop, the owner came out and took his cap off in a sweeping gesture with his arm, as he bowed to Turiddu. "*Buongiorno, Signor Turiddu!*" the man said as Turiddu passed him by without even looking at the man to acknowledge his greeting.

As soon as Turiddu and Paulo were well past the storefront, the owner spit on the ground and whispered through clenched teeth, "May God cast you into hell with the rest of your devil brothers!"

Turiddu pointed out Giovanni Falucci's place. "We need to get two weeks' pay from Falucci."

"I don't think he owes two weeks boss; I collected from him last week; I remember I collected last week Saturday," Paulo said.

"Shut up! I say he owes two weeks. Keep your mouth shut."

Giovanni Falucci made wooden crates. He had a profitable business selling crates to the farmers who came to the docks to ship their produce off to Europe or North Africa. It was easier for a farmer to buy the crates at the docks—by not packing his produce at his farm, it made the load lighter for the horses and he could pack more produce onto the wagon at the same time.

"Ah, Falucci, how's the crate business this week, eh?" Turiddu greeted the man as walked through the door.

Falucci shrugged his shoulders and said nothing.

"Well, you know why I'm here. You owe for two weeks, signor."

"Two weeks? I paid last week, Vanucci. The jackass standing next to you collected from me already last week. Go ahead," Falucci shouted at Paulo, "tell him you already collected."

Paulo shrugged his shoulders. He knew if he stood up for the man, Turiddu would punish him—so he said nothing.

Falucci bit his bottom lip. He started to shake his fist at Turiddu but then thought better of it. He walked to the counter where he kept his money, he opened the drawer and took out two weeks' payment and threw it on the counter. "You want it—come and get it."

Turiddu calmly walked over to the counter and took the money; he handed it to Paulo to count.

"It's all here, boss." Paulo said.

"Good! Keep up the good work, Signor Falucci! I'll see you next week and, by the way, say hello to that beautiful wife of yours for me, eh!" Turiddu smiled and walked out the door.

Turiddu left Falucci's store and started towards the next stop on his list—when suddenly he stopped dead in his tracks.

"What's the matter boss?" Paulo asked.

Turiddu pointed at a large wagon parked not far from where they stood. "Look who's come to the docks to sell his produce! It is Signor Giuseppe Vazanno! My father's great friend, the man who can do no wrong—Giuseppe Vazanno!" Turiddu said sarcastically.

Immediately Turiddu's first thought was about Adriana Vazanno. *His whore daughter must have lived! I can't believe it! If she had died, surely I would have heard about it, and besides that, Vazanno looks too calm and happy. Damn it! The whore must still be alive.*

"Come on, Turiddu; let's finish our collections; the sun is

getting higher and soon we won't be able to tolerate the heat out here. Come on; remember, you said we have to get the collections to your father today?" Paulo said fervently as he tried to get Turiddu to leave Vazanno alone. The thought of what Turiddu did to the young Vazanno girl sickened him still when he thought about it.

"Shut up and follow me." Turiddu spit on the ground as he boldly walked towards Giuseppe Vazanno's wagon. "You know, Paulo, my father is so stupid! He gives everything away. It's bad enough he feeds the beggars on the streets as he listens to their sniveling excuses . . . but worse, he gives the best of everything away—everything rightfully mine—to his equally stupid, faithful friends—like that *bastardo* right there!" Turiddu said pointing out Giuseppe Vazanno to Paulo.

"Ah, Signor Vazanno! How are you, my friend?" Turiddu shouted out as he held his hand out to Giuseppe.

Not expecting to hear his name , Giuseppe turned around quickly. To Turiddu's delight, Giuseppe's face betrayed his surprise and immediate disdain at seeing him standing behind his wagon. Speechless for a moment, he stared at Turiddu and then returned to his work of unpacking crates—ignoring him completely.

Santo Padua, who was helping Giuseppe unpack their shipment, also turned quickly when he heard the unfamiliar voice. When he saw who it was he looked away, pretending not to have heard Turiddu's greeting.

Turiddu ignored the slight and smiled—he enjoyed seeing how uncomfortable Giuseppe and Santo were. "I see you are having a very good year, Signor Vazanno! Your lemons look the perfect color and, *mamma mia,"* Turiddu said, shaking one hand up and down, "look at the size of them! You are a very lucky man indeed, signor. Thank God for your good fortune!"

Giuseppe continued working, ignoring Turiddu's false attempt at flattery.

When Turiddu saw that Giuseppe was avoiding him altogether he said, "By the way, I understand your son had quite a celebration a few days ago! My father and mother told me all about it! I'm sorry I could not come and celebrate with your beautiful family; my work kept me away. Your son is to be ordained a priest, yes?"

Giuseppe's face flushed. The more Turiddu talked about his family, the angrier he became. Turiddu was not invited to Antonio's celebration and Giuseppe knew his friend Vito never mentioned anything about it to his loathsome son. Turiddu had gone too far now. Giuseppe stopped what he was doing and turned to face Turiddu squarely. "Yes, my son is to be priest soon. Now, if you don't mind, I have to finish unloading my produce before the noon sun is upon us. Good day, Turiddu." Giuseppe tipped his cap to Turiddu and turned away from him again.

Turiddu smiled triumphantly when Giuseppe turned away from him. "Well, you are right about that, the sun is getting hotter now, isn't it? I have to get back to work myself. After all, I must be about my father's business. You know how it is . . . my father is getting older now; he is giving me more and more responsibility with the family business."

"You're a lucky man, Turiddu, to have such a great man for your father," Giuseppe said sincerely. "And every man in Sicily envies you that!"

"I am aware many men do envy me, Giuseppe, but I'm not sure how many of them envy me because I am my father's son," Turiddu answered dryly.

Giuseppe was done with Turiddu. His narcissistic nature sickened him; when Turiddu spoke disrespectfully of his father, Giuseppe could contain himself no longer. "I'm very busy right now, Turiddu. Please give your father my blessing and respect when you see him today." Giuseppe again turned his back on Turiddu; he jumped up on the wagon and started helping Santo lift all the crates and move them closer to the back of the wagon.

Suddenly, the smile was gone from Turiddu's face; he felt rage swelling in his gut. *How dare the bastardo Giuseppe Vazanno turn his back on me! He's dismissing me as if I am nothing more than a poor, ignorant peasant!* he thought.

That worthless piece of merda! I should have killed his daughter when I had the chance; that would have taken the arrogance out of that bastardo! Looks like I have to finish what I have started, he told himself. A smile crossed his lips. *Yes,* he told himself, *I look forward to finishing the job I started.*

Turiddu and Paulo finished their collections and headed

back to Turiddu's office. Once inside, Turiddu closed the door and sat down close to Paulo.

"Would you like a drink, my friend?" Turiddu asked Paulo.

"Sure, boss!" Paulo answered enthusiastically. Usually, Turiddu dismissed him as an afterthought as soon as the work was done.

Turiddu poured Paulo a shot of whiskey and handed it to him. "*Salute!*" Turiddu said as he downed his shot.

Paulo repeated "*Salute*" and downed his drink. Then Turiddu poured them another shot.

"Paulo, I have a special job I want you to do for me. It's very important and no one—not even my father—can know what it is I am going to ask you to do. Do you think you can keep this job a secret from everyone—even my father?"

"Yeah, sure, boss," Paulo responded cautiously. He was becoming more and more disgusted with Turiddu's way of doing things; he not only mistrusted him but was starting to loathe him.

"Good. I want you to ride to Catania; there is a man there, his name is Battaghlia. I want you to deliver a letter to him for me. This is very important, Paulo," Turiddu leaned in closer to Paulo, "absolutely no one . . . no one . . . must ever know of it. Do you understand what I am saying to you? Do you understand how important this job is?"

Paulo fell silent. He had never been farther than Corleone. The thought of traveling all the way across the island scared him. But still, he was afraid of Turiddu and what he might do to him if he did not comply with his request. Paulo answered, "Yeah, sure, boss. You can trust me."

CHAPTER VI
THE AFTERMATH

MIDAFTERNOON, 4 MARCH 1911

MARIA WAS ANGRY. She was angrier than she had ever been with her daughter Adriana.

Thank God Nella and the others were here to help me, she kept telling herself, *and absolutely no thanks to Adriana!*

Maria sat for a while at the kitchen table; suddenly she got up, took her apron off, and started for the door.

"Where are you going, Maria?" Nella yelled after her sister.

"I'm going to go and find my useless daughter! When I find her I'm going to give her a thrashing!"

I cannot believe Adriana would do this to me! She knows how important this day is for her brother, Maria thought as she walked towards the barn. Just as she finished hitching a horse to a small wagon, her son Antonio rode into the barn with Santo Padua.

"Where are you going, Mamma?" Antonio asked.

"To look for your sister . . . she hasn't come home . . ." But then suddenly her voice trailed off upon seeing Antonio and Santo. Instinctively, she knew something was wrong.

Just then, Giuseppe and Sevario came into the barn followed by Gaspano. "Where's everyone going?" Giuseppe shouted happily.

Upon seeing her husband and the others, Maria felt a sense of panic choking her. She jumped down and ran to her husband. "Where is Adriana?" Maria asked frantically. "Is she with you, Giuseppe?"

"What do you mean? I haven't seen Adriana at all today except for this morning. We came back early because we are all starving . . ." Giuseppe stopped. Suddenly it occurred to him what his wife was saying to him—Adriana was missing.

"Adriana! What do you mean you haven't seen her? She left early this morning . . . she had your supper and . . ." Maria started to scream out frantically. "Giuseppe! Adriana was supposed to bring you your supper before noon! What do you mean you have not seen her all day? What are you saying to me? Where is my girl?" Tears were streaming down Maria's face.

"Stop it! Stop it, Maria . . . there is a good explanation, I'm sure of it. Adriana is very responsible. Surely, she would not disobey you today or any day for that matter. Something must have happened. She most likely is helping someone with something. Don't worry! We will find her . . . we will find her. I promise you that," Giuseppe said, trying to reassure his wife.

Giuseppe started shouting orders to his brothers, Antonio, and Santo. "Me and Sevario and Gaspano will go to the south orchards and you," he said to Antonio, "and Santo go to the north orchards. We'll go there first and if we don't find her there then we'll all head for Balestrate."

Immediately the men started to get back on their horses. Giuseppe turned to his wife then and hugged her; he kissed her forehead and said, "We'll find her. Don't worry, Maria. I'll find our daughter. She's fine. I promise you," he said.

Antonio and Santo followed Giuseppe out of the barn. "Follow me with the wagon, Santo." Antonio looked back towards his mother to make sure she was far enough away not to hear him. "We may need the wagon in case there has been an accident. Don't say anything to Mamma or Papa . . . just wait until Mamma is back in the house and then meet me at the north orchard."

***

Antonio rode ahead of Santo along the road leading to

Balestrate. The north orchard ran parallel to the road and he thought it better to follow the road all the way into the village before going into the orchard itself. He reasoned his sister may have come upon someone in need of help on the roadway or in the village—and simply lost track of time. *She may even be on the road itself now,* he thought. *Perhaps she has been injured.* His mind raced from one scenario to the next, not believing any of them could possibly be true. *Not today,* he told himself. *This day was too important to Adriana; nothing would have kept her from returning home immediately to help with the preparation. Nothing, that is—unless she had no control over what has happened to her.* Antonio's thoughts rambled on causing him to imagine every sort of scenario. His head was pounding with pain as sweat poured down his forehead under the fierce heat of the early afternoon.

Antonio scoured the low-lying shrubbery and trees along the dirt road to Balestrate; *If she has met with an accident she may have fallen into these patches of bushes,* he told himself. Finally reaching the village, he went up and down every street. He went into every shop along the way, asking the owners and patrons if they had seen his sister that day. He asked as calmly and casually as he could under the circumstances: he did not want to alert anyone to the fact that his sister was missing— that was unheard of in Balestrate. He knew all too well how the village women loved to gossip about the young girls in the village and did not want his sister to be the object of their gossip.

Finding no trace of Adriana in the village, Antonio left Balestrate riding slowly over the bridge leading out of the town and back towards his father's orchards. Just as he reached the main road, Santo rode up with the wagon.

"Santo, take the wagon around the outside of the orchard. I'll go through the interior of the orchard crisscrossing it from north to south—if you see her, fire one shot out immediately. I'll keep an ear out for your signal and you for mine."

Santo nodded in agreement.

***

The heat was almost unbearable. It was well into midday, at a time when most men would be taking a rest. Antonio passed a small clearing in the north orchard where he knew the workers took their rest, but it was entirely empty. Of course it was, he told himself. His father had told everyone to go home early.

Antonio took off his leather vest and pushed it down into his saddlebag. Removing it brought him some relief from the heat; he wiped his brow with a kerchief as he continued to ride through the orchard. Suddenly something caught his eye. It was white and lay just a few yards or so off in the distance. He kicked his horse hard into a gallop. As he got nearer the white object he recognized it immediately. It was a satchel—the type his mother used to pack food into. Then he saw the bread and cheese scattered across the ground and two flasks emptied of their contents nearby.

Antonio's heart began to beat uncontrollably as a feeling of dread came over him. The sight of the spilled wine and scattered food was an ominous sign. He got down off of his horse and picked up the satchel. He looked around the area quickly, frantically—but saw no sign of his sister. Then, he saw another clearing just to his right.

He walked into the clearing holding his horse's reins; he noticed immediately a grove of cypress trees surrounded by some low-lying shrubbery farther back in the area. He walked quickly towards the grove of trees. As he got closer, his eye caught sight of the stone bench situated in front of the trees. A feeling of dread came over him like a pall covering a casket, and he picked up his pace and started running towards the stone bench. He felt as if he could not get enough air into his lungs . . . and suddenly he saw what he did not want to see: one small, bare white foot sticking out from behind the stone bench. Antonio ran towards it. He gasped as he rounded the bench and there, lying on the ground nearly naked and looking barely alive, was his sister.

"Oh, my God," Antonio screamed as he bent down next to Adriana. He began yelling out her name but she did not move or show any sign of life. He quickly dropped to his knees beside her and then picked her up into his arms. He felt her heart beating against his own; he knew then she was alive.

"Adriana! Adriana!" he kept repeating but he could not rouse her to consciousness. He laid her down gently on the ground and, removing his own shirt, he covered her. He ran to his horse to retrieve a flask of water; he wet his kerchief with it and then placed the cool cloth on her forehead; then he poured the rest of the water—gently—over her face.

Adriana began to cough violently and then appeared to be choking on something as she opened her eyes suddenly to consciousness. Antonio sat her upright, leaning her against his own chest. A trickle of blood came out of her mouth. The sight of the blood frightened him deeply but at the same time he felt a sense of relief knowing she was alive.

"Adriana! Adriana! You're alive. Praise God, you're alive! Praise God!" he repeated over and over again.

Adriana, roused to wakefulness, looked up at Antonio. Now, for the first time, Antonio could see the full extent of the injuries to her face and upper body. He wanted to scream out in shock and horror at the sight of his little sister, but instead controlled himself. *Her face!* he thought. *Her beautiful face has been trampled and beaten as one might see done by a crazed and rabid dog! Who would do such a thing to an innocent angel?*

Adriana could open only one eye. The other was swollen shut completely. Blood oozed from her mouth. The side of her face where her eye was swollen shut was also swollen and already turning a deep shade of black and blue. Antonio laid her back down gently.

Adriana grabbed at his arms frantically as if begging him not to leave her.

"I'm going to get a cover for you—something to keep you warm. Don't be afraid, Adriana—I'm right here next to you. I swear I will not leave you."

Adriana let her arm drop to her side.

Antonio ran to his horse and removed the saddle blanket; then he ran back to his sister to cover her with it. "I'm here, Adriana. I'm here with you now. I won't leave you. I won't leave you."

Antonio saw her clothing scattered about the ground around her. He quickly picked up her outer blouse, her stockings and shoes. As he did, he shook his head from side to side and began to cry quietly—he did not want to frighten Adriana. *Oh my God! What has this monster done to you, my innocent angel! Who would commit such a crime?* Suddenly, Antonio was overcome with rage—a feeling he had never experienced before. He looked up to the heavens and said out loud, "Why, dear God? Why? How could you let . . ." But he stopped his rant, knowing full well this was not the work of his God but the work of the devil himself.

Antonio managed to put Adriana's stockings on her feet and then her shoes. Her skirt was intact; it was her outer blouse and chemise that had been ripped from her. Keeping his own shirt about her little body, he gently lifted her in his arms and carried her to the stone bench.

"Antonio..." Adriana managed to whisper.

"Shh . . . shh . . . don't speak, Adriana. Save your strength. Just squeeze my hand if you can hear and understand me."

Adriana squeezed his hand weakly.

"I'm going to call Santo to bring me the wagon. He's close by and can be here in an instant."

"No!" Adriana managed to say out loud. "No! No, Antonio!" Then, as if every bit of her strength had been exhausted by speaking, her head fell back against Antonio's arm and she appeared to be in a state of unconsciousness again.

Frightened, Antonio began shouting her name again. Finally, she opened one of her eyes and looked up at him.

"What are you saying, Adriana? Of course, we must get you home to Mamma . . ."

"No." Adriana said and then began to cough again as blood poured from her mouth. She rested a moment and then found her voice. "No, I cannot see Mamma or Papa or anyone else. You must leave me here to die, Antonio. I have been desecrated. I have been dishonored. I am not fit to enter into our parents' house again."

Antonio shut his eyes against a deluge of tears streaming down his face. He knew his sister had been attacked brutally, but the thought of rape...was completely unthinkable. *How could it be? How could anyone in the village, anyone . . . any man in all of Sicily commit such a crime against an innocent? No,* he told himself *. . . it is impossible.* Finally he regained his composure. He knew the reality of what Adriana had said. He asked her the one question he knew he had to ask. "Who? Who did this Adriana? Do you know his name?"

"Yes," she whispered. "Yes. I know his name."

"Who, then?"

"I will not tell you unless you vow you will never tell another soul who it was, Antonio."

"What are you saying to me, sister? Whoever did this has to be punished for his crime. No, I will not promise you that. The man must be brought to justice! He must be made to pay for the sin committed against you!"

"I tell you, Antonio, no one on this earth—other than me and you—must ever know the truth of today. If you do not promise me this I will refuse to go home with you; I will stay here and die rather than tell anyone what has happened to me today."

"Adriana, why? Why are you protecting this animal? You must tell me!"

"You must swear, Antonio! You must swear to me you will never tell a soul what has happened to me here today."

Antonio put his head down. His heart was broken for his sister. But still he could not reconcile in his mind the fact she did not want the man punished for what he did to her. He felt confused and frustrated. But, realizing she would not tell him the truth unless he promised to keep her secret, he said, "I swear it. I swear your secret will never be revealed by me."

"You must promise me you will never as long as you live tell Mamma or Papa what has happened to me here today."

"Adriana . . ."

"NO! You must swear, Antonio." Adriana choked.

"Yes, I swear it."

Adriana lowered her head against Antonio's chest. He could feel her hand that was gripping his arm start to tremble. Without raising her voice or her head to look at him, she said quietly, "It was Vito Vanucci's son, Turiddu Vanucci."

"What?" Antonio exclaimed. "Papa and Vito Vanucci are like brothers! Are you sure you know it was Turiddu, Adriana? Could you possibly be mistaken?"

"There is no mistake. He proudly told me his name. He wanted me dead, Antonio. He did not think I would ever live to be able to tell anyone his name."

Antonio brought his hand to his mouth; he bit down hard on his fist. He bit it so hard that blood oozed from the bite. "We have to tell Papa!" he screamed.

"Antonio, no, we cannot. Papa will kill Turiddu. No matter what Turiddu has done to me, Don Vito—the most powerful man in Sicily—will be obliged to avenge his own son's murder—even if it is *committed by our father.*" Adriana said slowly between gasps of breaths. "If Papa kills Turiddu—and I know he would without a doubt—Don Vito will have to get even! I don't know this for certain—but I am not willing to take a chance. I cannot, I will not, take the chance of my own father being killed because of me. I cannot, Antonio. I cannot."

"But surely, Adriana, when Mamma and Papa see you like this they will know something terrible has happened to you. They are not stupid people."

"That is why we, you and I, will tell them this. When I knew I was alive, I began to think of the consequences of this day." Adriana choked again and spit up more blood. Once she cleared her throat—she continued slowly. "We will tell them that I disobediently climbed the bridge wall on my way back to the orchards after leaving Francesca and Cinzia at their lesson. We will tell them I wanted to pick wildflowers for the celebration tonight. We will tell them that I fell over the wall and landed among the rocks in the creek bed below. Most of my injuries look as if I took a terrible fall, Antonio." Finally she said with emphasis, "They will believe this story—*if you tell it.*"

Antonio sat quietly for a long time. He knew everything Adriana said was the absolute truth: Vito Vanucci could have the entire family killed just to cover up the scandal. "I agree with you." Antonio said finally. "But, still I have to take you home. Will you let me call Santo now?"

"Yes." Adriana said quietly; she shut her eyes then, knowing the humiliation and shame she would be suffering—even if her parents did believe her injuries were from a fall.

Antonio stood up then and fired one shot in the air. He left Adriana for a moment to go and wait for Santo to arrive with the wagon. Within minutes he saw him coming up the side of the road. He went out to meet him.

"Did you find her?" Santo asked excitedly as he jumped down off of the wagon to meet Antonio.

"Yes, but . . ." Antonio hesitated searching for the words to tell Santo about his sister's "accident."

"What is it?" Santo asked, suddenly feeling panic rise in his own throat as he saw the grave expression on Antonio's face. "What's happened? Is she all right?"

"Yes, she's fine." Antonio lied. "She's suffered a terrible fall. She was picking flowers up on the stone wall bridge leading into town when she fell off hitting her head against the rocks."

Santo knew Antonio was lying. He wanted to run to Adriana. He tried to push past Antonio but Antonio stopped him. "Leave it be, Santo. You must promise me today you will never tell Mamma or Papa where we found Adriana. Promise me you will tell them we found her lying among the rocks in the shallow part of the creek. Promise me."

Santo started to cry. "Why are you making me say these things, Antonio? Tell me! Tell me what has happened to her! Was it an animal? Did an animal attack her?" Santo cried.

"No, she fell from the bridge. She fell while picking flowers. She landed on the rocks below and that is how we found her."

* * *

"Antonio, I'm almost near the front of the farmhouse. I don't see anyone outside. Papa and the others probably haven't come back yet."

"Pull the wagon to the far side of the barn so that if Papa comes back he won't see us taking her into the house."

Santo stopped the wagon. He looked back to see Adriana wrapped tightly in the horse blanket; Antonio kept her face covered against his chest so that Santo could not see the condition of it. Santo's heart was breaking; he wanted to go to her and hold her but that was something he knew he could not do. "We're here," he managed to say to Antonio.

"Go inside and get Mamma. Bring her here but tell her to stay calm. Tell her only that Adriana fell and we found her under the bridge."

Reluctantly Santo climbed down out of the wagon. He ran towards the house and through the back door. Maria sat at the kitchen table, crying. When she saw Santo come in the kitchen and take off his cap—without saying another word—she knew they had found her.

"Where is she?" Maria said as she stood and then bolted

from her chair towards Santo.

Santo turned from her and started to walk towards the back door.

"Stop, Santo!" Maria yelled to him.

Santo stopped but still did not turn to her. She walked up to him and turned him around to face her. "What's happened? Tell me now or . . ."

"Adriana has had an accident. She fell from the bridge . . ."

Maria ran past Santo without letting him finish his lie. As she ran out the door she could see the wagon a short distance away. She began to run. When she reached the wagon she jumped up into the back of the wagon bed. To her horror, she saw Antonio holding Adriana in his arms—with the horse blanket covering her face. Her first thought was that her daughter was dead.

"NO!" Maria screamed. "*Mi figlia! Mi figlia! Mi figlia e mort!* My daughter, my daughter is dead!"

"Mamma!" Antonio said firmly, "Adriana is alive. She is hurt. That's all! She's suffered a terrible fall. We have to get her into the house and to bed." Then he asked, "Where is Papa?"

"He and the others have not returned yet."

"Good, then," he said to his mother. Then he yelled out to Santo to pull the wagon up close to the house.

***

"Papa!" Antonio said as his father rode into the barn, "we have found Adriana. She has had an accident; a fall."

Giuseppe jumped down off of his horse and started to run towards the farmhouse; Antonio ran after him.

"Papa, wait. Wait."

Giuseppe stopped to face his son. "What is it? I want to see my daughter!"

"Wait, Papa. Mamma asked me to tell you to wait until she can settle Adriana in bed. I assure you Adriana is all right. She will be fine."

Giuseppe pulled away from Antonio's grip as he had grabbed his father's arm to stop him from going any further towards the house. "Leave me alone! I want to see my daughter." Then he began yelling, "Maria! Adriana!"

Maria rushed out of Adriana's room when she heard

Giuseppe's voice yelling for her. She ran to the back door to greet him—and to stop him from seeing Adriana.

"Your daughter has been very disobedient!" she said angrily, trying to convince Giuseppe she was enraged. "If she wasn't in so much pain I would kill her with my own hands!"

"Let me see her then," Giuseppe demanded.

"Thank God for Antonio! He found her lying in the creek bed by the bridge leading into the village!" Maria said breathlessly as she felt panic enveloping her. "Please, I beg of you, Peppino, let me clean her up. She is very upset because she has disobeyed us. She is completely remorseful and humiliated. I assure you she is fine! Please give her just a few hours to recover. Her shame and embarrassment are punishment enough for now."

Giuseppe looked at his wife for a long time. More than anything, he wanted to believe her. "Do not hide a thing from me, Maria," he said sternly. "I want to know every detail of what has happened to my daughter."

Maria forced a smile and then kissed him on his cheek. "Oh my God, today of all days, do you think I would keep something from you? Please don't waste your time with this foolishness. There is still so much to be done for tonight. Go on now, you and the others get cleaned up. I will take care of Adriana and later you can punish her as you see fit." Maria smiled at Giuseppe reassuringly. "I have fresh bread and cheese waiting for you on the table out front. You and your brothers should eat something before you finish setting up all the tables for tonight."

Maria was convincing and Giuseppe believed her. "I'll be outside if you need me then." He turned from his wife and started to walk towards the others who were standing about awkwardly. "Gaspano, Sevario," he yelled, "get cleaned up; we have a lot of work to do."

* * *

As soon as Giuseppe and his brothers left, Maria looked at Antonio. "Go and get Nella for me."

Antonio left his mother to get his aunt. As he walked out of Adriana's room he saw Santo standing with his cap in his hand; he looked as if he had been crying.

"Come on brother. There is nothing more for us to do now."

Antonio put his arm around Santo's shoulder and hugged him. He had always known how Santo felt about his sister.

Nella walked into Adriana's room and put her hand to her mouth. "Oh, dear God, what has happened?" she asked in shock at the sight of Adriana's face.

"Get me clean linens—lots of linen. Tear up a bed cover into long strips and bring it to me as fast as you can. But first, put on water to boil. I will need olive oil, sweet oil, and honey. Go on. Hurry up and don't breathe a word of this to anyone. Do you understand me, Nella?"

Nella nodded her head in agreement and then ran out of the room.

Maria started to take off her daughter's clothes when she realized her blouse had been torn down the middle and her skirt and underskirts were stained with blood and dirt.

"Oh, my dear God," she exclaimed when she saw all the swelling and black and blue marks on her daughter's lower abdomen and thighs.

Nella came in then with the water and clean towels. Maria immediately covered her daughter's nakedness. "Put everything down here, Nella." Maria pointed to a table she had set next to Adriana's bed.

Nella then left to cut up some clean linen strips. As soon as she had cut up an entire piece of linen, she brought it in to her sister.

Maria looked up at her and said, "Nella, I need you to keep Giuseppe from seeing Adriana like this. Can you do that for me, sister?"

"Yes, of course Maria, but what has happened to her?"

"She fell. She fell from the bridge covering the creek as she left the village today. Antonio found her there."

"She fell?" exclaimed Nella. "What on earth . . ."

Maria cut her off. "Go on, Nella. Do as I have asked you to do."

* * *

"Adriana? Adriana?" Maria whispered to her daughter.

Adriana moaned and tried to turn her head towards her mother's voice.

Maria, relieved her daughter was alive, breathed a sigh of relief. "I'm going to clean you, Adriana," Maria said as she pulled the sheet that covered her daughter's naked body down to her shoulders.

Adriana's small body started to shake uncontrollably. Maria put her hand to her daughter's forehead and felt it burning with fever. Immediately, she put a cold cloth across her daughter's forehead. She covered her upper body warmly as she worked to clean the lower half of her body.

Maria gasped; blood was still oozing from between the girl's legs. Maria put her hands to her mouth to cover a scream. She knew. She knew exactly what happened to her sweet angel, Adriana. Maria was crying now and had to continuously push back an urge to vomit.

"Adriana! Adriana!" she whispered, "Tell me child, what has happened to you? Who has done this to you?"

But Adriana did not answer her. It was as if she had fallen into a deep sleep to protect herself from the reality of what had happened.

Maria stood immobilized, staring down at her daughter's body. "This is impossible!" she kept saying over and over again. "No one . . . no one in Balestrate would ever dream of committing such a crime. Who could have done such a thing to my daughter, dear God? Who?"

Maria wanted to scream but controlled herself.

By the time she had finished cleaning her daughter, washing her hair, putting sweet oil on her wounds, and then wrapping her scratches and abrasions with clean linen, she was exhausted.

"Mamma," Adriana whispered, barely able to open her mouth.

"Yes, my darling, Mamma is here. You are safe now. I will not let anything harm you, Adriana. You are with me now."

Nella knocked on the doorpost. "Maria? It's me, Nella."

"Come in," Maria said.

When Nella saw Adriana's bruised and swollen face she broke down in tears.

"Stop it, Nella. Please, I need you to be strong for me right now." Suddenly feeling a sensation of panic, Maria asked nervously, "Where is Giuseppe?"

"He tried to come in several times, but I made sure more and more people demanded time with him. He will be occupied for quite some time now. How is Adriana?"

"She has a fever. But her breathing is regular and she seems to be sleeping through her pain. Thank God for that."

"I will prepare the herbal for fever. Do you want anything else now, sister?"

"No, thank you, Nella. Thank you."

* * *

Maria managed to put the herbal medicine into Adriana's mouth and let it absorb there into her body. Within thirty minutes, her fever seemed to be reduced with the medicine. Maria got up and went to the kitchen.

The yard was filled with people. Everywhere she looked people were laughing and having a wonderful time. She spotted her husband sitting with Father Licolli and Antonio. She washed her own face in cold water and smoothed her hair back. She looked down at her apron to see it smeared with blood. Quickly, she removed the apron and threw it into the roaring hearth fire.

She put on a new apron and went to the door and waved at Giuseppe. Immediately he got up and ran to the door.

"How is she? Can I see her now?"

Maria smiled and put her hand to Giuseppe's face. "That girl of ours must be punished, Peppino. I know you have a soft spot for all your children, but Adriana seems to melt your heart entirely. She is sleeping now. But, in the morning you are going to have to decide on a punishment for her. She must be made to learn her lesson this time."

"Well, can I see her at least, Maria?"

"Let her rest. It will only upset you to see her bruises and then you will soften and she will never be punished! No, let her sleep for now, my love."

"Are you coming out now?" Giuseppe asked his wife. "No one has seen you yet and everyone is asking for you."

"Of course! I'm just going to change into the dress I have been saving for this occasion for a year now! I'll be right there, my love." Maria bent over and kissed him on his cheek.

Giuseppe smiled at her and then turned away to join the

others but then he slowed and stopped. He turned and looked at his wife and said, "Are you telling me everything about our daughter, Maria?"

"Yes, of course!" Maria said convincingly. "Go on now. I will be out as soon as I change my dress."

CHAPTER VII
THE VENDETTA

ADRIANA DID NOT get out of bed for two weeks. Her mother suspected she had suffered at least one or two broken ribs, because every time she tried to turn Adriana to another position, her daughter cried out in excruciating pain, "My side, Mamma, my side!"

Maria wrapped her chest tightly in gauze to prevent the bones from moving about; even though her daughter's breathing was restricted, she was better able to move her about with her chest stabilized. Adriana's fever continued for three days and nights and during that time she appeared as if in a coma. She neither spoke nor ate. Finally, on the fourth day, Adriana opened her eyes to see her mother standing over her. She could only manage to open one eye fully as the other was still nearly swollen shut. There was no more blood draining from her mouth; Maria managed to continuously rinse it by turning the girl's head to one side as she poured small spoonfuls of salt water into it and then let it drain out.

When Maria changed her daughter's undergarments she noticed there was no longer any spotting on them. Still, every time she did change them, she was forced to face the reality of what really happened to her daughter. Her heart broke a little more every day, until one day she could no longer control herself.

She left Adriana alone for a short time, making excuses to Nella that she needed to retrieve something from the barn.

Maria went into the barn and closed the door behind her, bolting it shut. The men were gone to the orchards, the children to the village for their lessons, and Nella was the only other person home with her other than Adriana.

Maria went to the back of the barn in between the tall stacks of hay. She stood there looking up to the ceiling of the barn as if she expected someone above to speak to her; to console her; to tell her perhaps that what happened to her daughter really was an accidental fall into a rocky creek bed. But no one spoke out to her. She felt isolated and alone. The very walls around her felt as if they were closing in upon her, and in the stone cold silence surrounding her, she began to scream. She screamed to God; she screamed towards heaven; she screamed out to all the angels and saints to please help her because, for the first time in her life, she was completely incapable of helping herself.

Maria cried, continuing to beg for God's mercy; she pleaded with him to take away everything that had happened to her daughter. "I'm begging you, Lord, I am pleading with you, please perform this miracle for my daughter! She is one of your little innocents! She is my innocent! You must take pity on me, God, and answer my prayer!"

In complete despair, Maria fell to her knees sobbing. Every emotion she had kept locked up in her heart for these past days seemed to emerge untamed from her lips, her heart, and her very soul. She beat her fists against the stone floor and then against her head; she pulled at her hair as if, somehow, tearing the hair out of her head would erase the sheer horror of what had settled upon her family and her home.

In exhaustion, she fell prostrate on to the ground. She lay there sobbing for what seemed an eternity, and then, finally calmed, she thought about what she must do. She stopped crying and managed to sit up in the middle of the floor. She wiped her face with her hands and fell silent. Finally, it had come to her. She was the matriarch of the family—it would be up to her to bring whoever did this to her daughter to justice. *The vendetta,* she thought, *yes, the vendetta. That is the only way! That is the Sicilian way and whoever did this is a Sicilian! He will pay. I will see to it if it is the last thing I do in my life—I will make him pay—with his life.*

***

It was nearly a week before Maria allowed Giuseppe to see his daughter. She made excuse after excuse why it was not a good time or a good day to see Adriana, and, because he loved and trusted his wife—he believed her. But, during the first week after the "accident" Adriana began to improve immensely. Most of the facial swelling had subsided and she was able to completely open the one eye that was swollen shut. Even though the bruising still remained, she looked much improved. But, before Maria allowed Giuseppe to come in and visit with her, she asked Adriana's permission.

"I can't keep your father away any longer, Adriana. Would you be able to see him today?"

"Yes, Mamma," she answered meekly.

"I have told him of the accident; he knows of your embarrassment and humiliation for disobeying us; he knows it was Antonio who found you lying in the creek bed."

Adriana nodded her head in agreement.

"Giuseppe," Maria called out, "Your daughter is asking to see you, my love."

Giuseppe rushed into Adriana's room. He went immediately to her bedside but was not prepared to see the condition his daughter was in. He gasped as he stared at her face and then he put his hand to mouth and bit down on it. "Oh, my God!" he exclaimed. "All this from a fall!"

Tears immediately started to flow down his face. He turned to his wife as if in disbelief.

"Maria! Tell me the truth; all this is from a fall?"

"Yes, Papa," Adriana said. "I climbed to the top of the wall as I was leaving the village. I wanted to pick flowers for Antonio's celebration feast. The most beautiful of all the spring flowers were at the top of the bridge. I am so sorry for all the pain I have caused you and Mamma and the rest of the family. I am completely humiliated and deserve to be punished severely."

Giuseppe knelt down next to his daughter's bed. He started to stroke her long hair and whisper how much he loved her. He couldn't stop crying and caused Adriana to cry herself.

"No, don't cry, Papa. I am recovering completely. I ask only you forgive my stupidity and disobedience."

Her father kissed her tenderly on her forehead. "There is nothing at all to forgive. You have and are suffering far too much for your simple crime of disobedience. Hush now. I want you to rest and completely recover, my angel." He kissed her again and then got up and went out of the room. Maria walked out after him. She watched from the kitchen window as he galloped out of the barn on his horse. To where, she did not know but understood his need to be alone.

＊

After four weeks of convalescing, Adriana's body was healing well, and outwardly she looked just like her old self again: young, beautiful, and healthy. Her ribs, although still sore, must have completely mended, her mother concluded, because she noticed Adriana was able to do all the things she normally used to do with stamina and determination; everything, that is, except go into the orchards.

Maria knew her daughter's outward scars would heal. She was not concerned about them any longer. The fever ceased, the lacerations healed, the swelling and black and blue marks were no longer visible. No, it was not the physical scars that worried Maria; it was her daughter's invisible scars that caused her to fear for Adriana's future. *Those are the ones that will eventually change my daughter from what she is to . . . what? My sweet, innocent girl! Oh, how my heart breaks for what you have come to know in such a horrible way.*

Hour after hour, day after day, night after night, and week after week, Adriana thought about how the "accident" had changed her life. Her life, deeply rooted in the Catholic faith and Sicilian culture and traditions, was over now. All was lost and it would never be possible for her to regain it again. She had lost her virginity, even though through no fault of her own, and no man in Sicily would ever take her to his marriage bed now.

And, to make matters worse, every time she thought about the sin committed against her by the monster Turiddu Vanucci, she could not help but think that if only she had covered her hair that day, he would not have been tempted to attack her. A seed of guilt began to grow in Adriana's heart and mind until it became a gnawing obsession. Then one day it came to her. *The perfect solution,* she thought. *I will tell Mamma and Papa on Easter Sunday.*

* * *

"Mamma," Adriana said as she walked into the kitchen and sat down at the table, "I have been thinking I would like to go to Easter mass tomorrow. It has been so long since I have been able to go to mass and I think receiving communion on Easter will help me very much."

"Adriana," Maria asked surprised, "are you sure you are up to going all the way to Palermo? Antonio is going to be assisting the priests at the cathedral tomorrow."

"Perfect, then!" Adriana answered. "I want to see Antonio serve the priests at mass; after all, he will be leaving the day after tomorrow to go back to Milano."

"If you think you are up to it, then yes, of course, you can come to mass with us tomorrow. We are going to leave midmorning because the bishop has asked Antonio to serve as deacon for the High Mass at twelve o'clock."

"I'll be ready then," Adriana said as she left the kitchen to go outside and milk the goats.

Maria looked out the window after her daughter. *She seems genuinely happy today! Perhaps God has answered my prayers after all.* Maria thought.

* * *

The mass was very long; it was solemn High Mass and there were three priests concelebrating, with Antonio who served as deacon. The church, decorated with hundreds of white lilies and flowers of every sort, looked majestic with vase upon vase set in front and on every side of the altar throughout the *Cathedral di San Marco l'Apostolo.*

Adriana and her family were able to secure pews in the front of the main sanctuary because they had arrived at the church over an hour before the mass was to begin. Adriana knelt and fervently prayed for God's help. She knew her mother and father would object to her plan at first. But, she also knew it was the only thing she could do to save her family from the ultimate disgrace that would come to them if she were to ever attempt to live a normal life in Balestrate.

The entire mass lasted nearly two hours. Adriana felt her stomach churning; no one had eaten anything since midnight and it was very close to three o'clock in the afternoon by the time the procession—led by all the priests followed by Antonio, then the acolytes, and then the altar boys—left the church. Adriana felt weak at times during the mass; waves of nausea plagued her especially when her brother filled the incense lantern and then blessed the altar, the celebrants, and finally the people. Sitting in the front row, the heady mixture rose up her nose and caused her to cough violently. It was everything she could do to keep down what little there was on her stomach. When the mass came to an end, she was relieved.

It took some time for the Vazanno family to reach the back of the church to greet the bishop, but by the time they did, Antonio had taken off his vestments and was dressed in his street clothes again. He joined his family to receive the bishop's special blessing given to the faithful once a year at Eastertime.

The bishop greeted Antonio first. The two exchanged an embrace and then kissed each other on both cheeks; then Antonio stood back and introduced his mother and father. Adriana stood behind them, waiting her turn to be blessed.

The crowd in the piazza was enormous! It seemed everyone from Palermo and, most assuredly, many of the towns and villages surrounding Palermo, had come to the Cathedral to attend mass.

Adriana looked into the crowd. The sun was shining beautifully overhead and she could see clearly all the finely dressed women and black-hatted men. She scanned the piazza from one side to the other and then back again. Suddenly, her heart seemed to stop mid-beat.

Antonio was standing next to her while the bishop conversed with Giuseppe and Maria. She reached out and grabbed his hand. He looked down at her and could see the look of sheer terror on her face. "What is it?" he asked.

She looked in the direction of the far corner of the square.

There stood Turiddu Vanucci surrounded by at least a dozen men, all smoking cigarettes, laughing as if at a fiesta, talking loudly, and generally making a spectacle of themselves. Turiddu Vanucci, dressed in a white suit with a white fedora hat on his head, stood in the middle of the group. He held a large black cigar in his mouth. Over one shoulder hung a black, woolen coat even though it was not appropriate for the weather.

"Come with me. Bring Francesca, too," Antonio said to Adriana.

She followed him without hesitation. When Giuseppe and Maria saw their children start to go back into the church, they both yelled out to Antonio at the same time.

"Antonio, the bishop is waiting to give the girls his Easter blessing!"

Antonio ignored their pleas and kept pushing Adriana into the church. He ushered her and Francesca through an oak door in the back of the church. As soon as they were in the corridor, he locked the door behind them. "Come on," he said indicating for her and Francesca to follow him.

When they reached the main sacristy, Adriana watched as Antonio fumbled to put the key into the lock of the door. He opened the door and led his sisters through the priests' vestment room and out the back of the church to where their wagon had been placed.

"Stay here with Francesca. I'm going to get Mamma and Papa so that we can go home as quickly as possible. Are you all right to stay here alone?" he asked Adriana.

The only gesture Adriana could manage was a frightened nod of her head. Antonio grabbed a blanket and told the girls to sit down on the floor of the wagon. Then he covered both of them with the blanket. "If you see anyone coming this way, cover your heads with this blanket. I will be right back, I promise you."

Antonio ran back quickly into the church and down the main aisle. He opened the door in the main vestibule at the entrance to see his mother and father still conversing with the bishop. But, to his shock and dismay, there stood Vito and Apollonia Vanucci . . . with their son, Turiddu!

Antonio was speechless.

"Ah, there you are, my son!" exclaimed Giuseppe.

"Yes, Papa," he said as he quickly walked up to stand next to his parents. "I'm afraid I'm not feeling well this morning. If you don't mind, bishop, I'm afraid my family and I will have to be leaving now."

"Did you say you also had two daughters, Signor Vazanno?" asked the priest.

"Yes, both of my daughters . . ." Giuseppe started to say both of his daughters were with him at mass but Antonio interrupted him immediately.

"Papa, I am really not feeling well."

Maria missed none of Antonio's drama. She sensed immediately there was something terribly wrong.

"Yes, we will take our leave now, Giuseppe," said Maria adamantly. Then, she turned to the bishop and kissed his hand. She kissed Vito and Apollonia but rebuffed Turiddu's attempt to kiss her.

* * *

"What is the matter, Antonio?" Giuseppe asked, concerned, as they walked down the aisle of the church to the main altar.

"It's not me. It's Adriana. She's not well. We have to get her home as soon as possible."

Antonio sat with Adriana in the back of the wagon. He had one arm around her and the other around Francesca. He could feel Adriana shaking uncontrollably next to him. By the time they arrived at home, her nerves seemed to have calmed.

"Adriana, go and change your clothes and wash your face, daughter. You will feel better once you have some food in you."

"Yes, Mamma." she said obediently. But, not wanting her mother to worry about her, she turned and said, "I am feeling much better now, Mamma. I just need to eat something. That's all."

* * *

The men sat outside, smoked cigarettes and drank espresso; even though it was a day of rest, still they talked about nothing but the orchards.

"I tell you there is something wrong with our yield this year, Giuseppe," Sevario said concerned. "This time last year, I swear we had twice as many lemons on our trees."

Giuseppe looked perplexed. "I think you're right. Tomorrow we'll go and inspect the trees; who knows? Perhaps we need to enrich the soil. We can do that first thing in the morning."

"Giuseppe!" Maria called out from the kitchen.

Giuseppe looked up and saw his wife was waving at him. "What is it?" he called out.

"Can you and the others come in for a moment?" she called.

The men all got up at once and started for the farmhouse. Walking in, they saw all the women sitting at the table.

"What's the matter?" asked Giuseppe.

Maria shrugged her shoulders. "Adriana wants to tell us something but insists the whole family be at the table."

Once everyone was seated, Adriana took a deep breath. She knew what she was about to say would shock her family but she also knew they would all—somehow—find a way to be happy for her. At least that was her hope. But, before she opened her mouth to speak, she quickly looked around to make sure everyone was in the room. That's when she saw Santo standing alone by the kitchen hearth. His arms were crossed over his chest and he looked upset—as if he knew what Adriana was about to say, she thought. She swallowed hard and closed her eyes a moment, begging God to help her speak.

"I have been thinking about something for a long, long time. Actually, since Antonio went away to the seminary," she started. She stopped then and looked directly into everyone's face. They were all staring at her; they looked as if they were holding their breath. They neither looked happy or sad but apprehensive.

Adriana looked down for a moment; she clasped her hands in her lap and held them tightly together to prevent everyone from seeing them as they shook uncontrollably.

"I have decided to go into the convent."

Maria gasped. Giuseppe leaned forward putting his hands on the table as if he wanted to try to persuade his daughter to change her mind.

"It is my decision and I know I will not change my mind. I have known for a long time that I have a religious calling from God and I can no longer ignore it. I am going to speak to the prioress at the Carmelite convent of St. Therese of the Child Jesus this coming week—in San Vito di Capo. I want you and Papa to go with me, Mamma," she finished, looking at her mother.

What relief! There, Adriana thought, it is out in the open now. Thank you, God! Thank you for giving me the strength to do what I had to do!

Maria first looked at her husband; the look on his face was one of shock; then immediately she turned her eyes to Antonio who caught his mother's look and quickly looked away, averting her stare. Everyone at the table remained speechless until Giuseppe finally spoke.

"Are you sure you have thought this through, Adriana? You will be giving up everything! The life at Carmel is very different from other religious orders; do you know that, child?"

"Yes, Papa. I know it very well; that is the reason I want to become a Carmelite, because of their prayer and contemplative life. It is a holy vocation, Papa; surely, you want the same thing for me as you do for Antonio?"

Giuseppe was speechless. He opened his mouth to speak but could not answer his daughter; after all, it was his decision to send his only son away to a seminary.

At first Maria, too, was speechless and in shock. But when Antonio had avoided her questioning look, she knew then, for sure, that he knew far more than he was telling her, and that made her angry!

"I cannot speak for anyone here at this table," Maria said, looking first at Antonio and then at her husband, "but I for one, think you need more time to think about this decision you seem to have made. I want you to think very hard about the life you will be entering, Adriana. It is not something you do one day and then change your mind the next. Understand, at Carmel you will only see your family once or twice a year! And, when you do see your family it will be from behind a grille! You will never be able to hold us . . . kiss us . . ." Maria's voice trailed off as she broke into tears.

Now everyone at the table had a look of anxiety on his or her faces. Maria pulled her apron up to her face and covered it.

Then, without warning, she got up and went outside, grabbing a shawl off a hook as she passed through the doorway.

Immediately, Giuseppe got up to follow her. But, Antonio stopped him. "No, Papa. Let me go," he said.

Santo Padua stared at Adriana as if she had just told him she was about to die. His mouth fell open as he dropped his arms to his sides and clenched his hands into fists. He wanted to yell out to her but knew he could not. Instead, he turned and walked out of the farmhouse and to the barn. He saddled his horse, mounted, and then kicked him hard with the heel of his boot causing him to bolt into a gallop away from the barn.

* * *

Antonio followed his mother without saying a word.

She walked on the road away from the farmhouse towards Balestrate. When she arrived at the bridge crossing the creek, she stopped and turned to confront Antonio.

"Is this where your sister fell, Antonio?" she asked.

Antonio put his eyes down.

"Come with me, Antonio, show me where you found your sister. Show me the rock upon which she struck the side of her face causing her one eye to swell shut." Without waiting for an answer, Maria started down the embankment towards the creek bed. She stopped when she reached a spot directly under the bridge. The water in the creek was quite shallow and she could clearly see the sandy bottom below. There were few rocks under the bridge—mostly larger boulders off to the side.

"So, this is where your sister fell, then?" She turned and confronted her son.

"Mamma, please, why are you doing this to yourself? Why are you torturing yourself so? Adriana seems very happy in her decision . . ."

Maria cut him off sharply. "Stop it, Antonio! Do you hear me? Stop talking to me as if I am some ignorant, uneducated, woman! You disappoint me, my son! You disappoint me!"

Antonio put his head down. He was no match for his mother's tongue when she was angry. He decided to let her rant and then calm. He would not try to reason with her now.

Maria looked at her son. Clearly she could see the pain he

was in and that, too, broke her heart. She sighed as she walked away from the creek and back up towards the bridge. There was grove of cypress trees only a few feet the other side of the bridge and Maria decided to go and rest her heavy heart there.

"Go back to the house, Antonio. I want to be alone for a while."

But Antonio did not want to leave her; he loved her very much and it also broke his heart to see her in so much pain.

When they reached the grove, Maria noticed the shrine that had been erected there by the townspeople. It was a wooden, enclosed shrine of a statue of the Blessed Virgin Mary holding a rosary and next to her, a statue of St. Rosalie, the patron saint of Palermo and all her provinces.

Maria smiled and said sarcastically, "Look there, Antonio, not only the Blessed Virgin but St. Rosalia too! Why didn't either one of them intercede when your sister was being brutally raped?"

Antonio's face shot up to stare at his mother's.

Maria's face took on a look of stony determination when she said, "Yes, Antonio, I know exactly what happened to your sister. I'm a woman, Antonio! Did you think for one instant I did not recognize what I saw on your sister's body?"

Maria started cry. "What I want to know is, who did this to your sister? And, if you know, you will tell me."

"Mamma. Please, don't torture yourself this way. I beg of you. It will come to no good."

"How dare you! How dare you tell me not to torture myself! Nothing I could ever do to myself could compare to the tortures your sister has suffered. Nothing, do you hear me? Nothing!"

"But, you don't understand, Mamma . . ."

"I understand this, Antonio: my husband, whom I love beyond all telling, took my only son and gave him away to the seminary. I could not interfere in that decision. Your father—the head of my household—said it was to be and I accepted his decision. But now, your sister, my daughter! No! No! I tell you—God cannot have another one of my children. I will die first! Do you hear me? I will die first!"

Antonio grew impatient and angry at his mother's lack of reason and control. In his mind, his sister was committing her life to a higher cause and he thought it courageous of her to choose the life of a religious—under the circumstances. "I think, in time, Mamma, you will come to realize what a blessing God is bestowing on you and our family by calling two of your children to religious life."

Maria walked to her son. She stood steel-eyed in front of him as she raised her hand and struck him across the face. The slap was so loud that all the birds nested in the trees above their heads suddenly took flight.

Antonio put his hand to his face and stared at his mother in shock.

"Your sister's body had been desecrated. Her life has been taken from her. She is no longer an innocent but rather has been—against her will—made into a woman; a woman no man in all of Sicily would touch now that she has been disgraced. Have you thought about that at all, Antonio? Have you? You talk about forgiveness and God's love! Well, let me tell you what your sister has to look forward to now." Tears were streaming down Maria's face now.

She continued, "You will return to the seminary and then go off somewhere—only God knows where—after your ordination; your father will return to the orchards with his brothers; and I will continue to take care of his household and our two daughters. But Adriana, oh, my sweet child, Adriana!" she said with a sigh. "My girl will go off to the convent and hide behind concrete walls and a grille—because of the shame she feels in her heart! Not because she has some calling from God, Antonio!" Maria screamed.

"And worse still, what if your sister is with child because of this monster's evil deed? Have you even thought about that? How long do you suppose the holy nuns at Carmel will allow her to stay there when they find out she's pregnant?"

Antonio started to cry now. He fell to his knees and covered his face with his hands. "Stop it, Mamma! Stop it!" he pleaded . "God would never let such a thing happen to Adriana! Never!"

"She had not had her show of blood this month, Antonio. It comes to her every month at the same time; it has not yet come this month."

Antonio sobbed into his hands as he knelt, hunched, on the ground.

Maria took her hand and put it on her son's shoulder. Then she cupped his face in her hand and made him look up to her.

"You have to tell me who did this to Adriana," she said. "We must avenge the sin committed against your sister, Antonio. We must. I cannot allow Adriana to go into the convent. Not yet, at any rate; if she has a true vocation, it will stand the test of time. But, she cannot go now. If she *is* with child, it will result in a terrible scandal when the convent forces her to leave. I will not allow such a humiliation to happen to her. I will wait and see what her condition is for sure. If she is pregnant, I will make arrangements for her to go to the mainland—in secret until the child is born."

Antonio looked at his mother in disbelief. He had not considered the possibility of Adriana becoming pregnant because of the assault. Now, everything his mother said made sense to him for the first time.

"Where would you send her?" was the only thing Antonio could manage to say.

"To Milano. You will be there at the seminary and my own mother lives there! Adriana could stay in the countryside with my mother. Once the child is born we can arrange for a midwife to take it to an orphanage in the city."

"What about Adriana? What if she wants to keep her child?" Antonio pleaded.

"No! No! I will not allow it. None of this is her fault! It is the fault of the devil and she will not be forced to live with a child spawned by a devil!"

"Oh, my God!" Antonio exclaimed. "Surely, you cannot possibly believe that an innocent child is ever conceived— conceived by the devil himself! Are you mad?"

"You speak like a priest already, Antonio. Surely, you have not seen what people are capable of doing to the innocent! I have seen girls in Adriana's condition whipped to death! It doesn't matter to the ignorant whose fault it is when an unmarried girl finds herself with child. They will *always* say it is the girl's fault! I know of one girl whose own father strangled her and threw her body into *Lago di Garda!* No! No! No! I will not let my sweet girl suffer any more, Antonio! I will not!"

Antonio stood up then. He looked at his mother and knew

she was right. As soon as the nuns at Carmel found out about Adriana's pregnancy—if she was pregnant—they would kick her out immediately. "I agree with you, Mamma. But, what can we possibly do now?"

Maria stepped away from her son. She stood with her back to him, her arms crossed over her chest. After a moment she turned back to face him. "Antonio, the only way is to tell me who did this to my daughter. This monster must be made to pay for what he has done. That is the only way. If Adriana is with child, I will send her to Milano; if she is not and truly has a vocation, I will allow her to go to the convent in San Vito di Capo."

"But I promised, Mamma, I took an oath to Adriana that I would not reveal who did this to her."

"As your mother, Antonio, I command that you obey me in this one matter . . . and I promise you, I will never speak a word of it to anyone—ever. No one will ever know except you and me. Of that I promise."

"It was Turiddu Vanucci. Vito Vanucci's son."

Maria let out a blood-curdling scream. "NO! NO! It cannot be! Not Vito's son!" Then she collapsed to the ground, screaming out the name, "Turiddu! Turiddu Vanucci!"

It was a long time before Maria was able to compose herself. She was in total shock that Vito Vanucci's son, her husband's godchild, had disgraced and violated her daughter. Antonio let his mother cry; he felt like crying himself.

Finally, Maria stopped crying. She wiped her face with the hem of her skirt. She stood up and said to Antonio, "It will be up to you to accept the vendetta, my son."

"What are you saying? No! No! I will not do that, Mamma."

"You must. I cannot give it to another soul; no one; not to your father or his brothers, not another man in this family. It has to be you, Antonio. It has to be you. If your father learns of this he will kill Turiddu with his own hands. Don Vito loves your father like a brother, but Turiddu is his blood—he would be forced to avenge his own son's death; he would surely kill my husband. The same would be true for any of your uncles."

"What about Santo Padua?" Antonio pleaded.

"He is in love with Adriana. He may be her only hope of marriage and a family. But even as good as Santo is and even as much as he loves her, he too may reject her—especially if she is already with child." Maria was crying again.

Antonio was surprised his mother knew of Santo's love for Adriana. He thought he was the only one who recognized it.

"Will you accept the vendetta, Antonio? Will you?"

Antonio shook his head. He, and only he, understood how his own mother could ask such a thing of him. Their culture demanded it of them and he knew he had to accept it. Finally he murmured, "Yes, Mamma. I will accept it."

CHAPTER VIII

THE SAMBUCA MAN FROM NAPLES

MONDAY 3 APRIL 1911

THE JARRING AND tossing of the boat awakened Antonio; it kept banking up against something. It was hitting something so hard, it caused Antonio's head to rise up and come back down on the lead piping that supported his berth. The jolt was so intense it nearly knocked him onto the floor.

Then a blaring blast from the ferry's foghorn rang out in the stillness of the night.

Are we in Naples already? Antonio thought. *Impossible! We cannot be! Perhaps the ferry has hit some rocks!*

That thought caused Antonio to jump up out of his berth and rush to the porthole window across the room. He saw clearly the ferry was docked somewhere. "But, where for God's sake; we're in the middle of the Tyrrhenian Sea!" he said out loud to no one but himself.

"All ashore who's going ashore! Last call for Isola Lipari!"

Ah, we have made an extra stop, he thought.

The cabin was pitch black. Antonio fumbled across the cabin, holding onto this and that until he reached the door; he remembered there was an oil lamp there on a table. He found it and lit it. The small cabin was immediately bathed in light.

My God, he thought, *how long have I been sleeping?*

His stomach started to cramp; suddenly, he remembered he had not eaten a thing since leaving Palermo early that day. He went to the small basin atop a dresser and poured some water into it; as he washed his face, he suddenly remembered what he was trying to forget—and sleep through. He heard his mother's voice saying, *Antonio, you must take this vendetta against Turiddu Vanucci; there is no one else who can make right what has been done to your sister.*

Oh my God, he thought as he looked at his reflection in the mirror above the washbasin, *what I have committed myself to? My own mother has asked this of me! I cannot, I must not! God, you have to show me the way,* he thought as he sat in a nearby chair. He put his head into his hands.

Immediately, the pounding headache he had before he fell fast asleep returned, only worse than before because he had not eaten anything in hours. *I need to get something to eat,* he convinced himself.

Antonio walked up the stairs to the top deck; he looked for a space to sit where he could be alone and think, but there were no empty tables. He thought perhaps he was missing one and decided to walk through the crowd to the other side of the deck. But there was not a seat to be had. He turned and walked down to the next lower deck. This room looked just as crowded as the one above, but then he noticed there were empty tables here and there, especially along the railing.

He walked quickly to one towards the back of the boat, and as soon as he sat down, he saw several other men come along and take seats at the other empty tables.

Within a matter of minutes, the deck was completely filled; everyone was yelling out to the *cameriere* at once to bring him or her something to eat or drink. Even though Antonio was hungry to the point of feeling sick, he decided he would wait patiently until one of the waiters was free enough before badgering him to bring him something to eat.

Besides, from where he sat against the boat's railing, occasional waves were high enough to splash up onto him—and the cold, salty water felt good against his face. He closed his eyes and tried to relax; finally, his headache started to subside.

"Excuse me, signor, is this seat taken?"

Antonio opened his eyes to see a fairly tall older gentleman with extraordinary blue eyes staring down at him. His first thought was, *My God, his eyes are just like my mother's.*

"No, no one is sitting there, signor," Antonio responded, "but, to be truthful, I really prefer to be alone right now."

The man tipped his cap and said, "Of course, signor. I understand completely. I have felt that way many times in my long life time but have never had the courage to say it!" The man smiled kindly at Antonio, put his cap back on his head, and then turned to walk away.

Immediately, Antonio felt a pang of guilt. He looked around him to see the deck completely full of people; he had never refused any man a seat in his life before.

"Signor!" Antonio called after the man.

The man turned around.

"Please forgive me, signor. I'm afraid I have offended you with by my truly terrible behavior; please forgive me. Will you join me, signor?"

"Why, thank you, signor, very much. But, I'm sure I will find a space on one of the other decks."

"Nonsense. I insist. Please join me."

The two men conversed politely for a time exchanging thoughts about the weather and politics on the mainland. A *cameriere* brought a large loaf of bread and a plate of cheese to the table, not long after Antonio managed to get his attention. "Please, I insist," said Antonio, "have some cheese and bread."

"Thank you, signor! And for your trouble I will gladly share something with you!" The man reached down and pulled out a tall bottle of black liquid.

"What is that, signor?" asked Antonio

"It is my specialty drink! It is *Sambuca*. Have you ever tasted it?" the man asked Antonio.

"No, I have never even heard of it. What is it, then?"

"Here, try some," said the man as he poured a small glass for Antonio and then one for himself.

Antonio lifted the drink to his lips but the man stopped him and then took out something from his coat pocket. He motioned for Antonio to put his drink down whereupon the man dropped three coffee beans into it. *"Con la mosca!"*

"'With the fly', signor?" Antonio asked.

"Yes, it is a salutation one says when adding the three beans; the beans are a symbol or wish for one's companion to have all measure of health, happiness, and prosperity! I suppose, the usual *Salute!* would serve the same purpose." The man laughed heartily then and downed his own drink. He saw Antonio had not tasted his yet and waved his hand at him to do so. "Go on, enjoy, signor! Enjoy!"

The thick liquid shot down Antonio's throat with a rush of heat from his palate to his gullet. He felt the results of it in his head immediately. And somehow, the feel of the liqueur on his head felt so much better than the dull headache. "Very good, signor. It reminds me of anise."

"Ah, very good! Yes, it is anise. Anise is the main ingredient along with elderflowers, oils, a little pinch of sugar, and of course, alcohol." The man shrugged his shoulders. "Anything added to alcohol tastes very good to me!" Then the man laughed out loud.

He has a good laugh, Antonio thought.

"You see, it was my own father who first made this delicious concoction in Sicily and then struck out on his own in Naples. That is how I have come to inherit this magnificent liqueur!"

"And what did you is say the name of this . . ." Antonio pointed to the black bottle, "this liqueur, signor?"

"Sambuca! Even the name I find delightful, don't you?" He asked Antonio.

"Yes, indeed. I do find it delightful, so much so, would you mind if I had another glass of it?"

"Oh, on the contrary! Please, it is not often I find a man so willing to drink with me!"

The two men drank several glasses of the liqueur. The stranger seemed at ease with the harsh alcohol and Antonio, although not used to it, seemed to welcome its effect on his emotional state. But the more Antonio drank, the more the thoughts of what happened between him and his mother began to again weigh heavily on his heart.

"Do you find life unpredictable, signor?" asked Antonio.

"Unpredictable in what way, my friend?"

"Well, please forgive my openness with you, signor, but I

have spent three quarters of my life, signor, preparing to enter God's service. And then, in just one short conversation, all the time I spent in preparation seems meaningless. Everything I had hoped and dreamed of is gone now, in just one instant!" Antonio started to laugh bitterly.

The stranger's demeanor changed in an instant. The young man sitting across from him was in trouble. Laughing is never an appropriate response to one's life being shattered into a million pieces. The stranger knew Antonio had not had that much to drink but still, revealing something so serious to a perfect stranger was an obvious attempt to ask for help.

"Tell me, what is your name, signor, if I might ask?" the stranger asked gently.

"Antonio. My name is Antonio Vazanno. I am the son of Giuseppe and Maria Vazanno from the village of Balestrate, in Sicily."

The man's jaw dropped. Momentarily, he fell speechless and simply stared at Antonio.

"Have I said something to offend you, signor?" asked Antonio.

"No, not at all!" answered the stranger. "I know of a man by that name Giuseppe Vazanno. And, I'm wondering if you might be the son of that same man? The man I know is also married to a woman by the name of Maria. But, the woman I know is from Milano, in northern Italy. Are you the son of that woman?"

"Yes! Yes, I am, signor. My mother is from Milano. How is it you know my father?"

"Your father saved my life, signor, once a very long time ago; and I will never forget. I owe your father my own life."

Antonio was the one surprised now. "What is your name, signor? And, how is it my father saved your life? Please, I want to know everything!"

"My name is Alfonzo Manricco. Your father, Vito Vanucci, Ciccinu Battaghlia and I all grew up together in Balestrate. My father moved to Naples when I was sixteen to make a better living for my mother and me. He started his own liqueur business there and that is how I have come to be the owner of this." He pointed to the bottle of *Manricco Sambuca*—nearly empty now in the middle of the table.

"But you have not answered my question; how did my father save your life?"

Manricco glanced down. He stared at his hands trying to decide what, if anything, he should reveal to Giuseppe's son. For some reason, Manricco suspected the man across from him was deeply disturbed about something. "Perhaps we can talk tomorrow . . . what is your name then? Ah, I remember now, Antonio? Is that correct? You are Antonio Vazanno?"

"Yes, I am Antonio."

"I will tell you everything tomorrow . . . after we've both had a chance to get some sleep after finishing off this bottle of devil's brew!" he said picking up the bottle.

Antonio smiled at Manricco. "If that is your wish, Signor Manricco. Yes, we can talk in the morning."

Manricco rose and tipped his cap to Antonio. He extended his hand to Antonio and they shook hands warmly. "It has been an absolute pleasure meeting you, Antonio. I look forward to continuing our conversation in the morning." With that, Manricco turned and walked across the deck and down the stairs.

Antonio could not believe he had met a man who had once been one of his father's best friends; beyond that, his own father saved this man's life! *'Your father saved my life.' Yes, that is what he said, I'm sure of it.*

Antonio started to get up but immediately was overcome with dizziness. *Not enough food and too much Sambuca,* he thought. He tried to get up again, but the same thing happened. He sat back down and put his hand to his head.

Suddenly, four men surrounded him. "We noticed you seem to be having some difficulty, signor. Are you feeling ill?" one of the men asked.

"Oh no. I am fine. I'm afraid I have had just a bit too much to drink. That's all."

"Well, I am a doctor, signor. I think you may need something to help your head."

"You are a doctor?" Antonio asked curiously, because the man did not look like a doctor. "And are these other men doctors too, then?" he asked.

"Oh no, signor. These three men are my brothers. We are traveling to Naples to meet another doctor friend of mine. Can I

at least get you a cool drink of water, signor? Do you think that
might help you?"

"Yes, thank you very much. A drink of water would be very
helpful."

One of the men left with the doctor and then returned in a
few minutes. He had a pitcher of water and a glass. The man set
the glass of water down on the table and squeezed some lemon
juice into it. "Here you are, signor. I think you will find this very
refreshing."

***

Manricco couldn't sleep. He could not believe he had just
met Giuseppe's only son. The last time he remembered seeing
Antonio Vazanno was when he was twelve or thirteen years old,
he thought. He remembered the day distinctly because it was
on the occasion of his own 30th birthday–the year 1903–and he,
Vito, and Ciccinu met at Giuseppe's farmhouse to celebrate.

Manricco smiled to himself as he thought about that day.

They had not met to celebrate his birthday, but rather to
honor Vito Vanucci. Vito's father had just died, thus making Vito
the Godfather of Palermo.

Manricco shook his head, thinking, *Our best friend and
blood brother, Vito Vanucci, Godfather of Palermo!*

He remembered how Giuseppe had insisted that the four
of them celebrate Vito's inheritance. *He even surprised us all
with the ring!* Manricco looked down at the ring on his finger.
Giuseppe had four rings made signifying their brotherhood.
*Each of us vowed that day never to take the ring off unless to
give it to someone in need of lifesaving assistance. But it was
Vito's gift that shocked everyone. It was that day he gave away
half of what he owned—to us!*

Manricco aroused himself from bed, and sat in a chair. He
poured himself another glass of Sambuca. *How generous and
kind my brother Vito is!*

As it turned out, Manricco reminisced sadly, *my own dear
father had died too. I had no choice—I had to leave my friends
and Sicily then—I had to take care of my own father's business.
Yes,* he thought, *that was indeed a sad time for me; I not only
lost my father but the constant company of my brothers, too.*

Manricco poured himself yet another glass of Sambuca. He felt the sting of tears in his eyes. *Stop it, you fool!* he scolded himself.

As it turned out, only Giuseppe was the recipient of the land Vito was giving away, with two conditions: any worker Giuseppe hired to work the land must be a full-blooded *Sicilian,* and a percentage of the fruit produced on the land must go back to the people. The rest of the profit Giuseppe was free to enjoy for himself—no strings attached other than all the money made from selling the fruit in Sicily must be kept in the Palermo bank, thus keeping even the Sicilian bankers employed. Otherwise, Giuseppe was free to export the fruit to any country of his choosing—but if he chose to export to a country with a history of domination over Sicily, the fruit must be sold at double the rate compared to other countries.

Then Manricco thought about Giuseppe's special announcement that day about his own son, Antonio. He remembered Giuseppe calling his son over to sit with them. He poured out glasses of red wine for all—including his son—and announced his son was going into the seminary school in Milano on the mainland. Everyone held their glasses high and said *Salute! I remember the look on the boy's face then,* thought Manricco. *He looked sad; very sad. He drank the glass of wine and then politely excused himself. Ah yes, I remember Antonio Vazanno.*

Then suddenly, he also remembered Vito's son! That was the day Turiddu embarrassed and humiliated Vito so very badly! He just seemed to appear out of nowhere—sitting upon a huge, black stallion. He was dressed all in black from head to toe including his hat; his hair was slicked back with oil. He began yelling like a madman when he rode onto Giuseppe's property. Then, just as suddenly, the man dressed in black fell silent and turned his horse to canter straight towards Adriana, Giuseppe's daughter.

They all stood up then to see what he was doing. But it was only Giuseppe who realized what he was up to. In an instant, Giuseppe began running towards the barn and in seconds was riding out to intercept the man. No one could hear the exchange between Giuseppe and Turiddu. But within minutes of Giuseppe's confrontation with the boy, a little girl got up from where she had been sitting—hidden from our view—and started to run towards the farmhouse. Two white goats ran next to her, as if guarding the child. Turiddu's horse bolted away from Giuseppe then and straight towards us as breakneck speed.

"Papa," the boy had said as he pulled his animal to a halt in front of his father, "Mamma told me I would find you here today. I need the money you promised me for the new saddle I ordered from the leathermaker in Naples. Mamma received a letter telling us the saddle would arrive tomorrow on the first ferry in from the mainland."

Vito's face turned expressionless, Manricco remembered. He must have been terribly humiliated and embarrassed by his son's actions, but not a hint of that showed on his face. Very calmly and quietly, Vito approached his son who was still on horseback. "Go home and wait for me there." That's all Vito said to the boy before he took off his cap and slapped the rump of Turiddu's horse. The animal bolted into a gallop—heading away from Giuseppe's farmhouse.

I cannot go back to sleep now! It is impossible, Manricco told himself as he stood up, put on his cap, and headed out of his cabin to take a walk, hoping the fresh air would cause him to relax enough to go to sleep.

* * *

After his stroll, Alfonzo Manricco was returning to his cabin on the main deck when he passed a small corridor and saw a man's feet sticking out from a doorway. Concerned, he went immediately to see what the matter was. Pulling back on the door, he saw Giuseppe's son lying on the floor—passed out completely. At first he thought it was the Sambuca but then he realized the young man's pockets had been turned inside out and that he had been robbed. He called for help and two stewards came immediately. The three men had to practically carry Antonio back to Manricco's cabin.

* * *

Antonio tossed and turned in a drugged stupor. He cried feverishly when he spoke of finding Adriana in the lemon orchard; he raved of the terror she had undergone during her brutal rape. He described her injuries and spoke of the animal who attacked her. He tossed this way and that; he hit his own head with his fists when he ranted of her attacker: *Turiddu Vanucci!*

Manricco listened in horror at Antonio's delirious account of his sister's assault, but when he heard Turiddu Vanucci's name, he too became angry. "Oh, my God, no! Not Vito's son!" he said out loud, nearly breathless with shock.

Antonio seemed finally to fall into a deep sleep as Manricco sat by his bedside. Even Manricco managed to doze off as Antonio slept. But within minutes, it seemed, Antonio was crying out again. "Adriana! Adriana! Who did this to you? What type of an animal could possibly do such a thing? Turiddu! Turiddu Vanucci!" he screamed out, throwing his fists into the air as if trying to hit Turiddu.

Still delirious, Antonio cried bitterly when he rambled on about his priesthood, of being ordained in December. How his father sent him to the seminary as a young boy. How he knew it broke his mother's heart. Then suddenly, he began again to scream things out—incoherent at first but then very clear. "No, Mamma! No, you cannot ask such a thing of me! I am to be a priest!"

Throughout the night Antonio kept pulling at his hair and pounding his fists into his head. He would cry, "I cannot do it! I cannot do it! Please help me, God!" Then, "Yes, Vanucci deserves to die! I have to kill Vanucci! I have to accept the *vendetta!* My mother is right, it is the only way."

Manricco, shocked at the rambling revelations of Giuseppe's son, knew now why the young man he first saw sitting alone at that table looked so steeped in thought and full of anxiety. At the time, he had no idea who the man was or why he looked so tortured but he knew now—something deep down inside of him knew—he had to offer Antonio his help.

How mysterious is fate, he thought, *how unbelievably mysterious it is.*

***

"Where am I?" Antonio asked as he opened his eyes to see his Sambuca drinking companion from the night before sitting next to him.

"You're safe here with me in my cabin, my son."

"Who are you again, signor?" But then he remembered. "No, wait. You're than man who sells Sambuca. I remember you. You're my father's friend . . ."

"Save your strength, Antonio. It seems you have been robbed and drugged. Thankfully, I could not sleep last night and went up to get some fresh air when I found you lying in an empty corridor."

"I don't remember anything at all, signor. I feel such a fool trusting in strangers to help me. I should have been more careful."

"Well," Manricco laughed, "I was a stranger to you, too! It is impossible to know all the time who we can trust and who we cannot. The important thing is I found you and that you are safe now."

Suddenly, Antonio felt entirely embarrassed. "I'm afraid I have been a terrible burden on you, signor. I really want to go to my own cabin now, if you will excuse me."

"Of course. I understand. But, I think it would do you a world of good to have some tea and refreshment before you go. Look," he said pointing to a tray he had the porter bring in, "I have taken the liberty of anticipating your hunger!" He smiled warmly at Antonio. "Won't you please join me?"

Antonio tried to sit up but immediately was overcome with dizziness. Manricco helped him to lie back down on the berth, putting several pillows under his head.

"There, there," said Manricco as he pulled a blanket over Antonio's legs. "Let me first give you some tea to drink, and then you can attempt to get up."

Antonio drank one cup of tea and then another. His head began to clear as the dizziness subsided. "I remember you telling me that you and my father used to be good friends. Can you tell me more about that, signor?"

"We are childhood friends! Your father, myself, Ciccinu Battaghlia, and Vito Vanucci were all raised together in Balestrate."

Antonio smiled at Manricco and asked, "How is I have never met you, then?"

"I met you once; you were perhaps twelve or thirteen. I came to your father's farmhouse to celebrate Vito Vanucci's inheritance. His father had just died and he took over the . . ." Manricco paused and asked Antonio, "You do know about the Society? The Society of Honorable Men?"

"Yes, signor. Who in Sicily does not know about it?"

"The reason you did not know me was because my father traveled during my childhood between Naples and Palermo. He had inherited the Sambuca business from his own father, and he often took my mother and me with him to Naples. But when he died, I had to go to Naples to take over the business. Finally, my mother also moved to Naples to take care of me, because I wasn't married." Manricco stopped talking for a moment and stared in deep concentration. Then he said, "But the bond between Giuseppe, Vito, Ciccinu, and me is very strong—so strong that nothing on this earth could ever break it. I assure you of that."

"But how did the four of you come to be so close?" Antonio asked, still confused because Manricco had not answered his question as yet.

Manricco fell silent then; he rubbed his chin as if debating what he should tell Giuseppe's son about his father's past. The problem was, he knew Antonio Vazanno was in trouble. And he knew he owed it to his old friend Giuseppe to help his only son.

Manricco thought, and then started slowly: "Your father is a very brave man, Antonio. Vito Vanucci owes his life to your father, and not just for one occasion but for two. If it weren't for your own father's persistence, bravery, and courage, Vito Vanucci would have died . . . twice!"

* * *

"We will always be blood brothers," Vito told Giuseppe. He took out his knife and grazed his fingertip with it; blood oozed out. "Here," he said, handing the knife to Giuseppe, "you have to do the same."

Once Giuseppe's finger was cut, the two boys put their fingers together and let their blood intermingle.

"Blood brothers forever, *m'fratello!*" Giuseppe said firmly.

"Forever!" echoed Vito.

Laughing at their show of bravado, the two boys began walking to their horses as they sucked the blood off their fingertips.

"What do you say we go to the Castellamare?" Vito urged Giuseppe. Anticipating Giuseppe's refusal, he said, "Don't say no, Peppino . . . I won't let you drown!"

"You're crazy, Vito! If I'm not back in the orchards when Papa returns from Palermo, he will kill me outright. Believe me, I'm not afraid of drowning as much as I am afraid of my father's hand."

"The problem with you, *m'fratello,* is that you let everyone else do your thinking for you. Are you a man or just a farm boy who follows orders all day?" Vito said mockingly, at the same time being careful not to offend Giuseppe too much. What he really wanted was to spend time with his friend taking a swim in the gulf with their horses.

Giuseppe was getting nervous. He knew Vito had a way of getting precisely what he wanted out of him; and he knew what Vito usually wanted meant trouble for the both of them. At the same time, Giuseppe wanted to please his best friend; after all, they had both just taken a blood oath for eternal friendship. Giuseppe stared down at his finger and began to think about what Vito proposed. He reasoned that if they left now and rode as fast as they could, they most likely would be done with their swim by noon. Giuseppe could sneak into the back of the orchards without his father seeing what time he had really returned. "Let's go. I could use a swim in this heat!"

* * *

The two reached the edge of the gulf in record time. It was Vito who entered the water first after climbing off his horse and taking the saddle off. Then he kicked off his boots, trousers, and shirt. He climbed back on his horse bareback and shouted, "Let's go! Let's go!" as he kicked his horse into the foaming surf. He glanced back to see where Giuseppe was. He saw him on the beach taking off his clothes and unsaddling his horse. Vito shouted back at Giuseppe, "Don't be afraid, Peppino! If you start to drown I will save you, my brother!"

"Go! Go!" shouted Giuseppe to his own horse as he too kicked him hard in the flank to catch up to Vito.

Riding their horses bareback in the gulf was something both boys were very experienced at; they each were skilled at staying on their mounts in the water. Wrapping a fistful of mane into both hands was the trick; holding on for dear life was the skill.

Giant waves lashed over the horses' heads and then onto the boys. There was a strong wind blowing into the gulf from the west off the tip of Africa, causing the waves to be quite high. Every once in a while one of the boys would lose his grip on his horse's mane and tumble backwards into the sea. Each boy was experienced in swimming bareback and knew what to do if a wave pushed him off his horse in the water. The first thing was to swim in the opposite direction of the horse to avoid getting kicked in the head by the horse's back hooves. After regaining his bearing, the boy would then swim rapidly up to the side of the horse and grab onto the mane once again. As soon as a good grip was established, it was quite easy to swing back up onto the horse's back.

Then it happened; a giant wave suddenly appeared, covering Vito and his horse completely. Giuseppe, swimming some distance from Vito, saw the wave coming and prepared for it by turning his horse sideways, bringing his head down close to his horse's neck and holding on as tightly as he could while holding his breath. As soon as the wave washed over them, they tumbled deep into the water. And immediately, both Giuseppe and his horse bobbed up again in the surf. He looked around quickly for any sign of Vito—but the only thing he saw was Vito's horse, swimming alone in the surf.

Vito never saw the wave. Caught unaware and off guard, he lost his grip when it crashed in on him. He tried with all his might to swim upwards but the current was too swift and he was dragged farther and farther out to sea. Nearly drowning because he could not catch a breath of air, he slowly began to sink toward the sea bottom. But just as suddenly, the grip of the current released him and he felt himself start to rise toward the blue sky above. His head came out of the water; he gasped for air; he was choking and trying to call for help.

Giuseppe saw him bobbing in the water and rushed headlong toward him. Gasping for every breath now, Vito tried to get his bearings when suddenly, like a bolt of lightning, he felt a hard kick to his head. Excruciating pain shot through him, and within seconds he was again drifting back into the deep blue of the sea.

Giuseppe saw what had happened. He knew where Vito was and swam as fast as he could toward Vito's horse. As soon as Giuseppe came near Vito's horse, he dove under the water. He held his breath as long as he could and then resurfaced to gasp for air. On his third dive, he saw Vito lying on a shallow reef, unconscious. He grabbed Vito and quickly brought him to the surface. He swam with all his might to get close to his own horse. He grabbed onto its mane and then threw Vito's nearly lifeless body on the horse. He climbed on behind Vito and kicked his horse as hard as he could, guiding them back toward shore.

Once on shore, Giuseppe pulled Vito onto the sand and began to pump his chest hard. Tears welled in Giuseppe's eyes; he knew Vito was about to die. He struggled to turn Vito this way and that, trying with all his might to get air back into Vito's lungs. Suddenly Vito gasped. He turned on his side and vomited out seawater. He lay his head on the sand and choked back tears himself. Blood was dripping from his mouth.

Giuseppe grabbed his shirt lying nearby and pressed it against his friend's face. "Open your mouth, Vito!" he ordered. "Holy Mother of God and all the saints! You have a hole in your head! That horse of yours kicked a hole in your head!" Giuseppe began to laugh so hard he was near hysterics. "Lucky for you, my brother, that horse didn't kick your brains out!"

Giuseppe sat down next to Vito, relieved his friend was alive. "I'm going to saddle the horses so we can get out of here."

But before Giuseppe was completely standing, Vito grabbed his arm and pulled him back. "Listen to me, Giuseppe, we're going to tell everyone that I tripped and fell against the big rock behind the *granaio di stampa olivastro*. Okay?"

"No, Vito! Not the olive presses!" exclaimed Giuseppe. "My father will kill me. There is no excuse for this one. We have to tell the truth. How stupid do you think people are anyway?"

"You're the *stupido*, Peppino. If we tell anyone we were swimming in the sea with these horses, we're both as good as dead. I'm not going to live just to die at my father's hand when he finds out I was swimming in the *mare*." Remembering their oath earlier that morning, Vito corrected himself, "I mean, my brother."

He waited for Giuseppe to continue his protest but thought better of it and added, "Just let me take care of this, okay?"

* * *

"Giuseppe, what happened?" exclaimed Vito's mother when she saw her son's bloodied mouth.

"It was my fault, Mama. Peppino found a wild boar in the orchards early this morning and came to ask my help to kill the beast before he damaged any of his father's lemon trees. Well, we killed the boar and buried him outside the south orchards."

"How does that explain your face, Vito?" his mother asked angrily.

"I was crawling in the rafters to put my rifle back when I slipped on the slick cisterns above the olive presses. I fell straight down, Mama, into the grinding olive presses. If it weren't for Giuseppe I would be dead right now. He caught me just before I fell between the grinding wheels of the press! He risked his own life to save me!"

"Oh, my God!" exclaimed Signora Vanucci as she ran to Vito to hold him in her arms. When she took away the shirt she screamed at the sight of Vito's missing teeth. "Holy Mother of God! Your beautiful face, Vito!" Encouraging Vito to stand, she assisted him to his bedroom. She helped him into bed and then returned to the kitchen to the waiting Giuseppe, patiently listening to Vito lie to his mother.

No sooner had Signora Vanucci reached the kitchen than Vito yelled out to her, "What will Papa do to me when he sees what I have done to myself?"

"I'll take care of your father. Stay in bed now and get some rest."

Giuseppe, now deeply worried about how his own father would punish him for his disobedience, told the signora he had to leave.

"Don't you worry about your father, Giuseppe, I will take care of him, too. I will go over to the orchards right now and tell him what has occurred this morning. He will be very proud of you, son. I promise you that. You're such a good boy, Giuseppe.

Thank God for you. It's always my Vito getting into trouble. If it wasn't for you . . . what would my boy do? I'm very proud of you! I will make sure your family and my husband knows how you saved Vito's life today." She kissed Giuseppe's forehead.

* * *

"So that is the first time my father saved Vito Vanucci's life; what about the second time?" Antonio asked the Sambuca maker. Signor Manricco considered a moment. "Ah, the second time. The second time is much more dramatic, and I hesitate to share with you the truth of it."

"No, I insist! I want to know everything you know about my father," Antonio said.

"Hmmm. The second time was when they were much older and Vito was already working with his father to form the Society of Honorable Men in Sicily. Are you sure you are prepared to hear what I am about to tell you?"

"Yes. By all means, please tell me everything."

* * *

Vito walked over the ridge and away from Giuseppe. His conscience nagged at him. He hated to leave his friend Peppino disappointed, but he had no other choice. He could not take him where he had to go. He did not want him involved in the dirty work he knew he had been raised to do. It would be better for Peppino not to become involved.

Vito reached the meeting place just as the sun was about to set. He stood in front of the barn waiting for his friends, Alfonzo Manricco and Ciccinu Battaghlia, to meet up with him. Within a few minutes he heard the sound of hooves and saw Alfonzo riding toward him over the ridge.

"Are you ready, Alfonzo?" Vito asked.

"Sure, why not? What do you think? I can't handle a simple deal like this?"

"Okay, okay, that's enough bravado from you. I don't want to remind you again . . . *omertà*, Alfonzo, *omertà!* This is serious business. I need to know you're with me all the way on this. I mean *all the way. Capisce?*"

Alfonzo dismounted his horse slowly and knelt on one knee. He took a cigarette out of his pocket and lit it. Inhaling deeply, he then blew rings of smoke up toward the evening sky. "My father is counting on me, Vito . . . just as your father is counting on you. Don't worry, *m'amico,* I'm ready."

"Good; where is Ciccinu?" Vito asked.

"He's going to meet us halfway there. I told him the roads we are taking."

The two young men rode off toward the hills. Not far from where they were to meet the contacts Vito's father had arranged for them, they encountered Ciccinu Battaghlia.

"Ah, you decided to join us, my friend!" Vito said to Ciccinu.

"I thought about not coming for a long time, my friend, but then I thought, 'what's going to happen to Alfonzo and Vito without me?'"

The three men laughed in camaraderie and turned toward Partinico, kicking their horses into a gallop now as the sun was starting to set. When they reached a small shack in a clearing just outside of Partinico, Vito took out a club covered at one end with an oil-soaked rag and lit it. Immediately, his flaming torch lit up the night sky.

"You two wait for me over there," Vito said, pointing to a grove of evergreens at the top of a small ridge. "I'll give you the signal when you should approach. Remember, I should be walking up toward the two of you with the men—wait until you see me walking toward you, understand?"

Both Alfonzo and Ciccinu answered Vito in unison: "Yes, boss!"

Vito rode away from them and rode out several yards; he stopped there and began waving the torch high in the air—a sign to the men he was meeting. Within minutes, Vito could hear horses moving in his direction. The night was black and Vito knew he wouldn't be able to see who was coming or how many were coming until they were nearly next to him. *Odd,* Vito thought, *where is the moon?* Then he looked up at the starless cloud-covered sky and realized the moon was in its first quarter and only a tip of its faint crescent shape lit the sky. *Ah, there it is.*

In an instant, two men on horseback were in front of Vito's horse.

"Identify yourselves," Vito demanded as he stood his ground in front of them.

"I'm here to buy a horse. There's no need for names, *amico*," said the man who appeared to be the leader, as the other man remained silent.

"I like to know who I'm dealing with. For all I know, you could be *polizia*."

"*M'nome Chiro . . . Chiro l'Forchetta*. Any more questions?"

"Yeah, why do they call you 'Chiro the Fork'?"

"Go ask the last guy I killed when I put one into his brains!" Both men started to laugh. Vito remained stone-faced. The man called Chiro said, "You got horses to sell me or not? You're wasting my time if you don't have horses."

"Sure. Sure, I got horses for you! Just show me the money first, signor; that's all I want to see first: the money, signor."

Chiro the Fork took a package out of his saddlebag and tossed it to Vito, who caught it in one hand. He opened the package and counted the money. "Ah, not enough, *amico* . . . the price was double what you have here."

"Let's see the horses. If everything is satisfactory . . . then I'll pay you the rest."

Vito smiled. "Sure. That's reasonable. But show me the money before I take you to the horses."

The man took out another package and unwrapped it. Bundles of *lire* were tied together neatly. "You see, signor, I have all the money. But I'm no fool! Show me the horses and I'll let you count the rest of the money."

"Okay, follow me," Vito said as he turned to ride toward the ridge where Alfonzo and Ciccinu were waiting.

'The Fork' and his henchman followed Vito. Without the light of a full moon and stars, it was difficult for him to make out the ridge where he had told his friends to wait. He held up the torch to get his bearings straight, but before he knew it they had nearly reached the top of the ridge . . . and Alfonzo and Ciccinu were nowhere in sight. Vito started to get nervous; they should have come out from behind the shrubbery by now. Suddenly he caught a glimpse of something coming toward them.

Next he heard the unmistakable sound of shotguns being cocked. Vito stopped and turned to see the two men behind him with their shotguns pointed at him.

"Get down, signor," said Chiro, "slowly. Don't try any of that Honorable Man bullshit on me. I've got a bullet with your name on it aimed straight at your head."

Vito dismounted slowly. As soon as his feet hit the ground, he looked again at what had at first caught his eye in the distance. It was Alfonzo and Ciccinu, stumbling toward him; both men had ropes tied around their necks and were slowly moving toward Vito, their hands tied behind their backs. As they got closer, Vito could see they were surrounded by four more men on horseback who were prodding them with whips, urging them to walk faster toward Vito. Once they were close, Vito could see they had already been beaten badly. Their faces were swollen and bleeding.

Vito stood next to his horse, his mind darting in a thousand directions at once, looking for options. Alfonzo and Ciccinu didn't have a chance of overtaking the men behind them. It would be up to him to get himself and his two friends out of this ambush.

"Take all of them over there," said Chiro, pointing to a small grove of oak trees.

The bandits dragged Ciccinu, Vito, and Alfonzo over to the trees and tied them there. Chiro walked up to Vito and said, "Do you know how much money I'm going to get for you, my friend?"

"Nobody is going to pay you anything for me, *friend*," Vito said sarcastically.

"Wait a minute, boys. Do I have the right man here?" Chiro said just as sarcastically. "If I am not mistaken, aren't you Vito Vanucci? Isn't your father Don Vanucci of Palermo?" The men all started to laugh as Chiro spit in Vito's face mockingly.

"You and your father! Big shots! Who cares about Sicily— only you and your father, my friend. You two sit around and make big plans for Sicily; all the while you take money from poor men like me and my friends here," Chiro said, pointing to his companions. "Real men, *Sicilianos,* own Sicily—not you and your Honorable Men!"

"My father won't pay you, signor; you might as well kill me now because I can assure you my father will not give in to your demands. But I can promise you this—you are as good as dead right now."

"Do you really think you and your father are the ones who should be running this island?" The man grinned at Vito, showing his yellow teeth. "I hope your father is as stupid as you are. He's next, *m'amico*. That's my plan."

Vito spit in the man's face.

The man slammed the butt of his shotgun into Vito's face; he started to walk away and then turned and hit him again, causing him to slump, with only the ropes around him holding him up. He kicked Vito hard in his face with his boot.

"This could have been quick, but I don't like that idea now. You need to learn a lesson before you meet your maker." Chiro ordered one of his partners to get Vito's torch; it was on the ground but still lit. "Bring me the torch! Hurry up!"

One of the men quickly picked up the torch and brought it to Chiro. "Hold him up against the tree," Chiro ordered.

Two men grabbed Vito under his arms and held him up straight with his back to the tree.

"Let's get you used to hell, *m'amico*," Chiro said as he started to push the lit torch into Vito's face.

A loud blast rang out.

Chiro suddenly grabbed at his back, which arched into a strange contortion; he then slumped to the ground. His jaw dropped open and blood spewed out. A second shot rang out and another man fell to the ground.

Now the remaining four bandits hit the ground, trying to escape being shot in the pitch darkness in front of them. With the lit torch back on the ground now, the men's bodies were illuminated against the blackness.

Another shot rang out.

A third man was struck in the head. He screamed out in agony and within seconds was quiet. The three remaining men got up and tried to run to their horses but the horses were gone now—and one by one, each man was hit with gunshot and each fell to the ground.

Giuseppe walked from the darkness and into the orange glow of the torchlight. Vito started to laugh. He was laughing so hard he began to choke. Now Ciccinu and Alfonzo were laughing, too.

"What in the hell are you doing here, my Peppino?" Vito choked out between bouts of laughter.

"I'm sick and tired of you always telling me what to do, you jackass! I hope you realize this is the second time I saved your life!"

"Oh yes, my dear friend, I do indeed know how many times you have saved my life! Let's just hope this is the last time, okay?"

Giuseppe untied them from the trees and brought their horses to them. "Do you think you can ride, my friend?" he said to Vito.

"I think I can manage that, Peppino, but I don't know about Alfonzo over there. It looks as if they really roughed him up."

Giuseppe helped Alfonzo up onto a horse behind Vito. Ciccinu was able to ride by himself. The four of them started slowly back to Palermo when suddenly Giuseppe told them to wait. He quickly rode off telling the other three again to wait for him. Within minutes Giuseppe came riding back with six other horses and shotguns in tow.

"I figured we couldn't go home empty-handed." He threw the two saddlebags full of money at Vito. "Here! Show your father the profits from your night's work."

Vito started to laugh again. He rode over to Giuseppe and said, "Now I owe you again, *m'fratello,* and not only me, but Alfonzo and Ciccinu too! You keep going like this and you might just live forever." Vito smiled and held his hand out to Giuseppe. The two men shook hands and Vito said, "I love you, my friend. No, not my friend . . . my brother!"

***

"If it hadn't been for your father's stubborn insistence to defy Vito's orders that day, none of us would be alive to talk about it," Manricco concluded. "I tell you truly, Antonio, your father is a hero and a very courageous man. And, all of us are deeply indebted to him for his bravery."

Antonio's head was pounding. He could not believe what Manricco had just told him. His own father had murdered six men! Could that be possible? *Why hadn't he ever told me about this? Why would he keep something like this from me? I'm his son, after all.* Suddenly it dawned on him: "Now I know why he wanted me to go away to the seminary. He never wanted me to know the truth of how he himself was made to become part of the

Society of Honorable Men," Antonio concluded.

"Oh no, Antonio; quite the contrary. After that night, your father was convinced that he never wanted to have anything more to do with the way Sicily had found her freedom. But, it was not only your father who was determined you would never become a part of it—it was Don Vito himself, as well!"

"What do you mean? What does Vito Vanucci have to do with me going into the seminary?"

"That's the reason he gave your father all the land he owns today. He knew your family, as good as they are, would never have been able to afford to send you to the seminary in Milano. After all, it is the most prestigious seminary school in Europe! So, by giving your father the property, a property your grandfather had worked since he was just a boy himself, and by paying for your schooling in Milano, Vito essentially was ensuring your father would be a very wealthy man for the rest of his life. That's how you father was able to afford your education, Antonio. It was through Don Vito's benevolence and love for your father."

Antonio was speechless. *Vito Vanucci gave my father everything!* "I did not know the extent of Don Vanucci's devotion to my father. But, surely, the reason my father sent me away to the seminary had more to do with the church than anything else; of that I am certain."

Again Manricco said nothing; he wanted to think carefully about what he would reveal to Antonio and how he would reveal it. The small cabin fell silent for a long time as both he and Antonio tried to think about everything they had learned in the past twenty-four hours about one another.

Finally it was Manricco who broke the silence.

"Your father is an extraordinary man, Antonio. Once he got a taste of what had to be done to belong to the Society of Honorable Men, he wanted no more part of it. Even though he understood and was grateful for how his father, Vito's father, and even Vito himself won the freedom of the *Sicilini*—still he knew one day it would change, and he was right. He knew the idealism upon which the Society was built would be lost on following generations. Vito's vision for Sicily was *la cosa nostra,* to keep all things Sicilian—Sicilian! But how can a country grow if it is not allowed outside of itself?

"Once those who did not directly fight for Sicily's freedom discovered all the wealth to be had just by being in a position of power, all would be lost. Giuseppe and Vito knew this and they were right. The *honor* upon which the Society of Honorable Men was begun has nothing at all to do with *honor* today. In fact—God help us—the exact opposite is true! Now the *Sicilianos* need to be delivered from that *honor* as it exists today!"

Antonio's head felt as if it would explode. "So the Godfather of Palermo paid the price of my priesthood? That's what you are telling me, Signor Manricco?"

Manricco smiled. He put his hand on Antonio's shoulder. "Listen to me, son; remember everything I have told you today—not just how it is you are able to attend a seminary in Milan!

* * *

Manricco knew he had to do something to help Antonio. The burden placed on the young man by his own mother was causing him the most distress and Manricco knew that trying to handle that request could mean the ruination of Antonio's vocation and his very soul.

"Here," he said as he took a ring off of his finger and put it into Antonio's hand, "I want you to have this. There is a man I want you to meet. You met him once, just like you met me many years ago; his name Ciccinu Battaghlia and he lives near Catania. He is a very powerful but wise man. He knows your father, and Vito, and myself very, very well. He will give you guidance if you are ever in need of it. You can trust him, Antonio. You can trust him with your life—especially since you are the son of Giuseppe Vazanno. He will help you; just show him this ring and he will understand that I sent you to him."

"But, Signor Manricco, what makes you think I am in the need of assistance?" asked Antonio, confused. "I'm returning to the seminary to finish my last months of preparation before ordination."

Manricco knew differently. He knew Antonio would never return to the seminary until the matter with his mother was settled—one way or another.

"Then take this and keep it anyway. If you think you may need counsel one day, then take it to Ciccinu. If you do not seek his help, then keep the ring for yourself. I'm getting old now and because I have not married and do not have a son of my own, then I give this ring to you as a pledge of my undying gratitude to your dear father."

CHAPTER IX

THE RING

14 APRIL 1911

ANTONIO SAT IN the Naples train station fingering the ring Alfonzo Manricco had given him. He got up twice to walk to the ticket counter to buy a one-way ticket back to Milan, but changed his mind each time. He knew, somewhere deep down in his heart, if he returned to Milan—to the seminary—he would never return to Sicily; he would be closing his eyes, his mind, his soul on the tragedy that had befallen his sister. The injustice of that, he knew, he could not live with. He had to find a way to help her and he could not do that if returned to the seminary.

If my vocation is true—if God Himself has truly called me to serve him—then it will not change if I wait until my sister is safe and justice has been served—on Turiddu Vanucci.

"A one-way ticket to Catania, Sicily, please."

"This train only goes as far as Messina, signor. You will have to purchase another ticket in Messina to go to Catania."

Antonio only had enough money for the ticket to Messina. "Just a one-way ticket to Messina then." Antonio pushed the money across the counter to the clerk.

"How far to Catania once I arrive in Messina?" Antonio asked the clerk.

The man shrugged his shoulders and then raised his palms up in a gesture of not knowing what to say. "This train only goes to Messina. I'm sorry, signor, that is all I know. I have never been to Sicily."

* * *

The train left Naples by midday. The conductor told Antonio they would not reach Messina until the next day—most likely sometime in the late afternoon—if the train did not encounter any problems.

"Problems? What kind of problems?" asked Antonio.

The conductor laughed. "I see you have not taken this train before, signor!" He laughed again and shook his head. "I will not even share with you the problems that *could* occur; no sense causing you worry. Let's just say, if all goes well, we'll be in Messina tomorrow afternoon."

The conductor looked at Antonio's ticket and then looked at how well he was dressed. "How is it you are in general seating, signor? You don't look as if you belong in this cabin."

"What's wrong with a general ticket, then?" Antonio asked.

"Never mind that. Follow me," the conductor answered.

He brought Antonio to a private cabin car; the seats looked bigger and more comfortable than the seats in the general seating car. "Here," he said as he opened the door for Antonio. "For some reason you look as if you belong in here instead."

"Thank you, signor!" Antonio answered. "But, are you sure this cabin does not belong to someone else?"

The conductor simply said, "Enjoy your trip, signor." Then he walked out, closing the door behind him.

Antonio was grateful for the peace and quiet. He eyed the long comfortable seat and gladly slumped down onto it. He let his head fall back and rested as he closed his eyes. At once, as was his habit now, he started to pray. Prayer helped him empty his mind of all his troubles and within minutes he fell asleep.

The shrill train whistle startled Antonio to wakefulness. He sat straight up to look out the window and see that the train was pulling into a station. *Impossible!* he thought. *It is not possible I have slept from Naples to Messina!*

"All out for Messina, Milazzo, Giardini-Naxos, and Catania! Last stop!"

Another conductor was walking the aisles of the train

announcing they had arrived in Messina. "ALL OUT!" he shouted as he clanged a bell over and over again.

Immediately Antonio grabbed his satchel and opened the cabin door to leave, but was met by passengers crowding the aisle; everyone seemed to be trying to exit at the same time. He sat back down to wait until the crowded aisle cleared. Within fifteen minutes it seemed most of the passengers had exited the train. Antonio picked up his satchel again and walked out onto the platform adjacent to the railroad tracks. The train was still steaming and began to roll, slowly, towards another set of tracks. Antonio presumed it was turning around to return to Naples.

Walking along the platform, Antonio followed the wave of people leaving the station; most of them walked directly to waiting carriages, but others were paying to rent a buggy for their ride into the town. Antonio thought about how much money he had left and knew if wanted to buy a ticket for a train to Catania, he most likely would not have enough money to pay for a ride into Messina. He saw a building he presumed to be the ticket office and walked in to inquire about the cost of a train to go to Catania.

"How much is a ticket to Catania, signor?" Antonio asked the agent.

"Two lire, signor. But the train to Catania will not leave until tomorrow morning now. The last train left just over an hour ago."

"What time does the train leave in the morning, then?"

"The first train leaves at 6:00 in the morning and one other at twelve noon."

Antonio reasoned he could probably find somewhere to sleep for the night in Messina that wouldn't cost too much but , then he remembered he also hadn't eaten anything since he left Naples. He needed to buy some food. He would walk to Messina and then return in the morning to board the train for Catania. He took out two lire from his pocket and pushed the money through the open window to the clerk. As he pulled his money out, the ring that Alfonzo Manricco gave him fell out of his pocket and onto the ground. Antonio bent over to pick the ring up but instead of returning it to his pocket he lay the ring on the counter as he took his ticket from the clerk.

"That is quite a magnificent ring, signor! It must be worth a small fortune!" the clerk commented.

Antonio quickly took the ring off the counter and shoved it into his pocket. Then he took his ticket and said, "Thank you, signor." He turned and started to walk away. Then, he stopped suddenly and asked the clerk, "I presume that road over there is the one leading to Messina; is that correct, signor?"

"The main road leading to Messina is to your right, signor. The left road leads back towards the sea."

Antonio nodded, tipped his cap, and then turned to walk towards the road on the right.

The sun was just setting as Antonio took off on foot toward town; by the time he had walked three-quarters of an hour, the dark roadway was only discernible a few feet in front of him. There was a quarter moon overhead and the sky was filled with clouds; when the moon shone down, Antonio could see the road and his surroundings readily; but, when the moonlight was obscured by cloud cover, the area around him was black as pitch.

Suddenly Antonio heard the sound of feet behind him. At first he thought himself imagining it, but as soon as the clouds covered the moon, he could hear the sound get closer and closer to him.

"Where are you going, signor?" a man's voice said in the darkness.

Antonio stopped and stood absolutely still. "Who are you that you would walk up to a man in the darkness of night? I assure you, I have absolutely nothing of value for you to steal from me."

Suddenly, the clouds moved away from the moon and Antonio was able to see not one man, but four. They did not look the way he expected at all; rather they looked like ordinary men, clean and dressed well. "So," Antonio said, "now that I can see you, what is you want from me?"

The man who had spoken to him first said, "Well, you must admit it is rather strange to see a man walking in the middle of the night down a blackened road—alone—without any companionship, signor. My friends and I," he said waving his arms out in front of the other three men, "are on our way to

Messina and thought you might want some companionship. After all, this can be a very dangerous road when you are alone at night."

"Why then are you four walking? Why aren't you on horseback, signor?"

"We are five men, signor. The fifth man is watering the horses not far from here. I assure you I'm not going to rob you; I just became curious seeing you walking by yourself. That's all." The man shrugged his shoulders.

"Thank you, signor," Antonio said sincerely while remaining skeptical of the man's motive, "but I assure you I am not afraid to walk alone here. I'm nearly to Messina now as I can see the lights leading into the city."

"Very well, signor. But, be careful. The night tends to bring out the worst in men, even those who are well intentioned in the daylight!"

***

Antonio turned and continued to walk towards Messina. He felt relieved the men were not robbers but instead seemed otherwise well-intentioned.

Alone now with his thoughts, he began again to think about his mother. He felt tears come to his eyes as he thought of the promise she made him make to her.

Oh my God, Mamma, he thought, *I love you beyond all telling; but I cannot—I will not do this thing you ask of me.* But there was one thing he knew for sure, and that was what drove his mother to conceive of such a terrible request.

If my sister becomes pregnant, he thought, *her life would be in complete ruins! There is no convent in all of Sicily, or Italy, or even the whole of Europe who would accept her under those circumstances. They'll take her in until the baby is born but then they will take the child from her immediately and put it in an orphanage for the rest of its life! They won't let her enter a convent—never under those circumstances. Even if she is not pregnant, no man will ever marry her now!*

No, he thought shaking his head back and forth in frustration, *no—my sister's life is truly ruined now all because of Turiddu Vanucci.*

Antonio felt the hard end of something hit the side of his head. Before he could even react, he fell to the ground, unconscious.

* * *

Antonio opened his eyes to stare at a dirty wooden wall with a large gaping hole in the middle of it. Immediately, he tried to raise his aching body from the floor but realized he couldn't move: his hands were tied behind his back, and his feet were tied together.

Where am I? he thought. He looked around the empty shack with its barren walls and broken-down furniture, and realized he was in a place most likely not near anyone—anyone who would be willing to help him. Then, he remembered. Someone hit him hard in the side of the head. And try as he might, he couldn't remember anything after that.

The more alert he grew, the more his head throbbed. Light filtered into the room onto his face through the hole in the wall. He closed his eyes against it hoping to stop his head from pounding in pain, but nothing seemed to help. The heat inside the room was unbearable and Antonio felt his stomach churn. He wanted to vomit but knew he had nothing in his stomach to give up.

A door opened behind him and he jerked his head around to see who or what was coming into the room. Three men came in and stood in front of him.

"What's your name, signor?" one of the men asked.

Antonio couldn't speak. He didn't know whom he was dealing with and was afraid to say anything. Finally, he managed, "Who are you?"

The man didn't answer him but instead turned to one of his companions and ordered him to untie Antonio.

As soon as Antonio was freed from the ropes, the man ordered the other two to help him up.

"Put him in a chair and then go bring some water," he ordered.

Antonio looked up at his benefactor and stared at his face. Antonio's mouth was so swollen he could barely get the words out. "Who are you, signor? Why are you helping me?" he slurred.

"My name is Mario Lucalla. I and my men came to this place after some local banditos tried to sell us this." The man held out the ring Manricco had given to Antonio. "Is this your ring, signor?"

"It belongs to a man I met on a ferry from Palermo to Naples. I was trying to get to Catania to meet someone whom I understood might be able to help me—if I showed him that ring," Antonio said as he pointed to the ring.

Lucalla rubbed his chin and stared at Antonio for a long time. Finally, he said, "And what man is it you are looking for, signor?"

"Signor Battaghlia. His name is Ciccinu Battaghlia and I'm told he lives somewhere near Catania."

"I see," said Lucalla. "I see."

A man came in with water. He handed the flask to Antonio who took it immediately but, before drinking, offered the container to the other two men.

"No, no, signor. Please drink! Drink!" Lucalla said. He waited until Antonio had finished drinking all the water before he said, "I think I can help you find the man you are looking for, signor."

"How is that, Signor Lucalla? Do you know Ciccinu Battaghlia?"

"I know this ring well," he said as he held the ring out in front of him. "The man you are looking for owns one that is identical."

"Who is that then, signor?" asked Antonio surprised.

"My own father. My father is the man you are looking for. My father is Ciccinu Battaghlia."

Antonio was shocked. How could it be this stranger who just saved his life was also the son of the man he was looking for? *It is impossible,* he thought, *impossible!* "How is it your name is Lucalla and your father's name Battaghlia?" Antonio finally asked.

"My father took me and my sister into his home when we were orphaned by the Messina earthquake of 1893; I was eight years old at the time and my sister was only two."

Antonio didn't know what to say. He was totally dumbfounded but at the same time very grateful that God was indeed watching over him. "I am at a loss for words, signor. If you had not come along, surely I would have died."

"How is it you were traveling alone on the road to Messina,

signor? Surely you must have thought of the dangers inherent in such an adventure."

"I had no money to buy transportation and spent the last of my money to buy a ticket to Catania on the morning train. I knew I needed to find some sort of shelter for the night in Messina, and quite frankly, I simply left everything in the hands of God."

Mario laughed out loud now. In between bursts of laughter he managed, "I'm sorry, signor. Please forgive me! But, God has not been down this road for a very long time! Whoever sent you there was definitely not well intentioned!"

Antonio looked stunned. "You mean the ticket agent gave me the wrong directions towards Messina? But, I thought as I walked I saw the flickering of lights signaling I was walking towards the city."

"Signor, you were on a road that leads straight to the sea. Because the road is higher than the sea, it looks as if you are heading straight for Messina when in fact, once you reach the top of the road's incline, you clearly see the sea below and the town of Messina jutting out like a peninsula just on the other side of the sea."

"So, I was tricked by the ticket clerk who must be working with those men who attacked me last night! He deliberately put me on that road just so I would be attacked by bandits!"

"I'm afraid you are entirely right, signor. Many of the clerks working in the train and ferry stations are just transient workers looking to make a few lire so that they can go off and gamble and whore. The one you met must be working with some of the local *banditos* who work around the stations looking for unsuspecting strangers to steal from.

"But, you got lucky, signor! If those *banditos* had tried to sell this ring to anyone other than one of my men, we would have never found you. They brought you here to die. No one comes out here to this desolate place."

"So how did you get them to tell you where I was, then?"

"Well, as far as I know there are only four men in all of Sicily who have such a ring: my own father who wears this ring every day; Vito Vanucci from Palermo; Alfonzo Manricco from Naples; and another man by the name of Giuseppe Vazanno, a lemon farmer from Balestrate.

So, which one of those three men gave you this ring to bring to my father?"

"Alfonzo Manricco. The man's name was Manricco and he is the maker of Sambuca. Do you know him?"

"Ah yes, very well, signor. Very well," Lucalla answered. "And, for Manricco to give you this ring, he must have trusted you completely because not one of the four men would have ever given it up to a stranger without a good reason. So tell me, signor, what is your reason?"

Antonio didn't know what to say. "I promise you, signor, on my father's name, I do not know why he gave it to me nor why he thought I was in need of help." Antonio put his eyes down then and continued, "But, I must admit, I do need help."

"I see. And can you tell me, signor, what your name is, then?"

"Antonio Vazanno. My father is Giuseppe Vazanno."

Mario immediately smiled broadly. He went to Antonio and put his hand out to him. "*Cugino*! Cousin!" Mario said enthusiastically. "Our fathers are blood brothers! That makes us cousins, then!" Mario took Antonio's hand and shook it and then he helped him to his feet and wrapped his arms around him. "Yes, I tell you we are related, my friend!"

"Will you be able to take me to your father, signor?" asked Antonio.

"Of course! Of course!" Mario said excitedly. Then he went to the door and yelled out to his men to saddle another horse.

"Come on, let's go. We can be in Catania by nightfall."

***

It was dusk when Mario Lucalla and Antonio rode onto Battaghlia's property. The farmhouse was surrounded by acres of vineyards and fruit trees of every sort. It seemed a paradise to Antonio—the lush green valleys were surrounded by high, majestic mountains and one in particular stood out to the west of where they rode.

"That's Etna," Mario said to Antonio. "We call her the jewel of the island. She's beautiful, no?"

"Yes, very beautiful, indeed. "

"Every once in a while she gives up her riches. She erupts, pouring lava down one side or another . . . but the result of all the ash she bellows out is what you see before you: rich, rich, nutrient-rich soil. The best in the world, I'm sure!"

"It's very different from Palermo, that is for sure. Here it is all green and bursting with color; in the west it is more brown and rocky; but, still, I cannot say the west is not without its beauty; especially along the coastlines of Palermo, Trapani, and San Vito di Capo!"

Mario rode into a large barn where several grooms were watering the horses. "Good evening, Signor Mario!" said one of the men.

"Good evening Vincenzo! How are you this evening? And, how is that beautiful wife of yours?"

"Very good, signor. Very good, *m'moglie e perfecto!*"

Mario laughed as he dismounted. "Come, signor," he said to Antonio, "come in and meet my family."

But before they reached the entrance to the villa, a young woman came out and ran to Mario. She threw her arms around his neck; he picked the young woman up and swung her around in the air. "How are you, my beautiful flower?" he said smiling broadly.

"I'm well," she said as he put her down on the ground, "and you, my brother, have you behaved yourself on the mainland?"

"Well, I'm here!" he said laughing.

The young woman looked past Mario to Antonio. "And, I see you have brought us a guest."

She stepped past her brother and extended her hand to Antonio. "Hello, my name is Franca. I am Mario's little . . ." she said with a smile, "sister. Welcome to our home."

"Thank you, Signorina Franca; my name is Antonio, Antonio Vazanno."

"You have a very interesting accent to your speech. Are you from the west then?"

"Yes, I'm from the province of Palermo and my town is called Balestrate. Although I doubt you have ever heard of it."

"Palermo—yes, of course. But you are right about your town. Please come in. Marietta will see that you are made comfortable. My father is not at home now but we do expect him to return soon."

Mario held the door open for Antonio; as soon as he entered

the house, Mario yelled, "Marietta! Marietta! Your favorite son has returned!"

A small elderly woman emerged from behind one of the many doors that lined the entryway to the interior of Don Battaghlia's villa. She looked as frail as a kitten at first but nearly leapt into the air at the sight of Mario. She ran like a small child to put her arms around his waist, for she was no more than five feet in height compared to his six-foot-plus stature.

"Mio figlio! Mio figlio! Mio bel ragazzo! Non si pio ` andare via e mi lascia per cosi `tanto tempo! Il mio cuore si spezza tutti il giorni non vedo il bello faccia."

"As you can see," Mario said smiling at Antonio, "she missed me!"

The woman told Mario she didn't want him to go away for so long anymore because her heart breaks every day she does not see his beautiful face.

Antonio presumed the woman was Don Battaghlia's mother, but she was not. She was the housekeeper he hired when he brought Mario and Franca into his house, when she was sixty-eight years old. Back then she had just lost her husband and her children in the earthquake that killed Mario's parents. The immediate bond between her and the two children was mutual; they each needed the love of the other.

"And this is Antonio Vazanno. He will be a guest with us for a time as he has traveled a very long way to see Papa. Can you make sure he is comfortable and feed him before Papa returns?" Antonio asked the woman.

The old lady walked slowly to Antonio and reached up and placed her hand on the side of his face. She patted it softly and said, *"Tu sei un uomo buono. Lo vedo nei tuoi occhi; siete turbati pero `. Vieni con men, vi faro ` qualcosa di special da mangiare!"* She told him she could see he was a good man by looking into his eyes, but that he looked troubled; but not to worry because she was going to make him something special to eat!

***

When Ciccinu Battaghlia returned home from the city, Mario was waiting for him. When he heard the front entranceway door open, he rose immediately to greet his father in the hallway.

"Papa, welcome home!" he said as he kissed his father on both cheeks.

"No! It is I who welcome you home, my son! How did everything go on the mainland?"

"Everything went as planned. But, we may have some additional negotiating to handle before the deal is completed."

Don Battaghlia laughed, "Additional negotiating? And, what exactly does that mean Mario?"

To continue their conversation, Battaghlia led Mario into his sitting room office and closed the door.

"The usual," Mario answered as he took a seat near the window. "Some people are harder to convince they need your protection. So far, the railway has been running well between the mainland and Messina, but once it has a few 'mishaps' the owners will soon realize—if they want to do business in Sicily— they will have to do business with us."

"I see," said Battaghlia. "Well, I have every confidence in you, Mario. They'll come around." He poured himself a glass of whiskey and took a seat near Mario. "You don't usually wait for me with open arms when I come in the door, Mario. What else is on your mind? And, please tell me you have met someone, you are in love, and you want to get married! Please, my son!"

Mario laughed out loud. "I'm afraid you will have to wait a bit longer for that, Papa." Mario sat back in the chair. "But, it seems I have met a man by the name of Antonio Vazanno."

"Vazanno? Giuseppe's son?"

"Yes, he's Giuseppe Vazanno's son. It was absolutely by chance and thank God it happened the way it did—or else, I'm afraid, the man would have surely died in Messina."

"What happened? Tell me everything. Is he here at this house now?"

"Yes, he's upstairs. Marietta fed him and then brought him upstairs to one of our guestrooms. I have no doubt he is sleeping now; he has been through quite an ordeal."

"What happened then, Mario?"

"It seems he traveled from Naples to Messina in the hope of finding you. He knew you lived somewhere in Catania and without a plan—or money—he set off to find you! I know it sounds fantastic, but believe me, it is even more complicated than that."

"Go on then."

"He is in some sort of trouble. He did not tell me what kind, but it seems your brother Alfonzo Manricco gave him this ring," Mario took the ring out of his pocket and showed it to his father, "and he told Antonio to come see you and give it to you."

"I see," said Battaghlia. "Well, for Alfonzo to send the man here, with his ring, yes, indeed Giuseppe's son is surely in trouble. Where did they meet?"

"Evidently, Antonio was traveling from Palermo to Naples and from there I do not know any of the details. I only just met him literally hours ago—and then it was only by chance. And, it seems our friends in Messina who still have not learned their lesson . . ."

"Leonardo Punnicci and his men?" Don Battaghlia interrupted.

"Yes, one of Punnicci's men tried to sell the ring to one of my men who took it from him and brought it to me. He knew it looked like something no one in Sicily would own. Sure enough, by the time we got done with Punnicci, he confessed he had beaten a man who was walking alone at night; they stole this from him and, as is their usual custom, in order to avoid being caught for their crime they left their victim tied to a post in an abandoned shack to die without food or water in the sweltering heat."

"They need to be taken care of, Mario. I don't want to hear the name Leonardo Punnicci again. Make sure you take care of that problem right away."

"Yes, Papa."

Battaghlia rang a bell and immediately Marietta opened the door to the sitting room. "Marietta, is our guest up and about?"

"*Si, Signor Battaghlia.*"

"Have him come down then. I want to see my brother's son again. It has been many years now."

Just then Antonio walked into the sitting room looking well-rested and in much better condition than when Antonio found him. But he still looked extremely ill at ease.

Battaghlia approached him immediately and put his arms around him to hug him. He kissed him on both cheeks and said, "Welcome! Welcome to my home! Please come over and sit with me and," he waved his arm in a sweeping gesture towards Mario, "Mario."

Antonio immediately felt better. He remembered only meeting this man once, a very long time ago when he was just a boy. But he remembered how he looked then and he could not believe he looked exactly the same now.

"I understand you have had a very bad experience here in the east? Mario explained how bandits along the road attacked you at night. Shameful! Shameful behavior. How are you now? Have you rested? Have you had enough to eat?"

"Yes, Signor Battaghlia. Your housekeeper has taken wonderful care to make sure I have had more than enough to eat and has made me quite comfortable. Thank you very much for you kind hospitality."

"Nonsense! You are the son of my blood brother, Giuseppe! You are a nephew to me, my boy," Battaghlia answered. "I remember well the last time I saw you. You were just a boy of perhaps twelve or thirteen then. As I recall, your father was preparing to send you off to a seminary on the mainland– Milano, I think. Is that correct?"

Now Mario Lucalla was completely taken by surprise–he had no idea the man he'd rescued was a priest. "You are a priest then, Antonio?" asked Mario.

"No, not yet. I will not be ordained until December . . . in Rome."

An awkward silence came between the three. Battaghlia could not even imagine what the young Vazanno could possibly want help for. The man before him was to be ordained a priest in just a few short months. Mario, too, felt confused that Vazanno's son came all this way seeking help from a stranger.

"So, tell me Antonio, what has brought you all the way to the east to see me?' Battaghlia asked, with growing concern.

"I'm afraid I have found myself in a terrible dilemma, Signor Battaghlia. You see something terrible has happened to my family . . ."

Before he could finish the sentence, Don Battaghlia stood up and went to Antonio's side: "Please, my son: what has happened to Giuseppe?"

"No, no, signor. It is not my father specifically. But, because of what happened, he will surely eventually suffer, too." Antonio put his eyes down. He had no idea what he should say, how much he should reveal, and whether or not it was even safe to talk in front of Mario Lucalla. "I'm sorry, I think I have made a grave mistake in coming here. I apologize completely for interrupting your household in such a foolish and dramatic way. If you will please excuse me, I really want to take my leave, signor."

Antonio got up to leave when Don Battaghlia stopped him.

"No, Antonio. I insist. Please stay. Sit down." Then he went over and poured three glasses of whiskey. He brought Mario and Antonio a glass and took a seat again. He motioned for Antonio to sit down too.

Once Antonio had taken a drink and seemed to have settled down a bit, Don Battaghlia said to him, "Let me assure you anything you say to me is in strict confidence. Anything you say to my son—it is like saying it to me. You have absolutely nothing to fear here. I would give my life for your father and he feels the same for me. You are his son and that same exact sentiment I extend to you. Now, please tell me why you have come all this way to Catania to see me, bring me Alfonzo's ring, and put off returning to the seminary. Very serious actions, my son; they indicate you must have a very serious problem."

Antonio looked up at Ciccinu Battaghlia and his son, Mario. He looked from one man to another and finally said, "I need help to avenge a serious sin committed against my family. I cannot tell you the sin or to whom specifically it was committed against, but I can tell you this: the man who committed the crime is Turiddu Vanucci, Don Vito Vanucci's son."

Battaghlia did not look surprised. His son, Mario, looked shocked.

"You mean the son of . . ." Mario started, but his father cut him off.

"Yes, Mario, the son of Vito Vanucci. I have never told you anything about the boy who is now a man; quite frankly, by now, I had hoped Vito's son would have found his way out of Sicily. But unfortunately, it seems he hasn't."

Now Antonio and Mario looked shocked.

"Vito is a courageous and good man. But we—that is, Giuseppe, Alfonzo, even Vito, and myself—have known for some time that Turiddu is something of a bad seed. He has been a bitter disappointment to Vito and, I am very sure, to his wife, Apollonia. But as a mother, I am sure Apollonia has found a way to look the other way when it comes to her son." Battaghlia took another drink of whiskey and then looked at Antonio, "So, tell me. How can I help you?"

"I have accepted a vendetta against Turiddu Vanucci."

Battaghlia didn't blink. He got up and took the bottle of whiskey from the table and poured each man another drink. Then he took a seat again and asked Antonio, "Tell me, my son, what happened?"

Antonio took another swallow of whiskey. This time it burned his throat as it went down his gullet. He felt a rush of heat rise from his middle all the way to the top of his head. Flushed from the drink, Antonio stood up, walked over and then sat down across from Battaghlia. "I cannot tell you exactly what he has done to my family, but . . ." Antonio paused choosing his words carefully, ". . . it is now in ruin because of Turiddu Vanucci. Even my own father does not know the true extent of the damage; but in time he surely will."

Mario Lucalla and Don Battaghlia looked at each other but remained silent, both trying to imagine the extent to which Vanucci had ruined the Vazanno family. Both knew that it could only be something disgraceful out of lust or a disgraceful act out of hatred.

"I realize I am being vague but be assured, what he has done is an abomination in our country and truly it is an abomination for the Society of Honorable Men."

Battaghlia stared down at his drink. He remained deep in thought for some time.

"I do not know how it is I can help you without knowing the exact crime. However, you have assured me it is a crime of sufficient enough magnitude that you have temporarily left the seminary and risked everything to come to me.

"You have to understand that my hands may very well be tied and I may not be able to do anything to help you. But, still, you have come to me in good faith and Manricco seems to believe that I can somehow help you. I will think about your request. I promise you I will give all the attention and support I am able.

But, what you ask is dangerous—even if the only thing I do is to give you advice.

"You have to understand my position, too. Not only is Vito my blood brother, just as your father is to me, but I have a position here in the east to uphold. If I were to get involved with Vito's son, the son of the Godfather of Palermo, there could be . . ." Battaghlia hesitated again, ". . . there could be a splintering of the east and west. That is something I will not let happen under any circumstances."

"Believe me, Signor Battaghlia, I do understand that. That is why I have chosen not to reveal to my father the extent of the damage done by Vanucci. I'm afraid the burden rests on my shoulders alone. All I ask is counsel from you, signor . . . Don Battaghlia. I do not want you, any more than my own father, to become involved in my problem. Rather, I was hoping you could give me advice on what to do. As you know, my father and Vito Vanucci are inseparable friends. But, still, my father and my family do deserve justice for the crime Vanucci has committed against us."

Ciccinu Battaghlia knew Antonio somehow had found himself in a desperate situation, which under the best of circumstances leaves little room for rational thought. He was asking for "help," which Battaghlia knew meant he was asking him how he should proceed to find a way to kill Turiddu Vanucci.

Mario looked over at his father anxiously; he had come to the same conclusion as his father; but still, Turiddu Vanucci was the son of the Don of Palermo. He could not read his father's face at all. He had no idea what his father's answer would be this time.

After many moments, Battaghlia spoke again. "I want you to give me one week to think about how all of us should proceed in this particular situation. But, you must promise me you will abide by my decision. Do you think you can do that?" he asked Antonio.

"Yes, I trust you will give me good counsel, Signor Battaghlia."

"Good. Give me one week; if you give me that much time, I promise you I will have a solution for you by then."

"Yes, Signor Battaghlia. I will gladly wait one week," Antonio answered.

"Good. Now go out into the garden and relax with me and my family." The Don looked at the mantel clock and said, "Ah, it is nearly time to take supper; another hour or so and it will be ready. Go on, take your drink out to the garden and relax. No, better yet—wait a moment."

Battaghlia went to the door and called out to his daughter, Franca, whom Antonio noticed had been working in the garden earlier that morning. She came into the room through the open glass doors leading from the garden. Strands of golden-reddish hair had managed to come down from atop her head, where she had pinned it up. The lovely tendrils framed her face and fell to her shoulders. Over her skirt she wore a long white apron that was completely soiled with dirt. She even had dirt on her face— but the sight of her was entirely appealing as she was quite a natural beauty.

"Look at you!" exclaimed Battaghlia. "Are you the daughter of Don Battaghlia or a common farmer?"

Everyone laughed.

"I'm working in the garden, Papa! You're the one who loves the sight of flowers all around you in the garden! How do you suppose all those flowers have managed to situate themselves there? Surely, not by themselves!"

"Do you think you can take some time out from digging in the dirt to show Antonio our horses and the stables?"

"Of course," Franca said smiling broadly. "I'll be just a minute." She walked back outside and took her apron and gloves off. She stepped back into the room and said to Antonio, "Come along then, follow me."

***

Once Antonio had left the room, Battaghlia went to his desk and pulled out a piece of paper. "Here," he said to Mario as he handed him the paper, "This came for me two days ago from Turiddu Vanucci."

Mario opened the envelope and took out the letter from Turiddu.

Caro Don Ciccinu Battaghlia,
My father sends his blessings and asks me to tell you

*he hopes you and all of your family are in good health!
My father has asked me to write to you as he is in need
of a favor from you if it is at all possible.. He requests
you send him a man from the east that is not known at
all here in the west. He has a job that he is in need of
being taken care of and requests the man you send to
him is not known at all here in Palermo. If you can send
him someone he will be very grateful and once again
indebted to you. The man you send will be well taken
care of for his services. If you know of such a person
please reply to this letter within the week by sending the
man to him or by sending a letter telling him you cannot
help him. Please send him to 19 via Gionetti, Palermo,
Sicily to a place called Petruccini Luogo, a bar owned
by my mother's brother, Geramo Petruccini. If I do not
hear from you in one week I will know you have decided
not to assist my father for your own reasons.*

Turiddu Vanucci

Mario finished reading the letter and looked at his father, "Why wouldn't Vito Vanucci contact you himself for such a thing?"

Battaghlia laughed out loud. "Yes, as you can see Turiddu is not only evil but stupid as well."

Now Mario laughed out loud. "The balls of a bull! Yes, that is for sure. So what do you plan on doing with that letter, now that you have it?"

"For this asshole to send me this type of a request he is definitely up to something. I want you to go to Palermo and find out. Leave now. It shouldn't take you any longer than a day and half by train. Go back to Messina and catch the train there for Palermo. Once you find out what the *demone* is up to, send me a telegraph. Palermo has one at the central bank there, as does our bank in Catania. If you cannot find out what's going on in one week's time, return home. I'm afraid we may not be able to assist our friend if that is the case."

Mario kissed his father on both cheeks and then the two men embraced.

* * *

"So tell me, Antonio Vazanno, why have you come all the way to Catania?" Franca asked as she and Antonio strolled through Don Battaghlia's stables.

Antonio hesitated for a moment, trying to think of a way to tell the woman about his business in Catania without divulging the details. "Well, I am here to meet with your father who happens to be a very close friend of my own Papa."

"Ah, I see. But really, that doesn't answer my question. Perhaps for your sake and mine as well, it would be better for both of us if I do not pursue the precise reason of your visit. But, that brings me to ask another question. Do you mind if I ask it?"

"I suppose we won't know that until you ask it," answered Antonio lightly.

"Do you work with your family, then? I understand your father owns vast orchards; lemon is the fruit, if I remember correctly."

"No, I don't really work with my family. Although I love working with my father and all my uncles, I'm afraid I am not cut out to be a lemon farmer. In fact, I am not going into the business at all . . . for many reasons . . . but one in particular."

"And, what is that, Signor Antonio Vazanno?"

"I am studying to be a priest. Actually . . ." Antonio hesitated again, the girl was exquisitely beautiful and there was something about her he was attracted to; although he could not name it, he knew it was not just the sexual attraction that occurs between two young people. When he looked at her directly to finish his sentence, he noticed a depth and sincerity in her eyes he had never seen before in a woman. "I am to be ordained in December. I am to receive my ordination in Rome."

"Ah, a priest!" Franca exclaimed. "That explains it!"

Antonio stopped walking and stood looking down at Franca. "That explains what?"

"You seem the type. Your demeanor; your distance; your perfect way of talking, acting . . . you seem the type of man who is very respectful and cautious around . . . people." Franca was going to say "cautious around women" but thought the better of it.

"Well, I find your ability to deduct such a complete and detailed opinion of me astounding after only speaking with me for . . . no more than five minutes at most!" Antonio said, smiling broadly at the young woman. He liked her very much. She reminded him of his sister, Adriana.

Franca put her face down; she felt silly at first and then ashamed. She blushed deeply at her foolishness. After all, she was flirting with him and, for all practical purposes, he was nearly a priest already.

"Come now!" Antonio said noticing Franca's embarrassment. He lifted her chin up to look at him. "You are exactly right! I can only tell you I am very pleased with your opinion. I mean that sincerely. I am a bit distant and standoffish around people. I truly don't mean to be but you have to understand I have been in the seminary since the age of thirteen. I assure you when you get to know me, you will think the better of me."

"I apologize." Franca blushed. "I'm afraid I have said too much. Please forgive me for being so rude."

"There is nothing to forgive, I assure you," answered Antonio.

"I naturally supposed, since you are the son of one of my father's friends, that you are . . . that is . . ." Franca was about to say that she supposed Antonio was an Honorable Man, like her own brother Mario Lucalla and her father, and presumably, Giuseppe Vazanno. But Antonio did not let her complete her sentence.

"Franca, now it I who must apologize. Would you please excuse me? Suddenly I am feeling the effects of my travels. We can perhaps speak later this evening, after supper. Would you mind that?"

"Oh no, not at all." Franca replied. "Is there anything I can...?" Franca's voice trailed off.

Antonio suddenly realized Franca was exactly right about him, but not for the reasons he had just told her. He was distant—not because of holiness or dedication to his vocation but because he had come to Catania to get help to commit the very sin he would take a vow against in December. He had come to Catania to find help to commit a vendetta! He was seeking help to commit murder! *I am no different from an Honorable Man, dear God! Please forgive me Father, please forgive me!*

CHAPTER X
THE HONORABLE
MAN FROM CATANIA

24 APRIL 1911

TURIDDU AND PAULO had just finished his father's collections. It was the end of the month and it seemed to Turiddu he was spending more and more time collecting rather than enjoying his life.

He was tired. But most of all, he was tired of taking care of his father's business.

"These stupid *Sicilianos*" Turiddu remarked to Paulo Aiuto who was helping him make the collections. Turiddu didn't trust anyone other than Paulo; he knew the thieves and bandits he hired to work for *him alone*—not his father—would steal the money and run as soon as they got their hands on it. "If they only knew there are no more foreigners coming over here from the mainland or anywhere else to take their businesses away from them! The Society took care of that problem twenty-five years ago!"

But Turiddu himself was stealing from his own father. He added a small percentage to the price his father charged each businessman. Then he simply kept the extra charge, reasoning that his father owed him that much for doing the work for him!

Turiddu and Paulo went back to his headquarters in the back of his uncle's bar located just a few minutes' walk from the docks. When they arrived, Turiddu asked Paulo again the same thing he had asked him every day since his return from Catania. "Are you sure you gave the letter to Don Battaghlia himself?"

"Yeah, sure, boss. The man took the letter from me. He opened it in front of me; he read it and then folded it into his pocket. Then he said, 'Go back to Palermo; tell Vito Vanucci I'll send the answer to him in one week's time.'" Paulo shrugged his shoulders as he looked at Turiddu.

"Go on, get out of here then. We're done for now. We'll finish the collections in the villages tomorrow."

Paulo turned and left Turiddu sitting behind his desk drinking a whiskey.

Turiddu was in a bad mood; worse than usual. He worried Battaghlia wouldn't send him—or rather, his father—a man to do a special job. That bothered him excessively because he needed a stranger—someone not known anywhere in the west—to get the job done. He needed someone to kill his father. And that person had to be completely unknown because as soon as the job was done, Turiddu would then kill him. Turiddu poured himself another drink.

And then, he thought, *there is the matter of that* bastardo, *Giuseppe Vazanno.* The thought of how happy and smug Giuseppe looked on Easter Sunday with his wife and family made Turiddu sick to his stomach. Then he thought about Giuseppe's son, Antonio. "That *bastardo* son of a bitch! So high and mighty with the Bishop of Palermo!" he whispered as he drank another glass of whiskey. Then he thought about Adriana Vazanno. The thought of her surviving that day in the lemon orchard enraged him. "That bitch should have died that day! How in the hell did she live?" he said as he threw his whiskey glass across the room shattering it into pieces.

There should have been a funeral for that bitch! But no, instead she survived a beating any man would have died from! he thought.

* * *

"Where do we start today boss, on the docks or the villages?"

"I got two collections left on the docks and then we can head out to the villages."

Turiddu and Paulo walked out of the bar and within a few minutes arrived at one of the two warehouses where they needed to collect. The first one was just across from the import/export dock. Turiddu had just opened the door to the warehouse when suddenly something caught his eye.

"Wait a minute," he said to Paulo. "Look over there. Is that Vazanno unloading his wagon?" he asked.

"I don't know boss. He's too far away."

"Come on, follow me," Turiddu said to Paolo.

The two men walked up behind Giuseppe who was standing with his back to the men. His brother, Gaspano, was in the bed of the wagon handing down crates of lemons to him. Suddenly, Gaspano stopped and stood up straight in the back of the wagon and stared at Turiddu.

"What's the matter with you?" Giuseppe teasingly said to his brother. "You tired already, old man?"

"No, you got company," Gaspano said as he continued to stare at Turiddu.

Giuseppe turned around and was surprised to see Vito's son standing there. "What can I do for you, Turiddu?" Giuseppe asked.

"Looks like," Turiddu said as he looked around Giuseppe at the tall stacks of lemon crates in the wagon, "you're having a very good year, Signor Vazanno."

"We're doing well. But not so much better than other years." Giuseppe felt irritated that Vito's son seemed to be prying rather than having a friendly conversation with him. "Is there something I can do for you today?"

"Oh, no, Signor Vazanno! No! I am just admiring how well your farm seems to be doing. Good thing you and my father are friends, eh, signor? Can you imagine how much you would be paying if you were not friends with my father?"

Giuseppe was angry now. He knew Turiddu's reputation well. The young Vanucci was actually despised by the people living in Palermo—but no one had the courage to say anything to his father because Don Vito was so well-loved and respected there. In the small businesses in and around the towns and villages of Palermo, everyone had had their fill of Turiddu Vanucci. They gritted their teeth every time he lied to them about the increase in protection money being *his father's* requirement. They knew Don Vito Vanucci well, just as they had known his father before him, and they knew he wanted little from the people and preferred instead to do *for* them. His son, Turiddu Vanucci, was the exact opposite.

Giuseppe said, "I apologize that I do not have the time to speak with you, Turiddu. As you can see, I am very busy now. But please, give my best to your father and mother."

Giuseppe turned his back on Turiddu and continued unloading the last few crates of lemons onto the dock.

"Yes, I will gladly give my father your best wishes," Turiddu said as he tipped his cap to Giuseppe's back. Turiddu started to turn and walk away but then he stopped and returned to face Giuseppe where he was stacking the crates. He stood in silence as he lit a cigarette, took a deep drag and then exhaled the smoke right into Giuseppe's face. "By the way," Turiddu said, "when I saw you on Easter, I did not see your daughters. Hopefully they are both well," he said sarcastically.

Giuseppe continued to ignore him.

"But, I did hear something . . . a rumor of sorts. I heard your oldest daughter—let me see, what is her name? Oh, yes, I remember now—Adriana, is that correct?"

Giuseppe just kept stacking the crates.

"Hmm . . . I heard she suffered a terrible fall a few weeks ago; or was it longer than that? I really don't remember. But I do recall, someone told me it happened somewhere around the bridge going into Balestrate. Is that correct, signor?"

Giuseppe stood up from the crate pile and faced Turiddu. He stood in front of the man, looking him directly in the eyes.

"My family is none of your business." Giuseppe pushed a pointed finger into Turiddu's chest. "I don't want to ever see you or hear from you again. You are nothing to me and we are only having this conversation out of respect for your father. I don't care if you are the son of my dearest friend, Vito Vanucci; it does not matter to me. And, the reason it does not matter to me is because you are a disgrace to my friend. Now, get away from me. I have work to do." Giuseppe turned away from Turiddu; he pulled the shipping paper out of his pocket and said to Gaspano, "Come on Gaspano, let's go. We're done here. Stop at the warehouse and I'll drop this off," he said, showing the paper to his brother.

Gaspano jumped over the wagon onto its front seat. Giuseppe climbed up next to him.

Turiddu walked up to Giuseppe's side of the wagon and said, "I'm sorry you feel that way about me, Signor Vazanno. I was hoping to persuade my father into talking to you about your beautiful daughter, *Adriana*." He said her name slowly and seductively. "You know it might be in your best interest to arrange, let's say, a nice agreement between your daughter and myself."

Giuseppe grabbed the horsewhip out of Gaspano's hand. Startled, Gaspano watched as Giuseppe turned towards Turiddu and raised the whip high above his head as if ready to strike him in the face with it.

Instead, he brought the whip down in a swinging motion, letting it land right on the lead horse's flank. The snap was so loud it sounded as if the whip broke in two. The animal whinnied in revolt, rearing upright. Within seconds, he was leading the other horse with him down the dock.

* * *

Turiddu was enraged at Vazanno's show of disrespect for him. But worse, he threatened to hit him. *That,* he told himself, *I will not tolerate. I think that bastardo has to go, along with my father.* As he walked back to the warehouses to finish the collections for the day, Turiddu thought about how Vazanno treated him, the more angrier he became.

"Are we going into the country now?" Paulo asked Turiddu once they finished their work on the docks.

"I want you to go alone. You don't need me anymore. Bring the money back here before sundown. The villages you don't get to today we can both finish up tomorrow."

"Yeah, sure, boss." Paulo said with a smile: it was the first time Turiddu let him go on collections by himself.

* * *

"Whiskey," Turiddu said rudely to one of the prostitutes who worked in his uncle's bar.

"There's a man here looking for you," the woman said before she turned to get the whiskey.

"Where is he?"

The woman nodded towards Turiddu's backroom office.

"Bring the bottle into my office then," he said as he walked away from her and towards his office.

Turiddu opened the door to see a man sitting in a chair in front of his desk. The man's back was to him so he could not see his face. But one thing that immediately caught his eye was the height of the man. He looked very tall for a Sicilian. Turiddu walked over to his desk so that he was now facing the stranger.

"Who are you, signor?" Turiddu asked.

Mario Lucalla stared back at Turiddu and said, "Who are *you*?"

"Turiddu Vanucci. I hear you are looking for me?"

"Ciccinu Battaghlia sent me here to you. I understand you—or your father—have a job for me here in the west," Mario answered.

Turiddu felt elated but controlled his emotion. The man in front of him was nothing more than a stranger who was about to make Turiddu—if all went according to plan—the most powerful man in Sicily. "So, tell me about yourself signor. Let's start by you telling me what your name is."

"Luca Petrolli," Mario answered. "Do you mind if I smoke, signor?"

"No! No, please. Go right ahead."

Mario took out a cigarette and lit it; he blew smoke up into the air and then offered Turiddu one, too. Turiddu refused. Instead, he opened his desk drawer and pulled out a bottle. "Care for a taste of the very best Sambuca in all of Europe?" Turiddu offered as he poured two glasses of Manricco Sambuca.

"I don't drink, signor. But thank you," Mario answered.

Turiddu scanned the man's face intently. He doesn't drink, Turiddu observed: that seems unlikely. He looks well-dressed, well-groomed; and he has the hands of a gentleman; they aren't calloused like a common laborer.

"You don't drink?" Turiddu said finally as he picked up the second glass of Sambuca after he downed the first one.

Mario simply shook his head, no.

"So tell me, signor, what proof do you have for me that the man from Catania has sent you here?"

Mario put his hand into his pocket to pull out a note from Ciccinu Battaghlia, but then stopped and said to Turiddu, "May I take the letter I have for you out of my pocket, Signor Vanucci?"

Without saying a word, Turiddu got up and walked around the desk. He stuck his hand inside Mario's jacket and pulled an envelope out of it. "Is this what you were about to show me, Signor Petrolli?"

Mario nodded.

Turiddu walked back around his desk, sat down, and opened the letter. The letter itself was sealed with a wax stamp with the letter "B" in the middle of it. Turiddu assumed it was Don Ciccinu Battaghlia's seal.

> *Caro Vito,*
> *I send you what you requested. His name is Luca Petrolli. He's a good man and can be trusted completely. He will be loyal to you. He has no family, according to him. When he has finished your work, you may keep him as he cannot return to the east for reasons I cannot discuss with you in this letter. Except—I will tell you this, if you have no further use for him after he completes the work for you, send him to Naples, as they are always looking for good Siciliano soldiers. He cannot return to the east—that would be too dangerous for me—and him. He knows he is not returning here. I hope he serves you well.*
>
> *Ciccinu Battaghlia*
> *1911 April*

Turiddu finished reading the letter and smiled.

"Well, it seems I have a new man at my disposal, Signor Petrolli!" Turiddu said enthusiastically as he got up to go to Mario, and extended his hand to him. "How do you feel about being a Vanucci family man, signor?"

Mario deliberately did not take Turiddu's hand; instead, he reached into his pocket and took out another cigarette. "This is

S.E. VALENTI   189

my only bad habit, Signor Vanucci."

Instead of feeling insulted that Mario would not shake his hand, he instead laughed. "You know, I think I will smoke with you, signor!"

Mario handed him a cigarette.

Turiddu took the cigarette and at the same time grabbed Mario's hand. "I will tell you this much, Signor Petrolli: you will earn a lot of money, very quickly; but, I also warn you, just as quickly you will find yourself dead if you ever betray my trust. Do we understand each other, Signor Petrolli?"

"It makes no difference to me who I work for or where I work. All that matters to me is the money." Mario blew smoke out just above Turiddu's head.

"Oh, you will be paid very well, my friend. Very well! Have you made arrangements for a place to stay here in Palermo, signor?"

"No, I just arrived early this morning," Mario answered.

Turiddu walked to the door and opened it. He yelled out to the woman who had given him the message about his visitor.

"Take my friend upstairs to one of the empty rooms. Make sure he gets everything he needs to be comfortable."

Then he turned to Mario and said, "Rest up tonight. Get something to eat and we will meet here tomorrow morning at dawn."

* * *

Mario was waiting for Turiddu outside of his office just before dawn.

When Turiddu arrived he was shocked to see his new employee already waiting. "I see you are prompt, Signor Petrolli."

"I'm eager to get the job done, signor. Although," Mario hesitated, wondering if he was going too far, "we still have not discussed that job or my pay as yet."

"Take it easy, my friend. We'll get to that. Take it easy!" Turiddu answered. "Come on and follow me. I have two horses already bridled and ready to go."

"No," Mario answered adamantly. "I want my own horse."

"Fine, not a problem. Get on this one and I will take you to get him at the stables."

Once Mario was on his own horse, the two men rode out of Palermo along a well-traveled dirt rode that, Turiddu told Mario, leads to all the towns and villages in the west. The two men rode in silence until they came to the coastal town of Balestrate.

"Follow me," Turiddu said to Mario, "and learn how to get into and out of all the villages along the coast." The two men rode for over an hour when Turiddu turned to Mario and pointed out an enclosed statue of the Virgin Mary on the roadside. "This is the beginning of the village of Balestrate."

They rode through the town and over the bridge. Before long, the two men had come upon the beginning of Giuseppe Vazanno's north lemon orchard. Turiddu led Mario over to a grove of cypress trees and dismounted. "Come on, sit down here. We'll take some wine and refreshment now."

Turiddu pulled out some cheese, bread, olives, and wine from his saddlebags. "Tell me, what do you think of this part of the country so far?"

"Nothing like the east; too brown for me. Not enough trees; too many rocks everywhere. How often does it happen one of your horses goes lame tripping across one of these rocks?" Mario asked as he threw a stone across from where they sat.

Turiddu laughed. "Who cares? If the stupid animal goes lame because he stepped the wrong way, then we just shoot him! That's all, we just shoot him!"

"Seems like a terrible waste of horse flesh to me," Mario said dryly without any trace of emotion.

"Yes, I agree, Luca . . . may I call you by your first name, signor?" Turiddu asked politely.

Mario shrugged. "It doesn't matter to me what you call me."

"Well . . . Luca, then . . . according to what I've been told, the west was just as green as the east at one time; but those *bastardo* foreigners from *Inghilterra* came in and drilled the shit out of the Sicanians for sulfur. Took down every tree in their path! That's why everything looks so brown and rocky."

Mario, bored with Turiddu's attempt at small talk, changed the subject. "So, tell me, signor, why have you sent for me? What type of job do you have for me?"

"I need to know I can trust you first, my friend. Tell me, Luca, what type of assurance can you give me?"

Mario looked Turiddu right in the eye without giving him the satisfaction of a blink, and said straight out, "I do the job, I get paid and I don't ask questions. Show me the money and I give my assurance: the job will get done."

"You're telling me that you have no reservations about *who* I might be asking you to get rid of, then?"

Mario shrugged his shoulders. "I don't get involved with the *who* or the *why*, signor. Knowing as little as possible is better for everyone concerned. I'm in the business of getting paid for my work. But," Mario said seriously, "I warn you, signor, I don't answer questions either. When someone asks too many questions about my motives, I figure they don't trust me and when that happens, the deal is off the table."

Mario was convincing. Turiddu believed him. "Take a seat, my friend, and we will talk about the job I have for you."

"You see all this land?" Turiddu began, as he swept his arms out in a waving motion. "All this land belongs to one man."

"Who is that?" Mario asked.

"His name is Vazanno. He's a man who has taken advantage of my father for years. He has successfully tricked my own father into thinking he is a friend to him. That he would die for him! And, my father, in his stupidity and softness, believed Vazanno. He gave him all this land and all the property on it. A huge farmhouse, stables, barns, all the orchards, everything!"

"And you feel your father should not have been so generous to this man, this man . . . what did you say the man's name is?" Mario asked innocently.

"Vazanno. Giuseppe Vazanno!"

"So, he is the man I am to kill. This man by the name of 'Vazanno'?"

"Yes. The sooner the better."

"That's no problem. Does he live near here?"

"He lives just the other side of that ridge over there." Turiddu pointed in the direction of Giuseppe's farmhouse. "He lives in one of the finest farmhouses outside of Palermo. All these orchards–these are all his."

"I'll watch him for a couple of days and get the job done within the next couple of weeks. How much money is in it for me?"

"I'll give you free passage to America and two *mille* lire."

Mario was shocked. *Two million lire! How can one man's life be worth that much money?* he wondered. "That's a lot of money, signor, to get rid of one man. What else do you want done?"

"You're very clever, Luca! I like that. Yes, there is someone else." Turiddu said. He looked around him as if afraid someone else besides the two of them could possibly hear what he was about to say. "I want Vito Vanucci killed too."

Mario felt his pulse drop as though all the blood from his head suddenly drained out of it; his hands started to sweat as his mouth went as dry as hot sand. *It's impossible!* he thought. *This jackal wants his father killed—his own father! The Don of Palermo! I must be dreaming; he cannot have said what I thought he said.*

"You want me to kill two men, then: Giuseppe Vazanno and Vito Vanucci. This Vanucci is the Don of Palermo, no?"

"Yes, that is right, Vito Vanucci, the Don of Palermo; my own father. Do you have a problem with that?" Turiddu asked.

"I will need to see the money before we make the deal," Mario said as pulled out another cigarette and lit it. He turned away from Turiddu because he did not want him to see his hands shaking.

"No problem. I will show you the money tomorrow. Come on then, let's have some wine and seal the deal."

Turiddu seemed almost giddy to Mario. He tore open the wine flask and drank one long gulp of wine; he wiped his mouth with his sleeve and handed the flask to Mario. Mario took the flask and pretended to drink from it while Turiddu pulled out bread and cheese from his saddlebag. The last thing Mario wanted to do was to put his lips onto the flask where he had just watched the devil himself drink.

Mario handed the flask back to Turiddu who then took another flask off of his saddlebag. This one, not yet opened, he threw it over to Mario. Mario broke the seal and took a long drink from it. He needed something desperately to calm his nerves. Turiddu continued to drink the entire flask of wine he had, and then looked at Mario and asked, "Have you finished that flask, my friend?"

"No, my friend, here," Mario said as he handed his flask back to Turiddu. "Go ahead, drink up."

Turiddu was singing as he lit a fire. When he finally got it started he turned to Mario and said, "I'll be right back." He got up from his kneeling position and walked off into the woods. Within no more than a half hour, Mario watched as Turiddu returned holding two dead rabbits. He had killed them with a knife and then proceeded to gut and skin them in front of Mario. He took a wooden branch and put the rabbits on it to cook over the fire. Mario was sick to his stomach now.

"I have to relieve myself," Mario said as he got up and walked off toward the woods. "I'll check on the horses and make sure they are watered."

"Go ahead, my friend. I'm surprised you lasted this long!" he said as he laughed. "I'm glad you thought about the horses, I must admit, I am neglectful when it comes to my own."

Mario wanted to kill Turiddu with his bare hands. He felt as if he could not stand one more minute in his company. He made up his mind that he would head back to Palermo immediately, no matter what.

"I'm afraid I am going to have to return to Palermo tonight, signor." Mario said to Turiddu.

"What for?" Turiddu asked suspiciously.

"It's my horse. He's splintered his left hoof; if I take his shoe off he'll be in a lot of pain and may go lame. I'm going to take him back to Palermo tonight."

"We can get him fixed in Balastrate. I know a good blacksmith there . . ."

"No, I'm going back to Palermo. I'm not taking a chance on my horse going lame. Can I walk into Balastrate and get another horse to ride back to Palermo?" Mario asked.

"Come on, I'll show you the way." Turiddu said, irritated. "You are really that concerned about a stupid animal?"

Mario didn't answer him.

Turiddu walked next to Mario but was so drunk from the wine that Mario suggested he sit on his horse and he would walk both animals into the village.

Mario had placed a pebble under his horse's shoe in his hoof so that the horse looked as if he was favoring his left foot.

As they passed the north lemon orchard, Turiddu started to brag about what he had done to Giuseppe's daughter.

"You know, Vazanno has two daughters. The one, the older one, her name is A-d-r-i-a-n-a," he said slowly as he pronounced her name seductively. "What a beauty that one is!" He put two fingers to his lips and kissed the tips. "Long, brown, wavy hair! So long it covers her back all the way down to her waist!"

Mario wanted to vomit but he controlled the urge.

"Huge black eyes that pierce a man's soul, I tell you," Turiddu said as they crossed over the bridge. "You know, my friend, I was her first lover! That's right! And you know where we made love? Right back there," he said as he turned around in his saddle and pointed towards the lemon orchard, nearly falling off of his horse in the process.

Mario swallowed hard. He wanted to cut Turiddu's throat then and there but knew he could not do so without consulting with his father first.

"You were her lover? You mean she and you were in love?" Mario asked not because he wanted to hear another word out of the devil's mouth but because he needed to know everything before he talked to his father.

"No, she hates me! Her father hates me, too! No, I took her! I beat the shit out of her until she was unconscious and then I took her! I never thought the little whore would ever live to tell of it—but she did! Can you believe that, Luca? Can you believe some girl no more than five feet tall and less than half my weight—lived after I was done with her?"

Mario did not open his mouth. He kept walking straight ahead. He neither wanted to look at Turiddu Vanucci nor hear his voice. It took every ounce of willpower Mario Lucalla had but he completely drowned out Turiddu's voice. He just kept walking until he came to the place Turiddu pointed out as the farrier's place.

As Turiddu got down off of his horse, he slipped and fell to the ground. He passed out, dead drunk. Mario put his limp body back onto the horse and tied him there. Then, after removing the pebble he got on his own horse and hit him hard into a gallop.

Turiddu's head bounced hard against the side of his horse as Mario galloped both animals all the way back to Palermo. When they arrived back at the stables behind the bar and Turiddu's office, he untied him and eased him down off of his horse.

Turiddu was still completely passed out in his drunken state. Mario hoped he would die. He left him there on the ground in the stables, lying near his horse.

Mario sat outside the Palermo bank waiting for it to open. It was early morning and he saw a woman walking down the street towards the bank. As she got closer, Mario saw her take keys out of her pocket as she approached the front door of the bank.

"Good morning, signorina!" Mario said to the woman who was obviously not a signorina. The woman blushed and put her eyes down.

"Excuse me, signorina, do you know if there is a telegraph machine in the bank?"

"Oh, no, signor. We do not have a telegraph here, but there is one in the post office, over there." She pointed just across the street from where they both stood.

"Do you know what time the post office opens?" Mario asked politely as he smiled broadly at the woman.

She smiled back. "Yes, signor. There should be someone opening . . ." Just then a man opened the door to the building across the street. "There he is. That is Signor Carducci. He always opens the post office when I open the bank."

"Thank you, signorina. I hope you have a wonderful day!" Mario said as he tipped his cap to her and then turned to walk across the street.

Relieved to be alone, Mario thought about what he *must* tell his father. It needed to be absolutely clear exactly what Turiddu Vanucci had already done and what his plan was. The telegram read:

> *Two men must die STOP a lemon grower STOP a godfather STOP*
> *One Innocent already attacked STOP Ruined for life STOP Not fit for*
> *marriage now in Sicily STOP Await your decision STOP*
>
> *Mario Lucalla 25 April 1911*

Mario waited for the telegram to go through. He sat down on the floor and decided he would wait until his father sent him an answer. He didn't care if Turiddu Vazanno himself walked into the post office and saw him sitting there on the floor. He was determined to stay until he received an answer from his father.

Mario sat for two hours. Several telegraphs came over the wire but none were addressed to him. Then finally, the man taking down the messages sent across the wire yelled out, "Is there a Mario Lucalla here?"

Mario jumped up and ran towards the man. "I'm Mario Lucalla."

"Well, here is the message. I hope it makes more sense to you than it does to me."

> *Do what I have taught you to do STOP My brothers must not be allowed*
> *to leave Sicily STOP I alone will now take on the obligation STOP*
> *the devil must answer for his grievous sins STOP*
>
> *Your father 25 April 1911*

Mario read the telegram and then shoved it into his pocket. He knew what he had to do. His father had taken the vendetta away from Antonio and onto himself. Mario walked slowly back towards the bar and Turiddu's office. As he passed one of the three livery stables along the way, he tossed the telegram into the farrier's burning hearth.

*　*　*

"Where have you been all morning?" Turiddu asked Mario when he walked into the office.

"I had some things to take care of. When do you want the job done?"

"What job?" asked Paulo who was sitting in one of the chairs in front of Turiddu's desk.

"Paulo, go and bring me an espresso and one for our friend here," Turiddu said pointing to Mario, "Luca Petrolli! He's here visiting from the east. He'll being staying with us for a while."

Paulo got up out of his chair and walked past Mario.

"I would prefer you don't discuss our business in front of

anyone. Am I clear on that, Luca?"

"Sure, whatever you say. When do you want the job done?" Mario asked.

"My father visits Vazanno almost every Sunday. He usually spends the night and returns at dawn to Palermo, the same time Vazanno and his brothers go out into the orchards to work."

"Well, getting rid of your father won't be a problem, especially if he's alone traveling back to Palermo. But Vazanno might be . . . more difficult. How many brothers go to work with him?" Mario asked.

"Three. Two are his relations and the other man was raised by the Vazanno family."

"So, four men." Mario said.

"Yes, the four of them go off together every morning to work in the orchards."

"Is there a time when Vazanno is ever alone for any reason?" asked Mario pretending to be interested in Turiddu's plan.

"They are always together. Those *fili di puttana* are tighter than any family I know of."

"What about a diversion of some sort?" Mario asked.

Just then Paulo came in with two tiny cups of espresso. He set the cups down on the desk and then took a seat next to Mario. He put his hand out to him and said, "My name is Paulo Aiuto."

Mario went to take his hand but Turiddu yelled out, "Paulo, go and get the morning receipts. Take them over to my father's house and then wait for me there."

Paulo got up and shoved his hands into his trouser pockets. He tipped his cap to Mario and then turned and walked out of the room.

"What kind of a diversion?" Turiddu asked Mario.

"Well, what if you pay some idiot to go after Vazanno when he and his brothers arrive at the orchard? Have the idiot tell Vazanno his wife needs him at home? Make up something like his kid is sick and that she wants him to return home as soon as possible?"

"Yeah! Yeah," said Turiddu, "that would work."

"This way I can get rid of your father first and then go after Vazanno once he is separated from his brothers."

"When do you want to do it, then?" asked Turiddu.

"When can you have the money ready and the ticket to America?"

"The money is no problem." Turiddu walked over to a tall cupboard. He opened it to reveal a steel chest on the floor. He turned the lock and opened the chest. Mario was shocked at the amount of money that lay in the chest. "I will arrange for your passage to America on one of the cargo ships that come in from the mainland on its way to America. Tell me when you want to go and I'll take care of the rest." Turiddu answered.

"This coming Monday, then. You and I can ride out to Balastrate together and you can wait for me to get the job done. Once it's done, we can ride back here together and get the money and I'll get on a ship. If there is a ship docked here that day, that is . . ." Mario asked. "Oh yeah, that's not a problem. There are cargo ships leaving Palermo every day during the week. I will make sure I make the arrangements for you for the next one leaving Monday night." Turiddu had no intentions of giving Luca Petrolli any money; he had no intentions of letting Petrolli get away to America. As soon as Petrolli successfully killed his father and Vazanno, Turiddu would have his men ambush and kill Petrolli for killing his father. That was his plan.

"Are you sure you will be ready this coming Monday? That doesn't give you very much time to make plans," Turiddu said to Mario.

"I know my job and how to do it. Let me worry about the details. Just make sure you've got my money and passage to America arranged by then," Mario answered.

Turiddu smiled. He could not believe his good fortune. Finally, he would be rid of not only Vazanno but his father, too.

"There is one more thing I need from you though, Turiddu," Mario said.

Turiddu was surprised. "What do you mean? I thought you had everything under control."

"Tonight, late after midnight, I want you to ride out with me to the Vazanno farm. I want to know exactly where and when Vazanno leaves his house and exactly where your father will be traveling on his way back here to Palermo," Mario answered.

Turiddu stared hard at Mario. He was naturally suspicious of everyone; especially since he rarely, if ever, told the truth.

"Yeah, sure, we can do that. No problem," said Turiddu. "You want to leave tonight after midnight? Right?"

"We can leave around two or three in the morning. I just want to get out to Vazanno's to watch when he and his brothers leave the farmhouse and what route they take to get to the orchards. I don't want any of the locals to see me riding with you. The less I'm seen around here the better," Mario answered.

That made sense to Turiddu, but for some reason he felt uneasy with the plan. "I'll meet you here at this office after midnight, then. We'll have something to eat before we head out to Balastrate."

Mario agreed with the plan. "I'm going to get some sleep for a while. We'll probably be up most of the night now."

As soon as Mario left, Turiddu took out the whiskey bottle and poured himself a drink. He sat thinking about Mario's plan. It sounded good, but still . . . there was something about it that made Turiddu nervous. Turiddu got up and went to the office door, opened it, and yelled out, "Paulo!"

***

Mario and Turiddu left Palermo at two o'clock in the morning.

"Did you arrange for someone to catch up to Vazanno and tell him his wife needed him at home?" Mario asked.

"Yeah, I got a guy in mind. He just started with me and he's from Balastrate. Vazanno knows him from the village but doesn't know he's with me now. He'll gladly lie for money. No problem."

Turiddu was nervous, and it was a feeling he rarely—if ever—felt. There was something wrong but he wasn't sure what. Mario acted the same: calm, deliberate, and serious. There was no reason to suspect he was going to do anything other than what he had been hired to do. As they rode throughout the night, Turiddu managed to convince himself he was being too cautious. Luca Petrolli was nothing more than a cold-blooded killer hired to do a job.

"You know, if everything goes well, I want to go to America myself," Turiddu said to Mario.

"Oh, yeah? Where in America?"

"I have a partner in a place called New Orleans. It's not near the big place everyone goes, New York, but it's supposed to have weather like we have here in Sicily. Maybe when I get there I can look you up. Maybe we can do business together in America. Hey, what do you think about that?" Turiddu asked Mario.

"I heard a lot of things about America; some of it good, some of it bad." Mario shrugged his shoulders. "But, yeah, we could probably do business together over there, too."

Turiddu now regretted wanting to kill the man he knew as Luca. Maybe they could be partners in America. *Maybe I will have to rethink killing this guy if everything goes as planned,* he thought.

The two men arrived in Balastrate and rode directly though the town, over the bridge and down the road leading to Vazanno's orchards; Turiddu rode ahead leading Mario to Vazanno's farmhouse.

When they got there, Mario pretended to check out the layout of the property; he walked slowly around the barn and the house; then he went back to where Turiddu was waiting for him and got back on his horse. "Let's ride back to the orchards now," he said to Turiddu.

***

They eventually reached the border between the south and the north orchard.

"Let's ride through this orchard," Mario suggested, pointing to the south border.

Turiddu stared at Mario. Something told him not to go into the south orchard.

"No, let's go into the north orchard. Vazanno just finished fixing all the irrigation pipes we broke in the south orchard. I'm positive he'll be working in the north one."

"Lead the way then," said Mario, "no matter. I just want to get a feel for the layout of the orchards."

Mario followed Turiddu into the north orchard. He slowed his horse down so that he was directly behind Turiddu. Once they made it to a clearing, Mario said, "Turiddu! Turiddu!"

Turiddu stopped and looked back at Mario.

"Let's stop here. I have to relieve myself."

Turiddu stopped. He watched as Mario got off his horse and disappear behind some shrubbery. He looked up at the sky. No wonder it was so dark, he thought to himself, the moon's in its quarter and the sky is full of clouds.

Suddenly, he was being pulled off of his horse by something around his neck. Mario had thrown a thin lasso around his neck with expert precision. Within seconds, Turiddu was on his stomach with Mario on top of him, tying his hands behind his back. As soon as Mario secured his hands, he tied his feet together. Then, he brought the ligature around Turiddu's neck back and secured it to his hands and feet that were already tied together. Every time Turiddu tried to move his hands or his feet, the ligature around his neck became tighter. He finally stopped struggling and lay still on his stomach.

Mario knelt atop Turiddu. The sheer weight of his body upon the rope attached to Turiddu's neck caused Turiddu to choke and gasp for air.

Mario took out his knife. He held Turiddu's head back by his hair and could see Turiddu's eyes bulging out of his head. He was gasping hard now trying to get air into his lungs.

"This is payback, you *bastardo*! This is payback for what you did for Adriana Vazanno and her family. Antonio Vazanno sends you this with his blessing!"

Mario raised the knife in his hand so that he could plunge it into Turiddu's neck.

"Boss! Boss!" yelled out Paulo Aiuto.

Just then, Mario saw four men on horseback riding hard towards him and Turiddu.

"Shit!" Mario said as he tried to finish his grisly task.

But it was too late. Turiddu's men were riding hard and if Mario didn't leave now, he would surely be caught.

Mario quickly stabbed at Turiddu, trying desperately to aim for his neck.

Turiddu, hearing his men coming towards him, felt a sudden rush of adrenaline; with all his might he began kicking and pushing at Mario to try to get him off his body.

The knife plunged into Turiddu's head just above his ear. It only pierced his scalp. But the top of Turiddu's ear was sliced off.

Mario had no choice now. He jumped off Turiddu and

whistled for his horse. In an instant he was on him and galloping away into the darkness.

* * *

Paulo immediately cut the ropes that bound Turiddu's hands, feet, and neck. At once Turiddu collapsed back onto the ground, gasping like a fish out of water. The side of his head and his ear were bleeding; his face was as white as bleached linen.

"Boss!" yelled Paulo as he turned Turiddu over on his back. "Can you breathe? Can you hear me?"

"That *bastardo*," Turiddu choked, "that *bastardo* tried to kill me."

"Who? You mean Petrolli?"

Turiddu nodded his head as he held his neck. "I want him dead! Do you hear me, I want that *bastardo* dead!" he choked.

Eventually Turiddu lay still, staring up at the sky; then he closed his eyes trying to get as much air into his lungs as possible. Suddenly, he choked and turned quickly to one side as he gave up everything in his stomach. When finished, he gasped and took in a deep breath. After a few more minutes, he looked up at his men and said, "Get my horse."

* * *

Mario kicked his horse in the flank with his boot; he rode him hard through the countryside, avoiding the main road back to Palermo. He had to get to the railroad station and quickly. He knew Turiddu and his men would be looking for him everywhere around the villages and towns surrounding Palermo but hoped it would not occur to them to look for him around the railroad stations between Palermo and Messina. After all, he reasoned, Turiddu knew Mario was riding his own horse and to him it made logical sense that Turiddu would be looking for him on horseback somewhere. Mario, not certain as to whether Turiddu had survived the ligature and then the stab wound to his head, was worried. If Turiddu lived, he knew it would be bad. But, at this point he had no other choice but to return to Catania as quickly as possible.

It took him longer than he expected to reach the Palermo

rail yard. The terrain between Balastrate and the station was rugged and rock-strewn; Mario had to circumvent a large area of ground in order to protect his horse from an accidental twist of leg or the loss of a shoe. When Mario reached the station, he maneuvered his horse around the back of the cars—this way he would not be seen by anyone in the station or standing on the platform waiting to load their animals for a trip to Messina. Quickly, he looked for an empty car. He was lucky! Finding one between the sheep and cattle cars, he pried the wooden door open. He backed his horse up a good distance, and then broke him into a gallop towards the open car. With one leap, the horse jumped and landed right where Mario hoped he would. Within minutes of their unusual boarding, the train whistle sounded. Mario let out a sigh of relief. But still, he knew the worst was yet to come.

CHAPTER XI

GIUSEPPE VAZANNO'S FARMHOUSE

MIDNIGHT, 05 MAY 1911

GIUSEPPE OPENED HIS eyes. He listened intently. There, he thought, *I did hear something.* He raised his head from the pillow. *A horse . . . no,* he thought, *horses.*

He got up quietly and crept to the window. He peered out, keeping his head low. He could only see a corner of the barn and, from his vantage point, he could not see anyone. But he knew where the voices were coming from. *Men,* he thought, *more than three or four*; that he was certain of. He crept back to the bed and said to Maria, "Wake up! Maria! Wake up."

Maria turned over and said, "Gius . . ."

"Shhh." Giuseppe put his finger to her lips. "Men, outside. I don't know who they are, but get the girls in the tunnel. Hurry up. I'll go see what they want."

"Peppino, no!" Maria urged. "Let me go with you."

"Get Adriana and Francesca into the tunnel, now!"

Giuseppe got up and quickly pulled his trousers on; he walked to the kitchen and grabbed the shotgun, which was always loaded and lay next to the hearth. He looked out the kitchen window but could see nothing. He heard his wife rousing his children in their bedroom behind him. Slowly, he walked across the kitchen to a side door that led out to an area in front of the barn. He opened the door a crack and peered out.

Oh, my God, he thought, *at least ten, maybe more!*

* * *

Maria quickly but softly stepped across the floor to Adriana's room. "Wake up, Adriana," she whispered, "wake up!"

"Mamma . . ."

"Shhh . . . shh! Someone is here. There might be trouble. Help me move Francesca's bed so we can open the tunnel door," she whispered.

Together, Adriana and her mother shoved Francesca's bed just enough to open up the tunnel door. "Gather some things, Adriana. Hurry up! Pack your sister's things, too. I'll get Francesca up. Hurry, now!"

Maria shook Francesca awake. "Mamma!" she said gleefully as if it were morning and she was getting up.

"Shhh . . . shhh . . . you have to get up! Adriana is waiting for you," Maria said to the girl.

"Mamma? Mamma? I don't want to go . . ." Francesca started to protest.

Maria gently gathered the child from her sleeping posture and sat with her on the side of the bed as she watched Adriana fill two satchels full of clothes and items for grooming. "Is this enough, Mamma?" Adriana asked her mother.

"Yes. Now get down in the tunnel."

Adriana did as her mother told her. As soon as Maria was sure Adriana had her footing on the cold dirt floor, she handed Francesca down to her.

"Stay quiet. I'm closing the door. Go to the end of the tunnel and stay there until I come for you. Do you understand me?"

"Yes, Mamma," Adriana said nervously. "What is it, Mamma? Who is here?"

Maria motioned for her daughter to come up the ladder. She bent her body down into the opening and grabbed Adriana by the face pulling her up closer. "I love you, my daughter. Take care of Francesca. I do not know what is happening, but there is some sort of trouble. Go to the end of the tunnel and stay there until I come for you. Stay safe and take care of your sister." Then Maria kissed her daughter on her cheeks and moved away from the opening. In an instant, the tunnel door came down, leaving

Adriana and her sister standing in complete darkness.

Francesca started to cry.

Adriana immediately put her arm around her sister. "Shhh . . . don't cry. Come with me."

The girl followed Adriana as she went to the shelf where the oil lamp was kept. In an instant, Adriana lit the lamp and soft light illuminated the storage room.

"You have to follow me, Francesca. Sit down. I'm going to put your shoes and stockings on."

As soon as Adriana and her sister had their shoes on, Adriana started for the tunnel attached to the storage room.

"No!" Francesca yelled out. "I'm afraid of going there, Adriana!"

"I will be right next to you Francesca, I promise you. But, right now we have to obey Mamma. We have to go to the other end of the tunnel."

The crying girl buried her head in Adriana's nightdress.

*** *** ***

Maria quickly put a skirt and a white chemise on over her nightdress; then she wrapped a shawl around her shoulders. She went to the kitchen door that faced the front entrance to the farmhouse. She did not see her husband.

Suddenly, she heard the sound of men's voices and then, to her horror, she saw several men dragging Giuseppe across the dirt towards the big oak tree. Immediately, she ran out of the house.

"Stop! Stop! What are you doing to my husband?" she screamed at the top of her voice.

Turiddu motioned for some of his men to intercept Maria. "Go get her and bring her here," he said.

Maria had grabbed another shotgun as she ran out of the house. She stood her ground when she saw the men running towards her. "Stop right there or I will kill you! I swear I will shoot!"

Giuseppe yelled, "Ride to Gaspano's house . . . go Maria . . . go!"

Maria would never leave her husband, especially when she saw they were now tying him to the tree.

Turiddu saw the woman was holding a shotgun on his men. He turned and walked to where his men were standing. He said to Maria, "Give me the gun or I will shoot your husband right now. You don't have any other choice. Give me the gun."

Maria threw the gun down in front of her. "You devil!" she seethed. "How dare you come to my house? You are nothing more than the devil himself! You are going to burn in hell forever, Turiddu Vanucci! Do you hear me? Forever!" she screamed.

"What a beauty you are!" Turiddu said mockingly. "Not quite as beautiful as your daughter, Adriana, but still a real beauty!"

Maria spit at Turiddu who had walked closer to her; close enough that her spit landed on his chest.

Turiddu slapped her hard across her face after he wiped the spit off his shirt. "Shut up, you stinking Milano bitch!" Then he turned to the men standing with him and told them to tie her hands and bring her over to the tree.

Giuseppe was yelling now. "Leave my wife alone, you *bastardo*! You touch my wife and I swear I will kill you with my bare hands!"

Turiddu walked back and, with the butt of his shotgun, hit Giuseppe directly in the face. Immediately Giuseppe slumped over with only the ropes holding him still against the tree. Then Turiddu took his boot and kicked Giuseppe in the stomach.

Maria screamed.

Turiddu slapped her again in the face and warned, "If you scream one more time, I will kill your husband right here and right now."

Turiddu instructed one of his men to get a pail of water and throw it on Giuseppe to revive him.

Turiddu stood in front of his captive waiting for his men to secure his chest against the tree so that Giuseppe was standing upright against it.

"So, where is your son, Giuseppe Vazanno?"

"My son? My son, Antonio?" he said, surprised at the question.

"Do you have another son?" Turiddu answered sarcastically. "Yes, your *bastardo* son, Antonio; you know, the holy one; the one who is in the seminary at my father's expense. The one who is to be a priest!" Turiddu screamed.

"My son is not here!" Giuseppe yelled. "He left after Easter to go to Milano; he's been gone a month already. What does all this have to do with my son, anyway?" Giuseppe demanded.

Turiddu walked over close to Giuseppe's face. He stood staring him in the eye and then pulled off the kerchief tied around his neck. "You see this?" he seethed through clenched teeth. "See this, my friend?"

He walked over and grabbed a torch from one of his men. He walked back to Giuseppe and said, "Maybe you can't see in the dark, eh? Here," he said as he held the torch so close to Giuseppe's face his hair nearly caught fire, "here, now can you see?" Turiddu said as he pulled his shirt collar down so that Giuseppe could clearly see the severe bruises that encircled Turiddu's neck.

Giuseppe stared at Turiddu's wound, completely confused as to why he would be showing him bruises around his neck. "What are you saying? Are you saying my son, who is in Milano, came back to Sicily and tried to strangle you? Tried to kill you? That's impossible. You are wrong . . ."

Turiddu bent down closer to Giuseppe and Maria and pointed to his neck again. Then he stood and kicked Giuseppe in the stomach with his boot.

"Another second and my throat would have been sliced from ear to ear. Your son paid someone to do this to me! He paid a killer to do this!"

Maria eyes opened wide; she felt as if she could not breathe. Antonio, my Antonio, please dear God . . . I pray it isn't true.

"You both look so surprised!" Turiddu sneered. "Just another second or two and my throat would have been cut from ear to ear. Your son didn't hire a very smart killer!" Turiddu laughed.

"Turiddu please, I beg of you, there has to be a mistake," Giuseppe pleaded.

"Oh, there is no mistake, my friend! And to prove that to you, I will tell you exactly what he said to me before he tried to put his knife into my brain!" Turiddu pointed to the top of his ear. "He whispered into my ear, 'This is from Antonio and Adriana Vazanno!'"

Turiddu turned his attention to Maria. "What's wrong, Signora Vazanno? Suddenly, you have lost your tongue for screaming?"

Maria spit in his face. Turiddu laughed this time and said, "Your daughter is much like you, signora. She spits just like you!" he said as he continued to laugh loudly.

Giuseppe stole a look at Maria. His face had shock on it as if, for the first time, he realized what had really happened to his daughter. Suddenly he knew. The accident was no accident at all. Now he knew the truth. It was Turiddu who had committed the crime against his daughter. His wife knew. Antonio knew. But they did not tell him. Instead of anger . . . he realized, too, why they had not told him.

Maria put her eyes down.

Giuseppe smiled at her and said in front of Turiddu, "Our children are not here. God has spared them from this devil. You did right, my love."

Maria knew at once that Giuseppe realized now why Turiddu had come to their farmhouse and why he was looking for Antonio and Adriana. She smiled at him.

"Don't fight this devil, my love. Our children are safe!"

Turiddu was enraged at the exchange between the two of them. He walked to Giuseppe and hit him once again in the head with the butt of his shotgun. "Shut up, you lying *bastardo*! Every word that comes out of your mouth is a lie." Then he walked back to Maria, whose hands were tied behind her back as she knelt on the ground. He crouched down in front of her and seethed, "Where is Adriana?"

"My daughters are not here!" Maria screamed at him. "I swear to you they are not here. They are in Milano with my mother. They returned to Milano with my son to visit with their grandparents." Then she screamed out at the top of her voice, "You are the devil himself, Turiddu Vanucci!" Then she spit at him again only this time—right in his face.

"Why, you stinking whore!" he said as he wiped the spit off of his face. "I'm going to teach you exactly how you are going to respect me and, believe me, you're not going to like it!" he taunted.

Turiddu turned and walked towards the farmhouse with the torch. Maria looked at Giuseppe. He mouthed to her the words, "The tunnel?" She gestured yes by nodding her head at him. Quickly, he put his eyes down so that none of Turiddu's men could see they had managed to communicate.

"Adriana! Adriana!" Turiddu could be heard screaming out her name as they watched the flame of the torch go through each room in the farmhouse.

Then for a brief moment everything went silent. "Where are you, whore?" he screamed out at the top of his voice. The sound of crashing pots and glassware shattering against the stone floor could be heard. Then, within seconds, one room and then another went up in flames.

Turiddu walked out the farmhouse; he stopped and turned and threw the torch back into it. Immediately, that entire room was also in flames.

Giuseppe looked at Maria and she at him. It was obvious to both of them that he had poured kerosene throughout the house.

* * *

Turiddu continued to beat Giuseppe unmercifully.

Maria continued to scream out in horror.

When he couldn't get any information out of Giuseppe he told his men to go and gather all the small farm animals. "Not the horses, we can use those," he said.

One by one, Giuseppe and Maria were forced to watch as Turiddu and his men tied the feet of their rooster, eight sheep, and four lambs together and then threw them into the blazing fire—alive.

Giuseppe begged Turiddu to stop. "Please, I beg of you! Please, I'll do anything you want. Do you want the property? Do you want the orchards? Everything is yours, I swear it!"

"No, it's too late for that. The damage is already done. I want your son ANTONIO VAZANNO and your whore daughter, ADRIANA!"

Giuseppe slumped down in desperation. "I told you," he said crying hysterically, "My children are not here! I swear it! I swear it!"

"Since you don't seem to give a damn about your animals, then perhaps your wife will loosen your tongue."

Turiddu ordered his men to take Maria to the barn. Three men dragged her to the barn. Giuseppe could not see where they had taken her. But, within minutes of Turiddu and his men disappearing, he heard his wife's pleas. She was begging for mercy. Then he heard her say, "Please, have mercy on me! Please kill me now."

Giuseppe screamed. But Turiddu even ignored Paulo's screams to stop; that Giuseppe was calling for him. Turiddu continued to ignore everyone as he attacked Maria over and over again.

* * *

Adriana came to the end of the tunnel. She sat on the ground beneath the tunnel door. She listened as a familiar voice screamed out obscenities at her mother and father. The voice was unmistakable: it was Turiddu Vanucci.

She heard her father screaming out to him not to hurt her mother. She heard Vanucci scream at him to shut up! The acrid smell of kerosene fire filled her nostrils; she heard the frantic cries and bleats of the farm animals.

But when she heard the sound of her mother's screams she could not contain herself any longer. She bolted upright, and Francesca fell to the ground. Adriana pushed with all her might against the opening to the tunnel; she heard its hinges creak; the door suddenly opened upwards, stopping partway as if wedged against something preventing the door from falling open.

The light from the night sky flooded into the darkened tunnel. Smoke drifted over her head covering the bright stars, and then began to drift down into the tunnel causing her to cough violently.

Adriana saw her house in flames. She saw a man tied to a tree but slumped over, helpless—as men continued to strike him about his face and stomach with their fists and the butts of their guns.

Then, she heard her mother's sweet voice crying out, as if in unbearable pain, begging God to have mercy upon her.

Adriana dug her fingernails into the earth. She kicked her feet to climb up the slippery damp earth to escape the hole she was in. She wanted to run to her mother's rescue.

Something was holding her back. She tried again and again to lift her small body out of the hole, but she was caught on something. She bent down to see what was hindering her from getting out of the tunnel. It was her sister.

Francesca was clutching onto to her legs with all her might. She was shaking uncontrollably. Adriana thought immediately she was having a convulsion, but she was not. She clung to Adriana in a state of pure fear.

I love you, daughter! Take care of your sister, Francesca! Adriana heard her mother's words as clearly as if she were standing right next to her then. She knew what she had to do.

Quickly, she reached up and grabbed the inside handle of the tunnel door. She pulled it down as hard as she could. It slammed against its frame with a bang. She was again completely surrounded in pitch-blackness. She felt her whole body shaking; she reached down and felt for Francesca; she felt her hair. She put her hand on her sister's head and whispered, "Francesca? Francesca?" The little girl didn't say a word. She was neither crying nor talking.

Adriana, frightened that something was wrong with Francesca, knelt in front of the child. She felt for her face and knew she was breathing. She pulled her sister next to her and held her tightly. Then she picked her up and started to back into the tunnel.

The height of the tunnel at the exit was nearly five feet, but as she managed to go deeper into the narrower part of it, its height diminished. When Adriana could no longer carry Francesca easily, she felt her way to an inside wall and sat down.

"Francesca, talk to me, my angel," Adriana whispered.

Francesca put her arms around Adriana's waist and her head on her sister's chest. She held onto Adriana's body as if it was her only lifeline. She made not a sound.

Adriana began singing softly to the child. As the night wore on, Francesca loosened her grip on her sister. But Adriana continued to sing and when she thought she could not sing another note, she began to pray.

***

Paulo was sickened by Turiddu's brutality against Maria Vazanno. He had to get away from him—and from Vazanno's farm. He backed away slowly, trying not to make a sound. He didn't want Turiddu to see him leaving. Once out of Turiddu's sight, he turned and started to run in a panic down the road towards Vazanno's orchards.

Suddenly he stopped. If Turiddu found him running away, he would kill him without even asking him for an explanation. *There is no escaping that monster,* he thought, but still, he could not make himself go back to Vazanno's farmhouse. Instead, he went down to where the horses were tied. He sat down on the ground and put his head in his hands, and wept bitterly.

Sometime before dawn, Paulo heard footsteps coming towards him. He looked up to see Turiddu standing over him.

"Come with me," Turiddu said.

Paulo got up; he started to follow Turiddu but his legs buckled under him. He was shaking. He was sure Turiddu was going to kill him for leaving the farmhouse. He managed to follow Turiddu across the high, grassy area just to the side of the barn where Turiddu had taken Maria Vazanno. To Paulo's dismay, Turiddu walked into the high grass and pointed to the woman's body that lay motionless on the ground. Turiddu pointed and said, "If she's still alive, kill her."

Paulo swallowed hard. "Yeah," he stuttered, "sure, boss."

"Come on—and before you take care of her, we have to take care of Vazanno."

Paulo followed Turiddu. He still wasn't sure if Turiddu was going to kill him or not. But at least he knew he wasn't going to kill him until he got rid of Giuseppe and Maria Vazanno.

Turiddu went to Giuseppe. His body was slumped forward from the waist where he was still tied by ropes to the tree. Turiddu yanked Giuseppe's head up by his hair and stared at his face. Giuseppe opened his eyes momentarily and then closed them as if in a dead faint. "This *figlio di una cagna* is still alive! It's impossible to kill these *bastardo* Vazannos!"

Then he turned to Paulo and said, "Kill him."

Paulo nodded.

"I'm taking the men to Trapani tonight. I don't want my father to know I had anything to do with this—not yet, anyway. Kill them both and get rid of the bodies. I don't want anyone to know where their bodies are, you understand me?"

"Yeah, sure, boss."

"So, you and the other men are going to Trapani tonight?" Paulo asked.

"I got a couple of more things to finish up in Balastrate first. Vazanno's got brothers. They all have to die. I'm going to take care of Gaspano first and then the other one . . . I can't remember his name but he's got a house just over the ridge on our way to Trapani. When you're done with Vazanno and his *putana*, meet me at the fork in the road leading to Trapani and San Vito di Capo. If you're not done getting rid of the bodies by noon, then the others and I will head for Trapani. Get there when you can. We'll be at the usual place waiting for you."

"What about your father?" Paulo said nervously.

"Shut up! That's my problem and I'll take of it." Then Paulo watched as Turiddu went around on horseback, yelling at his drunken followers to get up. "Come on, you jackals; we have more work to do."

Turiddu and the other men rode off in a cloud of dust; as soon as they were gone and out of sight, Paulo fell to his knees. He put a shaking hand to his mouth and wiped it; then he wiped away the tears that were streaming down his face. "Damn you, Turiddu!" he screamed. "Damn you!"

Paulo got up and walked over to Giuseppe. He untied the ropes around his hands and feet and then he untied the rope that was holding him to the tree. Immediately, Giuseppe slumped to the ground as if dead. Paulo ran to the well and pumped water feverishly into one bucket and then another. He ran back to Giuseppe and poured the water over his face and upper body.

Giuseppe gasped. He opened his eyes and immediately started to try and move his body backwards and away from Paulo.

"It's all right; it's all right," Paulo said to Giuseppe, holding up his hands as if in surrender.

Giuseppe blinked and then stared at Paulo in disbelief. He stared a moment longer and then he croaked, "Where is my wife?"

"She's alive. I'll take you to her."

Giuseppe started to try and stand up but fell back down again. Paulo went to him to try and help him up, until Giuseppe pushed him away. "Get your filthy hands off me, you *bastardo!*" he screamed.

"Look, stay here. I'll bring her to you. Stay where you are." Paulo turned and started to run towards the barn and once he reached it, he went around to the side of it, out of Giuseppe's sight.

Shortly, Giuseppe watched as Paulo approached him with two horses; on one horse was a human form. Then he recognized her: it was Maria. He got up and started to run towards Paulo, falling every few steps. Once he reached the horse, he went immediately to his wife's body and took her face into his hands. "Maria! Maria!" he cried. When she didn't move or speak, Giuseppe knew. "She's dead! You killed her!"

"No, she's alive. She's been beaten badly and . . ." Paulo couldn't say the word 'rape' so he didn't say anything.

But Paulo knew there was no time to waste. He told Giuseppe again, "She's alive. You have to take her and get out of here now. I'm supposed to kill you both but I'm not going to do that. But you must get out of here now, or I'll have to kill you to save myself." Paulo's voice cracked as he wiped tears from his eyes. "I'm not fooling you! Get the hell out of here and get out of here now! I will give you five minutes to get whatever it is you think you might need and then you have to go."

Giuseppe looked at his wife. Her face was swollen and bruised; her arms and legs were bruised but she didn't appear to be bleeding. He struggled to get to the barn. He brought out the small wagon; he piled empty flasks and blankets in it and then led it to where Paulo stood next to Maria's limp form draped over the horse. He went to her and tried to move her into the wagon, but it was impossible for him in his condition. Paulo came over and lifted her down off the horse and gently placed her in the wagon. He helped Giuseppe hitch up a horse.

Once the horse was secured, he said to Giuseppe, "Now, get out of here. Don't look back; just keep going. Vanucci is supposed to meet me on the road to Trapani—up where the road forks off up to San Vito di Capo. Don't go near there. Stay in the *campagna*. Stay away from the main road."

Giuseppe covered his wife and filled three flasks with water. Then he got up into the wagon. Paulo threw a shotgun up to him.

"Ha! Ha!" Paulo said as he hit the horse's rump.

The horse took off with a jolt. As they passed the burned-out house, Giuseppe looked over to where he knew the tunnel door was. He wanted to stop and get his girls more than he wanted to breathe—but he also knew Paulo Aiuto was one of Turiddu's men and he did not trust him. *What if this is another of Turiddu's tricks just to find my girls?* Giuseppe thought. *No, I will not give up my daughters. Sevario or Gaspano will find them. They will know where to look.*

Giuseppe looked back to see Paulo pointing his shotgun at him. He heard Paulo shout out, "Just keep going. Don't turn around. I swear I will kill you if you come back."

* * *

Turiddu and his men were not far from the bridge leading into Balastrate when he suddenly stopped.

"That looks like Gaspano Vazanno!" he said to one of his men. "Follow him. I want him dead, too. When it's done, come back here. I'll be waiting right over there in that cypress grove."

* * *

After Paulo made sure Giuseppe did exactly what he told him, he started out towards the road that leads to Trapani, which is just on the other side of the village of Balastrate. As he began to cross the bridge, he heard his boss call out to him. He turned to see him waving him over to a grove of cypress trees not far from the bridge.

"What happened? Are they both dead?" Turiddu asked anxiously.

"Yeah, sure. They're gone. That's for sure."

Turiddu looked at Paulo suspiciously. For some reason he didn't believe him. "What did you do with the bodies?"

"I poured kerosene on 'em, lit a match, and . . ." Paulo lifted his hands into the air, indicating an explosion. "Believe me, nobody will ever recognize them," Paulo lied.

"Good job. I'm just waiting for the men to come back. I can't believe my luck! We were just about to cross over the bridge there when, lo and behold, who's going over it before us?"

Paulo shrugged his shoulders. "Who?"

"Gaspano Vazanno!" Turiddu started to laugh and shake his head. "That stupid *bastardo* won't know what hit him!"

Paulo felt as if all the blood was draining from his head. "Maybe I should go and see if the men need my help?"

"Sure! Go ahead. I'll wait for you here."

Paulo wanted to get away from Turiddu; the very sight of him sickened him now. Then he thought, *He sends everyone else to do his filthy, dirty work while he sneaks back and hides in the shadows. God, I hate him!*

CHAPTER XII
THE BAPTISM

05 MAY 1911

"WHERE ARE YOU going? The sun isn't even up yet, Gaspano!" Nella asked her husband as he was putting on his trousers next to their bed.

"It's nearly dawn. The sun will be up any minute now. I'm going to Balestrate . . . to church. I'm going to make arrangements for Angelo's baptism."

"What about going to work? Should I meet you at Maria's this morning or wait for you to return?"

"No, wait for me here. I won't be long. I'm going to 5:30 mass and will ask Father Licolli then. Which Sunday do you want?"

"As soon as possible, Gaspano. Angelo's almost three months old! Father is going to be angry we put it off any longer," Nella answered.

"Yes, I agree. But don't worry about the priest; I'll make up some excuse for the delay; although, I have to admit, even I don't know why we have waited this long!" Gaspano said, laughing. "Oh, well. As long as it is done, that is all that matters." Gaspano leaned over and kissed his wife on her head. "I'll be back right after mass and we can go to Giuseppe's house together."

"Wait, I have some *buccellati* I put away at Easter; I want you to bring them to Father. He loves my fig cookies." Nella got up from bed and ran to a storage area behind her kitchen. She came back with a large package tied with a ribbon. "Here," she said, "Father will love these."

* * *

"Ah, Gaspano Vazanno! How wonderful to see you at morning Mass!" exclaimed Father Licolli.

"Here," Gaspano said as he handed the package of cookies to the priest. "My wife made these especially for you! She knows how much you love fig cookies."

"Grazia! Grazia!" Father Licolli said as he tucked the package under his arm. "Come with me to the rectory. Do you have time for an espresso?"

"Actually Father, I would like to sit with you as I must make arrangements for my son's baptism."

"How old is the child now, Gaspano?"

"Oh, not quite three months old. I know we should have had him baptized much sooner but the orchards have been keeping my family very busy this year."

The priest looked at Gaspano with a twinkle in his eye. "Now you know as well as I do, Gaspano, there is no excuse for postponing an infant's baptism. Neither you nor I know when the Lord wills us to come home to Him. That is an indisputable truth, my friend."

"I know, Father. And we are more than ready now. Is there any time within the next few weeks you can baptize the boy?"

"Come into my office, then. I'll take a look for you. Besides, my housekeeper should be in the kitchen by now and she can prepare something to eat before we start our day."

The two men walked from the church to the rectory where the priest lived. As Father Licolli came into the back door, he saw Pina Licovolli, his housekeeper, preparing espresso over the kitchen hearth.

"Pina, please bring an espresso for Signor Vazanno, too. We'll be in my office."

The woman kept working, giving little notice to the priest. But as soon as Gaspano took a seat across from the Father Licolli in his office, Pina knocked on the door and then entered without waiting for an answer—carrying a tray with two espressos and a small plate of *dolci* on it. She placed the tray on the desk and then walked out without saying a word.

"It was good to see you in church this morning, Gaspano. I know I already told you that, but it does the soul much good to take frequent communion."

"Yes, Father, I know that." Gaspano answered as he prepared his espresso by adding several small spoonfuls of sugar to the tiny cup. "But the orchards demand so much from us."

The priest turned and took a large ledger from among several others lining the bookshelf behind him.

"Work! Laboring by the sweat of our brow . . . ." the priest said thoughtfully. "Just think of it, Gaspano: if the first man and woman had never sinned, none of us would have to labor! All day long we would simply offer glory to God! Just as the angels do . . ."

"Yes, Father," Gaspano answered, not quite sure what the priest was trying to say.

Without looking up at Gaspano, the priest opened the ledger and turned to the last entry in it. "It looks as if we can baptize the boy this Sunday. Will that be acceptable to you, Gaspano?"

"Oh yes, Father! Yes! My wife and I were hoping that would be possible."

"Good," said the priest. "What did you name the boy?"

"Angelo."

"*Perfecto*! What a beautiful name! And, what is his date of birth?"

"The fifth day of February, Father."

"Who will be the Godparents then?"

"Santo Padua will be Godfather and Adriana Vazanno will be Godmother."

"Ah, Giuseppe's daughter! How old is the child now?"

"She was just sixteen in December, Father."

"Very good. Very good! I remember like it was just yesterday when Santo's mother left him here alone. He had lost his father in a terrible mining accident and then his own mother died of grief! What a terrible tragedy." Father clucked his tongue against the roof of his mouth. "But, all praise be to God, your family took the boy in. And, he looks to have grown into a fine young man, too!"

"Yes Father. That is certainly the truth. He is a very good man," said Gaspano.

"You see this book, Gaspano?" asked the priest rhetorically. "Every child born in Balastrate for the last two hundred years is recorded here. Not only their births and baptisms, but First Communions, Confirmations, and marriages, too! Yes, the lives of everyone living and dead in our little village are recorded here. I suppose I should find a safer place for this book other than the library shelf behind me. But God has seen fit for the book to survive this long, and I don't think I should needlessly worry about what might happen in the future, eh?"

The two men laughed together, enjoying the light mood of the early morning.

"Nella will expect you for dinner then, on Sunday, Father. You will come?"

"Of course! Of course! I never miss a Sunday meal made by one woman or another in Balastrate; all the women here are experts in satisfying a man's palate!"

A loud pounding could be heard at the door.

Father Licolli looked up, startled. "Who on earth could that be?" he said to Gaspano.

Gaspano stood up immediately and went to the office door and opened it. Three men pushed the door completely open and rushed into the room. They were carrying shotguns.

"What is the meaning of this?" demanded Father Licolli, who immediately came out from behind his desk to face the intruders directly.

Gaspano jumped in front of the priest, as if to shield him. "I'll take care of this, Father."

The first man into the office took his shotgun and struck Gaspano in the head with it. "We don't have a quarrel with you, priest. Go on! Get out of here!" ordered the gunman.

"I know you!" Father Licolli said. "You are the first son of Signora Albergetti! Your mother comes to mass every day here, in this church! How dare you strike down an unarmed, defenseless man! How dare you!"

"Shut up or I will shut you up," answered Albergetti. "Now do as I tell you to do, and you won't get hurt."

"I will not leave my own house. Never." Then the priest bent down to tend to Gaspano who had slumped to the floor when he was struck.

In the background, the housekeeper was screaming and crying, "Leave this house of God. Get out of this house, I tell you!"

Albergetti told the gunman standing next to him, "Go and take care of that!"

The man went into the hallway and slapped the old housekeeper hard across the face. "Now get out of here before I slit your throat."

The woman turned and ran out the back door of the rectory, and the man came back into the room and stood next to the other two.

Albergetti pointed his shotgun at the priest. Gaspano quickly pushed the priest aside and then put his body in front of his. "Surely, you don't have a quarrel with this innocent priest. Leave him alone, I beg of you."

"Come with us. Get up and follow us," the leader said to Gaspano.

Gaspano immediately stood. But just as quickly, the priest was on his feet, too. Now it was he who stood in front of Gaspano. "Tell me what it is you want. I will give you anything. I have money and some of the things here in the rectory that are quite valuable. Just take everything you want and leave us alone."

"Nope. It won't work that way, priest. We want Gaspano Vazanno."

"What for? What has he done to you?" asked the priest.

"We got our orders. Vazanno dies today. You either come with us," Albergetti said to Gaspano, "or, we will kill both you and the priest."

"Orders?" said Father Licolli. "What are you talking about, 'orders'? From whom do you have these orders?"

"Turiddu Vanucci."

"No! That's impossible. He is the son of Vito Vanucci! You have made a very terrible mistake, signor," said the priest.

Then Albergetti nodded to the two other men to grab Gaspano by his arms. The priest pulled a poker from the fireplace hearth and struck one of the men in the head with it. Immediately a shot rang out. Albergetti fired his shotgun right into the priest's torso.

"Oh, my God! Oh, my God! What have you done, you devil!?" screamed Gaspano.

A second shot rang out as Albergetti shot Gaspano in the head.

Gaspano's body now fell next to the bleeding priest who was mortally wounded. The priest laid his hand atop Gaspano's head. He whispered, "God bless you, Gaspano." Then he looked up at the three men standing over him and said, "May God have mercy on your souls." He closed his eyes then, and his head fell to one side.

"Take Vazanno's body," Albergetti demanded. "Put it on his horse."

* * *

Soon, villagers could be heard screaming and crying as they rushed from their homes towards the rectory. The housekeeper had alerted the villagers of the trouble by ringing the town's bell. Word spread like wildfire.

Two men carried Gaspano's body out of the rectory and laid it over his horse. Then they mounted their own horses and took off toward the bridge leading out of Balastrate. Waiting outside of town, Turiddu watched as the two men approached the bridge, leading the horse with Gaspano's body on its back. He watched them ride off towards Gaspano Vazanno's farmhouse.

Turiddu waited. Thirty more minutes passed and then he saw them: his three men were riding towards the cypress grove.

"It's done, boss. Vazanno's dead and we just left his body at his farmhouse."

"Did you have any problems?" asked Turiddu.

The three men looked at each other.

"Well, what happened?" Turiddu screamed.

"We had to kill the priest, too."

"What priest? You don't mean Licolli? Not Father Licolli?"

* * *

Paulo Aiuto watched in horror as the townspeople carried the priest's body out of the rectory and laid him down in the middle of the square. He shook his head in disbelief. *It is impossible!*

They did not kill Father Licolli! It is impossible! he thought. His stomach lurched. He walked away from the square and behind a building; he vomited once and then again. His whole body was shaking. *Oh my God,* he thought, *I will never be forgiven! I will never be forgiven!*

CHAPTER XIII
THE DECISION

CICCINU BATTAGHLIA READ the telegram from his son, Mario; his facial expression at first was one of relief as he had been waiting anxiously for news from Palermo. But within seconds, his expression turned to disappointment and then, scathing anger.

Immediately after reading the telegram, Battaghlia balled the paper up into a wad and was about to throw it out, but thought the better of it. He went to his writing desk and sat down to draft a return telegram.

A courier from the bank had delivered the telegram to Battaghlia. He waited in stone silence. He dared not ask the details of the telegram; after all, Ciccinu Battaghlia was the Godfather, the head of *La Famiglia* over all of eastern Sicily; the courier felt privileged just to have been invited into the entryway of the Don's villa.

When Battaghlia had finished reading the return note, he handed it to the courier.

"Here, send this immediately. There is no time to waste."

The man left, and Battaghlia knew he now had to tell Antonio the truth. Especially since he had just given his son the power to kill Turiddu Vanucci. It was a decision he did not want to make, but he had no choice. Turiddu had hired a man to kill his own father along with Giuseppe Vazanno. He could not let that happen. He would never allow that to happen.

"Marietta! Marietta!" Battaghlia called out from his office.

The housekeeper appeared immediately. "Ask our guest to join me here in my office. Bring us some refreshment, too, please."

The woman disappeared just as quickly as she had arrived. Within minutes, Antonio was knocking on the open door to Battaghlia's office.

"Come in, Antonio," Battaghlia said when he saw him. "Please, take a chair over here by the window."

The two men took chairs just a few feet apart by a large window that overlooked the villa's gardens. Antonio immediately knew there was something wrong. But still, he waited for Battaghlia to speak first.

"When I told you I would give you my answer in one week . . . I truly thought I would be able to give you advice. But, it seems, something has happened to change all that."

"What has happened? Have you heard news from Palermo? From my family?"

"Yes. Yes, I have news to share with you but I'm afraid it . . ." he hesitated, "isn't good."

"Then tell me, signor. Please. It is better to know than not know," Antonio answered.

"You are a wise man, Antonio Vazanno, just like your own father."

Marietta came in with a tray and set it on a table between the two men. She started to pour an espresso for Battaghlia but he waved her away. "Thank you, Marietta. That will be all for now."

Don Battaghlia took the original letter he had received from Turiddu Vanucci asking for a good man, from the east, to do some special work. Antonio read it with interest. "It seems Turiddu most likely wrote the letter and used his father's name and reputation to get you to cooperate with him."

"Very astute. You are exactly right. I have known Vito for as long as I have known your own father; he would never ask his son to write to me—he would write me himself."

"What do you think it means then?"

"Unfortunately, I know exactly what it means, Antonio."

Antonio sat in silence. He knew that whatever Battaghlia had to tell him was important and it had something to do with his family. "Go on, Signor Battaghlia. What have you found out?"

"I sent Mario to Palermo last week. He took the train from Messina to get there; we both thought it would be a better and faster route. He went undercover and posed as the man Turiddu asked me to send . . . for the special job."

"And . . ." Antonio said.

"And . . ." Battaghlia handed the telegram he had just received to Antonio. "Mario sent me this telegram just this morning. You can read it if you want but, in essence, Turiddu wants a man to assassinate two men . . ." Battaghlia poured himself a glass of whiskey. "Your father first, and then, his own."

The color drained from Antonio's face. He could not believe what he was hearing. "Are you sure there is absolutely no mistake about that?" Antonio managed to get out.

"None." Battaghlia pointed to the crumpled piece of paper he had given Antonio. "Read it."

Antonio read the telegram. His jaw dropped open. When he read the terse description of what had happened to his sister—which Mario now knew—he broke down in tears.

Battaghlia walked to Antonio and put his arm around his shoulder. "At least now I understand everything," he said to Antonio. "I would have done exactly as you have done, had I been in the same circumstance."

"Now what?" Antonio asked.

"Now I will tell you what my decision is."

Battaghlia sat down again and poured them another drink. "I have taken the vendetta from you—from whomever gave it to you in the first place."

"That is not what . . ."

"I understand that. You have no sin on your soul. You came here for advice, not to hire a murderer to kill someone. But, now that I have this information," he pointed to the telegram in Antonio's hand, "everything is different."

"No! No one needs to be killed . . ."

"Yes. Turiddu must be killed. You have no say in the matter. This is entirely my business and the business of the *famiglia*. The reason the Society of Honorable Men was formed was to prevent just this type of thing from *ever* happening again. I am the one obligated to avenge my brothers' attempted assassination by the enemies of honor!"

Antonio put his head down in his hands. "There must be another way! Turiddu could be brought to trial, he could be . . ."

"No! You don't understand our ways, Antonio. Your own father did not want that for you and so it is—and should be. Vito and I know what must be done, just as our fathers knew and risked their lives to make sure *la Cosa Nostra* would never die."

Antonio shook his head in disbelief.

"Is there any other way, Signor Battaghlia?"

"No. It has already been done. My son Mario is taking care of Turiddu Vanucci as we speak. I expect him to return home within a few days now. As soon as Mario returns, I think it will be entirely safe for you to return home."

"But, what about Vito Vanucci? Won't he rebel against his own son being assassinated—by you, his brother?"

"No. I will show him the proof of his son's cruel intentions. He will mourn bitterly for his loss but he will know I did what had to be done. That is our life, Antonio, and I realize you do not understand it—nor do I want you to understand it. It is the life we have chosen freely—it is not your life—nor your father's, nor your family's."

Antonio had tears running down his face. Battaghlia sat next to him and again put his arm around his shoulder.

"I'm sorry this is so disturbing to you, Antonio. Someday . . ."

"No. It is not *la Cosa Nostra*. It is my sister. What will become of her now?"

"I want her to come here. She can live with my children and me no matter her circumstance. Franca and she are nearly the same age and Marietta is wonderful . . ." Battaghlia hesitated, as he hated to think that Adriana may be with child, but knew it was a possibility, "with children, if it comes to that."

Antonio put his head against Battaghlia's shoulder and cried.

* * *

Mario rode up to his father's villa just before midnight. He tried to be quiet so as not to disturb anyone in the house, even though he knew he was going straight up to his father's room to wake him.

Battaghlia heard the knock at the door. "Come in," he said.

When he saw Mario standing there, he knew instinctively something had gone wrong.

He got up and pulled on a nightshirt. "Come over here, son. Sit with me. Tell me how things went in Palermo."

When Mario had finished, Battaghlia got up and walked to the window. He took out a cigar and lit it, then he poured himself a tall glass of Sambuca. He poured Mario one too, and the two men drank silently.

Finally, after a few thoughtful moments, Battaghlia said, "It is going to be very dangerous for Antonio here in this country. He cannot stay here. Since Turiddu knows it was I who tried to trick him—with you—it is not safe for you to stay here either. I will arrange your passage to America immediately."

"America, Papa?" Mario said. "Why America?"

"I have tried to assassinate the son of a Don. There may be terrible repercussions associated with that. My greatest fear now is what Turiddu is doing to the Vazanno family. He has already raped and tried to kill Giuseppe's oldest daughter and now . . ."

"Do you think he will . . . ?" Mario stopped. He did not have to ask such a stupid question. He knew just how far Turiddu Vazanno would go to get what he wanted. "How can we find out what has happened in Palermo since I left there two days ago?" Mario asked.

"I will send another man there immediately. While I wait for his report, I will arrange for a cargo steamer to take you and Antonio to America. Get prepared. As soon as there is a ship available, you will be leaving."

"How long do you think I will have to stay, Papa?"

"I don't know son; I don't know. Let's wait until we find out what happened after your attempt on Turiddu's life." Battaghlia shrugged his shoulders. "Who knows? Perhaps you scared him enough to scuttle his cowardly plan; perhaps not. At any rate, I will wait for my man to return from Palermo before I make a final decision. For now, go to bed. You need your rest, as do we all, now."

Mario kissed his father on both cheeks and hugged him tightly. "I'm sorry I failed you, Papa."

"Nonsense. You got closer than most mortals would have

in an attempt to kill that Turiddu Vanucci—the son of Satan himself."

* * *

The next morning, Mario and his father waited for Antonio to come downstairs. Battaghlia let him sleep the night before because there was nothing Antonio, he, or Mario could have done in the middle of the night anyway. Besides, the day before had been hard on him and on Antonio, and he wanted Antonio to get as much sleep as possible.

Eventually Antonio came into the dining room to eat something, but Marietta entered and spoke to him: "Signor Battaghlia would like you to join him in the sitting room." Then the housekeeper turned and walked to where Don Battaghlia and his son, Mario, were waiting.

"Signor Antonio is here, Signor Battaghlia," Marietta said as she opened the door to the sitting room and then stepped aside to let Antonio go in.

"I will bring more espresso and *dolci*, signor," Marietta said as she closed the door behind Antonio.

Antonio saw the looks on both Mario and Don Battaghlia's faces. He walked over to where the two men were sitting and asked, "What has happened?"

Mario related every detail of what had happened. He apologized again for failing to kill Turiddu. But, as he explained, Turiddu somehow prepared his men to be on the lookout in case things did not go exactly as he had planned. So when he did not return to a prearranged meeting place with his men, they came looking for him.

"What do you suppose Turiddu will do to my family now?" Antonio was worried; he was afraid of what Turiddu would do now in retaliation.

Mario and his father looked at each other; both men put their heads down and did not speak.

Finally, Don Battaghlia said, "I have sent a man to Palermo to find out what's going on there. He should be back by midnight tonight or early tomorrow—before dawn. We will have our answer then."

Antonio put his own head down as if in deep thought. Slowly

he said, "Thank you, Mario. You risked your own life for my family and me; and the same to you, Signor Battaghlia. I will be forever indebted to you both."

The three men hugged each other.

"I need to be alone for a while. Do you mind if I excuse myself?"

"Of course not, Antonio, of course not. Let me call my groom and he will prepare a horse for you right away."

"Thank you, Signor Battaghlia, but I think I just want to walk right now."

Antonio walked out to the gardens and then looked out towards the vineyards; he put one foot in front of the other and simply started to walk aimlessly. His thoughts were in turmoil. *There is nothing now that can be done to make things right for me and my family. Dear God, please help me find a way,* he prayed.

As he walked, he thought about his mother and her pitiful plea for help. She felt so powerless to make things right for her sweet Adriana. He understood her. *She only acted out of love, that's all,* he told himself. *Isn't it amazing what even the best intentioned among men are capable of doing when they are desperate!*

Antonio stopped and looked up at the clear blue sky. *Dear God, what have I done? I know you forgive every sin when one is remorseful for it, but dare I ask you for forgiveness? It is not just my sin now, but two other men I have led into sin!*

"Do you mind if I walk with you?" Franca asked innocently.

Antonio jumped back surprised. He didn't hear her coming up next to him.

"I'm sorry! I'm afraid I have surprised you . . . perhaps even scared you." Franca felt sincerely sorry for surprising Antonio.

He did not want company. He wanted to be alone with his thoughts. He felt exhausted and looked forward to an afternoon of prayer and reflection. "Hello Franca," he said politely, "you're right. I didn't expect you here this afternoon."

"I see you want to be alone. I understand. Perhaps another time," Franca said as she turned to walk away.

"No, wait. Please. It's just that I . . . well, it is just that I have many things on my mind. I always find it helpful to walk and try sort things out when I feel overwhelmed."

"I understand completely," Franca said and then smiled warmly at him. "I have many things I should be doing myself this afternoon. Don't get lost out here. Just look up and you will see the tall bell tower atop our house."

Antonio felt guilty. He liked Franca. He did not want to offend her in any way. She was a warm, intelligent woman and he did not feel threatened by her beauty. She reminded him even more now of his sister, Adriana.

"Please, would you like to walk with me? Actually, I am a bit worried I might just get lost! You're right about that."

"Of course, it will be my pleasure."

* * *

Antonio and Franca walked through the vineyards until they came to a beautiful clearing by a babbling creek. "Let's stop here for a while and rest. The water seems very refreshing," Antonio suggested.

Franca took a seat on a grassy knoll under a huge oak.

Antonio sat down beside her and then laid back to rest on his crossed arms behind his head.

"So tell me, Antonio Vazanno, how do you feel about returning to the seminary and your ordination in December?" Franca asked.

Antonio was surprised by the question. He never talked about how he felt about anything, much less about his vocation, to a stranger—a beautiful stranger at that. "I feel good about that, if it happens," he answered.

Franco looked down at him surprised. "What do you mean, 'if it happens'?"

Antonio sat up, pulled his knees up, and wrapped his arms around them. "I guess I mean until my family's problems are solved, I'm not quite sure what I will be doing in December or any other year for that matter. I can't very well continue on with my life when their lives are in turmoil."

Franca nodded her head in understanding. "I know what you mean. I love my father very much. If anything were to happen to him . . . or Mario . . . I don't know what I would do. I suppose I wouldn't want to live."

"Oh no! Don't ever say that," Antonio said. "God gives us only those things he knows we are capable of taking. He is such a good God. If anything were to happen to your father or your brother—you should be sad and unhappy—for a while. But, God has given you your own self to care for and love first."

"Now, you do sound like a priest!" Franca said with a laugh. "How is it you want to be a priest?" She added quickly, "That is, if you don't mind my asking."

"No, I don't mind at all. It was actually my father who decided for me. He sent me away to Milano to the seminary school there when I was thirteen. I hated it at first, I suppose because it wasn't of my own choosing. But as time went on, I came to love the intellectual challenge and then the spiritual growth that somehow developed in me."

"You don't have to enjoy stimulating intellectual conversations to be a priest," Franca said. "When did you discover you had a vocation to the religious life?"

"Good question," Antonio said as he laid his head back down on the grass. "Last year, I think. I went on a pilgrimage to the Holy Land; several of us went with some senior priests and a few of our professors. I never realized I would be so enchanted and my soul so renewed visiting the sites of Christ's passion and death. For me, the experience made my life meaningful. I realized for the first time the responsibility priests have for the people of the church." Antonio shrugged. "For me, my vocation became real then."

"So, you are completely happy now? You accept your vocation and all that goes along with that? You know, never being with a woman; never having children?"

"Yes, completely," Antonio said without hesitation. "I believe my life is meant to be dedicated to God and the Church. The reason I am here in Catania has been a revelation to me. I know now what every man and woman is capable of and, for the first time in my sheltered life, I realize that no one is perfect—just being human makes us vulnerable. Without God, we are nothing but weak creatures left to falter in a sinful world."

Franca looked at Antonio, surprised. "I am afraid I do not share your philosophy about the world, Antonio; to me the world is a beautiful place—not a sinful one." Franca got up.

"We had better be getting back. My father will wonder what has happened to you."

Antonio got up and started walking alongside Franca.

"There was a time when I, too, thought I would enter a convent; it was after a man that I loved very much died. We were to be married but he died of influenza a year ago."

"I'm sorry to hear that," Antonio said sincerely.

Franca stopped and turned to face Antonio. "But, I knew that entering a convent, sheltering myself away from the world, was not the answer for me. You should experience the love of a woman before you make your commitment to God. There is no sin in that."

* * *

Just before midnight, Battaghlia's messenger came back to the villa. Mario and his father had been sitting in the garden, waiting for his return.

"What has happened, then?" Battaghlia asked.

"The day after Vanucci's assassination attempt, he took a couple dozen men and went to the Vazanno farmhouse. The house and everything in it was completely destroyed, including Vazanno's animals. There has been no sign of Giuseppe Vazanno, his wife Maria, or their two young daughters, Adriana and Francesca. Everyone presumes Turiddu murdered them all and then got rid of the bodies somewhere.

Gaspano Vazanno was shot dead while he was visiting with the parish priest in the village of Balastrate. No one knows where his body is either. But, there were several witnesses to his murder because he was gunned down in the priest's house next to the church. No one has seen his widow, Nella Vazanno, or any sign of their three small children.

They didn't burn down Gaspano Vazanno's farm but they did take all of his horses. But for sure, all the bodies are missing and most people think they have all been buried in a mass grave somewhere."

"What about the other brother, Sevario Vazanno?"

"No sign of him anywhere or of the adopted brother, Santo Padua, who lived with Sevario. Like I said, the rumor is that all the Vazannos have been murdered, except for Giuseppe

Vazanno's oldest son, Antonio, who is said to be somewhere in a seminary in Milano on the mainland."

"Do people say who murdered the Vazannos?"

"No one knows for sure. But the rumor is Turiddu Vanucci had something to do with their murders and the burning of the oldest brother's farmhouse."

"Why do people suspect Vanucci?"

"It seems the *bastardo* has been bragging about attacking a young girl and leaving hints the girl was Vazanno's oldest daughter, Adriana Vazanno."

"She is missing, too?"

"Like I said, there is not one Vazanno anywhere to be found in western Sicily right now."

"Have you heard anything else?" Ciccinu Battaghlia asked.

The messenger hesitated.

"Go on, what else?" Battaghlia demanded.

"There's talk that you started a war with Vito Vanucci and that Sicily may be completely divided between the east and west. They're saying you want to be Godfather over all of Sicily."

Ciccinu shook his head back and forth. "Oh, my God! I have to somehow get word to Vito."

"Evidently, Turiddu's father Vito doesn't know anything about all of this—so far anyway—because he's been on the mainland for the last two weeks on business. But, he is due to return home sometime this week."

"Anything else?"

The man shook his head no. "That's it, Godfather."

"You did a good job. Thank you, Luigi. Go on and get something to eat and get some rest; you look as if you haven't slept since you left here two days ago."

"Thank you, Godfather. You know I am always at your service." Luigi walked to the Godfather and kissed his hand. "May I leave now, Godfather?"

"Yes of course. Go on and get some rest."

When Luigi left the room Mario said, "Do you want me to tell Antonio what we have found out, Papa?"

"No, let him sleep. I will tell him in the morning. But, now it is of the utmost urgency you both leave here as soon as possible."

CHAPTER XIV
PAULO AIUTO'S BETRAYAL

07 MAY 1911

WHEN PAULO ARRIVED to see the townspeople carrying Father Licolli's body out into Santa Anna Piazza, he became queasy at the sight. He knew then there was no limit to Turiddu's evil. After Luca Petrolli's failed attempt to kill Turiddu, Turiddu had told Paulo he had hired him to kill Giuseppe Vazanno and his father, Vito Vanucci. Now they would have to do the job themselves. He could only assume Don Vanucci was next.

He knew then he had to try and stop him from killing any more innocent people—especially his own father, Don Vito Vanucci.

Paulo waited and watched carefully, hidden behind a tall building near the Piazza di Santa Anna; he watched until Turiddu's men rode out of town with Vazanno's body draped over his own horse. As soon as the three men were out of sight, Paulo returned to the bridge just outside of Balastrate where Turiddu was waiting for him. He was shaking so badly he could hardly hold the reins of his horse, much less the shotgun in his right hand. But he had to keep Turiddu from becoming suspicious.

"There's a really big problem now in Balastrate, boss," Paulo said, anticipating Turiddu's angry response.

"What do you mean? What the hell has happened? How did those stupid jackasses mess up killing Vazanno?"

"That's not the problem . . . they did kill Vazanno. The problem is . . . they also killed the village priest along with him, Father Licolli!"

To Paulo, it looked as if all the color drained out of Turiddu's face right before his very eyes.

Turiddu was smart enough to know the killing of Vazanno could be explained to his father a thousand different ways, but the murder of Father Licolli could never be explained away. Even the most hardened of criminals in Sicily would never think of killing a priest in cold blood!

Paulo was right! Now, Turiddu had a very big problem! The killing of the Vazannos was one thing, but the murder of Balastrate's beloved Father Licolli was quite another! Turiddu was in trouble and he knew it.

"Maybe you should go to Trapani and then down to Marsala for a couple of days until this all blows over," suggested Paulo, hoping Turiddu would take the bait.

Turiddu looked at him suspiciously. "And where are you going to be, then?"

"Nowhere. I'll stay here and take care of business. When your father asks me where you are, I'll tell him you went to Trapani and then Marsala for the monthly collections. I'll tell him you left a week ago and left me here to take care of the local collections. It's a perfect alibi. Your father doesn't know you hired these *bastardos* from the hills to take care of this Vazanno business. Nobody, especially your father, will even know you might be remotely connected to the priest's murder."

Turiddu was pleased with Paulo's suggestion. He smiled at Paulo. "You're a good man, Paulo. I'm going to take good care of you when I run Palermo."

"Go on then and get out of here!" Paulo said, relieved Turiddu didn't want him to come west with him and the other men. "I'll handle everything right here with your father. You can count on me, boss."

As Paulo watched Turiddu ride off, he couldn't get his words out of his mind. *I'm going to take care of you when I run Palermo! What the hell is that madman thinking? Is he going to kill me too?*

Paulo knew then he had to try to stop his boss from killing any more innocent people—even Vito Vanucci.

* * *

Turiddu met up with the men who killed Father Licolli and Gaspano Vazanno that same night. They gathered in an old abandoned barn he'd often used as a meeting place for his men when they went out to Trapani. The place was located on the shoreline, not far from Erice.

The men were already sitting in the barn when Turiddu rode up.

When Turiddu came in, he told the men to stay seated. Then he walked over to a desk in the middle of the floor and took out a bottle of whiskey. He grabbed some glasses and put them on the desk, too. Then, he poured each man a drink and offered each one a cigar. Only one of the three men took the cigar and he lit it eagerly.

"So, how did it go today?" he asked. "I heard you had some trouble in Balastrate. Paulo tells me you killed a priest. So how many of the Vazanno brothers did you kill after we left Giuseppe's farm?"

The three men looked at one another. The man whom the priest recognized as Signora Albergetti's son said, "Just Gaspano Vazanno."

"You didn't find the younger one, the one they call 'Sevario' then?"

"No. After we left Balastrate we came here directly; I mean, it was bad. You should have seen those people, boss! They wanted to tear us apart limb from limb because of the priest. We didn't have any other choice but to get out of there as soon as possible."

"Sevario's place is not far from Balastrate; you must have passed it riding out of Balastrate?"

One of the other men said, "We'll find the last brother! We can go back, boss."

"It's too late for that," Turiddu said. "By now he knows what's happened to his two brothers and he's long gone, most likely headed for the coast to get to Africa." Turiddu laughed. "He could be right here in Trapani—right now—paying some *bastardo* to take him anywhere just to get off this island.

"I'm not worried about him right now. There's time for him. But, I got another job for you three."

"Yeah, sure, boss, what is it?" answered Albergetti.

"It's worth a lot of money. But, if you take it on, you have to be willing to leave here right away; Sicily, that is. You can go anywhere you want, but my guess is you will want to go to America where you'll have work—if you want it—with my partner there." Turiddu paused. "It's my father: Vito Vanucci."

The three men fell into dead silence. Two of them averted their eyes from Turiddu; only Albergetti stared at him in disbelief.

"I can't do that," Albergetti answered. "Your father's the Godfather of Palermo; I for one won't accept the vendetta. Killing a lemon farmer and his brothers is one thing, but killing the leader of the Honorable Men is another. No, I'm out," he said finally.

"You're turning down a lot of money, my friend. Perhaps you would like to think about it a while longer?" Turiddu asked calmly.

The two other men sitting next to Albergetti looked at him to answer. "No, I don't need to think about it, I'm not killing *my own Godfather,*" Albergetti answered adamantly.

Turiddu, without blinking an eye or even changing his position, shot a hole through the desk and into the stomach of Albergetti. He fell backwards onto the ground, holding his wound, crying out in agony.

The diversion gave Turiddu time to stand up behind the desk and shoot the other two men before they had a chance to react. Then, calmly, he walked from behind the desk and stood over Albergetti. "I'm sorry you did not take me up on my offer, signor." Turiddu fired one more shot and watched as Albergetti's head fell to one side.

Turiddu opened the door then. He motioned for the men who waited outside to come in.

"A couple of you, get rid of these bodies. I'll take the rest of you into town. Meet us at the *Porta Stretta* when you're done with this."

Four of Turiddu's men stayed behind to get rid of the bodies of the men Turiddu had just murdered; the rest rode with him into Trapani to the *Porta Stretta*.

"Get a drink," Turiddu ordered to the men who followed him into the bar. "When the others get back here, let me know."

* * *

All the men were now in Turiddu's back office, with Turiddu seated at his desk. "I don't know what's gonna happen, now that those pieces of *merda* you men just buried have killed the priest in Balastrate," Turiddu said to his men with a smile, "but, I think there's gonna be hell to pay for it!"

Turiddu got up out of his chair and poured himself a glass of whiskey. His back was to his men. When he turned around, the men looked anxious and he knew they were nervous about whether they would get paid for all the work they had already done over the last two days.

"Don't worry, men!" he said laughing.

Turiddu took two large saddlebags from a cupboard and opened them onto a table in the middle of the room. "There," he said, "is that what you were worried about?"

The men started to relax and smile; then they were laughing out loud, slapping one another on the back; they were openly relieved Turiddu was keeping his end of the bargain.

"There's enough money here to cover the Giuseppe and Gaspano Vazanno jobs, but . . ." Turiddu hesitated a moment and then walked over to the table covered in money and said, "I've added an extra 500 thousand lire to each man's take."

The men stood with their mouths open; that was more money than they would have ever expected to make in anyone's lifetime.

One of them stepped forward then and asked, "So, what are we expected to do for all this money, Vanucci?"

"Both the Vazanno brothers you killed still have family in Sicily. I want them all dead. Giuseppe Vazanno had three children: Antonio the oldest son, and Adriana and Francesca, his two daughters. Gaspano Vazanno has a wife and three kids. All his kids have to be killed—even the infant. They all have to be killed."

The men looked at each other. Many of them shrugged as if to say it didn't matter to them who they had to kill for that much money; others rubbed their chins thoughtfully with their hands, as if unsure they could murder children.

"Then, there's the matter of the youngest Vazanno brother, who somehow escaped our guns. He lives with another man named Santo Padua, who was adopted by the family and, as far as I'm concerned, is also a Vazanno."

Someone said, "I don't know about the others, but I'm in. Whoever doesn't want in on the deal now, they don't get the extra money, and those of us left here split their share."

"There is one more man," Turiddu said.

Now the men looked at each other again; a sudden silence fell over the group. Someone else stepped forward and asked, "Who is it, then?"

"Vito Vanucci."

There were four men standing in the back of the room. When they heard the Godfather's name, they glanced at each other quickly and then looked away.

Then Turiddu said, "Whoever is in on the extra 500 thousand lire, come forward and get your money. Whoever isn't, you're free to leave."

Every man in the room came forward to get his share of the money. They all knew staying back was suicidal. They all took their money and stood back, waiting for further instructions.

"Some of you men need to go up and down the western coast; look for families traveling together with children—especially families trying to get to the north coast of Africa or to *l'isola di Malta*. The rest of you men, take your money and head out looking for the Vazannos throughout the hill country and the provinces in central Sicily; if you don't find the family there, keep going until you reach the east. Just make sure you find them. They're out there; just find them."

"So what happens when we do find them and . . . and get rid of them just like you say? How do we get word back to you?"

"Don't worry about that. If you find men willing to help in the search, give them some of your share of the reward money; that's up to you. But, I'll be in Palermo. Find your way back to Palermo or get word to me there; that's where you'll find me. When . . ." Turiddu looked down for the first time, "when Vanucci is dead, believe me, I'll be the first one to hear about that. Now, get out of here and get to work. I'm going back to Palermo; I should get back there tonight sometime."

***

Paulo was waiting behind the stables at Don Vanucci's farm.

He felt physically sick; he knew he was about to betray Turiddu but had no idea if Don Vito would believe him. If he didn't believe him, it would mean certain death for Paulo; if he did believe it, there was still a close certainty that he would kill him anyway. Either way, Paulo Aiuto knew he was a dead man.

I'd rather be dead anyway, thought Aiuto. *My only hope now is that God will find mercy on my soul for what I am about to do, and forgive me for what I have done while in the company of Turiddu Vanucci, the devil himself.*

Paulo smoked one cigarette after another; he came to the Vanuccis' farm right after he left Turiddu in Balastrate, and had been hiding behind the Godfather's stables ever since, trying to get up the courage to speak to Vanucci when he returned home from the mainland. As he lit another cigarette, he told himself over and over again how stupid it was to be waiting here—at Vanucci's farm—not even knowing when the Don was supposed to be returning home!

He sat like a wounded animal in the high brush behind the stables. He knew at any minute one of the Don's men could discover him there and shoot him on sight. He didn't care.

Over and over, he thought about what he would say and how he would say it, finally breaking down into tears knowing there was no good way to tell Turiddu's own father that his son was an assassin—and that he, the Godfather of Palermo, was his next target.

Paulo watched the sun set and then rise again as he waited in the tall grass behind Vanucci's stables. Finally, hunger and thirst had taken their toll, and Paulo decided to leave the farm, get something to eat, and then return again later.

He stood up to leave when suddenly, he saw a figure in the distance; it was Don Vanucci riding back towards the stables.

Immediately, Paulo ducked down again.

He listened as Vanucci rode into the stable, "*Whoa, ragazza, whoa.*"

He listened to the sound of water being pumped from a well somewhere in the stable; then he heard the Godfather again, *"Non c`e` ragazza! Prendo l'acqua per voi!"*

Get up! You have to go into the barn! Paulo's brain urged him on. He walked inside.

"Who the hell are you? How did you get in here?" Vito Vanucci shouted as he grabbed his shotgun out of its scabbard, which was still hanging on his horse.

"My name is Paulo Aiuto, Godfather. I work for your son, Turiddu Vanucci."

The Godfather walked immediately toward Paulo without taking his gun off of him; he walked around him towards the door, looking for any sign of men outside. No one was there.

"Where's my son, then?" He asked Paulo.

"I'm here alone. I am asking permission to speak to you, Godfather." Paulo hesitated, knowing what he would say next would seal his fate. "I have something to tell you about your son, Turiddu."

Suddenly, Don Vanucci recognized Paulo as one of the men who hung around his son like flies attracted to waste. "Yeah, now I remember seeing you with my son. You're one of those ignorant *banditos* he pays to follow him around everywhere he goes. Yeah, I recognize you. So, what do you want?" Suddenly, it also occurred to Vito Vanucci that this man might be standing before him to tell him something tragic had occurred; that his son might have been in an accident or, worse, that he was dead. "What's happened to my son?" he demanded.

"I have information you should... that is... I have something to tell you about Giuseppe Vazanno and his family."

Vito's facial expression changed completely. At first he looked startled to see a stranger standing in front of him on his property—he thought immediately about how he would severely punish the men who were supposed to be guarding his villa—and then he got angry. How dare this nothing of a man have the guts to confront him at his own home, on his own, unaccompanied by his son! But now, when he heard his old friend's name, his expression changed to one of anxiety and fear. "What do you mean? What about Giuseppe Vazanno? What do you know about him or his family?"

"Something terrible has happened to . . ."

Vito lifted his shotgun and struck Paulo in the head with the butt of the gun. Paulo immediately fell to the ground, holding his head. Vito stood over him, ready to strike again. "What have you done to Giuseppe?" he demanded.

Paulo held up his hands to shield himself from the butt of the shotgun. He started to cry. "Please, Godfather, please! Giuseppe is alive, I swear it. He and his wife are alive!"

A look of relief came over Vito's face. He said, "Get up."

Paulo staggered up to his feet. He fell backwards once as the blow to his head caused him to nearly lose consciousness. When he finally got to his feet, he found a wooden pole and leaned up against it.

"Start talking or you're a dead man!" Vito pointed his shotgun at Paulo's head.

"Something has happened. Gaspano Vazanno. He's been killed. He was killed yesterday, shot dead . . . on the order . . . on the order of your son."

Vito felt the blood drain from his head. Suddenly, his heart seemed to stop and he felt as if he could not get enough air into his lungs. "Go on; finish it," was all he could manage to say.

"Turiddu took us, a band of maybe twenty men, to Giuseppe Vazanno's farmhouse the night before last. He tortured Giuseppe and his wife, and then burned the farmhouse to the ground."

Vito's face was chalk-white. "Where is Giuseppe now?"

"I don't know."

Vito fired a shot into Paulo's leg. He fell to the ground, screaming in excruciating pain. "Tell me where Giuseppe Vazanno and his family are now!" Vito demanded.

"Turiddu wanted me to kill them both and get rid of the bodies. Instead, I let them go," Paulo managed to get out as he cried in agony, holding his lower leg which had nearly been severed with the gunshot. "I watched them as they left Balastrate headed for San Vito di Capo; I'm not certain that's where he went . . ." he choked, ". . . but he went in that direction."

Vito walked over and put his shotgun's barrel into Paulo's mouth. "Tell me everything and do not leave out one thing." Slowly, he slid the shotgun back out of Paulo's mouth.

"Something happened a few weeks ago. This guy shows up

and nobody knows who he is. All I know is Turiddu was waiting for him. He told us his name was Luca somebody, that he was from Catania and that your son Turiddu hired him to do a special job here in Palermo. Next thing I know, Turiddu tells me and a few other men to wait for him one morning outside of Vazanno's north orchard. Sure enough, when Turiddu doesn't show up to meet with me and the other men, we go looking for him—just like Turiddu told us to do. We finally see Turiddu and this Luca man off in the distance but realize there is something wrong. The closer we get, we can see this guy is trying to kill your son. We ride up and the man takes off on his horse."

"So what does all this have to do with Giuseppe?"

"The man called Luca was hired by Turiddu to kill Giuseppe Vazanno and . . . then to kill you."

"Go on," Vito said through clenched teeth.

"It turned out this Luca was first hired by Antonio and Adriana Vazanno to kill Turiddu, your son.

"Antonio . . ." the Don said in obvious shock. ". . . Adriana Vazanno? But why?"

Paulo put his eyes down then. He looked up at Vito and pleaded with him to kill him because the pain was now unbearable.

Vito took his shotgun and hit Paulo in the head again with it. "I said tell me everything, you *bastardo.*"

"Your son raped and tortured Adriana Vazanno two months ago; he found her walking in the orchards where she was taking some food to her father. He beat her so bad—he thought he had killed her. When he found out she didn't die, he became some sort of madman; he went completely crazy, burning with hatred for Vazanno. That's when he hired this guy named Luca to kill Vazanno."

"And me, don't leave that part out, *bastardo.* Then what happened?"

"I already told you!" Paulo screamed out.

"Tell me again."

"This guy was supposed to kill Vazanno and you four days ago now. But, instead, this guy tries to kill Turiddu but didn't get the job done. Turiddu was so enraged he took a couple a dozen men to Vazanno's farmhouse two days ago and, like I said, burned it to the ground. He left me the job of finishing off Vazanno and his wife. Then, he took the men and went looking for Vazanno's brothers. They found Gaspano Vazanno going into Balastrate just before dawn yesterday morning. Turiddu sent three of the men to follow him and kill him."

"So they did manage to kill my Gaspano, then?"

"Yes, but the worst of it is that while trying to kill Gaspano, Father Licolli got in the way and they shot him, too."

"No!" screamed Vito as he walked closer to Paulo. "No, not Father Licolli!"

"Yes, this man called Albergetti shot the priest because he stepped in front of Gaspano. Then when the priest was shot, he shot Gaspano too."

Vito put his hand to his forehead, rubbing it in complete disbelief. He walked back to a small wine barrel nearby and sat down. Paulo could hear him crying, even though his face was turned away from him. For just one minute, Paulo thought perhaps Vito Vanucci might spare his life then.

After what seemed an eternity to Paulo, Vito Vanucci got up and walked back to where he lay now on the ground. "Where are Giuseppe's and Gaspano's children?"

"I don't know. Turiddu was going to send men out looking for them; he also was going to send men out looking for the younger brother, Sevario Vazanno, and the other man they call Santo Padua."

"Where is my son now?"

"He's in Trapani. He wanted to establish an alibi so that you would not think he had anything to do with the killings of the Vazanno family."

Vito went to the front of the barn and fired off several shotgun blasts.

Within seconds, the stable was surrounded by dozens of men. "Where the hell have you *bastardos* been?' he screamed at the men as they entered the stable.

"What's happened, Godfather?" Vito's lead *capo* asked.

"Meet me at the docks. Take this piece of *merda* back to my son's office there. Put him in the office and take care of him there. Tell my brother-in-law I want to meet with him, too—at my place on the docks. Carry this guy out the back so that my wife does not see anything."

"There's one more thing you should know, Godfather," Paulo said as the Don's men were carrying him out.

"Wait," Vito said to his men. "What is it, you stinking piece of *merda?*"

"Turiddu has a partner in America. His name is Benjamin Meyer."

"In America? What are you talking about?"

"Turiddu's been stealing lemons from the Vazanno orchards for over a year; he's partners with a guy from a place called *Nuovo Orleens, Luanna, America.*"

Vito raised his hand in the air and said, "Get him out of here."

* * *

Vito rode to the docks and waited for his men and his brother-in-law to come to him at his office in Palermo.

His brother-in-law came in while the men waited outside. "Godfather," he said as he went to Vito and kissed him on both cheeks and then his hands. "What can I do for you?"

"Is Aiuto dead?"

"Yes, Godfather."

"Before you killed him, did you get out of him the names of all of the thieves working for Turiddu?"

"Yes, Godfather."

"Bring Aiuto's body here to my office. I want the devil to see his number one man's brains spattered all over it when he walks in."

"Yes, Godfather."

"You are to say nothing to Turiddu except that he is to come to me here immediately when he returns from wherever he is. Have him followed. If he tries to leave Palermo instead of coming here, kill him."

"Yes, Godfather."

"Then, I want every one of the men who Aiuto fingered to be killed right away. If you can't find them here in the west, send men into the Sicanians. If you can't pull them out of their rat holes in the mountains, then send men to their hometowns and torture their family members to give them up; if that doesn't work, send men all the way to the east."

"Yes, Godfather."

"I want every one of Turiddu's gang of thieves to be found and killed. Do you understand me?"

Vito's brother-in-law put his eyes down. "Yes, Godfather."

"Go on. Go back and wait for Turiddu to arrive at the bar. When he gets there, remember: he is not to go back to his office. Send him here first. When I'm done with him and if he's still alive, I will send him back to you. Just make sure he doesn't take anything out of there worth anything—including any money he might have in there."

Vito's brother-in-law bowed to Vito and then turned and walked out.

* * *

Turiddu arrived back at the docks around midnight that night. When he walked into his uncle's bar, his uncle was waiting for him. "Turiddu, wait! I have to talk to you."

"Yeah, what do you want? Make it quick, I'm tired. I want to get home to bed."

"You are to go and meet your father at his meeting place here in Palermo."

"Are you *pazzesco?* It's after midnight! My father's home in bed, you *idioto!*"

"Go to your father—now, Turiddu," his uncle said between clenched teeth.

Turiddu looked stunned. "What's going on, Uncle? Has something happened at home?"

His uncle turned and walked away. He went to a door in the back of the bar and walked out, slamming the door behind him.

Turiddu looked around and noticed over a dozen of his father's men scattered throughout the room. His hands started to sweat as a feeling of doom came over him. He walked to the door and then out onto the street. He mounted his horse and turned in the direction of his father's meeting place. He looked back to see at least a dozen men following him.

* * *

"Sit down," a voice in the dark commanded when he opened the door to his father's meeting place.

The voice was all too familiar to Turiddu. "Papa?" he called out quietly. "Papa, is that you?"

"I said to sit down, Turiddu. I have something to show you."

Turiddu sat down and immediately his father lit an oil lamp, casting shadows across the room. But one thing caught Turiddu's eye immediately. In the corner was the corpse of Paulo Aiuto staring blankly up at the ceiling with a huge hole in the middle of his forehead.

Turiddu gasped.

"You recognize that man, Turiddu?"

"It's Paulo. It's Paulo Aiuto."

"That's right. He's one of your *bastardo banditos*. He told me everything, Turiddu. He told me everything you have done. There is no use trying to deny it," Vito said resolutely, "I know everything."

Turiddu started to shake uncontrollably. He knew there would be no reasoning or even trying to lie to him now. "I can explain . . ."

"Shut up. You have lost all your rights. You cannot speak, you cannot move right now without permission from me, and I do not plan on giving you that permission—ever again."

Sweat was pouring down Turiddu's head. In a final act of defiance, he screamed out, "Go and kill me, old man! Go ahead! I want to die! I'd rather die than be your son one day longer."

"Oh, you will get your wish, Turiddu. I promise you that," Vito said.

Realizing he had gone too far now, Turiddu changed his attitude immediately. "Papa, I'm sorry! I didn't mean for this to go this far . . ."

Vito stepped forward. He was holding a thick club in his hands; without even a moment's hesitation he swung, hitting his son squarely in the jaw—knocking him off of his chair and onto the floor.

"I didn't give you permission to speak," Vito said standing over his shocked and shuddering son..

Turiddu started to cry.

"Get up! Get up, you crying coward. I want to fight you like a man. Do you think you can do that, Turiddu? Do you think you can fight like a man?"

"Papa, please. I don't want to fight you," Turiddu pleaded.

"Get up!" Vito commanded.

Turiddu struggled to his feet. His head was bleeding from the first blow to the side of his face and blood obscured his vision. His head was spinning so badly, he stumbled backwards before he could right himself. Just as he finally regained his footing, his father struck him again with the club, this time to Turiddu's stomach. Immediately Turiddu bent over, vomited, and then fell to the floor, holding his midsection, crying out in pain.

"You tried to kill my friend . . . my brother, Giuseppe Vazanno, and his family! You did kill Gaspano and the priest Father Licolli! You have to answer for these sins, Turiddu. This time, you will not be able to escape. This time you have to answer for all these sins!"

Turiddu heard his father's voice as if it was an echo; but the one thing he heard as clearly as day was, *you tried to kill Giuseppe Vazanno and his family*.

"What kind of an animal are you? What kind of an animal did my seed bring forth from my own loins? No," Don Vanucci seethed as he stood over his son lying on the floor crying like a baby, ". . . you are not an animal—but you are, without a doubt, worse than an animal!"

Turiddu covered his face and continued to sob on the floor, hoping his father would relent, after seeing him in such an apparent state of remorseful distress.

"If you think I am moved by your tears, Turiddu, you are mistaken. Your tears mean nothing to me—just as you mean nothing to me now."

Turiddu stopped crying and lay perfectly still on the floor. He was shocked his father seemed able to read his thoughts.

"Get up off the floor," demanded Turiddu's father.

Turiddu watched as his father walked over and sat down behind his desk.

Slowly, Turiddu lifted himself up off the floor.

"Come over here and sit in front of me," Don Vanucci commanded in an ice-cold voice.

Turiddu sat directly across from his father. He watched as his father stood up then and took a shotgun off the wall. He loaded it in front of Turiddu and then walked back to the desk and sat down.

"My inclination is to kill you, Turiddu. I want to end your life because it was I who gave you life. I blame no one but myself for what you have become. Your mother had nothing to do with what you are now." Vito Vanucci wiped tears from his eyes. "When I think of your mother and what you have done to her, it makes me want to strangle the life out of you."

Turiddu stared at the shotgun that lay on the desk in front of his father.

"But, I cannot kill you. I cannot kill you because it would kill your mother and I love her more than anything or anyone in this world. I cannot kill you because I believe it is a sin to kill one's own flesh and blood; just as God did not kill Adam or Eve for their sin. Instead, he took everything from them. He left them naked and in pain. Everyone, everyone, has to pay for their crimes, Turiddu—there are no exceptions!"

Suddenly, Turiddu felt elated. He was not going to die! His father's reaction only served to convince him further of his father's inherent weakness as a leader. But, he kept himself still, not wanting to show his profound relief.

"You are no longer my son nor your mother's. Sicily is no longer your country. From this precise minute, you are no longer allowed to live here. You have no money, no inheritance, and no family. As far as I am concerned, you were never born."

Turiddu swallowed hard. *No money? No inheritance? How am I to live?* he thought. Then, he mustered the courage to speak, "What do you mean, Papa? Where am I to go without any money?"

"That is your problem, not mine. I have instructed the men of *la famiglia* they are to shoot you if they see you *anywhere at all* in Sicily after the next twelve hours."

"Where am I to go, then? How am I to leave Sicily without money?" Turiddu's hands were sweating. *This is impossible . . . surely he will let me see my mother?* "What about Mamma? Can I see my mother before I leave?"

"No. Now get out."

Terrified, Turiddu staggered from his father's office. Slowly he limped past several of his father's closest guards who all pointed their shotguns toward him as he passed. The first place he went was back to his uncle's bar; he had money put away in a safe there.

"Get out," Turiddu's uncle said to him when he walked in the door.

"I just want to get my things from the . . ."

"Get out," his uncle said as he looked up at the clock. "I would shoot you now but your father gave orders we could not fire one bullet at you until 12 noon today. You have ten hours left of your life here in Sicily. If I were you, I would make good use of those few hours."

Turiddu walked backwards a few steps toward the door he had come in. Then, when he knew he was close to the door, he turned and walked out of his uncle's bar. He remembered he had put money away in the stables at his father's house. *That's it!* He thought. *The money under the cistern in the barn!*

Turiddu went out to get on his horse—but the animal was gone. He turned to go back into the bar to confront his uncle—but then thought better of it. Instead, he walked around to the back of the building and climbed into his office. The room had been emptied of everything, including the safe where he had hidden most of the money he had managed to skim off of the profits belonging to his father. He looked around to make sure no one was looking to see what he was doing, and then he pulled out one of the drawers in the desk where he had waxed an envelope to the back of it. He ripped it off quickly and stuffed the money into his shirt. Then he pulled up a loose floorboard and removed the small pistol and some bullets he had stashed there. He climbed back out the window he came in, and quickly walked toward the outgoing cargo ships docked at the far end of the pier. He needed to get on a boat and he needed to do it before noon.

* * *

"Where's this ship going?" Turiddu asked a crewman as he watched him stack crates of cargo atop wooden pallets.

"New York, America," the man answered.

"How much money you want to get me on this ship before it leaves?" Turiddu asked.

"Show me how much you got and I'll let you know if it's enough," the man answered as he continued to stack crates.

Turiddu showed the man 500,000 lire.

"Stay here," the man said to Turiddu as he grabbed the money out of his hand.

Turiddu started to protest but knew he had no other choice; there were no other vessels on the dock and by the time they would arrive—if they did arrive—it would be too late for him to try to get aboard.

After a few minutes the shipman came back with work clothes and boots. "Here," he said, "put these on. If anybody sees you in the clothes you're wearing, they'll kill you just to steal your clothes."

Hiding behind some pilings, Turiddu changed into the old clothes; he threw his own clothes and leather shoes into the sea. When he had changed, the man motioned for him to come over to him. "When this pallet goes up, hang on. It will be lifted to the ship's deck. Once you're aboard, start taking the crates off like the other men on deck. Nobody will bother you after that. Just follow what the other men are doing. Keep quiet; don't talk to anyone. If you're lucky, you'll make it to America in one piece."

CHAPTER XV
SAN VITO DI CAPO

05 MAY 1911

GIUSEPPE DROVE THE small wagon into the *campagna*. He dared not head for the main road leading into the village or toward Palermo. Better he stay on the small, grassy trails in the countryside rather than risk meeting any of Turiddu's faithful followers.

Why this one man wanted to help him he did not know; but as he drove away from him he prayed to God in grateful thanksgiving for Paulo's faint but courageous heart.

Giuseppe did as he was told. He kept driving the wagon toward the coast. Every few minutes he looked back at his wife in the bed of the wagon; he couldn't tell if she was alive or dead. She lay motionless under a thin blanket that shielded her exposed skin from the burning sun overhead.

Finally, after what seemed an eternity, Giuseppe looked back and did not see Paulo following him. He immediately looked for any sign of a spring or a running creek. He looked up at the low-lying mountains surrounding him and saw one with just a hint of snow still atop it. He headed in that direction and sure enough, he found a small running stream.

Immediately he stopped and climbed into the back of the wagon. He took the cover off his wife's face; he could see she was still breathing, but only barely. He started to cry as he held her in his arms. Her eyes remained closed. She moaned and then went silent. Her face and body felt on fire.

Giuseppe pulled his shirt off and soaked it in the cold creek water. He bathed her face and upper body with his wet shirt; she opened her eyes then and looked up at him. She started to talk but he said, "Shh . . . shh . . . we are alive. I'm going to take care of you, I promise. Just be still, Maria. Be still."

He cupped water in his hand and poured a few drops gently into her mouth. She sucked the water readily at first, but then began to choke. Giuseppe held her up straighter in his arms; when he did, blood poured from her mouth.

She opened her eyes again and then her head fell backward.

"Maria! Maria!" he screamed as he tried to revive her, thinking she was dead.

She moved her head to one side and then tried once again to open her eyes.

"Thank you, God! Thank you, God!" he said out loud.

After he cooled her body with the cold water, he washed her face and then gently placed her back in the wagon. He attached the blanket cover to the top posts of the wagon so that the covering was a few feet above her head rather than directly on it. He thought this a better way to keep the sun off of her and yet let air circulate around her.

He filled the water flasks he took from his barn, made sure his horse was watered, and then began again in a westerly direction, hoping to come to the coast before nighttime.

* * *

The sun went down and the air seemed remarkably cooler; Giuseppe knew he was near water: he could taste the salt in the air. Suddenly, he came upon a coastline. "Thank you, God!" he said again, as if needing to speak to God aloud rather than in silent prayer.

Maria opened her eyes at the sound of Giuseppe's voice. "Giuseppe, Giuseppe," she managed to say. But her voice was barely audible and Giuseppe did not hear. She tried to sit up; she braced herself against the side of the wagon and said louder, "Giuseppe?"

Immediately Giuseppe stopped the wagon and ran to the back. He climbed in and pushed his body close to hers. "Maria, Maria! You are awake!"

"We are alive then, Giuseppe?"

"Yes, Maria, yes, we are alive. Here, take some of this water." He squeezed water into her mouth. The cold, clear water seemed to revive her sufficiently so that she opened her eyes and tried to sit up.

"No. Stay where you are. Just rest. I will get help for us soon. But I need you to be well before we move on."

Suddenly, Maria sat up out of Giuseppe's arms. "Our daughters!" she screamed. "Adriana and Francesca? Where are they, Giuseppe? Where are they?"

Before Giuseppe could even try and console his wife, she fainted dead away; the loss of blood and fever left her with no reserve whatsoever.

Giuseppe now knew how desperately ill his wife was. He had to find help for her, and soon—or else she would surely die.

* * *

Giuseppe saw he was on a rocky coast; to his left was a mountain. It was one of the tallest in western Sicily and he knew immediately he was near San Vito di Capo. And he knew there was a convent at the top of the town. But from where he stood, it would take him hours, if not a full day, to travel all the way to the base of the mountain and then from there to the top of it. No, Maria would not live through that. He needed to get across the gulf and then climb the mountain from the other side; he knew where he was. It would take him less than one hour to get to the Convent of St. Therese from the other side of the gulf.

Giuseppe left Maria in the wagon and walked down to the rocky coastline. He could see a small boat not far from where he stood. The night was bright with stars and a full moon. He knew if the fisherman looked his way, he would see him. Giuseppe waved his arms in the air. But it was impossible for the man to see him from his current vantage point. There was a large rock sticking out of the water not far from where he stood. He jumped into the water and swam to the rock.

Climbing up out of the water, he stood and began shouting,

"Help! Help!" He waved his arms back and forth and continued screaming, "Help! Help! Over here! I'm over here. I need your help!"

The man waved back to Giuseppe. He appeared to be pulling his net back into his boat. Within a minute or two, Giuseppe saw the man begin rowing his boat towards him.

"*Grazia, signor! Grazia, signor!* Thank you, oh, thank you, signor!" Giuseppe managed to say as he struggled to hold onto the side of the small fishing boat. "My wife is very ill. Can you please help me? I need to get her up there," he said pointing to the Convent of St. Therese, "to the convent infirmary."

The old man looked at Giuseppe suspiciously. In the middle of the night he finds a man standing atop a rock waving his arms and screaming for help; then suddenly, the man jumps into the water and swims out to meet him as he is rowing towards the rock where the man stood! "This is a fantastic story, signor!" said the fisherman. "Where is your wife, then?"

"Please, signor, she is over there." Giuseppe said as he pointed towards the coastline where he had left Maria in the wagon.

The man helped Giuseppe into the boat and together they rowed toward the shoreline.

When the fisherman saw the terrible condition of Giuseppe's wife, he felt immediate remorse for not believing his story.

"Your wife is very ill, signor. Come, I will help you lift her into the boat."

***

Giuseppe pounded on the wooden door and then pulled on the rope attached to a large bell above the door. He continued pounding and pounding until a small slot opened in the middle of the door. Two small eyes stared at him.

"What do you want here, signor? This is a convent," said the nun who opened the small peephole.

"It's my wife. She's very ill. Please sister, I need your help!"

The door opened.

A small woman, no more five feet in height, stood there dressed entirely in black with a long, brown scapular covering the front of her black habit. A stiff, white linen piece encircled her head, leaving only her face visible, and from atop her head hung a long, black veil that fell to the floor.

The nun looked up at Giuseppe and asked, "Where is your wife, signor?"

Giuseppe turned and pointed to Maria who was lying on a small cart the fisherman used to carry his catch back to his house after a night of fishing.

"Bring her in, signor," said the nun as she opened the door wide enough for Giuseppe to carry Maria in.

"Follow me, signor." The nun turned from Giuseppe and started down a long corridor. As they walked through the silence of the convent in the middle of the night, the only sound to be heard was the gentle clicking of the nun's rosary beads as she walked down the hallway. As they passed the convent's chapel, Giuseppe heard a bell ring. Then, in complete unison, women began singing. The heavenly, ethereal sound of their joined voices singing the ancient prayers of the Church immediately brought tears to Giuseppe's eyes. *My God, You have delivered us! You alone have delivered us from the devil's grip!* Giuseppe prayed in thanksgiving as he continued to follow the nun down the long corridors, deeper into the safety and peace of the convent walls.

Suddenly, the nun stopped and turned to Giuseppe. "You can go no further, signor." Giuseppe looked around the nun to several other sisters holding a long litter. They set it down upon the floor. The nun whom Giuseppe had been following said, "Please lay your wife down here, signor."

Giuseppe gently laid Maria on the litter. Maria moaned but did not otherwise speak.

"Mother will speak to you now, signor," the nun said as she opened the door to an office. Giuseppe walked in to see another nun, much younger than the one who opened the door for him, sitting behind a large desk.

"Signor . . ." the sister said as she stood up from the desk and walked towards Giuseppe with one hand extended.

"Giuseppe Vazanno, sister. My name is Giuseppe and my wife's name is Maria."

"Signor Vazanno, please come and sit here by the fire."

The nun was more than kind: she was open and inviting, and at once, Giuseppe felt comfortable sitting across from her. But, as soon as he was seated, the nun immediately got up and poured two cups of tea. She brought the tray to Giuseppe and offered him a cup.

Giuseppe cried. He put his head down into his hands and wept. The nun put the tray down and then stood near him. "Please, signor, can you tell me what has happened?"

Giuseppe told the mother superior of the horror that had transpired; he told her of his wife's repeated rape and beatings, of his own brutal beatings and slaughter of his farm animals, and finally of the complete destruction of his house. By the time he had finished recounting the terrible events of that night, he was nearly inconsolable.

"It is time you got some rest, Signor Vazanno. The doctor has been called and I am sure he is caring for your wife now. There is nothing more you can do right now except take care of yourself. You must rest and trust that your wife is in God's hands."

The mother superior went to her door and rang a small bell. In an instant, the nun who had opened the door for Giuseppe was standing in her office. "Please take Signor Vazanno to one of our guest rooms, sister. Make him as comfortable as possible and make sure he has some warm soup and bread before he retires. Thank you, sister."

Giuseppe stood then but nearly collapsed. Both the nuns helped him to his feet. He started to thank the mother superior and the other sister, but the mother superior took his hand in hers and said, "We are here for God. It is our pleasure to serve you, signor."

* * *

"It's a miracle this woman made it through the night, Mother. I cannot tell if she will live even throughout the day today. She has lost a great deal of blood; her injuries are extensive; I shudder to think what she went through." The doctor shook his head. "The best we can do now is keep her comfortable. Keep her warm; keep her hydrated—try to feed her soup every couple of hours and make sure she drinks water." The doctor went to his bag and pulled out a bottle. "Here," he said, handing the bottle to the infirmary sister, "put two drops on her tongue every four hours; this will stop most of her pain."

The mother superior accompanied the doctor as he left the infirmary.

"Where is her husband, then?" asked the doctor.

"I will send for him. He was in a terrible state himself when he came here late last night. I am hoping he was able to sleep and rest."

"Sister," the mother superior said to one of the nuns, "will you please ask Signor Vazanno to come here to my office to speak with the doctor?"

***

There was a knock at the mother superior's office door.

"Come in, sister."

The nun walked in first with Giuseppe following. His face, lined with anxiety, still looked as if he had not slept at all.

"Signor Vazanno," the mother superior said as she rose from her desk and walked to him. She took him by the hand and led him to a seat next to the doctor. "Please sit here, next to Doctor Abarazzi."

"Thank you, Mother," Giuseppe said. Then he turned to the doctor and extended his hand to him. The two men shook hands and then Giuseppe said sincerely, with tears welling in his eyes, "I cannot thank you and Mother enough. I will be forever indebted to you both for all you have done for me and my wife."

"Signor . . . Signor Vazanno," the doctor started, "I am afraid I cannot make any promises about your wife's condition right now. She has suffered some very severe injuries; so severe, I am afraid, that she may not recover fully from them."

Giuseppe was weeping now; he covered his face with his hands.

"I'm so sorry, signor. But, we will know more in a couple of days. That is . . ." The doctor was about to say they would know more in a couple of days *if* Maria lives out the next couple of days, but he stopped himself, seeing how distraught Giuseppe already was. "I will be here with your wife, signor; if she needs anything, between myself and the good sisters she will be well taken care of, I promise you that."

"Can I please see my wife, doctor?"

The doctor looked up at the mother superior. Men were never allowed in the infirmary. But under the circumstances, she decided to make an exception. "Yes, signor, I will arrange for you to see your wife right away," the mother superior said and stepped out of the room.

When the nun left the room, the doctor asked Giuseppe, "You do know that your wife had been severely raped and beaten?"

"Yes, doctor. I know everything."

The doctor shook his head back and forth. "What kind of animals did this to you?"

"They were not animals, doctor; they were devils from hell."

The mother superior came back into the room. "The sisters are arranging a private room for your wife, Signor Vazanno. So you can stay in the room with her for the duration of her stay with us."

* * *

Giuseppe was taken to his wife's bedside. He took a seat next to the bed and took her hand in his. She looked beautiful. The nuns had bathed her, washed her hair, and put her in a clean linen nightdress. *She looks like an angel,* Giuseppe thought. Her yellow-golden curls fell about her shoulders and tumbled down the side of her face.

"Maria," he whispered. "Maria." Maria did not open her eyes but turned her head in the direction from which Giuseppe's voice came.

He smiled then, knowing she sensed he was there; after several hours passed, Maria suddenly opened her eyes and looked up at Giuseppe. He had laid his head down on the bed and his black hair, so familiar to her, was just inches away from her own. She reached up and gently touched his head.

Startled, Giuseppe raised his head; his eyes met Maria's. The two smiled at each other.

"Giuseppe," she struggled to say, "we are alive?"

"Yes!" Giuseppe said. "Yes, my love! We are both of us alive!"

Giuseppe got up immediately and called one of the nuns into his wife's room. "She's awake! Can you please call the doctor?"

Within a matter of minutes the doctor was standing next to Maria's bedside. He listened to her lungs with his stethoscope.

Then he felt her forehead. "She is febrile."

"What does that mean, doctor? She spoke to me! She is awake! Isn't that a good sign, doctor?"

"I'm afraid your wife has a serious infection in her lungs. She has several broken ribs and because she cannot expand her chest to the full extent, I'm afraid fluid is building up in them. She has a fever now. All of these things are . . . well they are . . . not good signs, I am afraid."

"But, she will recover doctor, won't she? She will recover?"

"We will have to wait, signor. We will have to wait. Her life is in God's hands now." The doctor put his hand on Giuseppe's shoulder and walked out.

***

"Mother, I think it is time to call for a priest to give Signora Vazanno the sacrament of extreme unction," the doctor said.

"Does her husband know how serious her condition had become?"

"I am going to tell him now. He went to the chapel to pray."

"I will call the priest right away," Mother said.

The doctor entered the chapel to see Giuseppe kneeling in front of the main altar. He had a rosary in his hand and was praying silently. The doctor took a seat behind him and waited for him to finish saying the rosary. When Giuseppe got up and turned to leave, he was startled to see the doctor sitting in a pew behind him.

"Doctor, what is it?" Giuseppe asked anxiously.

"Come with me, signor. We have called for the priest."

***

Giuseppe walked into his wife's room quietly; he twisted his cap in his shaking hands. He approached her bedside and stared down at her near-lifeless body. Her skin was as pale as porcelain and she appeared to be in a deep sleep. He knelt down next to her bed and took her hand in his. "Maria," he whispered.

Maria stirred; he saw her try to open her eyes; she blinked several times and then turned her head to face him. She closed her eyes again as if even the act of keeping her eyes open was too much for her. Giuseppe squeezed her hand and leaned in closer to her. "Maria, it's me, Peppino. It's Peppino, Maria. Can you hear me, my love?"

Maria squeezed his hand. She opened her eyes again just enough to look up at Giuseppe's face. "I don't think I will live, Peppino," she whispered. "Will you stay with me? I'm afraid."

Giuseppe kissed his wife's forehead. "I will stay right here and I will not leave you, my love."

"Excuse me, Signor Vazanno," said a soft voice behind him, "the priest is here to anoint your wife."

Giuseppe not wanting to take his eyes off Maria's gaze said, "Have the priest come in, sister."

The nuns had prepared a bedside table for the priest to administer the sacrament of extreme unction. The priest took a small container of holy oil from his bag and placed it on the table.

"God's peace be in this place."

Everyone in the room except Giuseppe responded, "And in all who live here."

The priest put on a white surplice and, over that, a narrow stole; he took a small crucifix and put it to Maria's lips. Giuseppe watched as his wife actually kissed the crucifix; he was amazed at her ability to recognize the cross, in her condition. The priest took holy water and blessed Maria with it and then he blessed all those present as well.

"Can you hear me, my child?" the priest whispered as he leaned in close to Maria's ear.

Maria turned her head towards the priest.

"Can you speak, my child? Can you make your confession?"

Maria opened her eyes wide. She turned her head to look right at the priest. She felt for his hand and took it in her own, "Yes, Father," she said weakly, "Yes, I want to confess."

Giuseppe got up to follow the nuns out of the room.

Maria would not let go of the priest's hand. She said, "I want my husband to stay here with me, Father. Is my husband here?"

Giuseppe knelt down and took Maria's other hand in his; he said, "Maria, I'm here next to you, my love. I am right here and I will not leave you."

***

"I confess to God the almighty Father, the maker of heaven and of earth, and to you Father, that I have sinned. I have gravely sinned."

Maria gasped for air. She could barely breathe now, and with every word that came from her mouth, she choked and coughed up blood.

The priest knelt down next to Maria's side; he leaned his ear in so that it was very close to her mouth. "Go on, my child, confess your sins."

"I have gravely sinned against God, my husband, my family, and my faith."

"Go on, child," said the priest.

"I lied to my husband about a grave matter, a matter that I deliberately kept from him."

"What was the nature of the secret, my child?"

"I lied to him about what happened to our daughter. I told him she suffered an accidental fall, but instead she was attacked, raped, and brutally beaten by a man we knew well. His name is Turiddu Vanucci. I did not tell my husband because I was afraid he would kill him for the disgrace he brought upon our family."

Maria stopped as she began to cough violently. She regained her breath for a moment and managed to say, "Forgive me, Father, for I have gravely sinned."

"Is that all, daughter?" the priest asked.

Maria turned her head away from the priest and looked up Giuseppe.

"Not telling your husband the truth, daughter, was not a great sin. You were trying to prevent a greater sin from being committed by your husband."

"No! I have committed *a grievous sin*, father!"

The priest now looked over at Giuseppe who held his head in his hands, weeping bitterly. The priest felt immediate pity for him. Then he looked back again at Maria. "Confess then, daughter. Tell me your sin."

"My sin is great, father; not only have I sinned against myself but I am the cause of another's sin. I gave a vendetta to my own son! I forced my own son to kill another man! My son was to have been ordained a priest, father! I knew he would accept it . . . I knew it!" Maria was crying now. "Out of his love for his sister and me, he accepted the vendetta. I have caused the ruination of my soul and the soul of my own son! Do you understand now, Father?"

The priest looked quickly at Giuseppe and then back to Maria. He made the sign of the cross and said, "Daughter, are you sorry for this sin and all the sins of your whole life?"

"Yes, father. I am bitterly sorry for this sin. But I have more to confess." Maria turned from the priest and looked at her husband; she began stroking Giuseppe's hair. "I confess that I am guilty of loving my husband more than anyone on earth or in heaven. God forgive me because now that I am going to Him, I realize my love for Him should have been greater than my love of my husband or anyone on this earth. If I had loved the Lord the way I should have, I never would have asked my son to commit such a terrible crime against God! I am to blame for so much heartache, Father! I am to blame for everything that has befallen my family!"

"Daughter, I absolve you of all of your sins." The priest made the sign of the cross over Maria. "Now you must make a perfect Act of Contrition."

Maria, nearly breathless now, began to recite the Act of Contrition. "Oh, my God, I am most heartily sorry for having offended thee. I detest all of my sins . . ." As she prayed, her voice weakened and softened until it was inaudible to Giuseppe.

"Maria! Maria!" he said loudly, over and over again. When she did not respond, he bent down and took her face in his hands. He kissed her forehead and then her lips. "I love you, Maria. I have always loved you, and never in my lifetime will I ever love another, I promise you that."

Giuseppe held her close to him and continued where Maria left off: ". . . because I dread the loss of Heaven and the pains of hell; but most of all because I love Thee, my God, Who art all good and deserving of all my love! I firmly resolve, with the help of Thy grace, to confess my sins, to do penance, and to amend my life. Amen."

"Our help is in the name of the Lord," said the priest.

"Who has made heaven and earth," Giuseppe responded.

"Let us pray . . ." The priest finished saying the ritual prayers for the sick and dying, and then took his thumb and dipped it into the holy oil; he anointed Maria's eyes, her ears, her nose, her mouth, the palms of her hands, and the soles of her feet.

"By this holy anointing and by His most tender mercy may the Lord forgive you all the evil you have done throughout your whole life."

Finally, the priest leaned in close to Maria's ear and whispered, "Do not be afraid, my child. God is with you and all your sins have been forgiven. Do not succumb to the temptations of the Evil One, for God awaits you now to take you to His heavenly home."

The priest blessed Maria one last time and then got up and left the room, leaving her and Giuseppe alone.

"Can you ever . . ." Maria stopped to catch her breath, "can you ever forgive me for what I have done to you and our family?"

"There is nothing to forgive." Giuseppe leaned in and kissed his wife tenderly on her forehead. "You of all people know what I would have done if . . ." Giuseppe stopped talking.

Maria's head fell softly to one side. Her chest no longer moved. Giuseppe put his head on his wife's chest to hear the last beat of her heart before she expired. He held her in his arms until the nuns came in to prepare her body for burial.

* * *

"What is the date, sister?" asked Giuseppe.

"Today is the tenth day of May, Signor Vazanno."

"When can we bury my wife's body, sister?"

"Father will have a Mass for her soul tomorrow morning and we will bury her in our cemetery here at the convent, if you are in agreement with that."

"Yes, thank you, sister. Thank you for all you have done for my wife and for me. Can I ask you to do one more thing for me?"

"Yes of course, Signor Vazanno. Anything."

* * *

Maria Vazanno was buried in the cemetery behind the Convent of St. Therese of the Child Jesus on the eleventh day of May, 1911.

Giuseppe Vazanno left for Napoli that very day. The same fisherman who had helped Giuseppe and Maria the night he found them stranded returned to take Giuseppe across the Tyrrhenian Sea to Naples the evening of Maria Vazanno's funeral.

That same afternoon, the same nun who opened the door to Giuseppe Vazanno that first night, went to the village of San Vito di Capo to post the letters Giuseppe had written. One was addressed to Antonio Vazanno at the Seminary of SS Peter and Paul in Milano, Italy; the second was to Gaspano Vazanno in Balastrate, Sicily; and the third was to Sevario Vazanno and Santo Padua. That letter was also sent to their home in Balastrate, Sicily.

Giuseppe doubted any of the letters would ever reach their intended recipients.

CHAPTER XVI
THE REUNION

MAY 1911

"HOW MANY DAYS now since we've left Balastrate?" Sevario asked Santo.

"It was the fifth day of May, I think. We've been traveling now for five days—so today is the tenth day of May. Why?"

"I figure we have another week or so of travel, at the rate we're going. That means we won't reach Catania until the seventeenth or so."

"What does it matter how long it takes to reach Catania?" Santo asked.

"It's not the date I'm worried about. It's the time it's taking us to get there. Whoever is after us must have figured out by now we're not anywhere near Palermo or in any of the coastal towns along the western shores," Sevario said. "By now I have no doubt the men who are looking for us are not far behind; maybe just a few days away."

"So, what do you think we should do?" Santo asked. "Do you think we should take a chance on the main roads leading to the east?"

"No, I still think that would be a mistake. Whoever is out there is looking for a family like ours traveling together. Besides, that trouble we ran into in Salemi just might have been a trigger point for someone looking for us; we still don't know who those men were, and they could very well be working for the people who are after us."

"So, what do you propose then?"

"I'm going to ride ahead . . . to Catania. I can reach there much faster by horse—alone—than us driving this wagon across this no-man's-land at our current snail's pace."

"How long do you think it will take you to get there?" Santo asked.

"I'm going to take another horse with me; if I can ride straight though, I figure I can get there in two days at the most."

"When are you going to leave?"

"As soon as I make sure you and the others have enough to eat and drink for the next couple of days. I'm going to leave at nightfall and ride through the night. With any luck I can reach Catania in less than two days—and then, God willing, ride back here for you and the others with help from Battaghlia and his men. I figure I should catch up to you in no more than three days."

"Should I just continue due east then?" asked Santo.

"Yes. Just keep going in the same direction. I'll leave some markers for you along the way just in case you or I happen to lose each other's trail."

Sevario reached down into his saddlebag and pulled out a long red kerchief. "I'll leave pieces of this every half mile or so on the end of tree branches along my path. Just keep heading due east. I promise you I will be back as soon as I get help for us," promised Sevario. "I will leave markers along my way. Look for them and follow my course."

* * *

Sevario rode hard, and headed straight toward the east. Just as he had hoped, after two days, he could see the top of a mountain—covered white with snow. *Etna! That must be Etna!* he told himself. He kicked his heels hard and rode as fast as his horse would carry him towards the mighty mountain.

He reached Catania within hours. He went into the first bar he spotted. Breathlessly, he went to the owner and asked about Battaghlia.

"I'm looking for a man. His name is Battaghlia. Have you heard of this man?"

"Who are you?" the man asked suspiciously.

"He's a friend of my brother—best friends with my brother!"

"Who is your brother, then?"

"Giuseppe Vazanno. The two men grew up together and they are both blood brothers with a man named Vito Vanucci. Have you heard of Vanucci? He is from Palermo."

The man looked at Sevario, surprised. "Wait over there," the man said pointing to a table in the corner. "I'll be right back."

Sevario went to the table as instructed. A woman approached him and asked if he wanted something to drink.

"*Aqua, per favore, signorina.* Water, please, miss."

The woman stared at Sevario for a minute; then she turned from him without saying a word. She returned in short order with a large wheel of cheese, a loaf of bread, and flask full of wine. "Eat your fill, signor. The bar's owner will not go broke sharing some cheese and bread with a starving stranger."

Sevario bowed his head and took off his cap to the young woman. "You are very kind, signorina. Thank you very much." As he began to wolf down the bread and cheese, the woman put her hand to his arm and said, "Slow down, signor! You have all day to eat this meager meal."

"Uncle! Uncle Sevario!" a familiar voice yelled out loudly.

Sevario's eyes opened wide as he jerked his head quickly in the direction of the voice. He could not believe his eyes. Standing just feet from where he sat was his own nephew, Antonio.

"Uncle! Uncle, is it really you?" Antonio exclaimed as he ran to Sevario.

At the same time, Sevario rose from the table and ran to meet Antonio. The two men held onto each other, a thrill of emotion rendering them both speechless. Finally, Sevario pulled back from Antonio but continued to hold him at arm's length.

"Yes, it's me, Antonio! It's me, your uncle! What are you doing here? How on earth did you come to be in Catania?"

"It's a long story, Uncle; one we can speak of soon. Are you here alone?"

"No, your sister, Santo, and Zia are with me, too."

"Where are they then, Uncle?" Antonio asked confused.

"We have to go get them right away, Antonio. They are in grave danger."

"Come with me first. You need food and rest. We can talk on the way back to Don Battaghlia's villa.'

"You are with Don Battaghlia? You know this man, Antonio?" Sevario asked, shocked Antonio would be with the very man Sevario had traveled hundreds of miles to meet.

"Yes, Uncle. I know him well, now. I will tell you everything. Come now, I'm anxious to hear about my family."

* * *

Ciccinu Battaghlia hugged Sevario warmly. "I am very, very happy, Sevario, you are alive! Please sit here with me and tell me everything," Battaghlia said as he opened his arms towards a settee in his drawing room. Sevario sat on the settee with Mario Lucalla and Antonio, and Battaghlia sat across from them.

Sevario retold his story to Don Battaghlia and Mario Lucalla. He repeated everything, starting with the night he and Santo discovered Giuseppe's farmhouse burned to the ground. The truth in the telling of it was almost too much for Sevario to bear.

Antonio, tears streaming down his face, put his arm around his uncle and held him tightly. "Uncle, we can continue talking later. Do you want to rest for awhile?"

"No, Antonio, not now. Let me finish telling the horrors of that day and then we must leave right away to go back for the others. They are all in grave danger." Sevario took a drink of the whiskey that Cicinnu Battaghlia had poured for him. He swallowed the liquid, slowly letting it burn his throat—the sharpness of it soothed his nerves. He finished the glass and then asked for another. Don Battaghlia gladly poured another glass for him.

"When we could not find Giuseppe and Maria and after we found the girls, me and Santo became increasingly worried about the safety of Gaspano and his family. Immediately we went there—to Gaspano's farm. That's where we found him . . ."

Sevario stopped talking then; he began to weep bitterly. This time, no one stopped him. Instead, they all took another drink of whiskey—giving Sevario time to recover.

"I found Gaspano behind his house with a shotgun blast

to his head and his stomach. My poor sister-in-law was lying over his body, trying to revive him. His own children stood back watching their mother screaming and beating on Gaspano's chest to get up."

Sevario put his head into his hands. He could not continue.

"Come and lie down, Uncle, for just a few minutes. I promise you, while you rest, Mario and I will get the horses ready to go after Adriana and the others. Please, Uncle, you need to rest."

Antonio motioned for Mario to help him take his uncle up to one of the bedrooms on the second floor. As soon as Sevario rested his head on the pillow and closed his eyes, he fell asleep immediately. Sheer exhaustion had finally overtaken him.

Just one hour passed when suddenly Sevario bolted upright from his sleep. He saw Antonio sitting next to the bed.

"Antonio! We have to leave here now! Right now!"

"Everything is ready, Uncle. Mario and the others are waiting for us downstairs. We have a fresh horse for you. We can leave right away. Don Battaghlia's housekeeper has packed a good meal for you—one you can eat while we ride."

Within minutes, Sevario, Antonio, Mario Lucalla, and twelve of Battaghlia's best men were riding out of Catania on the westward trail Sevario had marked.

***

Meanwhile, Adriana was driving the wagon while Santo rode out ahead to make sure they were following Sevario's trail due east. He kept his shotgun at the ready, in case they came upon strangers. Sevario marked the trail, just as he promised, every half- mile or so. About midday, a day and half after Sevario left them, Santo spotted four men riding up on a ridge not far away. He turned around and headed back to the wagon to warn Adriana and the others. "I spotted four men on horses not far from here; they are most likely innocent, but I think we should hide the wagon for now."

"Where should we go, then?" asked Adriana.

"Follow me. There's a wheat field not far from here. We can hide the wagon there."

Feeling confident the wagon was well hidden in the tall wheat, Santo told Adriana to stay quietly with the others while he went to investigate the path the strangers were taking.

"Be careful, Santo," Adriana begged, "nothing is worth losing your life over. Please, don't let them see you."

"I'll be fine. I'd rather keep an eye on them than have them keep an eye on us. I'll be back before nightfall. I will also find out what town we're near; perhaps with any luck I can find some fresh bread and cheese for us to eat." Santo turned to leave but then stopped and rode back to Adriana. "Keep the shotgun ready. If it's not me coming at you, shoot first and ask questions later."

***

Adriana fed Nella and the children the last of their food. She climbed down out of the wagon to milk the goats; the children needed the milk as there was no fresh water to be had. Everyone ate heartily except Nella, who continued to refuse taking anything to eat.

"Zia, please! You have to take the milk; how else are you going to have the strength and good health to feed Angelo?"

Nella shook her head. "Why do you trouble me with this, Adriana? I have plenty of milk for the baby; he's constantly at my breast!"

"Here, "Adriana said adamantly as she handed a flask of the milk to her aunt. "Drink this."

Nella took the container reluctantly; after taking a few sips she handed the flask back to Adriana. "Here, I drank it. Now leave me to rest."

"Thank you, Zia. Thank you."

Adriana tucked the children under their blankets and made sure Nella and the baby were covered and comfortable. "I'm going to check on the animals, Zia," said Adriana. "I'll be just outside the wagon."

Nella opened her eyes momentarily and then closed them again, making no indication she even heard what her niece had said to her.

Before turning to climb down out of the wagon, Adriana looked up at the sky. The night was unusually black with just a few stars emerging here and there among the huge, billowy clouds floating above her head. *Perhaps it will rain tonight,* she thought. Adriana turned then to climb down out of the wagon, reaching for the shotgun as she began to descend to the ground.

Before her foot even touched the ground, she felt a hand on her shoulder.

Startled she turned and said, "Santo . . ."

Immediately, a hand covered her mouth. Frantically Adriana tried to scream. But the hand that covered her mouth and nose was so big that not a word could escape her lips. Then she felt another arm reach around her waist and pull her back from the wagon in mid-air. Whoever was behind her held her waist and mouth so tightly that Adriana could feel the breath leaving her lungs—and she could not get any air back into them. In desperation, Adriana bit down hard on the man's hand; she felt her teeth penetrate his skin.

"*Putana!* Bitch!" a man's voice screamed out as he finally pulled his hand away from her mouth. At the same time, the man let go of his grip around her waist.

Adriana jumped away from him instantly. She tried again to reach up for the shotgun just inside of the wagon bed. But just as quickly she felt herself thrown to the ground with a man's body on top of her. Within seconds she could see she was surrounded by other men as she lay on the ground. Suddenly, a gag was roughly put across her mouth. Then she felt another rag being tied around her eyes. Before she knew it, she was lifted up and handed to another man on a horse.

"I'll follow you," Adriana heard a man say, "with the wagon. "Take the girl back to camp. We need to find out for sure who she is before we take her all the way back to Palermo or kill her—whatever we need to do. We just need some type of proof she's the Vazanno woman Turiddu is looking for."

The man giving the orders to the other men climbed up onto the wagon's bench. Upon hearing a stranger's voice in the front of the wagon, Alfredo woke up. Immediately he jumped up, pulling back the canvas covering from the bed of the wagon. He stared at the stranger for a minute and then screamed out, "Who the hell are you?"

"Never mind that! Shut up and sit down if you know what's good for you," the stranger yelled back. "What's your name?"

"Go to hell *bastardo!* Get out of this wagon!" Alfredo demanded.

The man turned then and slapped Alfredo hard across the face, knocking him down onto Nella. Nella was startled to wakefulness. She looked up at the strange man sitting in the front of the wagon; she grabbed Angelo to her chest and held him tightly. Then she reached out to Alfredo and pulled him to her. "Leave my children alone!" she screamed.

"What's your name?" demanded the stranger of Nella.

Nella froze in fear. Cinzia and Francesca woke up then. Cinzia started to scream. Francesca remained silent in her terror.

"Shut up! Shut up or I'll kill you!" the man yelled gruffly at Cinzia.

"Cinzia, come here by Mamma. Come here. Stop screaming, girl," Nella frantically urged her daughter, fearing the man was about to surely kill them all.

The man shouted out again, "What's your name, woman?"

Nella clenched her teeth, pressing her lips together.

Suddenly, the man jumped into the bed of the wagon and grabbed Francesca in his arms. He put a knife to her throat. "Tell me your name or the girl's dead."

"Vazanno!" Nella screamed. "Nella Vazanno!"

The man smiled. He threw Francesca down next to Nella. He turned and jumped down out of the wagon. Looking back at Nella, he said, "Keep all of your brats quiet; I don't want to hear a word coming out of any of your mouths. Shut up or I'll kill you all."

The man grabbed the shotgun lying on the floor in the back of the wagon. Then he got into the driver's seat and started to drive the wagon toward where his men had made camp earlier that day.

Alfredo threw himself down inside of the wagon and crossed his arms over his chest defiantly. Suddenly, a thought came to him. He remembered something he had hidden in his bundle when he left his farmhouse. Quietly, he began to move his body across the bed of the wagon to a pile of bundles on the other side of the wagon. He kept looking up to see if the man was looking back at him. He wasn't. The man seemed confident he had captured his quarry, and kept his eyes straight ahead toward the darkness.

Reaching the bags, Alfredo began frantically searching

for the one he needed. All the bags looked exactly alike. He would have to go through each one until he found what he was looking for. He felt each bag on the outside, hoping he would feel the object first instead of having to go through each bag; suddenly, he felt it. *I found it!* he thought. In an instant, he opened the bag and pulled out a long hunting knife his father had given him. He managed to slip the knife effortlessly under his shirt—just in time. Suddenly his whole body was being pulled backwards.

"I told you to stay put, you little *bastardo!* You move again and I'll kill you!" The man threw Alfredo back next to his mother. Then he climbed back up to the front of the wagon. He began to drive off but kept looking back at Alfredo every few minutes.

Alfredo let his head drop down onto his mother's arm. His closed his eyes, feigning sleep. But like the stranger, he too kept opening his eyes every few minutes to keep an eye out.

***

Adriana could see nothing. Her eyes were still covered tightly and her mouth gagged. She was lying across the front of the saddle of the man who had taken her. She did not know if it was night or day until finally she heard the coos of some mourning doves above her head. *It had to be close to dawn,* she thought. Suddenly she heard her abductor yell out, "Whoa!" and bring his horse to a halt. She felt the rider jump down off his horse. She remained across the horse for some minutes until she heard the sound of another horse.

"Where's Geramo?" a stranger's voice asked.

"He's coming. It's taking the wagon longer; the woodland here is pretty dense. He'll be here. What should we do with the girl?" asked a man's voice not far from her hanging head.

"We'll wait for Geramo to decide. For now, just get her down and put her over there."

Adriana felt herself being pulled off the horse. The stranger began dragging her by her arms across the rough ground. Then he let her go and she slumped down on the hard earth.

She felt the man standing over her. Fearing the worst, she brought both of her untied feet up and landed them squarely in the stranger's groin.

"You filthy *putana!*" the man screamed in agony. He was just about to get on top of Adriana when the wagon pulled into the clearing.

"Get away from her, you *figlio di putana!*"

Adriana's attacker got up slowly and began then to back away from her. "What's the matter, boss? You want the *putana* all to yourself?"

"Shut up! Tie up the horses. We have things to get done before we start back for Palermo," Geramo demanded.

* * *

For two days, Adriana, Nella, and the children remained gagged and tied. The men took off the gags for them to eat twice a day and it was Geramo who took the women and children into the woods to relieve themselves—as he stood a short distance away with a shotgun at the ready, in case any one of them tried to escape.

"It's been two days, boss. When do you plan on getting these *bastardos* back to Palermo?"

"We leave tonight, as soon as the sun goes down. I figure we can kill the older woman and her brood and just take the girl back to Palermo. She's the only one Vanucci wants, anyway."

"You want me to take care of them now, boss?"

"Yeah, go ahead. Might as well get things started. I packed enough for us to eat for three days—we don't need any more mouths to feed, that's for sure. The sooner we get rid of the others now, the better. Take them off into the woods; kill 'em and bury the evidence."

The other three men went over to where Nella and the children were tied up. One man took Nella and another picked up Cinzia and Francesca, tucking one under each arm. The last man picked Alfredo up off the ground and pushed him to start walking ahead of him.

"Hey, what about the baby?" the last man said as the three of them began walking into the woods.

"Leave the *bastardo,* there's plenty of wild boar around here. He'll be gone by morning."

Somehow Nella managed to free her mouth of her gag. "Adriana! Where are you?" she screamed out loudly. "They're taking us away, Adriana! The baby! Adriana, they are going to kill my baby and my children!"

"Shut her up!" the man who was pushing Alfredo yelled.

The man holding Nella stopped and took a long knife out of his pocket.

Alfredo broke loose from the man herding him and ran to his mother. "Leave my mother alone! Leave her alone!" he screamed out at the top of his lungs. "Take me first! I cannot bear to see my mamma and sister killed first! Please, I beg of you, kill me first!"

The man holding Nella started to laugh. "No problem for me, you little *bastardo!* Come on then." The man let go of Nella and pulled a piece of rope out of his pocket. "This is the best way, boy. Quick and easy." The man pushed Alfredo to the ground and knelt down over him and began to wrap the rope around Alfredo's neck.

Alfredo looked wide-eyed up into the eyes of the stranger hovering over him. If he could have killed with his eyes, the man would surely have fallen over dead. But instead, suddenly, the man's own eyes opened wide. His face became distorted and he gasped loudly. Then he slumped over, falling down to the ground next to Alfredo. His mouth was opened wide and blood started to ooze out of it. Alfredo pushed the monster off him and quickly got to his feet. He looked around to see Santo, Sevario, and another dozen men surrounding him.

Alfredo began to shake uncontrollably. Tears ran down his face. He stood directly over the dead man's body and with one sharp kick of his boot hit his attacker in the side of the head. "There, you *bastardo!* You deserved more than one bullet to your chest!" Quickly then, he ran to his mother who was still tied and sitting on the ground now. He freed her hands and feet and she hugged him tightly.

Within seconds, shotgun blasts rang out and the other two men lay dead on the ground.

It was Mario Lucalla who came upon Geramo and Adriana. Geramo, hearing the shotgun blasts, had let go of Adriana and was walking in the direction of the gun blasts when suddenly Mario came out of the woods behind him on his horse.

"Where are you going, signor?" Mario asked loudly.

Geramo turned around, pointing his shotgun at Mario.

A blast of gunfire sounded. Geramo fell to the ground moaning in pain, letting his shotgun fall to the ground. Mario came closer. He stood over the man watching him hold his stomach in agony.

"Let me put you out of your misery, signor." Mario fired one final shot into Geramo and the agony was over.

Adriana watched as Mario seemingly cold-bloodedly shot her abductor. Not knowing Mario, she believed him to be another of Turiddu's henchmen out to find her and take the reward for himself. Even though she was still gagged and her hands still tied behind her back, she immediately ran into the woods away from Mario.

Mario looked back to see Adriana running and quickly kicked his horse into a gallop. As he reached her he managed to stop his horse in front of her—making it impossible for her to move any further.

"Don't be afraid. I'm here with Antonio and Sevario Vazanno."

Adriana's eyes opened wide when she heard the name of her brother. She stood still in shock.

Mario quickly dismounted and immediately took the gag from Adriana's mouth and then untied her hands. "My name is Mario Lucalla; I'm the son of Ciccinu Battaghlia. Your brother and uncle came to my father's house for help."

Adriana looked up into Mario's eyes; he stood much taller than any man she had ever known in Sicily. She found herself staring up at him, speechless; the deep blue of his eyes—*his eyes are the same as my mother's,* she thought, staring into them. Her glance then fell on his rugged, handsome face; the blackness of his hair—almost everything about him—suddenly stirred something inside of her she had never felt before, not even with Santo Padua.

Finally she managed to say, "You know my brother, Antonio? Where is he? Where is Uncle?"

"Come with me. I'll take you to them," Mario said as he mounted his horse and held out his hand toward Adriana.

With little reluctance, as if she could not stop herself even if she wanted, she reached her hand up to Mario. He leaned forward and picked her up, settling her body in front of his on the horse. The two rode off then to meet with Antonio, Sevario, Nella, and the others.

* * *

Adriana awoke early the morning after arriving at Don Battaghlia's villa. It was still dark when she awoke, yet she felt refreshed. It seemed an eternity since she had slept in a clean, fresh bed. As she looked out her window she could see rays of light coming up over the mountains behind the Don's villa. She washed and dressed, luxuriating in a small tub of rose-scented hot water that someone had placed in her room. The warmth of the water made her feel human again—and unafraid for the first time since the night of the fire. As she washed her body, she noticed a small rounded mound where her flat stomach used to be. She put her hand on the mound and closed her eyes. Tears fell down her face as she allowed herself to think the unthinkable. *Is it possible, dear God? Please don't let me be with child.*

After she dressed, Adriana went downstairs, hoping her brother or uncle—or even Santo—would also be up at such an early hour. But the house was quiet and seemed empty. *Everyone must still be sleeping,* she thought.

Her eyes fell upon a beautiful garden just outside of the Don's sitting room. As she walked out onto the terrace she saw at once the breathtaking view of acre upon acre of vineyards sloping down the hillsides of a tall mountain range—the range was so close she felt she could reach her hand out and touch it.

"Good morning, Signorina Adriana."

It was the voice of Mario Lucalla. Adriana turned quickly to see him sitting at a small table behind her with a cup in front of him.

"Please join me! I have an espresso waiting for you!" he said warmly.

Adriana blushed. She knew she should not engage in a conversation with a man who was not a family member—especially since the two of them were alone in the garden. She opened her mouth to excuse herself but not one word would come out. Instead, she slowly walked towards the table and took a seat across from Mario. Immediately, he poured her a hot cup of espresso and then took the lid off of a large sugar bowl.

"Sugar, signorina? My espresso is usually quite strong—I think you may prefer it a bit sweeter than I do."

Adriana sipped the espresso. "I find it refreshing, signor. I don't think it needs sugar at all."

Mario smiled at her warmly. For what seemed like an eternity, the two stared into each other's eyes; then finally, Adriana forced herself to look away.

"Did you sleep well, signorina?" Mario asked.

"Please call me Adriana, signor. Yes, I slept very well. Your home is very beautiful and you and your father have been most gracious and kind to my family and me. I do not know how we will ever be able to repay you."

"I assure you, there is no need. My father and your father are blood brothers; to me, you are family."

"*Grazia, signor*. Thank you, signor," Adriana said sincerely.

"Please call me Mario."

The two sipped their espresso, silently enjoying the beauty that surrounded them. Finally it was Adriana who spoke. "Tell me how it is you and my brother have come to be friends."

Mario sat up straight. He did not know how much Adriana had been told about Antonio's arrival in Catania and what part Mario himself played in the events that actually brought Adriana to his father's villa. "It is a long and complicated story, Adriana. But I think it is one you must discuss with your brother first."

Adriana was about to urge Mario to tell her about his relationship with Antonio, when she heard a voice say, "There you are, Adriana! I knocked on your door, and when there wasn't an answer I thought you were still sleeping." Antonio walked to the table and took a chair across from her. "I see you have finally, formally, met my friend, Mario Lucalla."

"Yes, I was just asking him how it is you came to Catania and how it is you two met."

Antonio looked at Mario quickly but then averted his eyes.

Adriana felt the tension immediately. "What is it, Antonio? What's wrong?"

"I think I must ask to be excused," Mario said. "I have to get to the stables and make sure our newly hired equestrian trainers know where everything is." Without saying another word, Mario got up and left the two.

Adriana knew instinctively Antonio and Mario were keeping something from her. "Tell me, Antonio. How is it you are here in Catania?"

"Come with me, Adriana. Let's walk for awhile."

* * *

Antonio and Adriana walked down the garden path and out into the vineyards in silence. Adriana knew her brother would tell her everything but she wanted to let him tell her only when he was ready. They walked for quite some distance until they came to a large oak tree in the middle of a clearing not far from the vineyard they were in. "Let's sit there."

The two sat under the tree; a warm breeze was blowing from the Adriatic Sea that was no more than a few miles from Don Battaghlia's villa.

"It's beautiful here, Antonio. So green compared to the west. Everything is so lush and fertile . . ."

"Adriana, I have something to tell you but I fear it will be the cause of much pain to you."

Adriana sat upright then turned to face Antonio. "No, Antonio. You must never be afraid of telling me anything. Nothing you could say or do would ever change my love for you."

Antonio fell silent for a moment as if searching for a way to begin his story. Finally he simply said, "Everything that has happened to our family, everything since the night our home was attacked—is my fault—entirely."

Adriana's face suddenly was drained of all color. "What are you saying, Antonio? How could any of this horror be your fault?"

"The day before I left for the seminary back in April—Easter Sunday, actually—after you announced you were entering the convent, our mother . . . Mamma . . . came to me. She knew—and I swear without me telling her—she knew you had been attacked by a man—that you had been disgraced."

"Oh, my God, Antonio! Don't tell me this!" Adriana said desperately.

"I promised you I would never tell a soul about what really happened that day in the orchard, but somehow Mamma knew. She knew everything. The only thing she didn't know was who attacked you that day. "

"Antonio . . . ."

"No, Adriana let me finish telling you everything. If I do not reveal everything now, I'm afraid I will lose my nerve and will never be able to tell you."

Adriana fell silent. She took Antonio's hand and said, "Go on, then."

"Mamma was beside herself. She felt you were throwing your life away by entering the convent; she knew the true reason for your decision. I tell you, Adriana, her heart was completely broken. But worse, she felt helpless. She wanted revenge. As much as I am against revenge in every sense of it—no matter how deserving—Adriana, I agreed with her. You were protecting a monster! I felt the same as Mamma, I tell you. Turiddu Vanucci needed to pay for what he had done to you."

Adriana felt her heart pounding in her chest. A feeling of doom began to descend upon her and suddenly she felt as if she couldn't breathe. "Tell me everything, Antonio, please."

"Mamma gave me the vendetta."

Adriana gasped. "No! Not our mother! She would not do that to you, Antonio."

"Yes. It's true. I wanted to refuse but she told me if I did she would then tell Papa. And she also warned me if I did not tell her who it was that brought disgrace down upon you, she would confront you that very day in front of Papa and the entire family." Antonio shook his head back and forth. "I tell you, Adriana, Mamma was not in her right mind. My greatest fear that day was that she would tell everyone anyway—whether or not I told her who was to blame and whether or not I would accept the vendetta."

"What did you tell her, Antonio?"

"Everything. I told her it was Turiddu Vanucci who attacked you. I told her you had made me swear to silence because you feared Papa finding out the truth."

"So Mamma knew everything . . . that's why you seemed so upset the day you left for the seminary."

"Yes. I accepted the vendetta that very day. I accepted the vendetta to kill Turiddu Vanucci on Easter Sunday. I am so ashamed of myself, Adriana, but I had to do it. If Mamma told Papa everything, he would certainly kill Turiddu. And, the chances of Vito Vanucci forgiving Papa for such a crime were uncertain. She said everything you had already reasoned to be true. I had no choice but to accept, Adriana. Please tell me you understand." Antonio looked pleadingly into Adriana's eyes.

"I hold nothing against you, Antonio. I promise you that. But how is it then you have come to Catania?"

That's the most fantastic part of this whole ordeal, Adriana. I met a man on the crossing from Palermo to Naples. His name was Alfonzo Manricco. I came to find out he grew up with Papa in Palermo *and* with Don Vito and Don Battaghlia! The only reason he was not involved with the Society of Honorable Men was that, like Papa, he didn't want to become involved in the darker side of *la famiglia*. One thing led to another, and he too, saw that I was completely distraught even though—I swear on my own soul, Adriana—I told him absolutely nothing about what had happened to you. But strangely, he too, like Mamma, somehow knew something terrible had happened to our family and," Antonio looked Adriana directly in the face, "I assure you his love for our father is as genuine as is Don Vito's love for him. I had no reason to doubt his sincerity in trying to help me."

"But if you did not tell him the nature of your distress, how did he know then?"

Antonio shrugged his shoulders. "That I cannot tell you. I do not know how he knew. But all I do know is that I woke up in his stateroom the next morning and he gave me a ring—the same ring our father wears—and told me to see a man by the name of Ciccinu Battaghlia in Catania. And he said if I showed Battaghlia the ring and told him it is from Alfonzo Manricco, he would help me no matter what it was I needed help with."

"Did you immediately leave for Catania when you docked in Naples, then?"

"Yes. I found myself here in Catania. After making inquiries, I found Don Battaghlia, who accepted me with open arms when he found out I was Giuseppe Vazanno's son and that Alfonzo Manricco had given me his ring as a sign that I needed Battaghlia's help."

"Did you reveal the nature of your distress to Don Battaghlia?"

"No. I swear it. I did tell him that I was given a vendetta against Turiddu Vanucci. I didn't tell him why or by whom I had received the vendetta. He simply told me he would think about what should be done. He assured me he knew Turiddu well and that he was a heartbreak and disappointment to Vito Vanucci. He had no reason to doubt I was given a vendetta against him, and he did not further question me about the matter. All he asked of me was that I give him some time to think about how the situation should be handled."

"Well, then, if that is all you said to him, how can you tell me all of this chaos we are in is your fault?"

"I didn't know immediately what transpired after I told Don Battaghlia I needed his help to kill Turiddu. But, unbeknownst to me until later, he sent his son, Mario Lucalla, the man you were talking to this morning, to Palermo to find out what, if anything, Turiddu Vanucci was up to, or what, if anything, he had done to our family that resulted in my accepting the vendetta against him. Mario told me later when he arrived in Palermo that he disguised himself as a man Turiddu had requested Don Battaghlia send to him to do a *special job*. Soon Mario found out the *special job* was to kill not only our father but also to kill his own father, Vito Vanucci!"

Adriana gasped again. "No, not our father, Antonio!"

"Yes, our father and his own father. And to add more insult to an already heinous plot, Turiddu . . ." Antonio stopped then. He took a deep breath and waited as if what he was about to say was the worst of anything he had already revealed to Adriana.

"Tell me Antonio. Tell me everything." Adriana urged sensing her brother's hesitancy.

"Mario told me Turiddu bragged about how he raped and beat you. He bragged about how he thought he had killed you for certain and was shocked to see you still alive. He even chided our father several weeks after he attacked you—asking him about your welfare."

Adriana started to cry. She wrapped her arms about herself and started to moan in agony. The story her brother was telling was crushing the life out of her. Antonio put his arms about her and held her tightly.

"Adriana, I'm so sorry. I have been a miserable failure. All of this could have been prevented if it weren't for me."

Adriana turned her face to look up at Antonio. "What do

you mean? What does any of this have to do with the men who burned our house down—who may have killed Mamma and Papa, and who for certain killed Zio Gaspano?"

"That's just it. It has everything to do with it. When Mario reported Turiddu's plans back to his father, Don Battaghlia ordered Mario to kill Turiddu. He came to me after he gave his son the order and explained to me what he had found out. But the trouble is, Mario's attempt to kill Turiddu was foiled. He could not finish him off because Turiddu had his men in waiting—probably suspecting Mario may have not been as sincere as he pretended to be.

Just before Mario was about to finish Turiddu off—just before he was ready to plunge his knife into Turiddu's neck—he told Turiddu he was killing him for what he had done to you, and that his death was the result of a vendetta from the Vazanno family."

"Oh, my God!" Adriana shrieked. "It was Turiddu then who burned down our house and took Mamma and Papa and killed Uncle!" Adrianna tried to convince herself she had not known who committed the crime against her parents, but now she knew for certain.

"Yes. It was Turiddu. And, now he is looking for all of us. He's posted rewards all across Sicily—thousands of lire for our capture or death."

Adriana threw herself into her brother's arms; she shook uncontrollably.

***

Don Battaghlia opened the door to his study to let everyone enter before him.

Adriana walked in first and noticed Mario Lucalla was already sitting in the room next to his father's desk. The two looked at each other instantly; Adriana felt a blush come to her cheeks and immediately put her eyes down. Santo followed behind Adriana and noticed the look Adriana and Mario exchanged. He swallowed hard but chose to ignore it. He sat just across from Adriana, who took a seat on a long settee. When Antonio and Sevario came in, both men took a seat next to Adriana—one on her left side and one on her right.

"What refreshments would you like?" Don Battaghlia said as he pulled on a long rope that rang a bell for his housekeeper. Within seconds, his housekeeper appeared.

"Whiskey, please," Sevario and Antonio asked at the same time.

"Wine for me," said Santo.

The Don glanced at Mario and asked, "The usual?"

Mario nodded in agreement. Then Mario said to Adriana, "Signorina Adriana, what would you like?"

Adriana quickly averted her eyes from Mario's; she said to Don Battaghlia, "May I have *aqua, per favore*?"

Santo noticed the exchange between Mario and Adriana again. His heart began to beat faster in his chest. *Surely that old man is not interested in Adriana?* he thought.

Don Battaghlia pulled up another chair beside his son Mario. "I hope you are all comfortable; my housekeeper will be in shortly with your refreshments." He hesitated for a moment and then said, "I wanted to meet with all of you this morning because, in light of what has occurred over these past weeks, I think it is quite necessary to make some decisions and make them rather quickly."

"What type of decisions, Signor Battaghlia?" Sevario asked first.

"It's obvious Turiddu Vanucci is determined to take revenge on your family," the Don replied to Sevario and the rest of the family. "He is actively planning and recruiting men to find and . . ." the Don hesitated, "and kill you when he does find you. That is most evident in light of what has just taken place these past few days."

Just then the Don's housekeeper came in and began to distribute refreshments to his guests. The room remained awkwardly silent as she passed out the drinks. When she was finished, the Don said, "That will be all for now. Please leave the wine and whiskey flasks on the table. I will ring for you if I need anything more."

As soon as the housekeeper left, the Don said, "I think it will best for all of you to leave Sicily as soon as possible."

Antonio spoke first. "Leave Sicily? You mean go to the mainland, then? All of us together?"

"No," the Don continued, "that would be too dangerous. What I suggest is that you and my son go to America, perhaps to the south to a place called New Orleans. And the rest of you also go to America, but I think to a place called New York. I have a sister there, her name is Maria Vespucci. She will take care of you," he said to Adriana, "and of course your aunt Nella and the children."

"You mean I will be separated from my brother again, signor?" Adriana said with obvious fear in her voice.

"It will only be for a short period of time, I promise you. I need to meet with Vito Vanucci myself. I need to find out how much he knows and how he plans to take care of his son's obviously misguided hatred and vendetta against you. But, until I can determine you all will be safe and free of his revenge, you must leave Sicily."

"I'm not going to America," Sevario said abruptly.

"What do you mean, my friend?" the Don asked.

"I do not know for sure where my brother and sister-in-law are. None of us know for sure if they are dead or alive. We have not found them, nor have we found any trace of their bodies. My brother needs me—especially because Gaspano is gone. I will stay to find my brother. If I find he is dead, God forbid," Sevario made the sign of the cross over himself, "I will go to America and join the rest of my family."

"You do understand that you are not exempt from Turiddu's hatred. You are a Vazanno. He has already killed your brother, Gaspano. There is nothing stopping him from coming after you."

"I'll take my chances. Besides, Santo can accompany Adriana, Nella, and the children to America. He's a grown man and more than capable of protecting the women and children."

Santo felt immediate elation; he smiled broadly at the thought of going to America with Adriana. But just as quickly, he suppressed his emotions, not wanting the others to suspect his true feelings for her. "Yes. I will go with them to America," he said seriously. "They must not travel alone."

"All right, then," Don Ciccinu said, "it is settled. I will arrange passage for my son and Antonio to leave right away. If all goes well, I will prepare papers for them within the week. It will take a little while longer to get everything ready for Adriana, Nella, and the children . . . and you, of course, Santo," the Don said directly to Santo, "only because it will take some doing getting birth certificates and identification for all of you, stating all of you are from Catania rather than Palermo."

"What type of papers will we need, Papa?" Mario asked.

"None. I will book you passage on a working cargo ship. That way you will have easy access to America without being scrutinized by port authorities. Men come and go constantly between here and America. They work a few months on the cargo vessels, get their pay, stay in America for a while, and then return to Sicily. There is a term they use for these men in America; they call them *WOPS*. It means "without papers.""

Everyone laughed except Adriana.

Santo continued to steal glances at her every now and then—trying to gauge her reaction to Don Battaghlia's proposal. She gave nothing away. Instead she remained stoic—seemingly unaffected one way or another.

"As soon as possible I will write to Alfonzo. He may have heard something from Palermo—either from Vito or, hopefully, Giuseppe himself. But I think the most important thing we must do right away is to get you all to safety. Once you are all gone, I will travel to Palermo myself and meet with Vito."

EPILOGUE

"SHOULD I WRITE to you, Papa, when we arrive in New Orleans?" Mario asked his father as the two sat drinking an espresso the morning before Mario's departure for America.

"No. I will know when you arrive. My men in New Orleans have already been instructed about when and how to contact me when you and Antonio arrive."

Just then, Antonio and Sevario knocked on the Don's door.

"Come in," Don Battaghlia responded. When he saw who it was, he stood immediately and invited the two men to join him and his son.

"Do you know yet when Adriana and the others will be sailing to America?" Antonio asked Don Battaghlia.

"If everything goes as planned, your sister and the rest of your family will be sailing for New York in just a few days now; perhaps in two but more likely three. It takes time for my men to get all the papers ready for six people to enter America; unlike you and Mario, they must have identification papers to enter America at Ellis Island. Don't worry, Antonio. They will be safe with Santo Padua, and their papers will all be in order. I promise you that."

The Don finished his espresso and then poured each man a glass of Sambuca. "*Salute!*" he said as he raised his glass in the air.

"*Salute!*" all three men responded.

Suddenly there was a knock at the door. "Who is it?"

Don Battaghlia's housekeeper entered the room. "There is a man here to see you, signor. He has a message for you but he would not give it to me. He insists he must give it to you personally."

"Fine, then. Show him in."

A young man walked into Don Battaghlia's study, hat in hand. He carried a bag in one hand, a letter in the other. "Don Battaghlia," said the man respectfully, "I bring you greetings from Alfonzo Manricco." With that said, the youth handed the Don the letter, and then unwrapped a large bottle of Manricco's Sambuca and extended that to the Don as well.

"Manricco!" said the Don, surprised. He took the bottle of Sambuca, thanking the visitor. Then he opened the letter hastily. His expression changed from serious to joyful as he looked up at the men standing in front of him. "Antonio, your father is alive!"

"Alive? My God, where is he? Is my mother with him?" Antonio asked excitedly.

"I'm afraid Alfonzo does not mention your mother, Antonio. But, I'm sure if she is with your father, she will accompany him here."

"I must tell my sister and Nella!" Antonio started to run out of the room but Don Battaghlia stopped him.

"Go and find the signorina Adriana," the Don said to his housekeeper. "Ask her to come here right away."

Adriana entered the room within minutes. "What is it, Don Battaghlia?" She looked around to see everyone smiling broadly and then smiled herself, in anticipation of the good news that was surely coming.

"Our father is alive!" Antonio said to Adriana as he ran to take her hand. "Papa is coming here . . . with Signor Manricco!"

Adriana swooned and nearly fainted away. Antonio grabbed her quickly and helped her to sit in a chair. Mario brought a glass of water to her immediately.

"Here, drink this, signorina . . ." Mario said gently.

Just then Santo Padua came into the room. He had met the housekeeper as he was coming from his room. She had informed him that a man had brought news from Naples. As he entered, he saw Mario Lucalla kneeling down in front of Adriana.

"What is it? What's happened?" he asked frantically, thinking something had happened to Adriana.

Antonio and Sevario went to him immediately. "Nothing! Everything is good! Giuseppe is alive and he is coming here to Catania!"

"That is good news," Santo said as he continued to stare in Adriana's direction, "but is Adriana all right?"

"Yes, she was simply overcome by the good news. That's all."

Mario glanced back to see Santo staring at him. He got up from his knees and went immediately to his father's side.

"All four of us—together again," said Battaghlia, full of emotion.

Everyone looked then at one another. Did Don Battaghlia say *all four of us?*

"Signor Battaghlia," asked Antonio, "do you mean the three of you: my father, Signor Manricco, and you?"

Don Battaghlia looked at the letter in his hand. He cleared his throat and then said, "Yes, I did say all four of us: your father, Manricco, myself, and Don Vito Vanucci."

"When is my father coming here, Signor Battaghlia?" Adriana asked, breaking the silence that had settled in the room.

Battaghlia walked over to Adriana and Antonio, who were now sitting next to each other on a settee across the room. He knelt down and placed a hand on each of their shoulders. "My children, I know this is painful to hear. But the earliest he could possibly arrive from Palermo is four days' time—one day after you leave for New York, Adriana, and several days after your departure tomorrow, Antonio."

Adriana lowered her head on the verge of tears. But she stopped herself, saying firmly, "I will not allow myself to cry. My father is safe and he is on his way here to Catania—the safest place for him in Sicily now."

"That's right, Adriana. I promise you: when your father arrives here and discovers his children are alive and in America, he will want to waste no time in going there himself. I will make sure your father gets there as soon as possible. You will have your reunion with him, Adriana! I promise you that!"

* * *

Just before dawn, Mario and Antonio were up and ready to go to the dock. Don Battaghlia came down the stairs shortly after them. Just as they were about to climb into the waiting carriage, Sevario, Santo, and Adriana appeared in the doorway.

"We're coming down to the pier with you, brother." Adriana said adamantly.

Antonio smiled. "Good. I was hoping you would. That goes for you too, Uncle, and you, Santo," he said as he smiled each of them in turn.

When they reached the pier where the cargo ships were docked, only dockworkers and ship hands could enter. "Well, I guess this is where we must part," Antonio said as he turned to his sister. Suddenly his eyes filled with tears. "We will see each other again soon, my sister—until then, Santo will take care of you. And just think—the next time we see each other, Papa and Mamma may be with us!"

"Oh, Antonio, I hope with all my heart that is true."

Adriana stepped away from Antonio so that her uncle and Santo could say their farewells to her brother. As she stood back from the men she suddenly became aware that Mario Lucalla was standing next to her. She looked up at him and noticed he was staring at her. She smiled at him and then immediately lowered her eyes, feeling a hot blush come across her cheeks.

"Adriana . . ." Mario paused for a moment, and then continued. "Adriana, I don't know when or if we will see each other again. But I want you to know that I find myself thinking about you . . . almost every minute of every day."

Adriana looked up into Mario's eyes. She felt her heart begin to beat faster. Then, suddenly and surprisingly, she felt the stir of passion arise within her. She looked away quickly, feeling an ache of guilt; she stood next to her brother, her uncle . . . and Santo! How could she possibly feel this way about Mario Lucalla? She admonished herself for allowing such a sinful feeling to arise for a man she hardly knew.

"Adriana, I know everything. I know what happened to you and I want to kill Turiddu Vanucci more than any man for that. Can you please try to see your way to thinking about me the way I think about you? Is that possible?"

Adriana turned away so that no one would be able to hear

what she was about to say to Mario Lucalla. She stood very close to him and said quietly, "You must stop this. I am not fit to be with any man now. I don't want you to think about me. Nothing will ever come of it."

Mario looked defeated, his face saddened by Adriana's words. "All right, then. I love you too much to disrespect your wishes. I will not speak of this again, but I want you to know I cannot stop my heart and my mind from thinking of you. That would be asking the impossible." Then he started to walk away but stopped. He walked back to Adriana and said, "I am a patient man. I will wait for you for as long as it takes."

Mario took Adriana's hand and kissed it. Finally, he picked up his traveling bag and turned and walked towards the gangplank to board the *Capricorn*.

Without anyone's notice, Santo had watched the exchange between Adriana and Mario Lucalla. For the first time he realized that Mario was indeed in love with Adriana. His heart sank as he watched Adriana rub her hand where Mario had kissed it.

He was about to walk away himself, but then he too suddenly stopped. *I'm in love with Adriana!* he told himself. *I have loved her my whole life! No one—least of all Mario Lucalla, an assassin—is going to take her away from me!*

Santo walked back to Adriana who was now holding her brother once again in a final embrace before he too would board the ship. Santo waited until the two let go of each other and then took Adriana by the arm. "Don't worry about anything, Antonio. I promise you on my life: I will protect Adriana and the others from any harm. No one will be able to get within miles of us, I promise you—even if it means I will die doing it."

"Thank you, Santo," Antonio said as he embraced him. "Thank you. I can think of no other man to whom I would entrust my sister's safety more than you."

* * *

Adriana, Sevario, Don Battaghlia, and Santo watched as the *Capricorn* sailed off over the horizon. The four turned then and climbed into the carriage that would take them back to the Don's villa.

Santo sat next to Adriana in the carriage. For the first time he let his hand fall upon hers as they rode in the back of the carriage. He held it softly at first and then embraced it firmly in his own. Adriana did not pull it away. Instead, Santo could feel her body move closer to his. He breathed a long sigh of relief. *She does love me,* he told himself. *She does love me.*

Two days after Antonio and Mario left for New Orleans, a man brought identification papers for the Vazanno family and Santo Padua to Don Battaghlia's villa. He told the Don that the steamship *Cara Napoli* was setting sail midday the next day and he had arranged third-class passage for all of them. Immediately, Don Battaghlia had his housekeeper send for Adriana, Nella, and Santo to meet him in his study.

"Good news!" Don Battaghlia said as Adriana and the others walked into the room. "You are all leaving tomorrow afternoon for New York!"

Santo and Nella were happy to hear the news, but Adriana could not hide her disappointment. Don Battaghlia understood. He knew Adriana wanted more than anything to see her mother and father before she left for America.

"Well, all of you must go now and prepare your things for the voyage. Let my housekeeper know if there is anything you need, and I assure you–you will have it!"

Everyone turned to leave the room.

"Adriana," Don Battaghlia called out, "may I speak with you for a moment, please?"

"Yes, of course." Adriana walked back to where the Don was seated.

"Please have a seat," he offered. Then he took her hand and said, "Adriana, much has happened to you. You have been more than brave these past months and I have come to not only admire your courage but feel a very deep affection for you–just as if you were my own daughter."

"Thank you, Don Battaghlia, but I'm afraid I have not been as brave as you think I have been," Adriana said as she smiled warmly at her benefactor.

"It is an unfortunate thing that me, my son, and your brother have come to know the circumstance under which you find yourself today. I tell you truly, if I were your father, I would not think twice about ending Turiddu Vanucci's life. I swear to you I would hunt him down and end him—just as he has ended so much of your happiness."

Adriana looked away. She knew exactly what Don Battaghlia was saying to her. She knew that he, along with Mario Lucalla and her brother Antonio, knew she was raped and brutally assaulted by Turiddu—and probably suspected she was with child. Her humiliation was complete now. She stood up and started for the door to leave, tears streaming down her face.

"No, wait, please," Don Battaghlia said gently. "I tell you this because I truly love you—just as your father loves you. I need to know what it is you want me to tell your father. He most likely knows most of the story—but he may not know the whole truth. What do you want me to tell him, Adriana—if anything—when he arrives here?"

Adriana walked over to the large plate-glass window that overlooked the gardens. She folded her arms about her and stood for a long time. Don Battaghlia did not disturb her; he knew she needed to think before she answered him. After a while she turned, walked back, and took a seat across from Don Battaghlia.

"My life as I once knew it has ended. My dreams of marriage and happiness no longer exist. It would have been better for my family and me if Turiddu had succeeded in killing me that day—but he didn't. And that is what I live with every single day—wishing he had."

Don Battaghlia reached over and took Adriana's hand in his own.

"I think I am with child," Adriana said as she looked deliberately into Don Battaghlia's eyes. "So now, instead of dying a honorable death—letting my father and mother believe I fell from a bridge— now I must live with the dishonor of not only losing my maidenhood to the monster Turiddu Vanucci, but for the rest of my life I will be reminded of my sin because of an innocent child. I am unmarried, pregnant . . . and a disgrace to my family. So when you ask me what you should say to my father, I don't have an answer for you.

"It may be my father knows the entire story—after all, he is traveling with Vito Vanucci, who certainly by this time knows what his own son has done to me. But it may be he knows only bits and pieces of the story."

Adriana shrugged her shoulders.

"No, I think it is better to tell him nothing. When I see my father again, I will know by the look on his face what he knows. I will wait until then."

"As you wish, Adriana. As you wish. Now, you best be going and gather your things. You and your family have a big day tomorrow. You're leaving for America and—I hope to almighty God—to a new and better life there. You deserve only the best the world has to offer, my child. I hope with all my heart you find it in America."

Adriana smiled at Don Battaghlia. She squeezed his hand tightly; then she rose and walked out of the room to pack.

***

ACKNOWLEDGMENTS

I WOULD LIKE to thank Amanda Rooker of SplitSeed: Ideas That Grow (formerly Amanda Rooker Editing) for her meticulous and diligent work in assisting me to develop a novel worthy of publication. Her editorial assistance was essential to this novel and I would not have achieved the level of believability in my storytelling without her. Thank you, Amanda, for assisting me in making my dream come true.

I would also like thank John Koehler of Koehler Books for the honor of accepting my work to be published. I am humbled and very grateful for this opportunity to showcase my book as a debut author.

CPSIA information can be obtained at www.ICGtesting.com
Printed in the USA
BVOW02s1043150716

455403BV00003B/137/P